Shady
Neighbors

·|||·

Thom Powell

Oct, 2016

Shady

Neighbors

‧╟‧

Thom Powell

For Lucky

Chapter 1

DEEP IN THE DENSE forests of Oregon's Cascade Mountains, a bald eagle basked in the mid-day sun. The stately bird stared intently at a subtle disturbance in the short grass below its commanding position at the edge of a large, marsh-rimmed mountain lake. Focused on the faint rustling of the grass, the eagle straightened its spine, lifted its wings, and then leapt from its perch. The large raptor gained speed as it plunged earthward, wings trailing back. In an instant, the wings spread flat, the rapid descent slowed, and the white-headed flier leveled out into a glide just a few feet above the lush growth at the edge of open water.

Talons protruded forward as the raptor closed on the location of its unsuspecting prey. In one silent, fluid motion, the raptor dipped, lunged, seized, and pumped upward with powerful wing beats. It firmly grasped a snake that never saw what hit it. The serpent writhed and wiggled, but could not free itself from the eagle's unyielding grasp. The bird steadily climbed with constant wing beats, gaining altitude, and then turning in the direction of its treetop nest on a distant ridge overlooking the lake.

But this meal would never reach the eaglets in the nest. An osprey, drifting in the thermals above the sub-alpine lake, was witness to the eagle's effort to clear the area with the morsel of prey locked in its talons. The challenging osprey dove toward the larger eagle, descending at great speed, announcing its charge in a series of shrill cries.

The noisy advance of the osprey caught the attention of a lone group of human visitors to the lake. A slender, middle-aged woman, sitting in a lawn chair beside the lake, lowered the magazine she was reading and searched the sky for the source of the commotion. Two children, balanced on a semi-submerged log and clutching large dip nets, peered intently into the shallow water next to the log, unaware of the wildlife drama that was unfolding overhead.

"Look!" called the woman as she gestured skyward. They all looked up in time to witness the dogfight's climax. The osprey, seeming to be no match for the larger, stronger eagle, closed in at high speed like a fighter plane descending upon a lumbering bomber. The eagle tried to evade the attack, but the osprey deftly adjusted, staying on course to intercept the eagle in midair.

The birds collided, feathers flew, and they both momentarily tumbled earthward before regaining level flight. The osprey circled for another pass. The eagle dove to gain speed, still trying to make a run for it. Straight above the three tourists, the birds met again. Colliding, the two raptors tangled with talons extended, again plunging vertically toward the lake some sixty feet below. In the melee, the eagle thrust its talons toward the aggressive osprey, and the snake was involuntarily released from the eagle's grasp. The avian warriors managed to extricate themselves from the tangle of talons, wings, and feathers, reestablishing level flight, now in opposite directions.

The disputed serpent, lost in the fray, tumbled earthward. It landed with a "plop" some fifty feet out from the shore where the two children stood astride the saturated log.

"Wow, cool," said the ten-year-old boy to his twelve-year-old sister. "Did you see that? It dropped the snake!"

The osprey circled, searching for the freed snake, which recovered from its impact with the water and was now fleeing the scene. The snake slithered shoreward in the direction of the tourists, somehow surmising that the human spectators were its best chance for sanctuary. The osprey first located, then attempted to pursue the lost prey, but the eagle challenged its advance with a counterattack. When osprey and eagle collided anew, the snake gained the few critical seconds it needed to make its break for shore.

The birds entangled themselves in more aerial combat, as the serpent drew nearer to the lakeside tourists. Neither bird dared to pursue the snake that had propelled itself to within a few yards of the human spectators. But, by fleeing in the direction of the people, the snake had unknowingly chosen to run another gauntlet, consisting of grasping hands and dip nets instead of razor talons and tearing beaks. The children's nets extended toward the snake, anticipating its arrival.

"Don't worry, Mr. Snake, we won't hurt you," the boy promised, as he lifted the snake from the water in his butterfly net.

"Amazing," the woman breathed as she rested her magazine in her lap and watched the children complete their capture of the snake.

A moment later, the snake was in the boy's hands. "I think it's hurt."

"I'm not surprised, after all that it just went through," the woman said. "I can't even believe it's still alive. That's got to be the luckiest snake on earth. What kind is it? Is it the usual red-sided garter snake?"

"No, it's something different, Mom. It's all different colors. Look at this greenish-blue part. When you hold it up to the light, it changes color. It's really cool. I've never seen one like this before." He confidently reached into the net as his sister peered over his shoulder. "Look!" the boy exclaimed, proudly holding up the snake.

Mom looked over the top of her sunglasses. "Wow, that *is* different," she agreed with patronizing interest. "Hey, we have to leave soon. I have to get dinner started. Do you want to bring the snake home?"

"No. It lives here. I wonder what kind it is, though. It's really strange."

The boy delicately released the snake into the water. The frightened creature had not yet forgotten its narrow escape from the eagle's claws and it had no desire to return to the open water. Immediately, it turned and swam back toward shore, slithering up the muddy bank and disappearing into the grass. Since the entertainment had ended, the kids returned to the log and resumed their search for newts. The mother lifted her magazine and returned to her article. Moments later, she felt an inexplicable tingle throughout her body. She was overcome with a sudden, queasy feeling in her gut. Her intuition told her that something was wrong. She set the magazine down in her lap and lifted her sunglasses for a better look. Anxiously, she scanned the trees and shrubs of the shoreline. Her concern was heightened by the unsettling realization that the woods had suddenly gone eerily quiet. No birds were calling, and no crickets were ticking. The kids were oblivious, but she had the disturbing feeling that they were being watched.

To the woman, the sensation was as palpable as it was ominous. She continued to scan her surroundings for any sign of movement. About a hundred yards up the lakeshore to her right, she picked out a solitary dark shape that seemed out of place amidst the solid green vegetation along the waterline. She squinted at it intently, trying to determine whether it was a shadow, a stump, an animal, or a person.

The more she stared, the more she thought she was seeing some faint movement in the dark silhouette. She finally decided she was seeing only shadows of forest branches swaying in the breeze. Then she noticed there was no breeze. Just as she tried to reassure herself that she was seeing nothing more than the motions of inanimate shadows, the dark form crouched down in one quick motion, disappearing behind the green foliage of the lakeshore. She gasped. The hair on her neck bristled as a wave of fright broke over her.

"*Something is watching us!*" she said to herself. While she was not at all sure whether the dark shape was that of a person or an animal, there was no longer any doubt in her mind that it just moved to conceal itself.

As always, her immediate concern was for the safety of her children. She knew very well that she was in an isolated part of the Mount Hood National Forest, even though she was only seven miles from her driveway. Certainly, there were no police any closer than three times that distance. Dangerous wildlife was not her chief concern; dangerous people were. The form she just saw looked more like a person than animal. Whatever it was, she has no intention of hanging around long enough for it to get any closer.

"Kids, it's time to leave," she declared, while folding her lawn chair and gathering her things.

"Could we stay just a little longer?" pleaded her daughter.

"No. We have to go now. I just remembered I have to get dinner started and I'm already late." She tried to sound matter-of-fact so she didn't transmit her alarm to the kids. "C'mon Jack, get your shoes on," she coaxed.

The boy jumped from the log to the shore, sat down next to his shoes and began to undo the laces.

"Let's do that in the car, dear. We have to go *now*." She was trying to sound casual. It wasn't working. The anxiety she felt was coming through in her tone.

Without saying anything more, she tucked her folding chair under her arm, took her daughter by the hand, led her in the direction of her son, then took the boy with her other hand. As they left the small beach and entered the trail, she looked back over her shoulder one last time to be certain that nothing was following them. She led them both up the short trail toward their minivan, which was parked beside the forest road. Her daughter noticed the backward glance and surmised its significance.

She did not share her mother's concern, but the girl was curious. "What did you see, Mom?"

"I don't know, I mean, nothing dear. Never mind. We have to go."

The girl was beginning to share her mother's anxiety, although she still didn't understand what her mother had seen that had so suddenly changed her mood. The denials were unconvincing to the perceptive girl, but she trusted her mother implicitly. It seemed to her that this was a good time to just be cooperative, so she climbed in the van quickly and quietly, sat in her customary seat behind her mother, and fastened her seatbelt without having to be told.

Moments later the minivan, loaded with kids and chairs, rapidly accelerated away from Squaw Meadow, leaving a plume of billowing dust that drifted out over the open water before settling onto the azure surface of the mountain lake.

Meanwhile, the dark form that was crouched on the far shore rose up, turned away from the lake and disappeared into the forest.

Chapter 2

"**H**ONEY, WE HAVE a faculty meeting tonight, so I won't be leaving for at least another hour," explained the gaunt-faced, middle-aged man sitting at a cluttered desk in an even more cluttered science classroom. His deep-set blue eyes were red and barely open from a long day in the classroom, but his day was far from over. "I should just barely make it home in time to pick up Jack and get him to his baseball game."

Sam Ward was an experienced, weather-beaten, middle-school science teacher. He had quit trying to hide the cynicism he felt about the administrative demands he viewed as unproductive or irrelevant, such as this obligatory Monday faculty meeting.

"It's the longest hour-and-a-half of my week," he confided to his wife over the phone. "It's supposed to be a meeting, but they insist on making it 'teacher training'. I'm not a hamster, and I don't need training."

Sam exhaled with a resigned sigh. "I had another kid fall off the defective lab stools today. The furniture in this classroom is falling apart. It's not even safe. I told the principal back in September, and she still hasn't done anything. When I mentioned it again today, she said there's no money to replace them. But, somehow, she managed to find the money to buy herself a new laptop. When someone gets injured, then they'll care. Of course, they'll try and blame me."

Sam paused.

"You're whining, dear," said his wife.

"You're right," Sam replied. "Sorry. I have a bit of a headache. I should have called in sick today. Anyway, I'll be home as fast as I can, but I have to stop and get gas at the Redland Store. Do you need anything from the store?" He fumbled for a pen, then grabbed a paper off the top of one of the disheveled piles on his desk. He scribbled a few words on the back of a student's homework sheet, folded it hastily and stuffed it in his pocket.

"What are the kids up to?" Sam asked as he was writing. He put down his pen and his sleepy eyes widened as he listened intently.

"Wow, that sounds scary. What do you think it was? Do you think it could have been a bear? They should be out of hibernation now that most of the snow is gone…so everything turned out okay?…Great…Well, all's well that ends well…Look, tell me more when I get home. I gotta get to the faculty meeting…Oh, is Jack there? Good, can I talk to him? " As he waited, Sam chalked the next day's lesson on the board: 'The Six Steps of the Scientific Method.'

"Hi, Jack. Mom says you went to Squaw Meadow today.

Was it fun? You what? You found a new snake?" Sam listened to a brief summary of the battle of the two birds and the narrow escape of the snake. "That sounds really cool. I want to hear more about it when I get home. Any idea what kind of snake it was?...What do you mean, 'You don't know'? You're the snake expert. Okay, I'll bring home another field guide and we'll try to figure it out tonight after we get back from your game." As he spoke, Sam returned to his desk and pulled a book off the shelf behind his desk. "I have a good one right here.

"Oh, Listen. By the time I get home, there'll be no time to spare. You'll have to have your uniform on. I'll change as soon as I get home and then we're off. We'll have just enough time to get to the game, but you have to be ready. Mom said she'll get you dinner, okay? And, if you have time, go out back and whack a few balls off your batting tee. We're going to need all the hot bats we can get. I don't have to remind you that, with all this rain, we haven't had a practice all week. I better go. Bye." He folded his cell phone, grabbed his briefcase, and dashed out the door.

Ninety minutes later, Sam worked his boxy, old Land Rover up a winding forest road that paralleled the course of a rushing river. Black basalt cliffs rose steeply from both banks of the river. As he geared down, the engine whined. He pulled in a driveway and rolled to a stop at the pumps in front of a brightly lit, freshly painted store adorned with an authentic western storefront. A banner extended across the top of the quaint storefront proclaiming, 'Grand Re-Opening.'

Sam got out, slammed the car door, and stepped back to admire the new store. He walked over to an older gentleman who was fueling a pickup truck. "Boy this looks great, Larry!"

"Thanks. Turned out great, eh?"

"Yeah, I'll say. I thought this day would never come. You did a fantastic job. You must be thrilled to finally be done. Congratulations!"

"We're pretty happy" the proprietor replied in a slow, country drawl. "We got the approval on the septic system last Friday. That's what was holding us up."

"First the new housing development in Carver, and now a new store up here in Redland. Man, if it gets any more built up around here, I'm going to have to move further out."

"You're already farther out than anyone else. Heck, Ward, you're backed up against the national forest. That's about as far out as you can get this side of Alaska. Any further out, you'll be on the Warm Springs Indian Reservation, and I'm pretty sure you're not welcome over there, paleface." Larry tipped his cowboy hat back on his head and smiled.

"You got me there, Larry," Sam agreed. "I guess my back is to the wall. Think you can see to it that your new store is the last new building around here for a while?"

"Don't worry. If everyone else has to go through the same 'permit hell' that I went through, then this county has seen its last new building."

Sam chuckled. "Another good point." He turned and headed for the store. He paused to browse the new bulletin board outside the front door that had homemade advertisements for tractors, barn builders, riding lessons, horse shoeing, lost pets, hay for sale, and housekeeping services.

An unusual sign caught his eye. Between the signs for

horse shoeing and free kittens, Sam spotted a hand-lettered sign reading, "Have you seen me?" Below those words was a rough sketch of a hairy, long-armed gorilla-like creature. He smiled.

"Great. Bigfoot. What next?" He mumbled to himself, in disgust. Toward the bottom of the notice, a small pocket of cardboard had been neatly affixed to the posting. It contained a stack of business cards. Sam began to walk away, but then thought better of it. He backed up and reached for one of the cards. He pulled it out and looked at it as he backed through the front door of the country store.

Moments later, he was standing in line at the checkout counter, humming to the tune "Big Yellow Taxi" as it played on the sound system inside the newly remodeled store. He was silently amused to think that he was probably the only one in the store who could name the band playing the tune. As a middle school teacher, Sam made a point to keep up with as much contemporary music as he could. This decades-old Joni Mitchell tune was being 'covered' by the L.A. band, Counting Crows. Sam's moment of musical appreciation was suddenly interrupted by a bump in the back. He looked over his shoulder to see a short, round man with a full head of black hair and a closely trimmed black beard. The man was wearing a satin baseball jacket. He turned around to face the man and his side-kick: a boy wearing an identical blue and white baseball jacket.

"Hey there, 'Ohio,' you ready to get beat, tonight?" said the bearded fellow, grinning mischievously.

Sam mugged a look of playful fear, "Uh-oh, the enemy. How you doin' Bart?" Sam looked down at the boy in the baseball uniform. "Hi, Matt." The boy smiled and raised his hand to offer a silent wave.

"Looks like you fellows have a game tonight," Sam observed. "Who are you playing?"

"You," Bart replied.

"No, we play Beaver Creek tonight."

"Not any more. They cancelled. Their school's spring music program is tonight. A third of their team is either in the band or the choir, so they can't play ball tonight. Randy called me this afternoon. Since he already had the field and an umpire, he wanted to at least scrimmage before our league game against you guys on Wednesday. Then we have a make-up game against you guys on Friday. If the rain holds off, I guess we'll be seeing your team a lot this week."

"Guess so. Obviously, I'm not quite ready for tonight's game. I still have to go home and change. I guess if there's anything to the whole 'early bird gets the worm' idea, then I'm in trouble."

"You sure are. I see you're still rooting for those hapless Cleveland Indians," Bart said, gesturing at Sam's baseball hat. "You better get along and get your own tribe together. The game starts in a little over an hour."

"I know. Don't worry. I'll make it. So, what do you think of this new store? Pretty fancy, eh?"

"Yeah, real nice. How long has it been open?"

"Less than a week. I kinda miss the old store with the uneven floors and pails in the aisle to catch the water from the leaking roof."

"Hey, 'Ohio', Randy and I are talking about golfing on Saturday. Do you still golf?" Bart asked.

"Golf?"

"Yeah, golf. You know, little white ball, long metal

clubs...It's supposed to stay nice through the weekend. We're going to the little nine-hole course in Eagle Creek. Thought you might be interested in getting beat on the links, after you get beat tonight, of course," Bart said with another grin.

"I wish I had time to golf. I have a lot of mowing to do. I haven't been able to mow in over two weeks because of all the rain. But thanks for the invitation."

"Well, you wouldn't have all that mowing if you hadn't turned your pasture into a baseball diamond. I bet you didn't think about all the maintenance when you decided to do your imitation of *Field of Dreams*. 'Build it and they will come,'" Bart intoned, imitating the low voice of James Earl Jones.

"That's the truth. All I do is mow grass this time of year. You know, they never once showed Kevin Costner mowing his baseball diamond in the movie. I will say, for all the trouble it's been, though, Jack's hitting and pitching has really improved, which you might find out for yourself real soon. You better hope we don't pitch him against you guys, tonight. I, for one, predict that my 'Field of Dreams' pays off, and he gives your boys a bad time tonight on the mound. And, if he gets a piece of one of your pitches, we'll be seeing your outfielders' backsides as they run for the fence."

"Doubt it," said Bart's son flatly.

"Next!" called the middle-aged brunette behind the counter.

Sam turned and took a large step toward the checkout counter. "Sorry, Sally, guess I was getting carried away trash-talking that troublesome customer who was annoying me in the checkout line."

"Take it outside..." Sally smiled as she rang up Sam's

box of automatic dishwasher detergent and two bottles of Gatorade.

Meanwhile, five miles further up river, the sharp "crack" of a squarely-hit baseball echoed off the steep green hillside in front of a lone boy. Standing at the edge of a mowed field, the boy set a ragged baseball atop a rubber batting tee. With a solid swing, he launched another long hit into the forest. He bent down, picked up another torn baseball, and put it on the batting tee. From the doorway of the distant house across the long yard came a woman's voice.

"Jack, your dinner is ready. Dad's leaving the store right now. He'll be here in ten minutes."

"Okay, I'm coming!" As soon as he said this, he swung the bat, sending this hit even further into the woods than the others. He watched it sail, then bent over to pick up the last of the torn baseballs. The last ball followed the others into the thick woods opposite the rustic log house from which his mother had called. He put the bat into his bat bag and started walking toward the distant house. Suddenly, a torn baseball flew out of the woods, landing with a soft thud and rolling to a stop only a few yards from the boy's feet. Jack stopped walking and turned to face the ball. He looked at the ball, then looked out in the direction of the forested hillside, then back at the ball.

He stood, silently staring at the woods, a puzzled look on his face. The woods were strangely silent. No birds chirped. The boy walked over to the ball, bent over, and picked it up while keeping a suspicious eye on the forest.

The eerie silence of the moment was broken by the

crackle of car wheels on a gravel driveway. The boy dropped the ball, grabbed his bat bag, and ran toward the house as a brown Land Rover pulled to a stop in front of the two-story log cabin.

Chapter 3

THE WARD HOUSEHOLD sat on five acres of nearly flat bottomland surrounded by the steep hillsides of the Squaw Creek canyon. No other homesteads were in view, but two other homesteads did occupy other parts of the same fertile bottomland of the Squaw Creek valley as it widened near its confluence with the Clackamas River. Squaw Creek is one of the more isolated of the forested canyons that slices through the mountains of the northern Oregon's Cascade Range. The once-forested bottomlands were logged around the turn of the century for the timber that fed the nearby sawmills in the once-thriving, now depressed 'timber town' of Redland. Situated on the flat, fertile ground where Squaw Creek emptied into the larger Clackamas River, Redland thrived as a 'timber town' for decades. Eventually, the supply of virgin timber was exhausted, and the timber-based economy of the Redland area suffered a steep decline.

Timber was no longer king in Redland but the soils were still fertile and the growing season was long. Now, deforested bottomlands of the area produced agricultural crops of hay, Christmas trees, and vegetables at the hands of a new generation of settlers. The Wards and other modern homesteaders were urban refugees, not only of the nearby city of Portland, but of the larger and more beleaguered cities of the American Midwest. Life on the frontier is never easy and while these 21st century pioneers drove pick-ups and sport utility vehicles instead of covered wagons and surreys, they were hardy, none-the-less.

The Wards were avid gardeners, even when they lived in the city of Portland. More than anything else, that is what drew them to this rural area thirty miles from the rainy streets of Portland. Their lifestyle change began when Sam was hired as a science teacher in the Redland school district. As he settled in to his new job, they spent weekends driving around the immediate area, looking for a rural property where they could put down roots. They knew exactly what they were looking for: the 'Newberg silt loam.' They had read soil surveys and knew this to be the very best soil that the area had to offer for farming and gardening.

Most of the ground around Redland was quite the opposite. Since the Cascade foothills were a volcanic landscape, the soil formed atop the ancient lava flows of the area had a bright red appearance. The earliest settlers, the ancestors of the Ward's former neighbor Bart Foster, platted the frontier town of Redland and named it in honor of its crimson soils. These agriculturally-minded pioneers quickly found that the most fertile soils of the area were not the heavy clay *Jory series* soils in the uplands, but rather the sandy *Newberg silt loam* found all along the creeks and rivers of the area.

Being as agriculturally-minded as the pioneers, Sam and Grace Ward had read of these exceptionally fertile soils in the local gardening literature. Mindful of their passion for gardening, the Wards focused their property search on the lush and loamy bottomlands of the Redland area. One rainy winter Sunday, they took a fateful drive up Squaw Mountain Road. Stopping at a "for sale" sign hanging on the fence of an overgrown hay meadow, they both instantly knew that this fertile but neglected piece of real estate would support their future home and garden.

The land deal was soon struck. Since money was tight, Sam determined that he would build the home himself. With only weekends and summers to accomplish this daunting task, the construction of their dream home proceeded slowly. Two years later, the log home was not completely finished but it was live-able. The Wards put their city house on the market, and relocated their young family to their isolated homestead along Squaw Creek, five miles upstream of Redland.

Now, eight years later, the Ward family was comfortably ensconced in the log home they built near the pristine rushing waters of Squaw Creek. Their gardens, and their two children Elizabeth and Jack, were flourishing.

Sam's teaching job was just six miles downstream on the unpaved Squaw Mountain Road, then another short jaunt down the main highway to the Redland Middle School. Not only was the Ward homestead close to his work, but both Sam and Grace relished their close proximity to the vast tracts of public land in the Mount Hood National Forest.

The Ward property shared a border with the national forest, so nature was more than just close to them. For the Ward homestead, nature was often an uninvited guest.

There were other downsides to living on the edge of the national forest. During the logging boom of the 1980's, log trucks were as common as mini-vans on the Squaw Mountain Road. Then the timber industry's bust of the 1990's brought an abrupt end to logging traffic. The road was not well maintained any more, but it wasn't getting beat up as badly by heavy truck traffic, either. For the Wards, and the handful of other residents along the road, this seemed a suitable trade-off. There was much less dust and noise now that the road was only used by a smattering of Forest Service fleet vehicles and the seasonal parades of weekend recreationists.

The bottomlands of Squaw Creek, like much of the landscape surrounding western towns, saw an evolving land use that began with virgin forest, then timber land, then livestock pasture, and finally homesteads for urban refugees. When their children got older and more mobile, it became clear to the Wards that another shift in land use was in order. Unlike the suburban neighborhoods of Sam and Grace's childhood, there were no playgrounds and precious few playmates to entertain their growing kids.

Beginning with a swing set, the Wards set about to create an array of play areas on their acreage that would serve to occupy, entertain, and even educate the children. They created trails along the slow-moving creek where the children could witness the constant changes inflicted on the riparian woods by the local beaver population. Side pools and rocky outcrops provided rich habitats for garter snakes, newts and other small amphibians. Trout and several smaller species of fish inhabited the pools in the creek created by the ever-changing structures of the tireless beaver.

Sam built a tree house in a large maple tree that had sprouted multiple trunks. Walking trails eventually encircled the property, connecting the various play centers and gardens throughout the homestead. As the kids got older, though, the types of play that interested them also evolved. Like many a rural female, their daughter Elizabeth had a fondness for horses from the earliest age, and by some stroke of good fortune, new arrivals built an opulent horse stable just two miles down the Squaw Mountain Road. Rather than owning a horse of their own, the Wards were able to lease an animal for their daughter's care and use, and she was soon learning all the details of training and grooming horses for show purposes.

Jack Ward, on the other hand, was a horse of an entirely different color. From the youngest age, he had two consuming, almost contradictory passions: nature and sports. His interest in nature was understandable, given his childhood surroundings. Indeed, both children learned to appreciate and identify birds from an early age. Their parents would position their high-chairs in front of the picture window, allowing the children to watch the birds at the feeder as they learned to feed themselves. Jack's first spoken word was "bird," and both children could identify bird species by name before they could pronounce their own names.

Once Jack learned from his father how to catch garter snakes in the pasture by pouncing on them with gloved hands, it became his favorite pass time. Even as a toddler, he would arise on sunny mornings and immediately head outside, still in his pajamas, to patrol the edge of the pasture for garter snakes. He loved to catch them, hold them, and inspect them, always letting them go precisely where he found them, ever aware that the snake had a home as he did, and that was where the snake belonged. Jack's favorite toys were rubber snakes. He had snake posters on his walls. His favorite books were about snakes, and his favorite television shows were about snakes. That is, snakes and sports.

As with many other kids, Jack spent too much time in front of the television, but the usual kid stuff didn't interest him. If there were no shows about nature to watch, he would be content to watch games and sports highlights all day long. He could watch the plodding progress of a televised baseball game for hours. Grace taught him how to read baseball statistics in the newspaper and it wasn't long before he was able to calculate batting averages to three decimal places in his head.

Though he was fascinated by other televised sports such as basketball, football, and soccer, baseball was his passion. By the time he was three, it became clear to proud father Sam that sports was more than just a passing fancy for his small boy. That realization forced another revision in the Wards' land use plan. First, Sam built the basketball court. He learned how to mix, pour, and float concrete in the process of building the court behind their small barn.

When he wasn't searching for snakes, Jack could be found shooting baskets on their home-made court. When basketball season concluded in February, Jack's coach asked Sam if Jack might wish to play on the 'Midget' level baseball team he was organizing. Given Jack's almost innate interest in televised major league baseball, the answer was obvious, and it was shortly thereafter that Sam was considering yet another change in the land use for the expanse of level land that comprised their back pasture.

A few days after Jack was invited to join the baseball team, Grace heard the rumble of a big diesel engine. She looked out the sliding glass door to see Jerry Harding, the neighbor with the big horse stable, rolling up the driveway on a large John Deere tractor. When he rumbled up to the parking area trailing a plume of diesel exhaust, Jerry hesitated then veered toward the back pasture where Sam was waving his arm.

As the tractor ground to a halt in the middle of the pasture, Sam approached it and put his arm on the step where Jerry's foot rested. After a few minutes of discussion, Sam stepped aside, the tractor engine revved, and Jerry's John Deere began annihilating thick tangles of blackberries and brush on the outer margins of the pasture. After an hour of 'brushing' the perimeter, the tractor left, only to return a half hour later with a different attachment, this one for tilling up the sod and turning it into bare earth.

Grace was more than a little annoyed to see Sam out there behaving like he was living the Oregon remake of *Field of Dreams*, yet she also knew it was hopeless to try and change Sam's mind about an idea once he had a plan and some momentum. He was a man of uncommon stubbornness and determination, which was a bit maddening at times like this, when she did not particularly care for his ambitious initiatives. Grace consoled herself by recollecting that the house in which they now lived was also a product of three years of the same tireless determination that she was now lamenting.

Over the course of the weekend, Sam graded, raked, seeded, and watered the formerly green pasture. It was now a broad expanse of smooth, bare dirt. Grace wasn't at all happy about the pasture's sudden disappearance, but she squelched her objections in the hope that her husband's mid-life fantasy of creating a baseball diamond was intended to nurture the children's athleticism.

Despite her misgivings, it surprised Grace to see what lengths Sam went to for this seemingly impulsive addition to their homestead. A chain-link backstop soon stood at the back of the pasture, base paths were lined out with chalk, and a pitching mound was formed from a heap of clay and dirt.

Such was the beginning of the baseball diamond two years ago, carved from the back pasture where Grace's son's passion for wild animals would intersect with his love of sports in a way that was destined to ripple through the entire rural community, and into the wild forestlands that surrounded it.

In the two years since the pasture was turned into baseball field, Jack's interest in baseball steadily increased to the point where it rivaled his interest in nature. Tonight was a game. Jack was sitting at a table in his baseball uniform eating his dinner. He stared intently at a tiny bird sitting on a branch outside the dining room window. The bird moved closer to a nectar feeder and inserted its delicate beak into the small hole to sip the sweet nectar from the feeder.

"Look, Mom! It's the ruby-throated hummingbird. It's back!" Jack said.

"I know. I saw it this morning, so I filled up the feeder. They showed up almost two weeks later than last year. I think it's because this spring has been so cold and rainy."

Sam breezed into the room, wearing his baseball coach's uniform. He opened the fridge and grabbed an apple and a Coke. "Jack, we gotta get going. Where's your bat bag?"

"It's outside next to the car. I'm almost done eating. Hey, Dad! Did you bring home a reptile book from school?"

"Sure did, but we don't have time for that right now. We gotta go! C'mon."

"Oh, Dad! Know what else happened? I was out in the field practicing my hitting before you got home. Just before I came in, I took a few of the old baseballs and hit them into the woods behind the backstop. But, when I turned to go back to the house, one of the balls came back out! All by itself!"

"You probably bounced it off a tree. That must have been quite a hit. Nice going. Think you can do that tonight against Bart's team?" As Sam was talking, he emptied his pockets into a ceramic dish on a table by the door. He rattled his change into the dish, as well as a wrinkled gas receipt and a small folded card. He hesitated and looked confused, then recognized the card as the one he took off the sign on the bulletin board at the Redland Store. He read the name and number, smiled a half smile, then put it in the dish.

Meanwhile, Jack muttered to himself, because no one else was listening, "I dunno...I don't see any way that ball could have bounced off a tree..."

"We gotta go or we're going to be late for warm-up and you know what that means. You're going to have to run laps." At that, Jack jumped up and yanked the uniform-protecting napkin out of his collar.

Minutes later, Sam was unloading gear from the Land Rover. He paused to survey the situation. The parking lot of the community ball field was filling up with pick-up trucks containing parents and children wearing baseball uniforms. The charmingly pastoral sports field was one of the joys of Sam's existence. It was nestled in a pocket valley surrounded by the same lush, green forested terrain that typified the whole area around the town of Redland. Players from both teams were warming up as Sam carried a bucket of baseballs over to the dug-out. Randy, the head coach, stood nearby with his hands in his pockets. Sam was pleasantly surprised to see Gary White in the corner of the parking lot, adjusting his umpire uniform.

"Great," he thought to himself. "For once we won't have to scramble to find the umpire."

Randy's voice could be heard from the dug out. "Has everyone run out and touched the foul pole?"

"I haven't!" yelled Jack, raising his hand.

"Well, Ace, let's get going! You're late! You owe me *two* laps, ya slacker!" Randy smiled a sarcastic smile as he looked toward Sam. Sam turned and smiled in return, then shook his head. "My fault, coach!"

"Good, you can gimme a lap, too. We've got way too many goof-offs in this outfit!" Jack took off running. Ignoring Randy's command, Sam picked up the clipboard and looked at the lineup card. He then turned to Randy and said, "I wonder who Bart is gonna pitch. I saw him at the store an hour ago, and he wasn't saying."

Randy changed the subject. "Did you see the story about Bart in the paper today?"

"A story about Bart? No. I haven't seen the paper yet today. What was it about?"

"I guess Bart is doing a big real estate deal. He's in with some investors who want to build a resort and golf course on some land Bart owns up at Squaw Meadow," Randy said.

"WHAT? Squaw Meadow? No way! That's Forest Service land."

"Nope. The article said there's eighty acres around the meadow that was homesteaded by Bart's grandfather. Bart's dad held title to the place all these years and when he died last year, he left it to Bart. Plus, there's a mining claim that covers half of Squaw Butte that's been in Bart's family for generations. They have a plan to make a ski area, golf course, and a gated community. Sounds like they want to do the whole she-bang."

"No wonder he's so interested in golf lately," Sam said.

"Yup, if this deal goes through, and it sounds like it's gonna, then things will be getting pretty 'up-scale' around here. You and I both knew this day would come, but I never figured it would be old Bart leading the charge. Progress is coming to Squaw Meadow," Randy proclaimed with mock sincerity as he thrust his fist into the air, as if leading a charge himself.

Later that night, Sam was sitting at the kitchen table, still wearing his baseball uniform from the game played earlier in the evening. He was reading the newspaper, studying one particular article very intently: "Local Realtor Signs Deal for Golf Resort at Squaw Meadow." Sam sipped a beer in the darkened room. He stared blankly at the newspaper story. He shook his head and quietly repeated Randy's declaration from earlier in the evening, "Progress is coming to Squaw Meadow."

Chapter 4

Sunrise illuminated a galaxy of dew drops on the outfield grass. A lone figure trotted through the forest behind the backstop of the baseball field in the Ward's pasture. The figure moved out of the woods into the open. Sam Ward jogged around the baseball field in his tracksuit. He stopped, stared at the ground before him, and bent to pick up a hawk feather lying in the trail.

Stepping back and looking skyward, Sam searched for a nest in the trees above. He saw none. In light of his kids' interest in nature, he scanned the ground for more feathers. but, finding none, he resumed jogging.

Across the field and inside the house, Sam's wife Grace was making breakfast. Jack and Elizabeth were sitting at the breakfast table. Jack, wearing his New York Yankees pajamas, flipped pages in a field guide to snakes. Elizabeth read a book on horses. Dishes clattered as Grace put the kids' breakfast in front of them. Sam walked in the door and presented the hawk feather to the kids. Jack's face lit up.

"Where'd you get that?"

"Found it in the woods. What kind of hawk do you think it is?" Sam asked as he sat down with a cup of coffee.

"Probably a red-tail," Jack speculated, stabbing the feather into the flower arrangement at the center of the kitchen table. Jack continued to flip pages in the field guide as he started to eat.

"Dad, I've been trying to figure out what kind of snake it was we found yesterday. So far, it's not in this book you brought home from school..."

"I saw it first," Elizabeth interrupted.

"Well, I caught it."

"Well, what did you do with it?" Sam said, imitating Jack's tone.

"I let it go."

"Well, it was certainly the humane thing to do, but that also means you're the only one who can make the official determination on what it looked like. Maybe you should start by writing down a description or drawing a picture of what you saw so you don't forget any important details. "

"It was about a foot and a half long and it was really colorful and changed colors in the sunlight. I've never seen one like it before," Jack recollected as he continued to flip pages in the field guide.

"That's called iridescence, when the light plays on the skin pigments and makes the colors change. Chameleons have that. It does sound unusual, but I would be surprised if the snake you found wasn't in that book. That particular book is supposed to be the best field guide on amphibians and reptiles of this area. It should have everything. Too bad you let the snake go, though. An important discovery may have just slipped through your fingers. Literally. Now eat your breakfast, nature boy. We have to be out the door in fifteen minutes, and you're not even dressed yet."

"It kind of looks like this one, but it says it's not even a snake. It's a lizard that has no legs and looks like a snake…" Jack's voice trailed off, as he flipped one page back and forth.

The father looked over his shoulder while sipping a cup of coffee. He pointed to a small map at the bottom of the page. "That says they're only found in central and southern California, so I doubt it would be that."

Sam turned around and left the room as the kids ate. A short while later, the kids were standing in the doorway with backpacks full of books, waiting for Dad. Meanwhile, Sam was frantically looking for his wallet. He found it in his jacket on the hook by the door. "Keys," he muttered, looking around again.

"Right there, Dad," Elizabeth said with a look of annoyance as she pointed toward the dish on the stand.

"Thank you. *Now* I'm ready. Let's go…" Sam mumbled to himself in a distracted tone as he picked up the keys. He paused at the key dish and picked up the card he took from the bulletin board at the Redland store the previous night. He looked at it with a wry smile.

"…Yeah, Dad, *let's*…" Elizabeth said impatiently.

Sam kept the card in his hand as he kissed his wife goodbye, then turned to walk out the door behind his kids. Sam held up the card for his daughter to see. "Look at this card I got off a bulletin board on my way home yesterday," he said to his daughter. "This guy is a bigfoot chaser. Recognize the name?"

Elizabeth looked at the card as they walked down the steps toward the car. "Nick Rollo! I think that's Jenna Rollo's dad!"

"Well it said on a sign I saw that he's a 'bigfoot investigator.' Is that crazy, or what? I had no idea there was such a thing. I wonder whether there's a test you have to take to get certified…" Sam's voice trailed off as he walked around to the driver's side of the Land Rover.

"I see him when he picks Jenna up after school. He always wears this hat," Elizabeth gestured with her hands to indicate a wide brimmed hat.

"I think you mean a *fedora*, you know, like Indiana Jones," Sam asked. "Does he also carry a big whip? It might come in handy if he ever *did* run into bigfoot."

Elizabeth smiled and rolled her eyes. She paused before opening the rear door of the car. "Hey, Jack was in the front seat yesterday. It's my turn!"

"You snooze, you lose," Sam retorted. "Tell you what, you can drive. Can you drive a stick?" His teen-age daughter let out a dejected sigh as she climbed into the back seat. The car engine started and they sped off down the gravel driveway followed by the ever-present cloud of dust.

The school bell rang, but the clatter of students, books, and chairs continued uninterrupted. Sam Ward, science teacher, began his daily performance. He clapped his hands twice with a slightly effeminate, theatrical flair, shouting, "People! Peee-pull!"

Some of the students smirked at his exaggerated gestures. The class began to settle. Mr. Ward continued his theatrics with a sarcastic statement. "Today, lay-dees and germs, you will be fascinated to know that we will be learn-ing the subtleties of *the scientific method*! Yay!!" An audi-ble groan rose from the eighth graders. "Now, now, try to contain your excitement. It's probably not as exciting as it sounds."

"No one cares about the scientific method. When do we study sex-ed?" a student interrupted.

"Never. Why on earth would I ever give eighth graders any information that they could use to reproduce them-selves?" Everyone laughed. "Okay, 'Mr. Negative,' you may not care about the scientific method, but that's because you don't know anything about it."

"But give me a chance, I can make this interesting. Have I ever told you I used to sell ice to Eskimos? I got a cold reception there, too. To continue, these are the steps of the scientific method..." Mr. Ward gestured toward the chalk-board. "Write this down please...(clatter of notebooks)... now let's see how we can make this interesting to a bunch of oversexed eighth graders...I know! Bigfoot! There's a kid who goes to my daughter's school. Her dad chases bigfoot. It says so right here on his business card. Is this guy crazy or has science missed something?"

"My grandpa saw bigfoot once!" a female student piped up. She was a brown-skinned girl, obviously of Indian heri-tage.

"Your grandpa IS bigfoot," called another student.

"Yo mama!" she snapped back.

Everyone laughed.

"Laugh if you want to." The smile disappeared from her face. "You laugh because it scares you, but the Yakama Indi-ans don't laugh. White folks think there is only one of them, and his name is 'Bigfoot.' In my tribe, they laugh at *that*.

How can you have just one of anything? In the Yakama tribe they laugh at you people and that stupid name: Bigfoot. How insulting is that? My tribe calls them "Ste-ye-hah'mah" which means 'Stick Indians.' The coastal tribes call them the sasquatch. Every single tribe has a name for them."

"Wow, Iris," Sam said. "I had no idea you were so knowledgeable on the subject. How did you come to learn so much?"

"My grandpa told me a lot about them. He said our ancestors have been living here for thousands of years and they know a lot about the forest people, but the white men think it's all imaginary."

Iris stared intently at her teacher. "Do you think they're all just imagining things when they talk of the forest people? Well, they're not! They're just another tribe. They're mysterious but they're real. They live in the forest, and they mostly move at night, so they can see real well in the dark. They don't trust the daytime people, and they just want to be left alone. The Yakama Indians know they are out there, but they leave them alone, because that's what the Stick Indians want. My grandpa said you white people believe the TV when they tell you there's only one, and his name is 'Bigfoot.' You think it's all a big joke. You people laugh, but you're the fools."

Iris folded her arms purposefully to indicate she'd had her say. The girl next to her held up a palm toward her and said, "You go, girl."

Iris gave her a high five and smiled. The classroom was completely silent. Mr. Ward stood by the chalkboard, frozen with a piece of chalk in his hand. He is momentarily speechless. "Could your grandpa come talk to us? Does he live nearby?"

"My grandpa died last year."

"I'm sorry," Sam said. "Thank you for sharing that, Iris. That's amazing. I must confess I never took the whole thing seriously either. I guess I always assumed that one would have been shot by now. If they were real, where are the bones? Wouldn't someone have found bones by now if they were real?"

"Have you ever found bear bones in the woods?" Iris asked. "Even animals don't just drop dead in plain sight and stay there. Things eat them. The bones get scattered. But the sasquatch aren't animals. They're people. My grandpa said they're too smart and too fast for hunters to shoot. And he said that's lucky for the hunters, because if you shot one, you wouldn't make it out of the forest alive. If anything, it would be *your* bones that would be found by the scientists."

Another student raised a hand. "Wasn't there a story in the paper recently about some guy who said he faked all the footprints as a prank?"

"If there was, then he's a liar. Sasquatch sightings go back generations among the Yakama people, and other tribes, too! My grandpa said the paper prints that stuff 'cause that's what white folks want to believe. Sorry." She raised her palms in a gesture of apology. "Children wouldn't sleep at night if they thought the woods had monsters. Neither would their parents. My grandpa used to say we're the monsters. He said the sasquatch were the protectors of the forest."

Another long and awkward pause overtook the classroom. "I must say, Iris, you raised some excellent points. Now *I'm* curious," Sam remarked. "And I admit, I'm as guilty as anyone when it comes to thinking of bigfoot, er, sasquatch, as a joke or a bunch of hoaxes."

"Okay, I have an idea. I'm really glad this came up. Here in Oregon, bigfoot is a bit of a local legend, oops again, *sasquatch* is a local legend. Heck, sasquatch sightings are as common as Elvis sightings. See, the humor just flows. Anyhow, real or not, the question is, 'Can we investigate this scientifically? How good is the evidence?"

"It's so easy to make jokes instead of taking it seriously. I have an idea though. You guys get the scientific method written down and we'll make sure everyone here understands how it is used. Meanwhile I'll try to get in touch with this sasquatch investigator. My daughter goes to school with his kid. I'll see if I can't get him to come in and talk to all of us. It'll be interesting to see what he has for evidence. We'll rate the evidence for ourselves. This is perfect. Now, get writing, everyone. The scientific method." Mr. Ward taped a yardstick on the board in a theatrical manner. "Right here! Right now!"

The students began writing. The classroom fell silent. From the back of the room came the same voice as before, "So, when *do* we get to study sex-ed?"

Mr. Ward buried his face in his hands, shaking his head.

Two days later, the classroom brimmed with chaotic motion that gradually increased in intensity as more students filed in, dropped their belongings, and came to rest on the vacant lab stools around the room. Some glanced suspiciously toward the unfamiliar countenance at the front of the room. The stranger, head down and focused on his task, ignored the uneasy glances from pupils as he worked, lifting cloth-covered bundles out of large Tupperware bins and setting them carefully on the demonstration table at the front of the science classroom.

"Uh-oh, a substitute" a student whispered to another.

"I don't think so," answered Iris. "That's Jenna Rollo's dad, the sasquatch guy. I bet I know what this is about."

"What?" asked a clueless male student.

"Figure it out," she muttered in an impatient tone.

A bell clanged loudly in the hallway and at that same moment, Sam confidently walked into the classroom, carrying two cups of coffee, one in each hand. He made his way to the front of the room, setting one cup down on the demonstration table in front of the guest speaker.

He set the other cup down on the corner of his cluttered desk, pushing a stack of papers aside to make room. He leaned against the edge of the desk and spoke the first names of individual students as he stared out across the classroom. Each time he spoke a student's name, a head lifted up, a mouth shut, and the room got slightly quieter. In less than a minute, the room was almost quiet. Sam raised his eyebrow and made one more expectant pause. The last rustling of students came to a halt. The room was now silent. Sam began to speak.

"I'd like to make an introduction," he began. "This is the guest speaker I promised you. This is Nick Rollo. Mr. Rollo is a bigfoot researcher. Right, Mr. Rollo?"

"Actually, I prefer to use the word 'sasquatch'. 'Bigfoot' is such a silly name. Would you go out with someone named 'bigfoot'?" Nick Rollo smiled.

"No, but I wouldn't go out with someone named Sasquatch, either!" Sam joked. "Oh, wait! I take that back. There was this one girl back in high school…" he added with a look of comedic confusion on his face. The class laughed.

"I *so* believe that," Iris piped up.

"I was desperate...you see, I was a complete nerd back then...unlike now."

"I'm not even going to touch that one," Iris added. "It's too easy."

"Is this a classroom or a TV sitcom?" Nick asked.

"Oh, we haven't even gotten warmed up yet," the black-haired girl remarked. Sam silently sipped his coffee, smiling as he leaned against the cluttered desk.

Then Iris added, "Aren't you Jenna's dad? I've seen you at the stable where Jenna rides."

"That would be me, alright. But promise me you won't tell Jenna I'm here to talk about sasquatch. She would freak."

"That'll require some hush-money," Iris shot back with now-familiar sarcasm, extending her open palm.

"See me after class." Nick smiled. He lifted his head to address the class at large. "Please call me Nick. And since when does a bigfoot researcher have spare cash for hush money?...uh...*sasquatch* researcher, I mean."

"Whatever," Iris said.

"If I may interrupt your banter," Sam said, looking straight at Iris, "might we get on with this lesson, here?"

Iris sat back on her stool, folding her hands on her desk in mock seriousness.

"Anyway, people, the other day's science class was a presentation of the scientific method, right?"

"Punishment is more like it," Iris muttered.

Sam raised his finger in her direction as a silent reminder that she should be quiet.

He turned to his guest. He said, loud enough for everyone to hear, "Make a mental note, Nick: don't ask them tough questions. They only respond with hostility."

Everyone smiled. Iris faked a scowl, began to open her mouth, and then changed her mind.

"Thank you," Sam said, acknowledging her restraint. "We also, much to Iris's dismay, made clear the difference between a hypothesis and a theory. And we talked about a null hypothesis." He gestured toward the definitions on the board: "Theory, hypothesis, and null hypothesis," he continued. "Today, you are going to apply that knowledge. Here's how. You are going to be asked to formulate your own hypothesis with respect to the bigfoot question." Mr. Ward paused and turned toward Nick. "I mean sasquatch," he said, and then made a slight bow. Nick grinned and returned the bow.

"I think you guys are beating that joke to death," Iris observed.

"That's not the only thing I'd like to beat to death..." Sam said, and turned toward the guest speaker. "Sorry, Nick. 'Miss Interruption' here hates it when our jokes are funnier than hers. She thinks she's the next Paula Poundstone."

"Lenny Bruce, actually," Iris corrected.

"Nick is here to show you what he has collected over the years by way of *sasquatch* evidence."

"Don't you mean *bigfoot*?" Iris deadpanned.

"That's enough outta you, young lady. Now class, before Nick shows you anything, you are going to state your hypothesis with respect to the sasquatch/bigfoot question. Does it exist?"

Nick interrupted, "They."

"Huh?"

"They. Not 'it,' *they*," Nick said again.

"There has to be more than one," said Iris. "Remember?"

A look of confusion on Sam's face turned to under-standing in an instant. "Of course. *They*. Do *they* exist?" He grinned sheepishly, then continued, "Or, you may offer the opposite hypothesis: *They* don't exist. It's got to be one or the other. Once you formulate your hypothesis, you'll formulate your *null* hypothesis, which is the opposite, you might say the antithesis, of your hypothesis.

"The idea here is that you mustn't be overly committed to one possibility. You must remain aware of the opposing scientific viewpoint. If your hypothesis states that there is no such thing as bigfoot...er, I mean *bigfoots*, I mean sas-quatches, I mean, whatever, then your null hypothesis is that they *do* indeed exist.

"Then we will show you all the physical evidence that Nick has collected. Good or bad, strong or weak, you will rate the quality of the evidence as critically as you like on the sheet I gave you. Then, you will decide whether the evidence you saw compels you to either accept or reject your original hypothesis. Everybody got that?"

"I'm not sure I do," Nick said with a confused smile.

"You be quiet. You're not even paid to be here," Sam teased.

Nick, now understanding the lighthearted classroom climate that Sam created, jumped in. "I'm glad you brought that up. I've been meaning to ask about a raise? I mean, aren't I the one doing all the work here...?"

"Yeah, but I'm the brains of this outfit," Sam said. "And you can start earning your *non*-pay, that is if the two 'duel-ing comedians' here don't wipe each other out, first."

"Ahem," said Iris. "*Two* dueling comedians?"

"My God! I think I'm going to regret I ever tried to do this." He forged ahead. "Okay, so, everybody understand what we're doing?"

No one spoke. He theatrically wiped his brow in mock relief.

"Good, now, write! I don't care what you say; just write your hypothesis, whatever it is: 'Yes' to bigfoot. 'No' to sasquatches. 'Yes' to sasquatches. 'No' to bigfoot.

"Just make your null hypothesis a statement that is the completely opposite point of view. There's a little more to a well-constructed null hypothesis than that. It's actually kind of a statistical thing, but never mind that right now. Just make two opposing statements and let's move on. And in the interest of time, I'm going to ask Nick to start showing you all the evidence he's collected, because he has quite a bit to show you. Where do you want to start Nick?"

"Well, let's start with what I consider to be the strongest physical evidence, and then go downhill from there. Everybody has heard of the footprints." With a magician's flair, he pulled a big blue cloth off the table to expose an array of large plaster footprints.

"As you can see, I have eight different track casts that have come from three different states. Now, these are all authentic tracks, at least as far as I know, but I'm willing to let you be the judge of that. It's always possible that somebody faked them, in fact science requires you to first and foremost, assume that they are fakes, unless you saw a sasquatch make them, which of course you did not. So even though footprint casts are some of the strongest physical evidence we have, they are not really very solid at all. But, there's one thing you can say for sure. These didn't all come from the same foot, even if it was a fake foot. Look at how different these tracks are. If some faker like Ray Wallace or some other dead guy is supposed to have made all the sasquatch tracks ever found, he better be able to show us more than one set of fake footprint-makers. These tracks are all quite different.

"Interestingly, some of these casts are pretty similar, but none are identical. These two were found by the same guy in eastern Oregon, a fellow named Paul Freeman. He died a few years back. He was old, and he knew he was going to die, so he gave me these casts in the hope that they would continue to be shown to people just the way I'm doing here today.

"Mr. Freeman found these casts in different places in the Blue Mountains east of Walla Walla, Washington, about two years apart. It was his feeling that they belonged to the same individual creature that he was tracking. I tend to agree, but don't let me influence your judgment. Granted, these could all be fakes. That is always a possibility. Still, I'll show you something important but you have to look very closely. They're called dermal ridges. They're in this track, here." Nick pointed to faint lines on one of the track casts.

"Dermal ridges are the tiny little patterns of swirls in the skin on your hands and feet. We call them fingerprints, but they're on your toes and your feet, as well. So the correct name for them is 'dermal ridges.' Now, look at this track. This came from a creek just down the road from here near Colton. If you look real close at this heel area, you will see dermal ridges all over the place. It's very rare to get this in a track because the track has to come from very fine mud. Otherwise, the dermal ridges don't get transferred from your foot to the mud.

"If they do get transferred to the mud, then, the person who makes the cast also has to pour the plaster in very carefully or the dermal ridges will be washed away as soon as the wet plaster hits the mud. I didn't make this cast. It came from another fellow named Ned Kaneaster. He spent many years gathering evidence of these creatures in the Colton area where he grew up. I once helped Ned with some remodeling on his house. A few months later, there was a rash of sasquatch sightings around Colton. He carefully searched the area around the sightings and found some tracks in a nearby creek bed, which he cast with plaster.

"He gave me one of the casts. I don't think he realized it had dermal ridges in it when he gave it to me. I didn't notice that the cast showed the ridges until a couple of years after Ned gave me this cast. I've shown this track cast to guys who study the dermal ridges pretty seriously. They were amazed. This may be one of the best examples of dermal ridges ever obtained. This track is either really valuable, or worthless, depending on how seriously you take the whole sasquatch mystery."

Sam stepped forward and leaned over the footprint Nick was holding. "Could you show us those dermal ridges again, please?"

"Right there, there, and there," Nick said. "See the pattern of parallel swirls?"

"Indeed I do. That is very interesting. Okay, people, you've seen the track cast evidence. Now rate it on your sheet and let's move on to the next category. This is interesting stuff, but we don't have all day."

Silence fell over the classroom. Heads bowed and pencils moved in unison throughout the room as students wrote on their sheets. Nick paused to marvel at the silent focus of a class that was so full of disorganized motion just a few minutes ago. He brought forward the next box, which contained a portable CD player and a stack of CD's.

"The next category of evidence is 'sounds', I have some taped noises here. Whether or not these are sasquatch calls is what you get to decide. I'll just play the noises for you, but first let me provide some background. People who live in remote places, like ranches and homesteads that border the edge of the national forest, sometimes hear strange noises, especially at night. Mr. Ward, I understand you live on the edge of the national forest. Have you heard any strange noises at night?"

"I hear stuff all the time that I can't identify. I assume it's owls, coyotes, or maybe mountain lions. I will add that every once in a great while, I hear something really loud and really strange, but I tend to assume that it's just people out there being rowdy."

"Good point," Nick agreed. "But, sometimes people have other strange things happen and, for whatever reason, they decide that they may have sasquatch activity around them. When I hear about such folks, I might ask for their permission to set up what we call 'camera traps.' They're motion-triggered waterproof cameras strapped to trees. They're set to take pictures of whatever wildlife passes in front of them. Since they have to be waterproof and battery-operated, they're expensive. I can only afford a few, and the outdoors becomes a mighty big place when you only have a few cameras to set out. So, even though I set up these cameras, I also have to use other methods of collecting whatever evidence there might be. Putting out microphones and taping nocturnal creature calls turns out to be one of the easiest ways of collecting some kind of evidence from these areas of interest."

"For instance, when somebody reports hearing very strange noises at night, I set them up with a voice-activated recorder and ask them to keep it handy. I set up a microphone outside their house ahead of time and leave it there. I also set up recorders and have them ready to go. Whatever I get for recordings certainly isn't the best evidence in the world because I never get to see what is making the noises. However, I do get some pretty interesting sounds."

Nick paused, looked over the classroom. "I've done this for several years now and have recorded three very interesting noises I brought here today to play for you. I've played these calls for two wildlife experts, and neither of them can definitely say they recognize the calls as some familiar animal. Of course, that doesn't prove anything. It just says experts don't know what they are. So, you listen to them and see what you think. Then rate the evidence on your sheet. Here's the first call."

Nick pushed the button on the boom box and a screeching noise bellowed from the speaker. He stopped the player.

"Here's the second one."

He pushed play again and the students listened intently to a loud pinging sound, similar to the sound of sonar pings on submarine movies. Once again, Nick hit the stop button.

"And here's the last one..."

A long moaning howl emanated from the speaker.

"I've heard that one coming from the woods behind my house several times. I assumed it was a wolf," Mr. Ward commented.

"I suppose it could be," Nick agreed. "Of course, there aren't supposed to be any wolves around here, so that would be a fairly big deal in itself. How often have you heard it?"

"Oh, no more than half a dozen times over the years: usually in summer, late summer. It comes from the hills in the direction of Squaw Meadow," Sam replied.

"Interesting. You should try to tape it. I can show you how to get set up."

Mr. Ward nodded. "I'd be willing to try. It's pretty far away, but when I hear it, I can't help but be impressed by how loud it is. It echoes off the nearby hills. It gives me chills just listening to it right now."

"Okay, those are the calls. What do you think?" Nick asked.

"I think they suck," blurted Simon, a red-haired student. "Those noises could be anything. The last one sounds like an air raid siren."

"Now, be nice," Sam said. "We have lots more stuff to show you. Good or bad, just rate the evidence. Remember, we're trying to be scientific here. Just rate the audio evidence on your paper now that you've heard it. Save the attitude."

Heads went down, silence blanketed the room as pencils scribbled. Nick paused to savor the silence. He looked at Sam, who was calmly sipping his coffee. Nick smiled and Sam winked.

"Let's move on," Nick said. "We have eyewitness accounts, then spoor."

"What's spoor?" Simon asked.

"We'll get to that," Nick said, "but first, let's do sighting reports.

"The eyewitness reports, or sighting reports, as we call them, give us a lot of information about appearance and behavior of these creatures, but they are also the easiest thing to fake, so they are the least scientific kind of evidence. In fact, 'sighting reports' are completely unscientific. They're basically just stories. They're interesting stories, and they show patterns, but they are utterly unscientific because there is rarely, if ever, anything tangible and concrete to back up the story. So when it comes to evidentiary value, they're worthless."

Nick paused, scanned the faces before him. "But here's what's funny. Stories aren't supposed to be admissible in scientific circles, ever. But they are in medicine. Medical researchers call them case histories. If a person has cancer and suddenly gets better for no known reason, they study the situation and call it a case history. It sounds a lot more scientific when you call it a case history, but it's still basically a story. There's no physical evidence to go with it, other than the change in their medical condition."

After the sighting reports, the last things Nick showed the eighth grade students were scat samples. "You guys are gonna love this. Or maybe be horrified, I'm not sure. Do you guys know what scat is?" Nick paused and looked around the classroom, but no hands went up. I'll give you a hint. It's very similar to another word that describes the same thing."

Sam cleared his throat, smiled at Mr. Rollo, and made a chopping gesture across his neck.

Iris piped up, "I think I know!"

"I knew you'd figure it out. Moving on..." Sam said.

"Yes...well...in the 'sasquatch biz,' as in all wildlife research circles, we call it scat. And, believe it or not, there are people who think they've found bigfoot feces, scat, that is. Some of them have even been kind enough to give me samples of what they found."

"My, aren't you fortunate." Iris said.

"Like it or not, wildlife biologists can learn a great deal about diet and general health by analyzing scat. Scat is but one kind of spoor. Spoor is anything animals leave behind. Spoor can be hair, teeth, dead skin, blood, or urine…it's all known as spoor. It would be nice if I had blood to show you. Blood would be the best kind of spoor to obtain because it would contain fresh, pure DNA of whatever creature left it.

"Scat is the worst, because it contains the DNA of everything that the animal ate before it left the scat. It may not be the best type of spoor, but scat is easier to find and recognize than just about any other kind of spoor. I have three samples, two of which are right here, in Ziploc bags that I have no intention of opening. People who know of my interest in sasquatch send me this stuff when they find it."

"These two I'm holding came from two different hunters. I don't recall how they came by it. I will say they were both very serious hunters who spent a lot of time in the outdoors. In science though, none of that matters. The only thing that matters is, how it tests out. And, I have not had these tested because testing costs money. This kind of thing has been tested in the past, always with the same, uncertain results. So, I just hang onto these things and show them to curious folks like you people. There's not much to see since they're kind of broken apart. However, this beauty, on the other hand…"

Nick reached below the counter, lifted up a tray, then pulled the cloth cover off to expose an eight-inch long feces that measured two and a half inches in diameter. The class erupted into howls of horror and laughter.

"That thing explains all the screaming you played us on those tapes!" Simon yelled.

More howls of laughter. Nick thought to himself that these middle school students certainly were easily amused. Amidst the pandemonium, he calmly stood with the tray extended. He looked at Simon and quietly said, "That was actually funny, kid. Mind if I steal that joke? I'll get a lot of mileage out of that line."

Simon smiled. After a pause to let the noise subside, Nick continued, "...if you look closely, you can see that this particular scat is almost entirely fur. So it's definitely not human. It could be bear. That's really about the only other possibility. I've seen a lot of bear scat, but never one like this. Anyway, there it is. It was found by a Forest Service friend of mine who knew I did the sasquatch thing, so he scooped it up and saved it for me in his Starbuck's coffee cup. 'Grande' size, of course. Good thing, too, because he had to carry it around with him for the rest of the day in his pack.

"He was in a closed watershed where Oakridge gets its water. That helped rule out human origin, but then, so did the size of the darn thing. Oh, and one more thing: the scat is completely dried out and I've had it for at least four years now. But the thing still smells really bad and I mean *really* bad. Now I would never force anyone to do this, but if there is anyone who actually wants to, you can come up and take a whiff of the scat. Don't blame me if you pass out, though."

As soon as Nick said it, about a dozen boys were out of their seats and crowding around, ready to take a whiff. Nick pulled the tray back and instructed them, "This is how you smell something that may be quite strong. You fan the air from it toward your nose. That way, you won't get an overly strong blast of smell."

Nick demonstrated by fanning the air above the scat toward his nose. "Now, line up and let's do this in an organized fashion. While we're doing this, the rest of you can finish your rating of the evidence. Then, we can wrap this thing up. Rate the spoor samples on your rating scale, whatever that happens to be."

The kids picked up their pencils and began to write. Sam and Nick glanced back at each other. Sam said, "I think you've seen about everything Nick brought with him, right Nick?"

"Well, there's much more of each kind of evidence but, yes, you've seen a sample from each category of evidence."

"With the time we have," Sam explained, "that's about all we can drag out. Now let's summarize. You will decide whether the evidence adds up to verifying or refuting your hypothesis. Since everyone's hypothesis will be a little different, you are going to have to reduce it to a simple 'yea' or 'nay'."

Then Nick added, "If there's one thing I've learned, it's that kids love to know what other kids think. The same thing is true with most grown-ups, really. Anyway, why don't we take a little poll of all the junior scientists in the room? I'll keep a tally up here on the board, and for simplicity's sake let's just make two columns. One is 'Yes, sasquatches are real' and the other is 'no, they aren't.' O.K.? So, based on the evidence you saw, how many say 'no bigfoot'."

Almost the entire class raised their hands. Nick counted the hands, and then wrote '24' in the 'no Bigfoot' column. "Skeptical crowd you have here, Mr. Ward."

"So it seems," Sam agreed.

"Okay, how many say 'yes, bigfoot/sasquatch?'"

Three hands went up. One of them was Iris. "Three. This is good. Mr. Ward you didn't vote. What do you say?"

"Hmm, shouldn't there be a third category? You know, the one that is every scientists favorite category: 'requires further study'"

"Oh, absolutely. Fine, we'll add that, but before we do, what would you say if you had to choose between these two?" Nick insisted.

"I guess I would have to say 'no', but I must say, I found the calls to be pretty interesting."

"Okay, one more 'nay'. That makes a total of twenty-five to three. And now: the third category. 'Requires further study'. How many feel that, yes or no, the matter deserves further study?"

All the students in the classroom raised their hands. "Ah, now there's a sign that you all are good little scientists. Twenty-seven for 'requires further study.' Now we just have to get funding for this further study. Good luck. But aside from that, let's look at the results of our survey, one more time. First, I must say, the people who voted 'no' are to be congratulated, because they are properly applying the scientific method. You see, the honest truth is, all of this evidence is, well, crap...at least from a purely scientific point of view.

"Now, don't get me wrong. I collected this myself, or I got it from people I trust. But I also understand how science works, and the way it works is this: if it is even possible that the evidence was somehow faked or mistaken, we must assume that it is. Since none of this evidence is irrefutable, we are required by science to conclude that there is no compelling evidence to support the sasquatch hypothesis. The bottom line is that none of this evidence holds water."

Two of the students sitting by Iris thumbed their noses at her in gestures of obvious glee. The guest speaker noticed the gesture.

"Now, before anybody gets up on their high horse, we have to look at those brave souls who dare to go against the grain. Because, it has to be said, that even though none of this evidence, technically, is very compelling, we have to admit that quite a bit of it is intriguing. Even though it is not good enough at present, I have a prediction to make. The evidence is not good enough now, but someday, I predict, it will be. We can't prove a thing right now, at least if we abide by the exacting standards of science, but something is definitely going on out there in the woods that we do not have a handle on. Personally, I think we are looking at a huge scientific discovery that is just waiting to happen. It definitely hasn't happened yet, but I think it will happen someday, and maybe one of the open-minded yet scientific souls in this very classroom might be the one to do it. And then who would get the last laugh, eh?"

The room was silent. Iris sat up proudly and folded her hands on the lab table in front of her. The bell rang. Students began to move en mass. The teacher yelled over the clatter, "Hold it people! Aren't we forgetting something? Mr. Rollo here just provided you with a most interesting presentation of the scientific method that I've ever seen. Might we show our appreciation to Mr. Rollo?"

The students stood and applauded in unison. Nick held up his hands in a gesture of thanks. Sam applauded as well, then stepped forward to shake Nick's hand as the students filed from the room. "Ya can't do any better than that, Nick. I can't thank you enough for a great lesson. I don't know about the kids, but you've definitely got me thinking."

Chapter 5

≋

AFTER THE STAMPEDE of departing students ended, Sam Ward turned to his guest speaker, who was catching his breath and resting on a lab stool.

"Watch out for those stools," Sam warned. "They fall apart."

Nick stood up.

"Want to get some lunch?" Sam asked.

"Yeah, as long as it's not cafeteria food."

"There's a Subway shop down by the high school." Sam looked at his watch. "If we hurry, we can get in and out of there before the high school kids invade at 12:30. It would be good to get out of this place for a while. I'll warn you I still have a few questions on the bigfoot subject. That is, if you think you can stand talking about bigfoot a little more. I'll buy you lunch to make it worth your while."

"You don't have to do that. I never get tired of talking about bigfoot. But I thought you were skeptical of the whole deal."

"I am, or at least I was. I must say, you've got me wondering."

"Who was that Indian-looking kid in the front row? She's a riot."

"That's Iris. Isn't she a trip? Smart as the dickens, and quite the 'wise guy'. She's always right there with you, too. I think she has a future as a stand up comedian."

"There seems to be a lot of that in your class. Did you catch that red-haired kid's remark about the screams and howls when I showed the scat? I've never heard anything funnier in my life. But, I will say, that Iris kid seemed to know her stuff."

"Yeah. More than you know," Sam said. "In fact, she was the one who first got me questioning my own assumptions that the whole matter was a myth and a joke. I tried to make a joke out of it when it first came up in class. She insisted that it wasn't the joke I was making it out to be. Truth be told, it was her challenge to my flippant portrayal of the matter that got me wondering whether there might be more to it.

"I'd seen your card, on the bulletin board at the Redland store, but I probably wouldn't have done anything about it if she hadn't piped up in her feisty little way. More than anything, that's what prompted me to give you a call and see what you had to say. By the way, do you get much response from signs on bulletin boards like that?"

"A fair amount, but not all of it's welcome. What I'm really trying to find are rural residents in isolated places who have several unusual events of one sort or another to report. That means they are getting repeat visits from the creatures. That's not always what I get, though. Sometimes I get calls from people who want to prank me. They think I'm a goofball who chases shadows and ghosts and they want to have some fun at my expense. Once in a while, I get a call from a TV or newspaper reporter. I've learned the hard way that it's best not to play ball with the media. You just never know what the editor is going to do to the story after the reporter is done with it. Even if the reporter gives their bigfoot piece a serious spin, the editor usually changes things around and makes me out to be some kind of fool."

"TV is even worse than print media. No matter what you say on camera, they will edit it into a laugh line that the anchorman will use between the weather and sports. But media notwithstanding, I do get some interesting stuff, and there does seem to be a definite pattern. For instance, people who live in isolated places and who also raise lots of animals seem to have more than their share of visits by these mysterious creatures, or maybe they just do a better job of noticing strange things that occasionally go on in the rural landscape. Some would say they just have better imaginations. For whatever reason, it seems that these isolated, rural, salt-of-the earth-type folks who raise animals consistently report the most interesting nocturnal happenings. Once I figured that out, I also figured out that there is a better place to put up signs than bulletin boards outside rural grocery stores. Wanna guess where that might be?"

"Adult video parlors?"

"See, that's why everybody in your class is a cut-up. They're following your lead."

"Sorry, I couldn't resist. Anyway, I really haven't a clue."

"Feed stores."

"Feed stores?"

"Sure. Feed stores. Think about it," Nick said

" Let's see. It's a place that would be visited sooner or later by everyone who raises any kind of livestock."

"Yup, it's the animal husbandry connection. People who live around animals seem to be attuned to the comings and goings of all the wild creatures around them. And, laugh if you like, but that actually seems to include bigfoot. Go figure. I think it also might have something to do with the fact that they are up and moving around at weird times of the day. Before sunrise and after sunset, these folk are out there fixing the broken fence, rounding up the loose goat, and so on. You know the old country saying: 'If it has testicles or an engine attached, sooner or later it's going to give you problems.'

"Well, while they're out there in the dark of winter dealing with their troublesome livestock and troublesome engines, they're also in a position to see more and hear more than the rest of us, if for no other reason than because they're outside more. We may live in the country, just like them, but they tend to *really* be in the country, as in lying in the mud setting a skunk trap under the chicken coop while the rest of us are inside watching TV or surfing the Internet. Plus, they have all their animal feed lying around in bins and barrels. They also have gardens, orchards, and so forth. Well guess what? These are what you might call 'unmonitored food sources' for you-know-who."

"You mean sasquatches are raiding ranches and farms for food? I thought bigfoot was supposed to live in the wilderness."

"Maybe they do, but they don't necessarily stay there. It's like the bank robber who was asked why he robbed banks.

His answer was, 'That's where the money is!' Well, when it comes to why the bigfoot would hang around farms at night, it's the same kind of reasoning: That's where the food is!

"A big surprise for me, was not just that these creatures do, indeed, exist, but that they operate a whole lot closer to where we live than anyone realizes. I wouldn't suggest bringing it up in your classroom, but what I think I'm finding is that sasquatches know a whole lot more than we realize about where the 'easy pickins' are found in the rural landscape. It only makes sense. Why chase down rodents and grubs in the wilderness when you can have fresh chicken, eggs, and vegetables with no particular effort? I think they feed on wild food sources as well, based on my limited scat analysis, but I've also seen probable bigfoot scat that was all cherry pits, or apples, or blackberries."

Nick kept going, "They may seasonally reside in the wilderness, to keep people at a distance, but they also seem to frequent farm and ranch country under cover of night. And at night, there is absolutely no way of defending the multitude of agricultural food sources. Farmers and ranchers seem to be feeding the local wildmen whether they mean to or not. But when it comes to kids, it's best not to bring that up. It's better to represent the situation as something that is far away from where they live. They sleep better at night that way. Truth be told, I see lots of evidence that they come in and fleece the farms and ranches for food. Especially in winter."

"Really? That's amazing. I must say it does make perfect sense. Why chase wild animals when you don't have to? It's the most efficient way for a sasquatch to feed the family."

"Sure. Think about it: free food for the taking...and lots of it. No one is watching after dark, which is when these bad boys operate. If one could just see in the dark, there's an amazing amount of food that people leave just lying out. And, this much I think I know: these operators can see in the dark as well as you can see in the daylight. Oh, and I'll tell you another interesting thing I've bumped into several times. You would never think of it but it's as obvious as hell. Outdoor freezers. They are the freezer section of Mr. Sasquatch's grocery store. Lots of rural folk have a freezer in an outdoor shed that is loaded with food. Smoke houses are another one. There are lots of them out there and, under cover of night, they get raided. It's hard to always be sure it isn't the neighbor kids, but when the ice cream bars and corn dogs get left behind, and a frozen deer quarter, or a bag of frozen smelt disappears from the freezer, I don't think it's hungry teenagers. Teenagers don't eat smelt. They don't even know what smelt are!"

"Neither do I." Sam said.

"They're little oily fish that migrate like salmon. The smelt runs, like the salmon runs, are fast disappearing but when the smelt run does happen, old-timers still scoop them out of the river with long nets. If you ask me, the things taste nasty but people catch 'em and freeze 'em. The point is, I know a guy who lives on the Sandy River who has had his frozen smelt disappear out of his outdoor freezer almost every year. He assumed it was local teenagers, but I think the teenagers are getting a bum rap. He had ice cream and popsicles in the same freezer. Ask yourself what teenager passes up ice cream and popsicles so they could feast on a big old bag of little oily fish? I think most people who are getting ripped off in this way don't even notice, or they do notice and they just assume they're being ripped off by their white-trash neighbors."

The pair strode up to the restaurant. Sam held open the door for Nick as he said as he said, "It's weird you should say that. When I first moved out to my place on Squaw Creek, the guy who owned the next place over, Doc Carter, accused me of stealing his apples. I was flabbergasted. I mean, *as if* I'm going to risk getting shot for his lousy apples when they're ten cents apiece at the local fruit stand. I couldn't figure out where this guy was coming from. Until now, I always assumed it was deer. He was such an ass about it. He said he knew it was me who was stealing his apples because the whole tree was getting cleaned off from top to bottom.

"I could only say that I was a bit mystified as to how deer or bear could get the apples from the top of the tree. I assumed he was exaggerating. It's kind of ridiculous, really. He must have thought I was going over there with some big orchard ladder and carting off hundreds of apples. And he was so nasty about it, I had no desire to discuss it with him and figure out what was really going on. I can only imagine what he would have said if I tried to tell him bigfoot was stealing his apples. Somehow, I don't think he'd buy it. Guess I can't blame him. I don't think anyone else would, either. It makes you wonder how many rural people are wrongly suspecting some shady neighbor of ripping them off."

"You could say," Nick interjected, "that one of their shady neighbors *is* ripping them off. People are just accusing the wrong neighbors. I guess my point is, a lot of country folks have neighbors that they didn't know they have."

"O.K., so tell me this," Sam challenged. "How does a sasquatch get the apples from the top of the tree. Wouldn't they be too heavy to climb the tree without breaking all the branches?"

"A guy up on Bauer Road outside of Colton told me he once looked outside just after dawn and saw a sasquatch shaking his apple tree, and the apples were falling like rain. I think that would do it," Nick replied. "Is this neighbor guy of yours with the apple tree still around? He might have other observations to share."

"No. Fortunately, the guy moved away. He was getting old and he moved back to town someplace. Just as well. Nasty fellow. Anyway, so you're saying that my area up Squaw Creek is a good area?"

"Are you kidding? It's huge! The best. You're only seven or eight miles from Squaw Meadow, right? That's an easy stroll for a sasquatch. I've gotten three eyeball sightings over the years from elk hunters up in that meadow, and there are countless stories from scared campers who've heard strange things or had their camp cooler raided at night."

As they sat down with their lunches at a table, Sam asked, "By the way, have you heard that the guy who owns a big part of that meadow is going to develop it?"

"No, I hadn't heard that. What's he going to do with it? It seems a little far out of town for a subdivision," Nick wondered.

"He's going to do a resort. Golf course, vacation homes, gated community, you know, the usual."

"Great," Nick replied sarcastically. "Just what the world needs: another golf course. What do they want to call it, Sasquatch Heights?" Rollo kidded.

"I bet they call it The Lodge at Squaw Meadow. I've noticed they always name the new development after the place that got destroyed by the development."

"I don't think they'll use 'Squaw Meadow', Nick told him. "They're trying to get that name removed from maps and place names. Apparently, in Native American languages, 'squaw' does not refer to females in general, as most people assume, but rather a specific part of the female anatomy, if you get my drift."

"I had not heard that."

"It's true," Nick explained. "What's more interesting is the number of other place names right around our area that refer to strange forest beings. The names date back to pioneer times when the local geography was being explored and named by the first white settlers."

"Like what?"

"Well, right here on the Clackamas ranger district, there is a Skookum Creek and a Skookum Lake. To the Chinook Indians who lived around here, Skookums were forest spirits, but by today's standards they're essentially synonymous with the sasquatch. Then there's Cultus Creek, Devil's Peak, Devil's Ridge, Spirit Mountain, and my personal favorite, Tarzan Springs. As far as I can tell, these are all references to the same enigmatic forest beings that we were talking about in your class. The landscape is full of references to these creatures. In other places, like right around here, you see places with names like Indian Ridge and Squaw Meadow. How did these names come to be? The Indians were either dead from disease or moved to reservations by the time the Cascades were being explored and mapped."

Nick thought a moment, then said, "On a historical note, gorillas were unknown to science until the early 1900's. Settlers in remote places like the Northwest didn't learn about the discovery of gorillas until much later. Meanwhile, what were local people supposed to call such creatures that they saw here in North America, before African apes were even discovered? My theory is that, when they bumped into these intimidating creatures, they assumed them to be vestigial Indians who had not been shipped off to the reservations. Miners and settlers with some knowledge of Indian words used the word "squaw" to describe the creature they saw when they were obviously female, that is, when they saw obvious breasts on the sasquatch.

"Few people realize," Nick continued, "that in the most remote areas of the Mt. Hood National Forest, place names were not assigned until the 1940's. That's when cartographers were making detailed maps of the area for the very first time. I'm fairly sure that place names were not based on the presence of actual Indians at that late date, but it's hard to be sure of how far back the names go. Anyway, the local Chamber of Commerce would definitely prefer that the real reason for some of these place names be forgotten. Bigfoot is definitely not good for business, unless of course, it stays firmly in the realm of myth, legend, and joke. So that's where it stays."

Sam wondered, "What if it was shown that they actually did exist? Wouldn't the sasquatch potentially qualify as an endangered species?"

"Are you kidding? It would be the ultimate endangered species! It would be beyond huge. It would also be an absolute disaster for whole industries like logging or mining. If a creature like bigfoot was shown to be real, it would be the spotted owl times one hundred. And that simple fact is the very reason why the spin-meisters and industry mouthpieces are going to do everything in their power to keep the sasquatch "hypothesis" as you call it, well out of the public eye. And, it turns out, it's very easy to do that just by keeping the whole subject in the realm of fantasy and humor. You better believe that big timber companies know plenty about the sasquatch. Recognition of the sasquatch would be an unmitigated disaster for loggers and anyone else who made their living in the woods."

"Boy, that sure raises some interesting possibilities as far as putting the brakes on development of Squaw Meadow," Sam thought aloud.

"Yeah, well, good luck. You're not the first person to think of that one. People have been trying to prove the sasquatch hypothesis for years. Men you've never heard of like Green, Krantz, and Dahinden made it their life's work, yet they got nowhere. Sounds to me like an uphill battle all the way." Nick said. "If they couldn't prove the existence of the sasquatch, I doubt you ever will. The creatures themselves seem so unwilling to cooperate that it leaves sasquatch researchers like me to wonder whether they really are there or if we're just imagining the whole thing. But then, you see such vigorous condemnation from industry and government, it starts to become suspicious. As Shakespeare once wrote, 'Me thinks the lady doth protest too much.'

"The opposition is so strong," Nick continued, "that it begins to seem that they already know as much as they need to know, and whatever they do know, it's not good. There's much more at stake than the loss of a little development here and there, or a few more clear-cuts. Listing of the sasquatch would threaten everything that the Forest Service, Bureau of Land Management, timber, mining, and development ever wanted to do. So, if you want to stand up and say that sasquatches really exist, they would fight you to the death. Literally. And they'll start by ridiculing you and making you look like a complete idiot in front of the community and the world. So, be prepared to be a laughing stock about one week after you decide to go public with your battle to 'Save the Sasquatch.'"

"Point taken," Sam agreed. "Forewarned is forearmed. What exactly do you think these things are, anyway? That kid Iris is Yakama Nation. She says that her elders think of it as a tribe. But it seems I'm hearing it described as everything from an ape to a spirit. Nick, what do you think?"

"That's the biggest question, of all." Nick commented. "The debate rages, I guess, having cut my teeth around some of the old guard like Renee Dahinden, John Green, and Grover Krantz, I tend to agree with that thinking. I think we're looking at the North American great ape. It's probably a descendent of a creature found in the recent fossil record called *Gigantopithecus blackii*. That animal was a huge pongid, better known to the average person as a gorilla. We know it from the fossil record from jaw and teeth remains that were collected by this famous anthropologist named Von Koningswaald back around World War II. Right now, most of the bigfoot enthusiasts think it's a species of apes. We call them 'Giganto' for short. But more and more, that too, is being challenged.

"There's a Russian researcher named Dmitri Bayanov. He says that some Russian researchers know of bigfoot-style creatures seen in the Caucasus Mountains in the southwest corner of Russia. It's Bayanov's feeling that they represent vestigial populations of *Homo neandertalensis*, or what we call 'Neanderthal man.' Now, if Neanderthals are spread out around the globe in other places as well, then that fact might also explain the bigfoot phenomenon as we know it today. Other guys insist that the best fit is *Homo erectus*, also known as 'Java Man.' That's another Von Konigswaald discovery. Or, there's *Paranthropus*, which is also know as *Australopithecus*. So far, they're only supported by fossil evidence. And right now all of these possibilities share the same problem, and that is they're thought to be extinct. But then, what do we really know? Everything is based on the mere handful of fossils we have collected on these various creatures.

"Back in Charles Darwin's day, it was thought that fossils that had been unearthed up to that point in time represented a complete picture of all fossil species there were to be found. What a laugh that turned out to be! New fossils are showing up all the time. Just in the past couple of years, a hobbit-sized hominid was found on an island in Indonesia, and then a new fossil species of hominid was just found in Denisova Cave in southern Siberia. They even got the DNA on that one, and they were able to determine that the hominid wasn't a Homo sapiens or a Neanderthal. And, that fossil was only 30,000 years old. When a fossil is that recent, I say, it probably isn't extinct. Heck, it survived the ice age and everything else, so it probably still exists...and the possibilities don't end there.

"The lunatic fringe of the sasquatch field contends these creatures are not from this planet at all, but rather some kind of visitors from another world. I gotta laugh. Not at their wild suggestion, but just the idea of being known as the lunatic fringe of bigfoot enthusiasts. How much worse can you get than being seen as crazy by the 'bigfoot believers' that the whole world sees as crazy?

"Maybe it's a double negative that cancels itself out, in which case you're sane! Ha! So, there you have it. If sasquatches are visitors from another world, then that sure helps explain how come we can't ever catch up with them, why they seem to manifest a spirit quality about them, and so forth. If a guy wants to be truly scientific, then you have to consider *every* possibility, in which case that suggestion is certainly a distinct possibility. There are, however, two huge problems with the alien connection." Nick paused to take a few bites of lunch, which had been sitting on the table for five minutes.

While he ate, Sam jumped in, "Let me guess: If one were to stand up and say bigfoot is a space alien, you're going to get laughed out of town even more than the 'mainstream' bigfoot people, who are already laughed at by mainstream science!"

"Precisely," Nick agreed. "You're playing right into the hands of your detractors. Credibility is forever lost; at least until someone can persuasively show that there are even such things as space aliens in the first place. That's the one thing that seems even tougher to demonstrate than bigfoot itself. And that, Mr. Science Teacher, is the other 'huge problem'. If sasquatch beings are extraterrestrial in origin, then kiss it off. It's a safe bet that if something is somehow able to travel across the galaxy to get here, then us earthlings are hopelessly outgunned. You haven't a ghost of a chance of catching them in any trick or trap. They'll head you off at the pass every time. Just like they always seem to do, as much as I hate to admit it. Believe me, pal, I've tried everything...at least I feel like I have. Hidden cameras, video cameras, aerial surveillance, you name it; I've done it all. Everything but digging a deep hole and covering it with sticks and moss."

"I saw that same road-runner cartoon," Sam smiled. "Boy, there's the most interesting aspect of the whole question, so far: How would you prove it? In fact, forget about proof, how would you even go about getting decent evidence? Proof is starting to sound like a virtual impossibility," he added.

"Yep," Nick agreed, "Proof is a mighty tall order. I'll settle for good evidence, any day. Even that is starting to seem impossible. Especially when you consider that people didn't start trying to prove this yesterday. People have been pursuing this with a passion since the late 1950's, and all we have is a bunch of plaster casts, and some arguable hair samples.

"I suppose, to be perfectly honest, that's why some of us favor the 'great ape' scenario. It makes the problem seem much more do-able. It's the same reason we hate the space-alien scenario. It seems hopeless. Truth be told, I'd rather pursue an ape than an alien, any day. How about you?" Nick asked.

"Man. I can't argue with that logic. No sir. Now I better get back to the middle school. America's youth awaits. We shall continue this conversation another day, Mr. Rollo. It has been *most* enlightening."

They shook hands and Sam hustled off, grabbing his sandwich to gulp a few bits on the way.

Chapter 6

WEARING THEIR BASEBALL uniforms, Sam and his son loaded into the brown Land Rover. Jack balanced a paper plate with a slice of pizza as he fastened his seat belt. Sam fired up the Rover and they bumped down the long driveway. Sam talked as he drove and Jack ate pizza, trying not to drip sauce on his jersey.

"They're going to hit you," Sam advised. "You can't strike everybody out. I'm not trying to discourage you. I just want you to be ready for the fact that, Sooner or later you're going to give up some hits. Every pitcher does. It doesn't mean you can't pitch. Every pitcher has bad nights. On other nights, everything you throw is a strike. Some pitchers say there's a voice inside their head that turns on if you listen and it tells you what to pitch. If you hear the voice, listen to it. It'll tell you how to win."

The Rover pulled into the rural baseball diamond surrounded by thick stands of timber. Forest crowded the outfield fence. Bart Foster, once again the opposing coach, had already started warming up his team. Balls flew back and forth between young players of both sides. Randy sent fly balls to his outfielders. A couple of miscreants ran half-hearted laps. Sam waved to Bart, who made a detour toward Sam's car.

"Who are you pitching tonight?" Bart gestured toward Jack in the passenger seat and smiled. "Hope it's not Mr. Fastball in there." Jack smiled back.

"Hi Bart," Jack said politely.

"I dunno," Sam said. He turned and looked at Jack.

"Think you're up to throwing tonight, big guy?"

"I guess so," Jack replied sheepishly.

They started unloading their gear and headed for the dugout. Sam called out to Bart, "Say, I saw in the paper you signed a big golf course deal. I guess it's time I took up golf, seeing how I'll be so near to a new course. Have you got a name for these new links?"

"Oh, we're kicking around a few names but we haven't settled on anything yet."

"Well, I think it's customary to name a new development after the thing that was wiped out for the sake of progress. So, I think that would mean the golf course should be called "Squaw Meadow.""

"I knew I'd hear about this whole thing from you. Do you teach the kids at school to oppose all forms of development that you don't make money on yourself?"

"If I did, your daughter would know. She's in my class."

"Say, how about we bet the meadow on tonight's game. Winner decides how to develop it," Sam suggested.

"Ha, ha. I have a rule I always follow when it comes to betting. I never bet more than I can afford to lose, and I never gamble for rights I already have. We've been planning to do something with that property since before my dad died. He was perfectly okay with it."

"Yeah, but a golf course? If I remember your dad, he would have rather seen something done with that land that would have done more for the whole area. Like a baseball field."

"We already have a baseball field, this one! A golf course will bring in more out-of-town money, and that money will get spread around to a lot of families if they want to work with this project, not against it. You could get a piece of the action if you accept this project instead of spending all your energy fighting it. Remember, pal, if you can't beat 'em, join 'em."

"Where have I heard that before? You sure you won't play tonight for the meadow?"

Bart smiled. "May the best man win," he grinned, turned and walked toward his team.

Time flies, balls fly, plays are made, and errors abound. The five inning game was now in its final inning. Jack had already struck out once and singled to shallow centerfield when he stepped up for what would be his third and final at-bat. The count went to full.

Jack displayed some good baseball judgment; he stepped out of the batter's box, took a deep breath and stared straight out toward center field past the outfielders. He looked up momentarily, just in time to see a red-tail hawk glide directly overhead. He looked out toward center field and saw a movement in the shadows. A voice inside him spoke. Jack decided that he was going to swing at the next pitch, no matter what was thrown his way.

The pitcher wound up, and Jack's metal bat made a full and solid "Clink!" A line drive shot whizzed past the pitcher's ear as the pitcher ducked for cover. The ball bounced once on the edge of the infield and took a high hop right over the head of the ten-year-old centerfielder, who raised his mitt in a half-hearted effort to stop the speeding baseball.

The team in the dugout erupted into cheers as Jack dropped his bat and ran down the base path toward first base. The outfielders turned their backs on home plate and raced to retrieve the ball as it continued to bounce and roll toward the woods.

Jack turned on the gas and continued around the bases and headed for home. The cheering got louder and louder as the ball came flying in from the outfield and the base runner bore down on home plate. Jack tromped on the plate as the ball bounced into the infield, well short of the catcher's mitt. Two runners waited for the batter to cross the plate and offer him high fives. The young boys shrieked for joy. The game ended with a three run homer.

Jack and Sam drove home from the game in silence. The father shook his head. He turned toward Jack, hesitated, and then broke the silence.

"You've never hit a ball like that before."

"I've been hitting off the tee every afternoon when I get home. I think the practice helped."

"Ya think? Man, that was some hitting. I can't tell you how proud I am of you." Sam paused as a huge log truck rolled by them in the other lane.

"That home run on a full count was really something to see. How'd you manage to stay cool enough to hit like that?" Sam finally asked.

"It was just like you said in the car on the way to the game, Dad."

"What did I say?"

"You said 'do what the voice tells you to do.' I heard the voice. It said, 'This is it. Your pitch. Be sure and swing.'"

"Are you serious?"

"I listened for the voice. I thought it said swing, so I swung."

"Where did the voice come from? Inside your head?"

"Not really. It actually seemed like it was coming from center field...from the woods beyond the fence, almost. It seemed so loud, I thought other people could hear it, too."

"On the way to the game we were talking about pitching. I didn't know there was a voice for hitting. This IS news. Mighty good job though, kid. I'm really proud of you." Sam turned onto Squaw Mountain Road.

"It was especially sweet to beat Bart's team. I was giving him a bad time before the game about selling the meadow. I told him we should bet the meadow on our game tonight. Your homer would have won us the place too! Too bad we never shook on the bet, eh?" Sam kidded.

"I know...hey Dad, you did shake."

"What do you mean?" Sam asked.

"You shook before the game at home plate. Right in front of the umpire, so you even got a witness," Jack answered.

"You think that counts?"

"It should. Well, it does to me, anyway," answered Jack.

They both smiled and quietly stared at the road ahead.

Chapter 7

JACK STOOD ALONE on the mound in the pasture-turned-baseball diamond behind his house. A bucket of baseballs sat atop a wooden crate to his right. A large, rectangular pitching target stood behind home plate. He pitched with focus and accuracy at the target. The bucket of baseballs gradually emptied as he fired ball after ball at the target. Half the pitches hit the inside of the rectangular hole the size of the strike zone.

When he exhausted his supply of balls, Jack collected them in the bucket at home plate. He picked up a metal bat and proceeded to toss the balls into the air and hit them into the outfield, in the direction of the distant house. Jack picked one of the balls out of the bucket and paused to inspect it. The seam, made from red twine, had begun to unravel and the cover was partially peeled back from the ball. Jack stepped out from beyond the backstop and turned. He tossed the ball up and smacked it into the woods.

Jack returned to his position behind home plate and continued hitting baseballs into the outfield. He found another ball in the bucket that had old, frayed seams. Jack again turned to hit the ball into the woods. As he raised his bat to hit the ball, there was a rustling of leaves in the forest. A baseball came flying out of the trees. It rolled to a stop only a few feet from him. He picked it up and examined it. It was the same ball with the split seam that he hit into the woods a few moments ago!

Jack stood motionless, staring into the woods with the bat on his shoulder and the ball with the split seam in his hand. He tossed the same ball into the air and hit it solidly back into the woods. Jack stood and waited, leaning on the bat with one leg crossed across the other. A minute passed, then he heard the flipping of leaves as something flew through the branches in the forest canopy. Again, the baseball emerged from the forest, flying through the air in a high trajectory, then bouncing twice on the grass and rolling to a stop near third base. Jack stood and stared at the forest in quiet amazement.

Just then, from the direction of the house came the crackling noise of car wheels on the gravel driveway. Jack turned to see his father's familiar brown Land Rover drive up and stop in the parking area in front of the house.

Sam got out of the car. He was too far away to be heard, so he lifted his arm and waved to Jack at the other end of the field. Jack dropped the bat and ran toward his father. Sam slammed the car door and paused, holding his briefcase, and pleased to see Jack running toward him.

Sam smiled warmly, "It's nice to have a welcoming committee! How you doin', big guy? Good to see you."

Jack did not smile back. His face carried a concerned, almost distressed look.

"What's the matter, Jack? You don't look happy," Sam said.

"Dad, I think somebody's in the woods. I hit the ball into the woods and it came back. Twice!" Jack said.

"You sure they're not just bouncing off a tree and ricocheting back?"

"No," replied Jack. "They didn't come back right away. And there wasn't any noise."

"Really. Well it is national forest back there. Maybe there are hikers back there. What are you doing hitting balls into the woods, anyway? Those things cost two bucks a piece!"

"Dad, you gotta see this. I'm not kidding."

Sam followed Jack back to the backstop where the bat and bucket of balls were still lying in the grass.

"Okay, watch Dad."

Jack picked up a ball and turned toward the woods. He began the motion of tossing it up to hit it into the forest.

"Hold it! What are you doing? That's a new ball. You aren't going to hit a new ball into the woods."

"They come back, Dad."

"What are you talking about?"

"I swear they come back, Dad. It happened just before you drove up the driveway. It happened a few days ago, too. I tried to tell you, but you wouldn't listen..."

Jack stared at his dad then looked away, feeling embarrassed. Sam was smacked by the same embarrassment for having been told by his own son that he didn't listen. Sam looked at Jack then looked at his own feet. Then he looked toward the woods and recalled Nick Rollo's surprising lesson from the other day.

Sam's view of the world was more than a little shaken by the fact that a person came into his classroom and presented a lesson that was not only better than anything he could have ever done with that particular subject matter, but also a lesson that caused him to rethink his view of what creatures do or do not exist in his own neighborhood.

He was confronted, in his own classroom, with the distinct possibility that he was wrong about science, species, and creatures. He decided this was no time to dig in his heels and be wrong yet again, especially in front of his own son. Sam looked at the bucket of baseballs.

"Kid," he said to Jack in a resigned tone, "I've already been schooled once today, so I'm getting used to being wrong. If you say the balls come back, fine. Show me. I'll just shut up and watch. But, here, let's be slightly scientific about this, shall we?"

Sam reached into the bucket and pulled out a soft red baseball. "Here, it's the only red one we have, plus it's old. We can spare it. Go ahead and give it a whack."

He tossed the ball to Jack who lofted it, then unleashed his hardest swing, sending the red baseball deep into the woods. They both watched it travel in silence. It ripped through the leaves and landed well back in the woods in the general direction of Squaw Mountain. They both stood in silence, staring into the woods. Meanwhile, Grace was looking out the sliding glass door off the kitchen, watching Sam and Jack as they stood there, intently staring into the woods.

The early summer sun was setting. The verdant green leaves of spring had a splendid orange glow as a low angle sunbeam broke through the clouds and illuminated the wall of lush green foliage blanketing the side of the canyon. The light of the deep yellow sunbeam on the lush tree-tops looked like fire engulfing a swath of the steeply sloping hillside above the two tiny, human figures. Standing in the doorway, Grace thought to herself that she was standing before a veritable picture of rural tranquility. Then she wondered what in the world those two were up to. She slid open the glass door and took a breath, and just before she hollered the call that dinners ready, something flew out of the trees and over the head of the two distant figures.

A large, dark bird flapped out of the trees, then soared silently right over the heads of the boys. Both of their heads turn to follow the path of the winged form as it cleared the trees. Their gaze followed it as it glided over the baseball field, then in the direction of the house. Grace watched as it veered toward a grove of firs at the other end of their property.

Jack looked at his dad. Sam looked back at Jack.

"What the heck was that?" Jack asked in amazement.

"You know what that was," Sam replied.

"A great horned owl?" Jack guessed.

"Uh-huh. No doubt."

"Where'd he come from?"

"Not a clue," said Sam. "But he wasn't holding our ball. And after the way the rest of this day has gone, I didn't rule out the possibility. Believe me, I looked."

From the direction of the house came the call, "Dinner, boys! Come and get it."

"What about the ball, Dad?" Jack hesitated.

"We'll come back and check for it after dinner. I'm starving."

They turned and walked back toward the house. Minutes later they were sitting at the dinner table.

"That owl was amazing. It flew right over the house. What were you guys doing back there?" Grace asked as she put a napkin on her lap.

Smiling, Sam replied, "I think Jack hit it with a baseball,"

"You hit an owl with a baseball? Jack!" Grace replied in a scolding tone.

"He's kidding," Jack interrupted. "Before Dad came home, I hit a baseball into the woods… and it came back. Twice! Somebody was out there. So, just now, I hit another ball into the woods to show Dad, and instead of the baseball coming out, an owl did!"

"Maybe you *did* hit an owl with a baseball. You should quit hitting baseballs into the woods. It's littering," Grace said.

"Mom, you don't get it."

"Jack thinks somebody is in the forest throwing the balls back when he hits them into the trees. He wanted *me* to see it happen, so he hit one into the woods, and a few seconds later, out flies this owl. I think it's possible that he came close to the owl, and it decided to clear out. I don't think he actually hit the owl because it flew just fine. It might have been a near miss though. Still, it *was* the weirdest thing. Maybe we should go out there after dinner and hit some more Jack, just to see what's up."

"Okay," Jack replied as he began to eat.

"Speaking of weird," Sam says to his daughter, "Jenna's dad was a guest speaker in my class, today."

"Really. What did he talk about?" Elizabeth inquired.

"bigfoot evidence," Sam replied between mouthfuls of food.

"Really? Bigfoot? Why?" Elizabeth asked.

"Well, we're studying the scientific method, and the subject of bigfoot came up. When I saw his name on the bulletin board at the Redland store, I saw he called himself a 'bigfoot researcher'. I told him I was looking for some material for a classroom lesson and he agreed to give a presentation to my eighth graders. Did you know the guy investigates bigfoot sightings? He brought all this stuff from his collection to show the kids. He was an excellent speaker. The kids loved it."

"Is he serious?" Grace asked.

"Oh, yeah. Dead serious. He showed us footprint casts, hair samples, taped calls, and even some other stuff I won't bring up at the dinner table. I had lunch with him afterward. He told me about bigfoot sightings right around here. He said Squaw Meadow is a bit of a hot spot."

"Ha! Well, Squaw Meadow is less than six miles from here. Do you think bigfoot plays baseball? Maybe that explains the baseballs coming out of the woods, eh?" Grace said with a laugh. "Are you sure this guy wasn't just pulling your leg?"

"No, I really don't think so," Sam replied dryly.

"Well, if bigfoot lives around here, then maybe you could get him to play on your baseball team. Some of the fielding on your team is pretty weak, Dad," Elizabeth added with a laugh.

"I think you're onto something, kid. I bet he could whack that ball a mile, if we could just get him to hold a bat. The hard part would be proving he's in the fifth grade," Sam said, smiling. "We don't need a bigfoot, we need a fifth-grade bigfoot." Everyone giggled as they ate. The subject seemed to evoke humorous remarks from everyone.

"Even if he can't hit," Jack offered, "he'd scare the other team so bad they'd all run away. We would win every game by forfeit. All we have to do is get him to show up." More laughter ensued all around.

"How do you know it's a 'he'?" Elizabeth asked.

"Good point," Sam added. "Jenna's dad says there has to be more than one. So, what we really need is to get daddy bigfoot's permission to put junior bigfoot on our team."

"This is starting to sound like Goldilocks and the three bigfoots. I wonder if they eat porridge," Elizabeth joked. "I have to write a creative story tonight. I think I just got the idea I need."

"You better leave out the part about porridge. That's plagiarism. Still, I can see how it all could make a good humor piece. When it comes to bigfoot, the jokes just keep on coming. You should have been there in my class yesterday. Nick had them rolling. And when he brought out that..." Sam paused and looked at everyone eating meatloaf around the dinner table. "...Oh, never mind. Just eat your dinner. This has gone far enough already."

After dinner, Sam and Jack returned to the baseball diamond. Sam was pitching to Jack, who was belting some of them solidly into center field.

"Nice hitting, Jack. You have really started to get a handle on it. When did you start connecting like this?" Sam called from the mound.

Sam pitched another one and Jack connected but he fouled it back, over the backstop. The ball sailed into the woods on a fly. "Oops, there's one for bigfoot," Sam kidded. "Now, we'll see if it comes back."

"Don't laugh," Jack said seriously. "I know you don't believe me, but the balls really did come back."

"Okay, we'll see," Sam offered. "I'll keep watching."

Sam kept pitching and Jack kept hitting, and soon the bucket at Sam's feet was empty and the baseballs were scattered throughout the outfield.

"Alright, slugger, let's pick 'em up. I'll start out in right field, you get the ones in left." Sam and Jack walked off in different directions and started throwing the balls in toward the pitcher's mound. They worked their way around the field until they retrieved the balls that were fouled behind the backstop. Suddenly, Jack stopped.

"Hey Dad, come here! You gotta see this! Here it is!" Jack hollered, as he stood, staring at the ground in front of him. Sam trotted over. There, at Jack's feet, was the red baseball.

"I'll be damned," Sam said quietly. His head jerked up and he looked toward the woods. He tipped his baseball cap back on his head and scratched his bald spot.

"See, I told ya," Jack reminded.

"How come I knew you were gonna say that?" Sam muttered, still staring in the direction of the woods. "Hey, who's out there?" Sam shouted toward the woods. Deep in the woods, a single stick snapped. Sam and Jack both look at each other. At this point, dusk was setting in. "Are you thinking what I'm thinking?" Sam said to his son.

"Well, I'm not going in there right now, if that's what you mean," Jack stated firmly.

"Me neither," replied Sam. "I do think we need to repeat the experiment. Gimme a ball."

Jack picked up the red ball and offered it to Sam. Sam refused it. "No, gimme a new ball. A white one. Jack walked over and picked one up. Sam picked up his coat near the backstop and pulled out a Sharpie marker. He wrote on the ball: Experimental ball. 8:45 p.m. May 18.

"There," Sam stated as he handed the ball to Jack. "Now belt it into the woods. As hard as you can."

With a solid 'clink' of the bat, the ball sailed deep into the woods.

"Perfect," commented Sam. "It's almost dark. I'm pretty sure that if there *were* any hikers playing jokes on us, they'd be gone by now. If we ever see that ball again, we have a genuine scientific mystery to solve."

"Do you think there's people in our woods, Dad?" Jack asked, sounding slightly fearful.

"No, I really don't. I mean, that's public land mostly, but our property line only goes back five hundred feet. The nearest trail is almost two miles away and that hillside right there is too steep for any kind of trail. In the ten or so years we've lived here, I've never seen any hiker or hunter on that hillside, but it is public land back there, so I suppose it's possible."

"It's just hard to accept that someone wandered all the way down here from Squaw Meadow through five miles of trail-less forest, just to spy on us while we play baseball." The whole while Sam was speaking, his gaze remained fixed on a single spot in the woods, his eyes squinting. "And if that's what they were doing, they certainly wouldn't give themselves away by throwing our balls back onto our field, would they?"

"Maybe someone is playing tricks on us," Jack suggested.

After a brief pause, Sam agreed. "Oh, I think you are definitely right about that. Whoever, or whatever is out there, it's playing a game with us, all right. It knows we're out here playing a game and it wants to play, too. Why else would it *return* the ball? It, or they, *want* us to know they're out there. *Obviously*. But I also feel like it's saying, *"You can't catch me."*

"What do you think it is, Dad?" Jack questioned.

"I don't know, but I'm starting to think that it's definitely a 'who,' not a 'what.' I mean, it's too clever. It's hiding, but it moves. It moves, but we can't hear it. And it moves fast, and only to chase a ball. It's gotta be a 'somebody', not a 'something'. It's gotta be. 'Course, I guess that depends where you draw the line. But, you know what's really weird, Jack? If this had happened even a couple days ago, I'd be thinking hikers or pranksters. But after listening to Nick today, *of all days*, talking about 'the sasquatch hypothesis' I find myself thinking about at least one entirely different possibility."

"You mean bigfoot?" asked Jack, puzzled.

Sam shrugged. Sam and Jack stood side by side, silently staring into the woods, as the last bit of daylight illuminated the western horizon.

"Maybe the jokes we were making at the dinner table... there's just no way..." Sam mumbled. They both turned and began walking toward the house. The log home glowed with a honey brown color. The lights inside it illuminated the solitary cabin, casting a circle of light on the surrounding meadow and the lush green foliage beyond it.

"Does it scare you, Dad?" Jack asked.

"Actually, no," Sam smiled, " It just makes me really curious. In a way, I think this is really cool to think about. In fact, it's so cool, that I *want* it to be true, although that's not very scientific. We have to investigate this as critically as possible. After all, I'm a science teacher...and we have a genuine mystery on our hands. If you ask me, this is the kind of thing that makes living out here worth it."

Sam turned and looked over his shoulder one final time as they walked to the house. He put his arm around his son's shoulder and led him toward the house.

"It's just really cool to wonder about..."

Chapter 8

SITTING AT HIS desk in the corner of the cluttered classroom, the teacher stared at the computer screen in front of him. The desk was piled high with papers, folders, books, and office supplies. He ignored it all. It could wait. Sam was accustomed to facing down formidable amounts of paperwork. "The work that *needs* to get done *will* always get done," he said to himself, "and the work that doesn't need to get done will winnow itself right off this desk and into that trash can if it is allowed to sit there long enough."

Collecting his thoughts and checking current events for science stories seemed more important than correcting assignments. The whole strange idea of bigfoot was still bugging him. As Sam sipped his coffee, he did a web search of the topic and scrolled through the very long list of websites. One such website discussed experiments with remote wildlife camera sets. Links on that site led to a company that made motion-activated, weather proof wild-life camera systems. Sam studied the manufacturers speci-fications and prices. Then he reverted to the bigfoot web pages and explored further links to personal web pages of bigfoot enthusiasts who had posted results of their own camera surveys.

Next, he perused a website made by a Texas group that identified promising locations for bigfoot activity, and cor-related them to certain forest types and geological strata. While bigfoot sightings in Texas seemed utterly improbable to Sam, the website presented a serious tone and a long list of links to related articles. Sam looked at the clock and noticed that he still had ten minutes before the onslaught of students. He continued to surf. He found an Oregon-based bigfoot research group with still more links and articles. Sam found one serious-sounding essay entitled 'Habituating Bigfoot by Provisioning.'

The latch on the classroom door clicked, and it slowly opened. Sam looked up to see the building principal easing into the classroom with the small, careful steps of a person afflicted with chronic back pain. He immediately tensed. He clicked the mouse to close the 'Oregon Bigfoot' website he was studying. It was a rare day when the building prin-cipal left the comfort of her office and its orthopedic desk chair, and when she did, it was never a good thing.

Wilma Lavelle, the school principal, was overweight and unsteady. Her unsteadiness could be attributed to a bad back that she injured in an auto accident some years back. No doubt it was further strained by her obese frame. Inwardly, it was Sam's cynical view that Wilma was so infirm that she would not venture down the hallway of the school unless there was the reward of inflicting some sort of misery on one of her subordinates.

If the news was good, or even neutral, she would have surely summoned Sam to her office, or more likely informed him of the situation in an impersonal note left in his mailbox in the office. For her to limp down the hallway on her unsteady frame and orthopedic shoes was an ominous sign indeed.

"This can't possibly be a good thing..." Sam thought to himself. He finished exiting his computer then looked up at his unannounced visitor with a blank look.

"Hi, Wilma. How are you this morning?" Sam offered, trying his best to sound cordial.

"Good morning, Mr. Ward," Wilma returned with stilted formality. "I'm fine, thank you."

There was no warmth in her tone, just a formality that bespoke a certain distance she wished to maintain, signaling that she was the superior who was about to address a subordinate on a matter of official business. Whenever Wilma addressed Sam as 'Mr. Ward', reprimand was soon to follow. Sam winced, trying not to be made to feel ill at ease. He tilted back in his chair, resting his head on the interlocked fingers of both hands. He said nothing. He just waited with a blank stare as Wilma Lavelle took a few unsteady steps into his classroom before stopping to lean her large frame on one of the lab tables. She pulled one of the lab stools toward her and carefully eased one leg of her infirm body onto the stool.

" I just got off the phone with a parent who expressed a serious concern about a lesson you conducted the other day," she declared in clipped tones.

Sam resisted the urge to say anything at all. He could see immediately where this was about to go.

"This parent," she continued, "says her child was distressed over this lesson you gave, that had something to do with, um, bigfoot. Apparently it caused her child to have a sleepless night."

"Am I allowed to know which child's parent we're discussing here?" Sam inquired.

"I'd rather not mention the name. I can only say that it's a student in your class. The parent asked that I not mention their child by name. They didn't want their child to suffer any repercussions from their complaint."

"Repercussions? Like what? I've been doing this for thirteen years. Do you really think I'm going to exact revenge on a student because a parent complained about a lesson? I think it's quite necessary to provide me with the context of what is starting to sound like a complaint, and that means knowing the exact source of the dissatisfaction, whatever that is. How can I be sure this alleged complaint is not a fabrication if the source is kept secret?

"Forgive my skepticism, but I am a teacher of science. The same is true in journalism, though. Anonymous sources are suspect, for good reason, I might add. If someone has a serious complaint, they should not be allowed to hurl it from the shadows of anonymity."

The thinly veiled animosity between Mr. Ward and his supervisor was now out in the open. Ms. Lavelle bristled at the suggestion that the complaint she was referring to was a fabrication. She was not about to acknowledge any validity to Sam's contention. The conversation had now assumed the character of a sword fight with parry, thrust, attack, and counterattack. Clearly, the relationship between the teacher and the principal was characterized by adversity, and this was just the latest duel. The sword fight continued.

"For now, Mr. Ward, let's just focus on this lesson. The parent I spoke with says that, according to their child, you delivered a science lesson two days ago in which you told the class that bigfoot was real. This is the message that this child brought home from school. This caused this child to have a sleepless night," Ms. Lavelle stated.

"First of all, no, I did not teach a lesson on bigfoot. I applied the scientific method to the question of bigfoot's existence. But, truth be told, I did not personally teach the students anything. I did have a classroom presentation by a guest speaker, who is also the parent of a student in this school. And the guest speaker showed the kids what he considered to be bigfoot evidence. The kids were invited to evaluate the evidence themselves. They weren't told what to think. I was completely neutral, if not downright skeptical of the whole matter, and I encouraged the kids to be appropriately skeptical as well, which they were. The gist of the lesson was…"

"First of all, Mr. Ward," Ms. Lavelle interrupted with rising hostility in her tone, "You should know by now that it is school district policy that I be notified in advance of any guest speaker. Second, we have an established science curriculum in this district, and bigfoot does not appear anywhere on that curriculum document. And third, Mr. Ward, I'm told you, or perhaps your un-approved guest speaker, displayed feces in this classroom, which students were encouraged to not just examine, but to smell! I don't know what kind of science class you think you're running, but I can tell you this: some members of the community are outraged and I cannot defend these actions or your decided lack of judgment in this whole matter. If there are repercussion from all this, I cannot defend you against them. I must say, I am even inclined to share the community's outrage. I fear you have not heard the last of this very matter. This sounds quite serious, I'm afraid."

"With all due respect, let's be accurate here. What you call 'community outrage' amounts to a single, anonymous complaint. What you call 'feces' is known in wildlife biology circles as 'scat' and it has genuine scientific merit in that field. Further, these are eighth graders we're talking about, not kindergarteners. Some of them are out there doing drugs or having sex. I think we can let them look at wildlife droppings in science class without irreparably damaging their fragile psyches."

"All I have to say is that I was teaching the scientific method to eighth graders in a manner that was engaging and age-appropriate. If someone is claiming to have bad dreams over the matter, I say, 'perfect.' That means my lesson was effective. It had a lasting impact! They'll get over it. But it also sounds to me like some parent would prefer to create a tempest in a teapot. Great. I guess we're heading for the next 'Scopes monkey trial.' I'll see if can I find Clarence Darrow to defend me. This mystery parent will want William Jennings Bryant. I guess we'll duke it out in court," Sam said, with defiance rising in his tone.

"I had hoped you would acknowledge your error and offer an apology, Mr. Ward. I find your comments to be most unprofessional, and more than a little offensive." The principal challenged, "I hope you realize this matter could cost you your job."

"How can I apologize if I'm not allowed to know who I'm apologizing to?" Sam retorted. He paused. He felt his face flush with anger. He closed his eyes and took a deep breath. "Look, Ms. Lavelle, I'm sorry to sound rude. I'm feeling somewhat ambushed here and more than a little defensive. From my point of view, I was simply trying to present a lesson on the scientific method that had some lasting impact. It's starting to sound like I did a little too good a job of that," Sam reflected humbly.

"I agree with that much," Ms. Lavelle acknowledged. "However, I believe your approach crossed a line of appropriateness, and decorum. Displaying feces in class, Mr. Ward! What am I supposed to say to concerned parents? I fear we have not heard the last of this."

"In that case, I'll contact a union representative and start preparing my defense. As far as an apology, I'll consider it, but not before I know who I'm supposed to apologize to."

"Very well. The parent did ask to remain anonymous."

"You aren't required to grant that request," Sam insisted.

"I'll contact him and see if they are willing to let me divulge their identity," Wilma replied.

"A moment ago, you said it was a 'her'. Now, it's 'him.' Which is it?"

Wilma flushed. After a pause, she curtly stated, "They wish to remain anonymous, for now."

"Well, then, I would further suggest that a face to face meeting with him or her would be in order," Sam said.

Ms. Lavelle shifted her weight on the stool as she prepared to leave.

"I'll relay the message, and I will be..." Ms. Lavelle suddenly dropped from view, straight down toward the floor, behind the lab table.

The lab stool hit the floor with a crash.

"Good God!" Sam muttered. He jumped from his chair and dashed across the room toward the fallen administrator. As he rushed to her assistance, he could see only the tips of her fingers, desperately grasping the edge of the table.

"Are you alright, Wilma?"

"I-I...don't...know. Just... give...me...a...hand"

Sam ran around behind her and put his hands in her arm pits. He gently applied steady, upward pressure. Wilma gradually hoisted her large frame back to her feet. She stood still, with both palms flat on the lab table before her. She wavered back and forth. Sam stood still, arms extended, ready to catch her if she fell again. He wasn't sure he would be able to stop her if she dropped back to the floor.

"Can I get you anything?" stammered Sam. "Should I call for help?"

"Just...give...me...a...minute."

Sam remained behind her, unsure what kind of assistance she required. She was on her feet, but she was pale and slightly dazed.

"Are you sure you don't need some medical help...?" Sam repeated.

After another minute, Wilma stood up straight. She raised her arms to straighten her hair and regain her dignity. Sam saw her wince as she lowered her arms.

Ms. Lavelle turned and slowly, carefully walked out of the room. Sam stayed next to her, ready to catch her if legs failed to support her. Sam escorted her down the deserted hallway.

Once she was safely returned to the opulent wheeled armchair in her office, Sam returned to his classroom and plopped down in the wooden chair behind his own desk.

Although the whole embarrassing incident happened while he was being reprimanded, he still felt terribly about the accident that had just transpired.

"I told her those stools were defective," Sam muttered to himself.

He slammed his eyes shut and put his head in his hands. He ran his fingers through his hair. He opened his eyes and hit his fist on the desk. The computer mouse budged from the impact and the sleeping computer screen lit up, displaying the website he clicked on several minutes ago. 'Habituating Bigfoot Through Provisioning' read the type at the top of the screen. Sam put his hands over his eyes. A loud bell rang; students began to fill the halls.

Great. Sam was just notified he was officially on the hot seat, complete with potential legal repercussions, and now he was supposed to be cheerful and positive all day long. He wanted to read the article but he wouldn't have time. Sam clicked print and the article began to slowly emerge from the printer atop the file cabinet to his right. The room was filling up with students. Sam stood up and took a deep breath. What else could go wrong, Sam wondered? He wouldn't find out until he got to his son's youth baseball game the next morning.

Chapter 9

THE ROVER CAME to a stop in front of a locked gate. A sign read "Fischer's Mill Athletic Fields." It was a quiet Saturday morning, overcast and cool; a good day to get some mowing done. It was his turn to get the outfield mowed and the infield dressed for the early afternoon game. Sam unlocked the gate, rolled it back, and then paused to look out toward the sports fields: a baseball diamond, a soccer field, and a picnic area, all tucked into an oblong expanse of flat ground between the hillside and the creek.

The parking area bordered the creek. Half a dozen picnic tables were lined up in the shade of the cedars and red alder trees between the parking area and the creek. Sam peered out toward the baseball field to assess its condition. The outfield grass was in need of attention. It was long and lush from the spring rains. The grass was nearly tall enough to conceal a baseball. The infield was also in need of attention. It was hard-packed clay with tufts of grass and weeds beginning to take hold on the margins of the bare earth around the bases.

"At least there are no puddles," Sam thought. He was pleased to see that the field was dry enough to play on, although the weeds suggested that he would probably have to drag the infield more than once to get it into playable shape. The kids would be arriving in just over two hours and the game would begin an hour after that. That left him barely enough time to complete mowing the outfield and drag the infield. Sam had to get going but he couldn't resist standing for a minute and surveying the field in front of him.

He loved this field. It was the picture of pastoral beauty. Just like his property, the ball field occupied the river bottomland that was surrounded by steep hillsides blanketed with tall firs. It wasn't virgin timber, but having been logged almost a century ago, the timber was impressive second-growth.

The Fischer's Mill Sports Fields was named for an old water-powered grist mill that the Fischer family once operated on Squaw Creek just upstream from the present ball fields. Owing to its location just above the confluence of Squaw Creek and the Clackamas River, Squaw Creek canyon widened considerably. The ball fields utilized every bit of the flat land between the creek and the steep hillside. The forested slopes of the river canyon crowded right up to the outfield fence.

Consequently, balls hit over the fence were seldom recovered. If the fielder didn't see exactly where the ball landed, it was lost in the thick forest undergrowth. Limbs from trees close to the fence would grow out over the outfield and had to be pruned back. Hawks used the over-hanging limbs as perches from which to hunt rodents and snakes in the grass. Deer could sometimes be seen peering through the fence during games, like pedestrian spectators stopping to catch a few innings of baseball at the neighbor-hood ballpark.

To play a baseball game at the Fischer's Mill field was to play baseball in a forest clearing. The delightfully rustic surroundings routinely charmed the parents of the vis-iting teams from town. They typically came from more densely populated neighborhoods closer to Portland, like the one where Sam himself used to live. Sam Ward shared their appreciation for this quaint, rural ball field wedged between the dark green hillsides and the sparking water of Squaw Creek. The country charm of the park was a big reason why Sam liked to help maintain the park and help coach the team. Best of all, it was only three miles down Squaw Mountain Road from Sam's isolated homestead.

Sam snapped back to reality. He needed to get busy. He unlocked the storage shed and checked the fuel level in the lawn tractor. Sam jumped on the tractor and put on the hearing protectors. The old John Deere tractor fired right up, which was a relief. He backed it out of the shed and headed for the outfield. An hour later, Sam was on his second-last pass and nearing the outfield fence. He was daydreaming as he looked up and noticed that some of the branches of the fir trees had grown longer and were overhanging the outfield fence. He probably wouldn't have time to prune them before the game. As he drove beneath an overhanging branch, the lawn tractor sputtered, and then the engine died.

This wasn't good, Sam thought. He cranked the starter once again but the engine didn't turn over. He jumped off the tractor and removed the gas cap. The tank was still half full of gas. As he was getting back on the tractor, Sam noticed a stray baseball in the outfield grass just ahead of the tractor. It was fairly common to find practice balls against the fence or in the corner of the outfield as one was doing the mowing. But, often as not, the whirling blades of the mower deck would find the balls for him. A ball would make a "thump" as it struck the inside of the mower deck, then it would come flying out the side discharge port, shredded and cut from its sudden contact with the rapidly rotating blades.

Sam tried to keep an eye out for stray baseballs as he mowed. If he could get them before the mower did, and if the baseball hadn't been there too long, they might still be useable on his home field. If the baseball had been sitting there a while, they would be dark-colored, wet, heavy, and useless. Sam was pleased this time to spot a ball that still had a white rawhide cover and bright red stitching, though it appeared to have some dark marks on it. Sam hopped off the dead tractor to pick up the ball. As he got closer to it, he could see that the dark marks on the ball were words. He picked up the ball and saw that it was indeed writing on the ball. When he examined it more closely, he froze. He couldn't believe what he saw. It read: "Experimental Ball, 8:45 p.m., May 18th." It was Sam's own handwriting.

Unbelievably, he was holding the very ball that he wrote on and had Jack hit into the woods at his house three days ago and three miles away! "But how could it have gotten here?" Sam wondered aloud.

He studied the ball. It was clean and undamaged, just as it was when he handed it to Jack three days ago. It was the same Rawlings brand baseball they had dozens of at home.

No doubt about it, this was the same ball Jack hit into the woods. It was also dry, which meant it had not been there very long. Maybe a few hours, maybe less. Probably not overnight or it would be damp.

Sam raised his head and studied the woods behind the outfield fence for signs of movement. Sun flecks lit the leaves of low shrubs beneath the dense shade of the forest canopy. Nothing stirred. He turned and looked toward the parking lot. His was the only car in the lot. He looked toward the creek. The picnic tables were empty. Swallows circled over the creek feeding on insects. A lone turkey vulture tipped its wings back and forth as it soared high above the open expanse of the soccer field. He was alone at the ball field. Nothing seemed unusual about the surroundings. Sam looked at the ball again. He felt a sudden chill. The hair on the back of his neck prickled. A feeling of being watched broke over him like a wave. He turned and again studied the edge of woods beyond the outfield fence.

Deep in the woods, a stick snapped. A dark shape moved through the branches. An instant later, a raven emerged from the trees, letting out its guttural cry, then flying directly over Sam's head, over the ball fields, then away toward the Clackamas River in the distance.

Sam called into the woods, "Who's out there?" No reply. "Who's out there?" he demanded. He stood still, craning his neck and listening intently. Minutes passed noiselessly. The sense of being watched faded. He began to feel foolish about shouting into the woods. Still, the ball he held in his hand seemed to be solid evidence that something strange was going on. How could this ball find its way three miles away from where it was left three days ago, Sam wondered. It seemed like this had to be a practical joke, but the more he thought about it, the more unlikely it seemed. Only his son was present when they hit the ball into the woods. It was a spontaneous move that was intended to show his son that there really wasn't anybody in the woods returning the balls that Jack hit into the forest. Now, it was the father who was struggling to process the evidence that somebody was trying to surreptitiously return their stray baseballs.

Nothing made sense. Sam reconsidered the facts. How did the ball get here? He saw his son hit it into the woods back at home. The ball was dry. It couldn't have been lying there very long. The ball was found only because he got off the mower. He got off the mower because it suddenly stopped for no apparent reason. He thought it stopped because he was out of gas, but it wasn't. So, why *did* the tractor stop running? Then, he heard a stick break, and a bird flew out of the woods at a most peculiar moment. Could the woods be haunted? Was he imagining things? Could this have anything to do with Nick Rollo's tales of bigfoot creatures? Sam's head was overwhelmed with the strange possibilities he was forced to consider.

Looking at his watch, it dawned on him that he had no more time to dwell on these puzzling events. He had a job to do and time was very short. He put the ball in the pocket of his vest and got back on the tractor. He turned the key and cranked the tractor engine. The tractor roared to life. Sam was relieved, though he couldn't help but wonder again why it stopped in the first place. Sam decided he didn't care anymore. He didn't have any time to ponder this mystery at the moment. He jammed the gearshift forward, then pulled a knob that engaged the mower. The whirling blades roared and he resumed mowing the outfield. He looked around frequently as he traveled the arcing path of the outfield, but saw nothing else that was unusual.

In another hour, the mowing was complete and Sam set about dressing the infield by dragging around a weighted piece of chain-link fence. The team members were arriving as Sam began dragging the infield. Sam thought about showing Jack the ball he found when he arrived. But, then Sam decided it might be better not to say anything until after the game. It would be too distracting. He had to help the other coaches get the warm-ups started anyway.

Being preoccupied with all the unusual events of the past week, Sam hadn't had time to attend to some of the more mundane details of his life, like checking to see who the opponents were going be in today's baseball game. As he hurried to finish dragging the infield he saw a familiar red Ford crew-cab pull into the parking lot of the ball field and he instantly knew who his opponent was going to be. Sam continued to circle the infield, with a plume of dust following behind, he looked again in the direction of the parking lot and glimpsed his former neighbor Bart Foster unloading his baseball gear.

Barton Foster III used to live on Squaw Creek just a mile downstream of the Wards' place. Two years ago he sold his place to the folks who built the horse stables where Sam's daughter Elizabeth now boarded her horse. The Foster's house on Squaw Creek was a historic homestead that had been in their family since the late 1850's. As such, it was the oldest homestead not just on Squaw Creek, but also in the entire Redland area. It was also a small house with cramped rooms and primitive amenities by today's standards. So, despite its charm and historic appeal, it came to be seen, especially by Bart's wife, as entirely unsuitable for a family of four who were also prominent and successful members of the community.

For the past eight years, Bart owned and operated Redland Ford, a dealership that his father, Barton Foster Jr. started in the late 1940's. It was as profitable for Bart as it was for his father. And, as his car dealership flourished, Bart III's family decided they wanted more living space than their cramped, but historic, homestead afforded them. Tearing down an historic homestead to build a bigger, more comfortable place was not an option. So Bart sold the historic homestead to the Harding family and bought hilltop acreage on the other side of Redland, in the neighboring community of Eagle Creek. There, the Fosters then built an opulent, six thousand square foot home with every modern convenience, not to mention a panoramic vista of Mount Hood and the whole upper Clackamas River valley. It was a showcase home, built especially for entertaining, and therefore, much more suitable for a prominent local family.

Back when the Fosters and the Wards were neighbors, they crossed paths often, especially since they each had an older daughter and a younger son who were about the same age. But beyond the fact that their kids played together and went to the same school, there was quite a bit of difference between the two families. The Fosters, on the one hand, were more than simply native Oregonians; they were the West Coast equivalent of 'Daughters of the American Revolution'. Their heritage dated back to the earliest days of the Oregon Territory. Their relatives arrived with the first wave of European settlers. The Fosters were successful local business owners. They were not only supporters, but generous contributors to local Republican candidates who campaigned for county and state offices. They were also devoutly religious.

The Wards, on the other hand, were recent transplants from the Midwest. Sam and Grace Ward were teachers. Like a lot of recent transplants to western Oregon, they were left-leaning liberals, though they had no spare money to offer in support of any candidate or cause. They lived in a modest log cabin that Sam built; they were enthusiastic organic gardeners, advocates of strong land use planning laws, and supporters of such liberal constructs as urban growth boundaries. The Wards were scornful of organized religion. On the rare Sunday when they felt obliged to attend a service, they journeyed to the Unitarian Church in Oregon City. In the eyes of the Fosters, the Wards were viewed with playful disdain as refugees from the Midwest, and still worse, 'earth people'.

Yet, there was one big expanse of common ground that was shared by the two couples: they were both very dedicated to their families and both men loved baseball. The children of both families benefitted from parents that took the education of their children very seriously. Both families were active in youth sports and viewed it as an important element in their children's development. Bart Foster and Sam Ward had even forged an early alliance and coached a couple teams together when their boys first began to play team sports.

It wasn't a match made in heaven, however. Both had strong feelings about coaching styles, Bart favoring the 'tough love' drill sergeant style embodied by coaches such as Bear Bryant or Vince Lombardi. Sam Ward's coaching style was more of a 'winning isn't everything', encouraging one which he saw as more suited to youth sports.

Sam aspired to the laid back style of Pete Carroll or Phil Jackson.

Their differences became greater as their kids got older, and although Sam and Bart still liked each other, neither family was heartbroken by the Foster's decision to relocate to more spacious quarters on the other side of town.

Living on the other side of Redland, the Foster's son now attended an elementary school in Eagle Creek, although their eighth grade daughter Ellie was back at the only middle school in the area; that being the Redland Middle School where Sam was the seventh and eighth grade science teacher. In typical small town fashion, one can never completely avoid other locals. This was particularly true in the case of Bart and Sam.

The two families' daughters were a year apart, but the two boys were the same age and in the same grade, though they now attended different elementary schools. Before the Fosters move to Eagle Creek, the youth sports there were not as well supported as they were in larger Redland. The whole sports community in the Eagle Creek community benefited from Bart Foster's rabid enthusiasm and dedication to youth sports.

Bart quickly assumed control of the youth sports programs in which his son was enrolled. It wasn't long before Bart was assembling stronger youth teams in baseball, football, and basketball than Eagle Creek had ever fielded in the past. This was a sore subject with some of the Redland parents, Sam included, because Bart was using his local influence to draw some players from Redland over to neighboring Eagle Creek. It was even seen as a betrayal of his heritage for Bart Foster to abandon the community that his ancestors established, simply because he wanted a more opulent house for his wife and family.

Sam didn't see it that way. He liked having Bart as a neighbor, but he knew his wife Judy well and he understood the pressures that Bart lived with. Sam was also able to stay philosophical about the loss of some talented players in the sports programs. Bart's dedication to youth sports was still a big asset to the sports programs of the larger community that included both towns. Sam recognized that Bart's 'get-tough' style of coaching appealed to some households although it was seen as distasteful to others. While Sam had learned to accept the loss of some players to Bart's teams, he also understood that the situation made for an obvious cross-town rivalry and that was actually a good thing. The teams scrimmaged each other frequently and it was always a big game in the mind of the two coaches when the two teams did meet in league play.

Today's game was no scrimmage. It was the big face off, a league game between the two cross-town rivals and former Squaw Creek neighbors. So far, the rivalry that persisted between these two former neighbors was quintessentially sporting. It was playful, good-natured, and ephemeral. That was about to change.

Bart hauled his bat bags across the parking lot and headed in Sam's direction. Bart nodded toward Sam then looked at the patches of weeds along the edges of the infield. He put down his bat bags and paused, faced the infield and planted his fists on his hips. He looked toward Sam and then extended an open palm toward the infield dirt with a look of disgust. Sam wheeled the tractor over to the edge of the infield where Bart stood. Bart opened his mouth to speak but Sam cut him off.

"I know, I know. I had some problems with the tractor. But it's running now. Got anybody who can help do the infield while I help with warm up?"

"Not really. We have our own field to maintain, you know," Bart smiled. "This is your field. What's the old saying? 'A lack of planning on your part does not constitute an emergency on my part'."

Bart's tone, as well as his words, seemed to be admonishing Sam in a less than good-natured way. Something else seemed to be going on in Bart's head but Sam didn't really want to get into it.

"Thanks anyway, Bart. I'll get it done. There's two other coaches who can warm up our team. They don't need me."

"You must have gotten a late start," Bart added, unaware that Sam had been working on the field for the past two hours. "Maybe you're spending too much time looking for bigfoot."

Sam turned the key and the tractor went quiet. "I beg your pardon? What the heck is that supposed to mean?" Sam asked incredulously.

"My daughter Ellie says you're into bigfoot now and that you're having bigfoot kooks like that guy Rollo come into your class to convince the kids that bigfoot exists. I don't think that kind of stuff belongs in classrooms, and I certainly don't think it qualifies as science."

Sam sat back in the seat of the lawn tractor, momentarily speechless. He wondered to himself what could possibly be behind this sudden burst of vituperation from his old friend and former neighbor. Suddenly, it clicked. Bart's daughter was in Sam's class. Some anonymous person complained to principal about Sam's use of bigfoot to spice up a dull lesson on the scientific method.

It seems a bit too coincidental that an objecting parent wanted to remain anonymous and then here's Bart at the baseball field, objecting to the mention of bigfoot in science class. Suddenly, Sam had a pretty good idea who filed the complaint with the principal.

"Um...Bart...I don't suppose you called the school principal and complained about this?"

"No," Bart replied flatly.

Sam knew Bart well enough to know when he was holding back. "How about Judy?" Sam shot back.

Bart stared at Sam and remained silent.

"Thanks a lot, Bart," Sam added sarcastically.

"She had no choice. You have no idea what problems that lesson brought into our household. Ellie had nightmares about monsters that night. Then she didn't want to go back to sleep. She was in tears. Ellie and Judy were up half the night. It disrupted the whole household."

"Wait a minute. Are we talking about Elle Foster, alias 'Miss Who-gives-rip about-science'? The same kid who spends most of the period texting other kids in the class with her fancy new iPhone? It's nice to know that *something* I'm doing in class is having an impact on her."

"If my kid isn't paying attention in science class, maybe it's because you're not teaching the kids any science. If you call bigfoot science, then I don't blame my kid for not paying attention."

Fortunately for Sam, he, like all middle school teachers, was used to being challenged and even insulted. He wasn't going to let himself get annoyed by rude remarks from a parent. Sam was, however, a bit surprised to suddenly see a nasty side of Bart that he had never seen before.

"Okay, look Bart, I had no idea your daughter was so emotionally fragile. If I caused any problems at home by bringing up bigfoot in class, I'm truly sorry. Maybe I'm a bit thick, but it never occurred to me that it would be any kind of problem. What I don't understand is, if you had a problem, why didn't you just call me? If the plan was to get your old neighbor Sammy here in trouble, it sure worked. I had to sit there and listen to an uninformed principal threaten to fire me over a science lesson that I thought was pretty valid, and even somewhat interesting to all of the kids."

Sam took a breath, and added, "If Ellie came home with the message that the woods are full of monsters, then she *really* missed the point of the whole lesson. That's not what it was about. It was about The Scientific Method, not bigfoot. Heck, I don't even believe in bigfoot myself, and I made that perfectly clear, I think. And, I also made it clear that, as far as science is concerned, there is no such thing as bigfoot. And you could have found that out if you asked me instead of complaining to my principal. I got such a raft of shit about it, and now I find out that my old pal Bart is the one who complained. Jeezus!"

"Yeah, well, I didn't make the complaint, my wife did, but I don't blame her. We have to look out for my daughter's education, and the science lesson she described sounded too kooky to ignore. You're supposed to be teaching according to some kind of school district plan, aren't you? Do they know you are teaching the kids about bigfoot?"

"I'm not teaching about bigfoot."

"That's not what my daughter says."

"I suggest you check out your daughter's story a little more thoroughly before you assume her descriptions are accurate."

"I trust my kid, and I listen to what she has to say."

"That's great, except from what I'm seeing, your daughter is not the utterly reliable source of information you think she is. You call it trust. I see it as manipulation."

"Well, I trust what my daughter says."

"Way to go, Dad, but we're wasting time, here. If you want this field to look any better than it does right now, I have to get going. I wish you would have called me first and heard my side of the story."

"I was too upset and so was my wife. We don't think you should be teaching our kid something in science class that isn't approved by the school district. I felt I had the right to complain and I felt they needed to know what you were doing in class."

Sam decided to say nothing else. There was no further point in arguing. Time was getting short and the kids were arriving for the game. He turned the key, started the tractor, put it in gear, and drove off. The cloud of dust rose behind the piece of chain-link fence he was dragging and enveloped Bart as he walked toward the backstop. Sam looked up at the sky. The clouds were thick to the west. He wondered whether his friendship with Bart would endure this disagreement. As if to answer his question, a chilly breeze blew across the field. An odd coincidence, Sam thought.

Fortunately for Sam, the umpire was late in arriving, giving him extra time to finish dragging the field. The game began fifteen minutes late. A light rain began to fall. The wind blew cold and from the west. Sam put on his jacket and while doing so, he felt a lump in the pocket of his shirt. It was the baseball with the writing on it that he had found while mowing. So much had happened since he found the ball that he completely forgot he still had it.

Chapter 10

SAM'S TEAM WAS at bat and so far, they were ahead by one run. From the dugout, Sam occasionally glanced at the outfield fence, and peered into the forest beyond. He wasn't sure why, yet he kept glancing toward the woods behind the center field fence.

He couldn't keep his mind on the game. He kept taking the baseball with the markings out of his pocket and handling it. He couldn't stop wondering how the ball got from his homestead to Fischer's Mill. He mulled over the possibilities. Could someone be playing a prank on him? How would the prankster have gotten the ball? He would have to have been in the woods on Sam's property. He would have had to know that Sam was going to be mowing the field. He would have had to spend lots of time waiting for Sam and watching his movements at both places. Who had that kind of time? Who would care that much about Sam? All in all, the whole idea seemed too unlikely to be possible.

What were the other possibilities? Just one really stood out, and it seemed even more far-fetched than the idea that someone was pulling a prank on Sam. It was the whole sasquatch possibility. To Sam, only a week ago, the whole subject was nothing but a myth and a joke. Then Nick Rollo came to his classroom and made the presentation to his class. That was the first time Sam even considered the possibility. Now, Sam was not only taking the possibility of sasquatch seriously, but also he was wondering whether one or more of these creatures wasn't somehow targeting him. The whole idea seemed ridiculous.

Nick Rollo portrayed the sasquatch as some sort of hidden ape that sparsely populated uninhabited regions of the continent. Sam did live on the edge of just such an unpopulated forest area, which is the only reason why he was even looking to the sasquatch hypothesis for an explanation. But something else didn't square. Nick Rollo confidently described the sasquatch as some sort of ape. The whole thing with the baseball was too clever to be the work of an ape. Apes don't hide, spy, pick up baseballs, anticipate a person's whereabouts, and carry them for miles then toss it in front of the same guy as he moves around the local area.

What Sam was seeing was intelligent work by a person, but a person who was both nowhere and everywhere at once. If it *was* the work of one of these sasquatches, then Nick Rollo had vastly underestimated their cunning and intelligence of these bad boys. If a sasquatch was behind this whole charade, then they have all the cunning, intelligence, and mobility of people. But, how could they stay so well hidden? Sam kept mulling over the possibilities. An amusing thought popped into his head. 'Nowhere Man,' Sam thought, just like the Beatles song. Suddenly, the loud *ping!* of a metal bat brought Sam back to the game he was supposed to be coaching. Dylan, his catcher was streaking down the first base line as the ball soared over the head of the second baseman, then right into the glove of the center fielder. Dylan was out, and the inning was over. The players around Sam grabbed their gloves and headed for the field.

Sam was distracted through most of the game. If he wasn't thinking about the strange outcome of his baseball experiment, he was thinking about his conflict with Bart over the complaint to the principal. At the bottom of the sixth and final inning of the game, the Redland Wildcat team was holding onto a three run lead. But anyone who has ever played in a youth baseball game knows that three runs can disappear in as many swings of the bat. Bart's Eagle Creek team was at bat. Indeed, they managed to even the score and get another runner on first when, with two outs, the first batter in their batting order was at the plate. The batter rapped a single to right field, and the runner took off, rounded second, and headed for third. The ball was thrown to third where it was caught by the third baseman. The runner was a full step behind the throw and it was clearly an out from the coaches' point of view in the dugout. But, as anyone who has ever played Little League also knows, the umpires' calls can be maddeningly arbitrary.

Teen-aged umpires are the norm, but whether they are young or old, there is still only one umpire on the field and they must cover play over the entire field.

So, if umpire doesn't scramble out from behind the plate to get closer to the base where the play is going to happen, they put themselves hopelessly far from the play, and the calls becomes more of a guess than a statement of fact.

"Safe!" came the call from behind the plate, and the parents in lawn chairs let out a chorus of groans. The entire Redland Wildcat team was outraged. Randy, the head coach, turned to Sam and said, "You want to talk to Jake or should I?"

They all knew the umpire. Jake Fischer was the son of Dean, the guy who owned the local John Deere tractor dealership. Sam taught Jake science three years ago, and Jake's sister Sophie two years before that. Even though he knew the whole Fischer family, Sam also knew it was futile to challenge the call. Umpires are taught not to reverse calls. Still, he felt justified in reminding his former student how he was supposed to conduct himself as umpire.

"C'mon, Jake, you're supposed to get your biscuit down that baseline and get closer to that play. The game is on the line! Making a call at third from behind home plate is not the way you're supposed to work."

"Sorry, Mr. Ward, but he guy looked safe to me. I heard what you said."

The next batter poked a shot right at the shortstop, who threw it to first base.

The throw was wild. It went sailing over the first baseman's head, and the runner on third took off for home. He scored! The Eagle Creek Indians took the lead. The next batter popped the ball up right to the first baseman and the side was retired. The bottom of the Redland batting order was up to bat; two strike outs and one grounder to the short stop and the game was over.

The Redland Wildcats were bitter with disappointment. The coach called a last huddle.

"Boys, we can't let the game get so close that it's decided by a single call from the umpire. We needed more runs than that on the scoreboard. Bad calls are a part of the game." The coach looked over the disappointed faces of his team. They wanted more. He paused, "You're always going to see bad calls. No shame in that loss, men. Be proud."

As Coach Randy was reassuring his team, his assistant, Sam, was having different thoughts. "That's the way things have gone all day. I should have expected this. It's been one of those days."

The kids lined up to shake hands with the opposing team and Sam followed his players through the line, high five-ing the opponents as they filed past. At the end of the line, Bart Foster and his assistants beamed. Sam shook hands as their gazes locked.

"Good game, Bart." Sam said. He forced a smile.

"Guess the best team won, eh Sam," Bart declared gleefully.

"With a little help from the ump," Sam mumbled out of the corner of his mouth.

As they shook hands, Bart held Sam's hand an extra second. He wanted to stay and talk about the game for a few minutes as they usually did. Clearly, Bart was basking in his triumph, which was particularly sweet in light of their disagreement before the game. Sam, on the other hand was in no mood to talk. He eased his hand out of Bart's lingering grasp, silently turned and headed back to his dugout to gather up the gear.

"C'mon Sam, it's just a game. No hard feelings!" Bart hollered as Sam walked away.

Sam raised his hand in a half-hearted wave without turning around. It dawned on Sam that he would look like a poor sport to any of his players who might be watching. He raised his head and turned around as he walked away. With a weak smile, Sam hollered, "Hey cowboy, we'll get ya next time."

It wasn't the loss of a close game, or the bad call that bothered him. He'd seen both plenty of times before. It was just the whole day, beginning with a chewing out by the principal, followed later by the realization that it was his so-called friend who complained about a lesson that, by the way, was very well presented by Nick Rollo, not even by himself. No one bothered to find out what was actually taught. They just took the word of a single and spiteful child, channeled through a self-important parent. Sam felt as if he had been hung out to dry by both his friend and his supervisor on the same day. Then the loss of a close baseball game due to a bad call was the icing on an already rotten cake.

The team members were getting in the cars as Sam put the bats in the duffel bag. His son, Jack, was getting in the minivan and his wife hollered to him across the parking lot.

"See ya at home, Sam. I've got Jack with me!"

Sam waved in acknowledgement. Then he turned back to the dugout. The rain that mercifully held off for the entire game began to fall.

"At least one thing went right today," Sam thought. "The rain held off and we got the game in."

Sam put on his coat. Then, he looked around the dugout and saw it was strewn with empty water bottles. Normally, he would insist that the kids pick up their trash and leave a tidy dugout but the matter slipped his mind. He had been too distracted. He resigned himself to picking up the trash himself. He had to lock the tractor shed anyway, so he took the armload of empty water bottles to the trash bin that sat next to the small storage shed. He shut the door to the shed and locked it. He looked around one final time and saw that everything was tidy.

Before he left, Sam sat down on the bleachers to collect his thoughts and be certain he wasn't forgetting anything. He surveyed the field for trash, lost mitts, or errant baseballs before he left the field and locked the gate. That thought reminded him of the ball in his coat pocket. He reached in his pocket and pulled out the ball and looked at it, and wondered anew how it could have traveled three miles on its own. That caused him to scan the forest beyond the outfield fence one more time. If he hadn't been so distracted, Sam thought to himself, he might have gotten the one or two additional runs he needed to win the game.

Then Sam had another thought: "Don't beat yourself up. It's just a game!" The thought was loud, and clear. So clear, Sam turned around to see if someone was there. He was alone. There were no other cars in the lot. Only his. Everyone else was gone. Yet the thought in his head was so loud, it was as if it came from somewhere else. Without knowing why, Sam looked at the woods beyond the fence in center field. He studied the trees for any sign of motion. All he saw were silhouettes of trees and shrubs.

One stump was right on the outside margin of the forest just behind the fence. Something didn't seem right but Sam couldn't quite figure out what it was. He kept scanning down the tree line toward the right field line. As his gaze took him to the edge of the field, it suddenly dawned on Sam what it was that was wrong. There wasn't a stump behind the fence. Those woods haven't been logged in almost a century. His head turned away from right field and back toward center field where the stump was. But it wasn't there. The stump was gone. Sam shut his eyes tight and held them shut for a long second. Then he opened them again. There was no tall stump. Did he just imagine that? Was he seeing things?

"What just happened?" Sam said aloud. He squinted at the woods, then stood atop the bleacher bench he had been sitting on to get a better look.

"Who's out there?" Sam yelled.

Sam jumped off the bench, walked around the backstop and across the infield, directly toward the center-field fence. The rain was falling harder now, almost a downpour. Sam tried to ignore it as he arrived at the center field fence. He stood at the fence peering into the woods at close range. He thought he should climb the fence and go into the woods and look around. Then he heard the snap of a stick off to his left, back in the woods, out of sight.

All of a sudden, Sam felt very afraid. Hair on the back of his neck stood up, rigid. It was getting dark; rain was now falling and Sam was getting soaked, standing there. He wanted to go into the woods but all of a sudden he thought better of the idea. "What if it's a mountain lion?" he thought to himself. Besides, it was too dark to see much and in another ten minutes it would be too dark to see his hand in front of his face.

Sam turned up his collar against the rain and walked briskly across the field and back to his car. By the time he got back to his car in the parking lot, the downpour had slowed to a soft drizzle. Sam turned to look at the woods one last time. It was too dark to see anything except the outline of the trees against the gray cloudy sky. He got in his car, started the engine and drove out the gate of the ball field. Once his car was outside the gate, he stopped his car and shut off the engine. After he had the gate locked, he couldn't help taking one last look at the forest beyond the center field fence. Sam stood in the fading light of the cold, cloudy dusk, peering at the distant, darkening woods. The rain stopped.

"I know I saw that stump, that...whatever it was...it was there. I'm sure of it."

An owl hooted from the woods. Sam smiled. The owl hooted again. Sam laughed out loud. Sam took a deep breath then he shouted into the night, in the direction of the outfield, "You're not fooling me! I know you're out there!"

The hooting ceased. Sam got into the Rover, started the engine, and headed home. Once he was comfortably driving down the highway, he turned on the radio; but all the while, he was thinking of the owl and the stump and the baseball. Suddenly a knowing smile came over his face.

Whatever it was, it was playing games with him. That had become increasingly obvious. The radio was tuned to the oldies station, which was playing a song by The Beatles. Sam remembered the song fondly from his college days. It was "Nowhere Man" from the "Yesterday and Today" album. It was The Beatles' first album of introspective material as opposed to their previous albums which were predominantly love songs.

As Sam's tires hissed on the wet asphalt, he listened and hummed to the song on the radio when it suddenly occurred to him that the song title seemed chillingly appropriate. "Nowhere man...eh?" he muttered aloud. Then he chuckled. "OK, Nowhere Man, you've got my attention. Now what do you want?"

Chapter 11

S AM PULLED INTO Redland country store on his way home. He saw a familiar face at the cash register.

"Hi, Sally. What's new?"

"Howdy, Sam. Not much. I saw your daughter yesterday. I didn't recognize her. She's gotten so tall."

"Yeah, she's pretty grown up, isn't she?"

"Yeah, she sure is...and pretty, too. You're in for a few headaches when the boys start comin' 'round."

"Headaches? I already have headaches," Sam quipped. "But as far as my daughter goes, I like Charles Barkley's way of dealing with the whole boy thing. His line goes like this, "I kill the first boy who shows up, then let the word get around from there."

"Yeah, I suppose that would work. Where's Charles Barkley now? In prison?"

"Maybe, but at least no one messes with his daughter," Sam smiled.

"Oh, by the way, I'll tell you what's new," Sally replied. "Have you heard about the big land deal that's going to happen out at the end of your road?"

"Yeah, but I think it's all talk. I don't really expect it to happen."

"The county planner was through here this morning. He said the whole deal had the blessing of the Forest Service. He also said that, if Forest Service approved it, the county would probably approve it, too. It's been a while since I've been up that Squaw Mountain Road. All I know is it's supposed to be on a big piece of property way up by there in some meadows below Squaw Butte."

"Yeah, I'm pretty sure the Foster family owns that land. They've held it since the 1800's. They used to pasture cattle up there in the summer. Plus they have a mining claim on Squaw Butte, so, if you put the two holdings together, it's a big chunk of the land they own around that mountain. The down side for the Foster family is that they're completely surrounded by government land. And, of course, the only road to their property up there is owned and maintained by the Forest Service."

A customer came to the counter. Sam smiled faintly, stepped back, and waited. When the customer left, he continued, "A few years back, there was talk of a land swap between the Fosters and the Forest Service, but they never could work out the details. Bart told me the Forest Service was never willing to pay what the place was worth. And you know the Foster family. They don't need the money. Meanwhile, the Forest Service has never approved plans the Fosters have for developing the place. It's a real standoff."

"I just saw Bart Foster at the ball field tonight," Sam continued. "My kid's team played his kid's team. We had a few words but he didn't say anything about a land deal." Sam added, "We mostly talked about education."

"I talked to him about it a little bit last week, though. I know he's had control of all the family holdings up there ever since his dad died, and he's been working on the details of some kind of development deal for a while now. Since he can't make a move without Forest Service approval, I figured nothing would ever happen. If he's got a new deal going now, he's either found a way around the Forest Service, or they are in on the deal with him. That's bad news for us, but good news for a few local businessmen."

"I guess we remodeled in the nick of time," she reflected. "Anyway, I thought you might know about it since you're the last house up there before the National Forest boundary," Sally said.

"...and Bart Foster used to be my neighbor. Now he lives in that new mansion above Eagle Creek. I'd ask him what's going on with his big development plans, but all of a sudden we're not on speaking terms. His kid is in my science class, and he thinks I'm poisoning her mind," Sam said with a shrug.

"Aren't small towns great?" Sally asked. "There's always somebody else to blame for your problems. Anyway, lemme know if you find out anything. Since you live on that road, you'll be the first to know if things start to happen."

As Sam walked out of the store to his old Land Rover, Sally followed him with her eyes and quietly said to herself, "See ya' Sam."

Fifteen minutes later, Sam got out of the car at his modest log cabin, gathered his groceries and headed up the steps into the house. His wife was sitting at the computer terminal, and their old golden retriever was sprawled out on the center of the small living room. Elizabeth sat on the sofa with a backpack at her feet, reading a novel. Jack, situated at the kitchen table, was absorbed with cutting pieces of construction paper and pasting them to a poster board.

" Hi kids. Tough game, eh, Jack. Can you believe that call Jake made?"

"I know. Justin was safe by a step and a half," Jack replied.

"I hate losing to Bart's team. Fortunately, he's as mad at me as I am at him, so at least I don't have to listen to him gloat."

"How come he's mad?" Jack asked.

"Long story. I'll tell ya later. Whatcha working on, big guy?"

"I'm doing a report on snakes. I have to give a speech about it Friday."

"Cool. Are you going to practice it for me so I can hear it?"

"Yeah, as soon as I'm done with the poster."

"Speaking of snakes, Grace, have you heard anything about a land deal that Bart Foster is working on with their land up at Squaw Meadow?"

"Sure have! Everyone in town seems to have heard about it. In fact, we got a letter from the Forest Service about it today. Look at this!" She waved a manila envelope in the air but didn't look up from the web page she was studying on the computer monitor. "You're not going to like it. They're announcing a series of town meetings to get public input. You know what that means."

"Uh-oh. Not the 'public input' meetings!" That means they've already got their scheme planned. Now they just have to jawbone the locals into line. You're right. I don't like the sound of this."

"The upshot is," Grace continued, still staring intently at the computer screen, "they want to improve the road beginning at the forest boundary, and going all the way up to Squaw Meadow."

"Yikes! I don't need to hear this right now!"

"I'm looking on the Forest Service website! It says they want to realign the road, which involves rebuilding two bridges, and moving a couple sections of road to the other side of the creek. It doesn't say *why* they want to do all this work but you know it either has something to do with the Foster's private holdings up there at the meadow or because they want to do a bunch of logging. Anyway, that's what this letter is all about. They're asking for public comment on the whole plan. They're saying they need to improve access for recreation so they're cutting some of the timber that got scorched in the forest fire two years ago."

Grace studied the words carefully on the computer screen in front of her. "Isn't it strange," she observed, " how that fire started up there under mysterious circumstances and now has become the reason they want to redo the whole road up to Squaw Meadow? Here's the weird part: most of the so-called salvage logging they're proposing isn't even their timber. It's on the Foster's land claim on the edge of Squaw Meadow."

"Oh, man, this is sounding bad," said Sam.

"But wait! There's more!" Grace added. "The website here says the Forest Service is making a new acquisition thanks to the generosity of the Foster family."

"What was the generous move? Selling them a new fleet of Ford trucks at cost?" Sam asked sarcastically.

"Worse," snapped Grace, still studying the computer monitor in front of her. "Get this. The Foster family is going to donate their land on Squaw Mountain, all of it, to the Forest Service, which they are going to make into an elk preserve. They want to remove the road to the top of Squaw Butte and call it 'R.A.R.E. III land' which, I believe is Forest Service lingo for the third go around of the 'Roadless Area Review and Evaluation,' which was started during the Clinton administration, back in the 1990's. They're basically saying they want to manage the land for certain kinds of recreation, namely hunting."

"Here's the map of what they want to do right here!"

Grace sat back in the chair and relaxed a moment. "I'll bookmark the website and send the link to your e-mail address." She paused, "Think all this sounds a little bit too generous for somebody in particular?"

"You bet it does," Sam replied, now looking over his wife's shoulder as she studied the map on the screen. "Sounds like my good buddy Bart Foster has just made a tidy deal with our pals at the U.S. Forest Service. And unless I miss my guess, it's bigger than they're making it sound."

Sam paused, and then observed, "They're making it look like they want to cut a little timber, you know, to create some local jobs and help out a few logger families in Redland. Of course, the real deal comes after they clear out all those pesky trees around the meadow. Bart told me himself that he's been trying for years to get some kind big of development going up there. I didn't take him seriously because I didn't think he had a ghost of a chance getting the Forest Service to go along with something like that. It's starting to look like he's finally got his ducks in a row."

"I can see it now," Sam continued. "A golf course, lots of vacation homes, maybe even a convention center. Wouldn't that just be the tidy deal? That meadow has got to be the biggest piece of undeveloped flat ground anywhere on the north half of the national forest, and the only way to get in and out of there, is right down Squaw Mountain road."

The husband and wife looked at each other and they both flashed on the mostly-deserted road in front of their property. "Sam, I just bet old Bart has finally found a way to get them to let him do it. I smell a land swap. Bart gives the Forest Service their old Squaw Mountain mining claims and they give him more of the meadow. Then the Forest Service improves the road, supposedly for recreation or fire access, or something else that sounds good to the public."

"It also just happens to help them sell the timber, not to mention improving the access for Squaw Mountain Estates or whatever Bart ends up calling it. What a great deal to get Uncle Sam to fix the road for you. They'll make it a nice smooth two-lane highway all the way to Bart's golf course. What do ya think they call the place, Squaw Meadow Resort? The Resort at Squaw Meadow?"

"Hmmm." Grace paused. "I don't think they'll call it Squaw anything. Too politically incorrect. It's gotta be something like, Alpencrest or Mountain View, or something like that. Get rid of those trees in the meadow, and that place will have killer views of Mount Hood. The whole scheme is too perfect. Man, the more I think about this, the scarier it gets. If they've already got Forest Service cooperation, it'll be next to impossible to stop them. And every visitor and worker and truckload of building materials is going to go right past our driveway. We are *so* screwed. This isn't funny."

"This fits with the kind of day it's been all day. Everything else I touched today has turned to mud. And everything else that has happened has had something to do with Bart Foster" Sam reflected ruefully.

"Why? What else has happened today?" Grace inquired.

"Well, for starters, I got chewed out by Wilma Lavelle for letting the word 'bigfoot' be uttered in a science lesson. She tried to pass the buck by saying she was just responding to a parent who complained that my lesson was somehow inappropriate for their frail little daughter. She wouldn't tell me *who* was doing the complaining, because, of course, I couldn't be trusted with that *sensitive* information. It didn't take me long to find out though. Care to guess who complained?"

"Not Bart?" Grace guessed.

"None other! Well, not exactly him. It was his dear spoiled wife Judy that ruined the party. Isn't that bizarre?"

"How'd you find out?"

"We played his team tonight at Fischer's Mill. And he couldn't resist making a crack about bigfoot. I put two and two together and I acted like I already knew it was him. He finally admitted they were the ones who complained."

"How did 'bigfoot' come up in science class?" Grace interrupted.

"Remember I told you I had Nick Rollo in as a guest speaker the other day? He showed the class his collection of tracks and stuff and we talked about the scientific method and scientific mysteries. Ellie Foster is in my third period class. When she got home she told her parents that they learned about bigfoot in science class. Bart says it was Judy who got indignant about it but I'm not buying it. I bet they both decided it was worth making a fuss over. Next thing

I know, our spineless principal who didn't even bother to find out what really happened, is in my face and threatening to 'can' me for teaching the kids about bigfoot in science class."

"He never misses a chance to mention what a pillar of the community he is, Rotary club president, owner of the Ford dealership, and lets not forget his sister is on the Redland School Board. Of course, Wilma was no doubt thrilled to be given an opportunity to dump some heat and trouble on a certain troublesome science teacher that she's never liked in the first place. I'm sure she was all too happy to oblige."

"You're starting to whine, dear," Grace kidded.

"Anyway, Bart's team won the game tonight on a bad call, made by the ump who works at the tractor dealership that does a lot of business with the Ford dealer..."

"Now you're starting to sound paranoid," Grace interrupted again.

"Speaking of paranoid, the weirdest things were happening at the ball field. The tractor stopped working for no reason. I found a ball that Jack and I hit into the woods right out there in the back yard then there was this owl that was on the ground but it didn't sound like an owl, I think the woods are haunted and I don't know what the hell is going on anymore!"

Grace stared at Sam in silent disbelief. She slammed her eyelids down and reopened her eyes, then gave her head one solid shake. "I didn't follow a thing you just said. What the heck are you talking about?"

"I don't' even know. All I know is that I've had one helluva bad day and that was before I got home and found out that the same guy who has been making my life miserable all day is apparently in bed with the Forest Service on a land deal that is going to turn Squaw Meadow into a zoo and our road into a freeway."

"That's where you're wrong because we're going to stop him. I don't know how, but if there's any possible way, we're going to stop him," Grace replied forcefully, her eyebrows down and face flush with determination.

"Well, it's looking like we're going to have to take on the U.S. Government if we're going to do it, because it appears they're running interference for him *and* his scheme."

"That's nothing new. The government has always favored business. I can't believe that it's taken so long for that chunk of private land to get developed. Don't get me wrong, I don't want to see that land get developed any more than you do, but I knew this day would come sooner or later. The Foster family has been trying to get the Forest Service to let them develop that property for years. Looks like they've finally figured out how to do it."

Sam paused, "Gotta hand it to them. It's pretty clever. It starts with a fire that they may or may not have helped start. Then they get the Forest Service to use the old 'timber salvage' story to cut out a bunch of timber to make room for a golf course and improve the view. That also gives them an excuse to pave the road all the way up to the meadow."

Then, Sam got a bit red in the face, "I bet they'll even plow it for them in the winter."

He paused, "The Fosters swap their steep timberland on Squaw Mountain for millions of dollars in road work and the right to develop their meadow up there. Bart gets to build the resort he's always wanted, the Forest Service gets timber revenues, and they both get a fancy new road. All we get is a whole bunch traffic, summer and winter on our quiet little road unless we figure out a way to stop them."

"Any bright ideas? How about we set up a lemonade stand at the foot of our driveway and cash in on the increase in traffic?"

"Very funny," Grace replied with an equal amount of sarcasm. "Sorry. I'm fresh out of ideas right now. Dinner's in the oven. Let's eat."

"Great idea. I *gotta* get something to eat."

Sam left the computer room and went into the living room where the kids were working on their homework. "How's the snake project coming, Jack?"

"I need a glue stick."

Chapter 12

THE SCHOOL DAY had not yet begun. Mr. Ward sat at his desk in an otherwise empty classroom at Redland Middle School. He sipped coffee while browsing Internet websites. In the search engine, Sam enters the words "best bigfoot book."

Seconds later a list of blue website titles appears: "Hancock House Publishers: The Most Bigfoot Titles and Authors Anywhere on the Web!" After clicking back and forth he settled on a book entitled *Big Footprints* by an academic at Washington State University named Krantz.

Sam added the book to his on-line virtual 'shopping cart,' then pulled his wallet out of his pocket. He typed the credit card number just as a student walked into the classroom, followed by an elderly gentleman. They both have the tan skin and facial features that belie their Native American ancestry.

Iris, the class comedian, smiled broadly as she approached his desk. "Mr. Ward, this is my uncle, Henry Threelynx. I told him about the lesson you did last week on bigfoot and he wanted to talk to you."

"Uh-oh," Sam thought. "Not this again." Sam extended his hand and smiled a sheepish smile and immediately launched into a round of *mea culpas*.

"Look, I'm really sorry. I didn't mean to cause any trouble. I was just trying to teach the kids about the scientific method. The lesson wasn't really about bigfoot. It was just an attempt to teach them something about the scientific method by considering a local legend which may or may not be real. I hope I didn't cause any problems. If I did, I'm very sorry." Sam was falling all over himself with apology. He added one last statement to his effusive attempt to derail another complaint. He looked right at Uncle Henry. "Personally, sir, I don't believe in bigfoot."

"Well, I do, so there sure isn't any need to apologize to me for anything. You must be thinking I came in here to complain. Nothing could be further from the truth. I came in here to say, "Thanks." I'm glad you had the courage to cover the subject in a science class. You see, I grew up on the Warm Springs Reservation. Now, I live here in Redland. I'm an archaeologist for the Army Corps of Engineers. My wife has family that lives on the Yakama Reservation. My people know a few things about the 'Itohiul', or as you call them, 'bigfoot'. When Iris told me about your lesson and the way you allowed her to explain the Indian perspective on it, I felt a need to come in here and have her introduce me to you, in case you wanted to know a bit more about the subject."

Sam was speechless. He blinked, looked at Iris, then back at her uncle. He smiled and stuck out his hand. "Sam Ward, sir. It's a pleasure to meet you. Sorry to sound so defensive. I got some complaints, you know, about my, uh, rather controversial choice of lessons."

"I'm not surprised. Anyway, sir, you won't get any complaints from me. Iris speaks very highly of you. She thinks you're funny and she says you make science interesting."

"She's a very good student. I wish all my students were as eager to learn as she is," Sam replied.

"That is good news. We value education very highly in our family," her Uncle Henry explained. "But I came in mainly to tell you how much Iris enjoyed the lesson and how much I appreciate you presenting that material in a science classroom. She mentioned that even though you hosted a speaker, you seemed kind of skeptical about the whole matter at the same time.

"I thought you might be interested to know that the various tribes who are represented on the Warm Springs Reservation are very familiar with the sasquatch. The Chinook people called them 'Skookums' which means 'wood spirits,' and 'Itohiul' which translates to the more familiar term "big footed creatures." The tribes of Kwakiutl Nation call them 'Bukwas'. Other tribes have still other names for them. The Yakama People call them 'Ste-ye-ha-mah,' which translates into 'Stick Indians." Sasquatch is an anglicized word that comes from 'sesquac,' a term once used in parts of British Columbia by the Salish and the Chehalis Nations. There are still other names. Suffice to say that all tribes in North America have names for these beings and know of their existence."

Digesting all this new information, Sam clarified, "I always took it for a legend that describes a purely mythical being, but you're saying bigfoot is a bit more than a myth?"

"The problem with the word 'bigfoot', as the white men use it, is that they take it for a single creature; a single solitary forest "monster," if you will. Indians understand them to be a race of beings, a tribe, just like all the other tribes that have inhabited these lands for eons. They are a very mysterious tribe, to be sure, but a tribe nevertheless. We understand that they wish simply to be left undisturbed in their native lands and we are all too happy to oblige them. They are beings that posses formidable powers. They can render one immobile and defenseless. It is wise to keep a distance from them, as much as possible. Yet, they are also occasionally curious and interested in the activities of us humans, so, they may sometimes come around and observe our actions and activities."

Fascinated by the words of Iris's uncle, Sam had many more questions but the time was almost upon them when the bell would ring and the stampede of students would begin.

"Have you ever seen a sasquatch?" Sam asked.

"To see a sasquatch is said by tribal elders to be a bad omen, so we do not try to observe them, but I have been around them and in their midst on several occasions. When I sense their presence I try to avert my gaze and leave the area lest I disturb or annoy them. Over the years, they have been seen by many on the reservation at different times and at different places. We know the areas that they frequent, and as I say, we avoid those areas when we sense their presence. They are not all nice, yet they are not all evil either. Like the rest of us, each has its own personality. Some are very peaceful and even kind to us. Others are ominous and even mean-spirited. A mean or angry sasquatch is a dangerous being to be around and certainly not something to trifle with."

"How can you tell the difference?" Sam asked.

"They make it very clear. There have been children in our tribe who have become lost, and, to our good fortune, the sasquatch has looked after them. More than once, the lost child has been returned safely to our midst, apparently with the help of the sasquatch. In other cases, some fearless braves have challenged the sasquatch with a weapon or actions. The results were not pretty. I know of one man who was hit in the forehead with a precisely and forcefully thrown rock. He survived, but he was seriously injured. That man has never since been the same."

"Forgive me if I ask the same question you may have already answered," Sam began, "but I know of a guy who studies their behavior, and he describes them as a population of apes. But you seem to be saying they're human. Is that true?"

"Yes and no," Henry replied. "We think of them as part human and part spirit being. They are both, but they are neither. Sorry to be so vague and contradictory but they embody characteristics of both ends of the spectrum. Whatever they are, they are most certainly not some kind of ape. Anyone who thinks that is probably judging them on the basis of their physical appearance. Their appearance is just one of the many ruses that they are capable of perpetrating. They are clever and powerful. They are sentient beings that seem to know our intentions and what is in our hearts. They seem to be present even when they cannot be seen. They can be seen by you, but only if they wish to allow it. It goes as they allow.

"To see one is to be chosen. Some in our tribe fear that it may also be, as I said, a rather bad omen. Not everyone within our own tribe agrees, but remember, these beings, whatever they are, are not all the same. We understand that there are not just different ones but different kinds. The whole matter is more complex than what people may even be able to understand."

Sam was transfixed as the elderly gentleman spoke, but suddenly, the loud clang of a bell broke the spell that Sam felt as he listened intently to the words of Iris's uncle. Henry paused, waiting for the clanging of the bell to subside. The hall outside the classroom was now filled with the voices and the commotion of many students moving about. Henry smiled and looked at Sam.

"It sounds like your work day is about to begin. I hope I did more than just confuse you. We Indians do not have all the answers to what these beings are. Whatever they are, we do know that they are real and they are much more than apes. Most Indians see them as the lords, the guardians, of the forest and all the creatures that live within it."

Henry paused and smiled. "I'll leave you to prepare for your students. It was a pleasure to meet you. Thank you for all you're doing for my young niece."

Henry extended his hand and Sam shook it. Sam fumbled for something to say as Henry turned to leave.

"Henry," Sam said, "Will you tell them I said 'hello'?"

"Tell them yourself," Henry said with a smile.

"Is there a way to communicate with them?" Sam asked.

"Yes." Henry replied flatly.

"Might I ask what it is?" Sam inquired.

"If I told you, you wouldn't believe me, but you're a bright guy. You'll figure it out for yourself. Sorry to be so oblique.

Don't worry. They're listening. " Henry extended his hand to his niece. She took it and they headed for the door.

"See you in science class, Mr. Ward," Iris said.

As they walked through the doorway, Henry paused, looked back at Sam and said, "Remember: *It* goes as *they* allow."

Chapter 13

S AM SAT AT his desk before a silent, but full classroom. His students were working intently on a quiz. He tried to focus on checking papers from the stacks of ungraded assignments on his desk, but the conversation with Iris's uncle kept replaying in Sam's head. What Henry said was truly incredible. As difficult it was to believe, it was also difficult to accept that he could be completely wrong.

Sam was trying to be as scientific as possible about assessing this kind fellow as a source of accurate information.

Could Iris's uncle just be wrong? Maybe so, but he was representing himself as a lifelong resident of the reservation and a highly experienced and competent outdoorsman. Beyond his own personal experience, he seemed to be speaking from the collective experience of many others who spent a great deal of time in not just remote places, but places that were off limits to white people.

The possibility that Uncle Henry was fabricating his descriptions of Native American beliefs seemed out of the question. Here was a guy who had nothing to gain by making up stories. Why would he want to impress some paleface that he was never going to see again? Why would he spin yarns in front of his niece?

His niece was about the nicest, most intelligent, and most sincere student in his class. And she certainly had the best sense of humor. It seemed that the uncle showed up largely because he appreciated what Sam was doing for his niece. Henry was sharing what he seemed to consider almost sacred information with Sam about the sasquatch mystery as a sort of favor in appreciation of the positive impact that Sam was having on Iris.

All in all, it seemed that Sam had managed to stumble upon a source of information that even dedicated sasquatch researchers like Nick Rollo did not have. Sam found himself wondering how Nick would react to the descriptions provided by Iris' uncle of how his Native American brethren viewed the sasquatch. The most amazing part of the whole matter was the big difference between the way the Indian regarded the creatures and the way Nick Rollo saw them. This thoroughly perplexed Sam. His scientific side favored what Nick was describing, yet Henry spoke with such matter-of-fact certainty and wisdom that it was very difficult to discount his opinions.

Being a science teacher, Sam was indeed skeptical of such things as sasquatches until a few short days ago when Nick Rollo's calm and reasoned assessment of the evidence gave Sam pause. Sam probably would not even have taken Nick's descriptions seriously if he hadn't had some very strange personal experiences of his own last night at the baseball field. While Sam's personal experiences were vague and open to multiple interpretations, they had him seriously wondering whether at least some of what Nick was saying was true.

Now, just a few days later, this guy strolls into Sam's classroom out of nowhere and challenges nearly every idea that Nick Rollo was offering. Still worse, he was challenging them not because Nick's ideas were outlandish or based on weak evidence, but because Nick's ideas were too simplistic.

Nick saw a population of dumb apes shambling almost aimlessly around North American forests. Whereas Henry saw the same evidence as pointing to a sophisticated and sentient group of beings that were somehow both spirit and flesh at the same time. And the worst part of the whole sticky mess was this: the strange events that Sam had experienced himself were actually much more consistent with Uncle Henry's view of the creatures.

It also occurred to Sam that apes didn't seem likely to retrieve baseballs his son hit into the woods or move baseballs into Sam's path. All in all, it seemed like Uncle Henry was 'spot on' about the capabilities of these beings, whatever they were.

Would he ever be able to even explain to Rollo what Henry had confided? Sam doubted it. He was thoroughly steeped in the ways and methods of science so it seemed foolhardy to even try to change Nick's thinking, especially when all he had to offer was the legends and anecdotal information of an old Indian. The more he thought about it, the more futile it seemed to even try to explain to Nick the things that Henry described. No, indeed, the only prudent course of action would be for Sam to keep his mouth shut. Maybe Uncle Henry was correct, but there seemed no hope whatsoever of convincing anyone, not Nick, not Sam's wife, not anyone, that there was any truth to views of a guy like Henry Threelynx.

Yet, Sam had experiences of his own which seemed to bear out this strange perspective. And that was the most ironic twist of all. Sam was the science teacher. Sam was the original bigfoot skeptic himself until a few short days ago, and now he had been exposed to a point of view that was stranger than the one held by any of the bigfoot believers he personally knew. Although he had some mighty strange personal experiences, Sam had not one shred of physical evidence to bolster his bizarre interpretation of this phenomenon.

Why was all of this suddenly happening to him, he wondered? The coincidences just seemed too numerous. Was there a purpose behind all these strange occurrences and this troubling information? He felt alone and forlorn, sitting at his desk in the corner of this crowded classroom. "Why me?" Sam muttered to himself. And, as quickly as this rhetorical question came to mind, the two-word answer came right behind: "Squaw Meadow."

A sunny, warm Sunday found the Ward's Land Rover heading out the driveway of their homestead with Sam at the wheel. His son Jack was riding shotgun. A flat, white box sat on the back seat. When the car reached the foot of the driveway, Sam began to turn right toward town as a matter of habit. He caught himself in the middle of the turn and put the car into reverse, then turned the wheel to the left and headed uphill toward the high country.

The Rover was soon chattering up the washboard of bumps on the Squaw Mountain Road. A dust plume billowed out from behind the dust-covered SUV as it navigated the unpaved road up toward Squaw Meadow and Squaw Butte.

"What's in the box?" Jack asked.

Matter-of-factly Sam replied, "Apple pie"

"What for?"

"You might say it's a gift," said Sam.

"For who?" Jack asked.

"The sasquatch, you know, the wild people," Sam replied.

"You mean the people who watch me play baseball?" Jack offered.

"That's right. The people who watch you and sometimes want to join in," Sam smiled.

"So, you think they're really there?" Jack asked.

"Something's there. Something *or* someone. The more I think about it, the more I think it's a 'someone.' Nick Rollo says there's bigfoot animals out there. I think it's ridiculous. Not the idea that something's out there, it's just the name. But how is anyone supposed to take the idea seriously when they give it such a stupid name. It makes the thing sound like some big, dumb animal or even a clown. If there *is* something out there, it's smart. *Real* smart. The other day an Indian gentleman came into the classroom and described the same creatures as part human, part spirit. He gave me several tribal names for them, but they're hard to remember. I've taken to calling it the 'nowhere man'. It's the name of a song by The Beatles, and I thought it kind of fit when I heard it on the radio the other night, so it stuck.

"I know that song. Elizabeth has it on her iPod. She plays it all the time. She's really into The Beatles."

"Right. So you know the song?" Sam asked.

"Yeah, Elizabeth said that the 'Nowhere Man' is a guy who doesn't listen or pay attention to anything around him. She says we're all 'nowhere men' at times," Jack said.

"That's very profound, son. I can't believe that a fifth grader is explaining the symbolism in Beatles songs," Sam replied.

"Elizabeth is the one who explained it to me. That's one of her favorite songs," Jack replied.

"Well, I'm impressed that you could remember and explain it so well. You make an excellent point. I guess we are the Nowhere Men, especially when we do make plans to turn some creatures' home into a condominium project without even realizing that the creatures even exist. And I still can't believe that it took a fifth grader to open my eyes to the reality of the whole situation. If you hadn't hit those baseballs into the woods, I don't think we'd be sitting here right now.

"Actually, I'll be a sixth grader in one more week," Jack reminded his father.

"OK, Mr. Sixth-Grader, so what do you think they should be called?" Sam asked.

"I call 'em 'watchers'. That's what they do, they watch, and it seems like there's two. Sometimes I can hear them moving," said Jack.

"I like that. I like that a lot." Sam said.

"So how do you know they like pie?" Jack asked.

"I don't. I don't know anything, but that pie represents the sum total of three conversations I had yesterday with three people who view the Nowhere Man, or as you say, 'The Watchers', in three completely different ways, and it all comes down to that pie.

"The first person, that is the first conversation, was with your mom. I told her what happened out back with the baseballs the other day. She laughed. She's sure we imagined the whole thing. I told her about the ball we marked up and how I found it at the Fischer's Mill field. She said somebody put it there as a joke. I tend to agree with her on that one, but I think it's 'the watcher' who's playing the joke.

"I told her," Sam continued, "about the whole bigfoot thing as Nick Rollo sees it. She just couldn't take that seriously. Well, I had this idea. You see, Nick says they live right around here, among other places. He says Squaw Mountain up here is a hotbed for this 'bigfoot activity' as he calls it. If there were such creatures and you could somehow prove it then they would be this incredibly rare and endangered species.

"Then we could get the whole area preserved as a critical habitat for an endangered species. That would stop the development of Squaw Meadow and probably a whole lot more. It could stop everything on the Mt. Hood National Forest, at least for a while, while they sorted it all out. Well, I explained all this to Mom and she thought I had gone completely crazy. She doesn't want to even consider such a preposterous idea. She actually got kind of nasty about it when I wouldn't give it a rest."

"I guess there's Nowhere Women, too," Jack offered.

"Yeah, I guess we all have the potential. Anyway," Sam continued, "that was the first conversation and the upshot was I'm crazy to even consider such a far-fetched possibility. The whole idea of mysterious creatures in the woods is fantasy, and just the idea of trying to prove it for some kind of political or scientific purpose is delusional.

"Next I called Nick and I told him I was beginning to see his point about bigfoot and I wanted to try and get good evidence that we could use to show the world that such creatures existed. I told him that my big concern was the development on Squaw Meadow and the area around it. He told me he has been setting cameras in the woods up there for a few summers now and he hasn't gotten anything. He puts bait out in front of the cameras and whatever tries to take the bait gets its picture taken. I asked him what he used for bait. He said he generally uses raw meat or raw chicken and he gets more pictures of bear or bobcat or martens.

"Then he switched to apples and he got deer, raccoon and possums to come around. The bait was stolen a few times but still no photos. He also had his camera torn off the tree and left lying on the ground. The bait was gone, but the camera hadn't taken any pictures. I told him I thought maybe the creatures he was trying to photograph were somehow too smart. He said he didn't think so. He said he just needed to do a better job of hiding the camera. That was my second conversation.

"Then I called an Indian guy named Henry Threelynx that I met through a kid in my science class. I think you know her, her name is Iris Crowe. Henry is her uncle. Anyway, I told him that I wanted to show that Indians or something lived in the woods up around Squaw Meadow as a way to stop this plan for a development. He said he didn't think it would work. So, I told him about Nick's camera traps. He laughed. He said they'd never fall for such an obvious trick. I told him Nick had one of the cameras torn down and the bait stolen, and he wasn't at all surprised.

"Then, I told him what Nick was using for bait and he laughed. He said Nick's wasting his time with the cameras and his bait won't work anyway. So, I asked him what he thought they liked to eat. He said they eat what we eat. He said they wouldn't eat raw chicken, but they might like a nice cooked chicken with a little paprika on it.

"Here's the funny part. Henry also said they have their pride. He didn't think much of Nick's suggestion to leave a pile of apples on the ground. He said they won't take food that's left lying in the dirt. He didn't think they'd be too interested in a hunk of half-rotten meat, either. He thought that would insult them. Isn't that funny? He said they probably wouldn't touch the apples but they would appreciate a fresh apple pie. He said that when he was a kid, his grandmother would always make two pies at a time and leave one of them out back on a tree stump, but not on the ground. The pie was a gesture of appreciation to the 'big hairy men' as she called them. They were the guardians of the woods and also guardians of her family."

"So you're going to set the pie out somewhere?" Jack asked.

"I guess," Sam shrugged.

"Are you going to put a camera on it?"

"Henry said not to. He said to just put out offerings for a while and skip all the tricks and traps. They're way too smart for all that. He said I would be better off just trying to establish some trust by simply putting out gifts without any strings attached.

"Nick certainly didn't agree. He thinks they're apes. I had to decide which way I wanted to go. I decided to go with Henry's 'wildmen' point of view. You know, 'The Watchers'.

Frankly, I don't think we have the kind of time we need for this little project. It sounded like his grandmother was leaving them gifts over a period of many years. Even so, Henry's ideas seemed to make the most sense, especially in light of what we think we're seeing around our homestead. When I made the pie last night, mom wanted to know why I was suddenly so eager to bake.

"When I told her what I was going to do, she said, 'You're going to put a perfectly good apple pie in the middle of the forest?' I said, 'Yup, but don't fret. I made two of them last night, one for us and one for "them"'. She said I was insane. Now that I'm crazy, I figure all we have to lose is an apple pie. So, here we are and here's the pie!"

"Yeah, but she didn't see the baseballs come back when I hit them into the woods," Jack said.

"If she had, she might not think this is so crazy. But why Squaw Meadow?" Jack inquired. "Why not leave it nearer to our house, or even down at Fischer's Mill?"

"I'm not sure," Sam shrugged. "I was going to leave the pie in our woods, but then I thought we should head on up to Squaw Meadow and have a look around, anyway. Bringing a gift of some sort seemed like a good idea. I can't say why, but for some reason, I'm beginning to think that all this strange stuff has something to do with the fact that we live so close to Squaw Meadow. I'm just feeling like there is something going on up here. I'm really not sure why. Besides, if our good buddy Bart gets his way, Squaw Meadow won't be Squaw Meadow much longer.

"I figure we'd better get up here and enjoy the place before they turn it into a golf course. And maybe, just maybe, while we're up here looking around, we can figure out a way to stop him," Sam said. He slowed the car as it descended a long hill. He rounded a bend and he brought the car to a stop at the foot of a small bridge.

"We're here." Sam stopped the car beside the road. They were in a narrow valley between steep mountain ridges. On one side of the road, the valley was flooded with an immense, shallow pond that stretched toward the horizon. Reeds and cattails emerged from the water along the edges of this long shallow lake.

Like most high elevation wetlands in the Cascade Mountains, the lake was created by past beaver activity. Squaw Creek, like countless other mountain creeks, was dammed by beavers to create long, narrow ponds that gradually fill up with sediments, eventually creating grassy mountain meadows where large beaver ponds once stood. The complex of meadows known as Squaw Meadow was midway through the gradual process of filling up with sediment. A large stretch of open water still existed down the center of the mile-long beaver pond, though the edges of the pond were already boggy wetlands with saturated soils supporting lush emergent vegetation.

Squaw Mountain Road bisected the Squaw Meadow complex. On the north side of the road, the succession from pond to meadow was virtually complete and the ancient beaver ponds had given way to a verdant mountain meadow featuring an impressive variety of blooming wildflowers. Gumdrop shaped Squaw Butte was situated at the top end of this northern meadow. 'Butte' is a regional term for a feature that is too big to call a hill but too small to be a mountain. No consensus had been achieved as to whether The Squaw was a mountain or a butte. This created a geographical contradiction that the locals seemed perfectly comfortable with: the Squaw *Mountain* Road led straight up Squaw *Butte*.

Before arriving at the butte, the Squaw Mountain Road dipped down and crossed the valley floor of the Squaw Creek drainage which was flooded with long, narrow expanses of open water. The edges of these ancient beaver ponds were already filled with sediment. This saturated soil provided a wetland environment dominated by cattails and yellow water irises. Elsewhere along the margins of the ponds, old landslides and rock fall left boulder-covered hillsides jutting almost vertically out of the water and extending upward for hundreds of feet, all the way to the ridge top nearly a thousand feet above the valley floor.

Surrounding the long expanse of open water was lush green vegetation with sprays of yellow blooms, and the steep, boulder-covered hillsides surrounding the ponds and meadows. Squaw Meadow was a shimmering oasis of fresh water and wildflowers surrounded by jade-green mountains. The forest road that the Wards traveled had a wide spot for parking in the meadow. A rock fire ring next to the parking spot was filled with broken glass, blackened cans, and a few half-burned pieces of wood. On the other side of the dirt road, the flowing water of Squaw Creek wound its way through a broad, grassy meadow. Majestic fir trees blanketed the hillsides surrounding the high elevation lakes and meadows. The June sun penetrated an azure sky and thin mountain air with an uncommon intensity for so early in the summer. The open water reflected the deep blue hue of the pure mountain sky. It was a joyous day to visit this bucolic patch of sub-alpine scenery.

Sam shut off the engine. Both doors of the car opened simultaneously. Father and son stepped out and looked around. "I can see why they want to develop the place. It sure would make a very nice wilderness resort."

"Where do they want to build?" Jack asked.

"There's a ton of possibilities here. It just depends on how much development they're allowed to do. They'd probably take the whole place if they can get it. The plan, I think, is that the Fosters will give the Forest Service their land on Squaw Butte back there, which is all virgin timber," Sam explained, gesturing, "and in return, they get most of the valley floor which would include the meadow on that side of the road and the lake on this side of the road. I think they want the meadow areas for golf courses. The lake is public but it doesn't get much use, so if the lake became private land, they could put a locked gate across the road and keep the public completely away from it. Since the Fosters already own part of this hillside over here on the west side of the lake, they could build lakeside homes and the houses could each have a little dock on a private lake. Heck of a deal, really."

"So what are we going to check out?" Jack asked.

"I thought we'd cut across the Foster's land and work our way to the back side of the lake," Sam suggested

"What are we going to do with the pie, Dad?"

"Well, I figured we'd take it with us and keep our eyes open for a good place to leave it. Since the west side of the meadow is what they want to develop, I thought we'd look that area over first," Sam suggested.

The two stood and looked at the open water by the campfire circle. Rough skinned newts floated motionless in the shallow water at their feet. "This is where I got the newts last fall," Jack offered.

"I believe it," Sam agreed. "Look at 'em all! There must be a hundred within fifty feet of right here."

Jack grabbed one and lifted it out of the water. He let it walk across his open palm until it got to the edge of his hand. He raised his other palm just as the newt stepped off his hand. The newt landed on his other hand and kept walking. Jack lowered his hand as the newt walked. As the newt reached the edge of his second hand, Jack lowered his hand to the water. The newt stepped off Jack's hand and plopped into the water.

"Let's start exploring," Sam suggested. "Last time I was up here we had a boat. It's easier to get to the far end of the lake by paddling but I know where there's a trail. We have to cut through Foster's land. It's not as steep as everything else, so people tend to cut across their land when they're trying to get around the lake on foot. I'm sure it's one thing the Fosters would like to stop people from doing. Once we get to the back of the lake, it's all public land."

The pair walked a short distance up the dirt road. Sam peered into the brush on the side of the road as they walked. He stopped. "Right here," Sam gestured, peering into the woods on their right. "This is it. The trail is right in there. I think we should go get the pie and lock the Rover. Once we get in there, we're not going to want to come back until we're ready to leave."

Jack waited as Sam hoofed it back to the car. Sam returned with the pie in a reusable grocery sack and a day-pack on his back.

"I brought some water and some lunch," Sam announced.

They ducked into the woods through a small opening in the dust-covered tangle of brush at the side of the road. Blackberry vines tore at their clothing and scratched the bare skin on their arms. Once they were through the dense foliage that grew along the roads, the forest opened out, making travel easier. The pair of hikers had entered the deep shade of the temperate rain forest. Beneath a dense canopy of Douglas fir, the undergrowth gave way to a surprisingly open forest floor.

The faint trail they were following soon became clearer, wider, and easier to travel. There were no discernible footprints or hoof prints, yet the trail still seemed rather firm under foot. Still further along, the trail was so well compacted that it seemed like it was even getting frequent use. Also odd was the fact that neither Sam nor his son had to stoop under branches as they trooped along.

The pair followed the trail, as it led them along a forested slope above the wide shallow lake that occupied the center of Squaw Meadow. The trail rose, dipped, and wound its way through the woods, always staying in the dense shade of the forest. After walking for half an hour, Sam stopped and peered through the trees and saw a point of land in the direction of the lake that jutted out to form a peninsula.

The lake itself could be seen only partially, when openings In the tree canopy lined up. Putting one's head in the right spot afforded brief glimpses of the sunlight reflecting off shimmering blue water in the distance.

"That looks like our picnic spot, right out there," Sam declared, pointing in the direction of the lake.

"How can you tell?" Jack asked.

"As I recall, it's the first place where you can see water through the trees, right after a long stretch of trail that stays away from the lakeshore. I'm pretty sure this is it. Follow me."

Sam led Jack cross country, downhill and in the direction of the shimmering water in the distance. What looked like an easy approach suddenly got very difficult. A patch of spiny, fibrous devil's club blocked their route. They paused and studied the landscape. Rather than try to penetrate the forbidding patch of devil's club, Sam led Jack on a detour that utilized higher, drier ground where the thorny devil's club could not grow in dense, impenetrable thickets. At last, the reflected light from the lake began to brighten the forest. They were on the final approach to their scenic lakeside destination.

Their persistence paid off. The pair emerged from the undergrowth; stepping right out onto the sun-drenched point of land that Sam held in his mind's eye. Sparking blue water surrounded them on three sides. Vertical basalt cliffs rose high above them on the opposite shore of the narrow lake. At the base of the cliffs, giant boulders extended from the base of the cliffs to the water's edge. It was a magnificent spot to take a break on a magnificently sunny day.

"Yes! How's that for navigation? I led us right to it on the first try!" Sam declared with unmistakable pride.

"How did you know this place was here?" Jack asked.

"I spotted it from the water a few years ago. It took me a few tries before I found how to get here by land. It's real easy to get lost. I haven't been here in a few years so I was a little rusty on some of the details. I remembered the big patch of devil's club, so when we got to that, I knew we were on the right track. Isn't this a great spot?" Sam asked proudly.

"It sure is," Jack agreed. Sam set down the pie he was carrying and took off his pack. Jack stepped up to the water's edge and peered into the shallow water of the pond.

"Look at all the newts in here, Dad! Wow, there are tons of them!"

Sam smiled at the delight in his son's voice. He looked around for a flat dry spot where he could lie down. He put his pack on the grass when he found a suitable spot, then he sat beside his pack. Sam fell backward, stretched his feet toward the water, and let out a long sigh. He raised his arm and put a hand over his brow to shield the sun and then raised his head momentarily to see what Jack was doing. "We should have brought a net," he said as he dropped his head back down onto the pack he was using as a pillow. "Are you going to try and catch the newts?" Sam asked.

"They're so slow I can catch them with my hand." Jack was now on his stomach with his hands in the water. In seconds, he was pulling newts out of the water and examining them, then delicately setting them back in the water and watching them swim lazily away. They spent the next hour relaxing on the grassy point in the sun. They ate peanut butter sandwiches, sipped cans of orange soda, and ate fish-shaped crackers.

Sam could have relaxed there all day but Jack began to get bored. "Let's start heading back, Dad."

Sam sat up and looked around. Damselflies and dragonflies hovered just inches over the water. In the center of the pond, small splashes marked the presence of trout that rose to stab at the low-flying insects. Sam rubbed his face. For a moment, he allowed himself a daydream of fly fishing for the rising trout and the thrill of their explosive strike, and after a good fight, a look at their bright colors before carefully releasing them. But, that was for another day.

"Okay," Sam agreed reluctantly, "let's go." Sam sat up and began to gather up their stuff. He put everything in the backpack, clipped the cover of the backpack shut, and stood up.

"Where to now?" Sam asked rhetorically. He picked up the pie in the eco-friendly grocery sack and looked toward the woods. "Next job is: find a place to leave this." Sam waved the pie in the air. Then he added, "First, let's find our trail outta here."

Jack waited for Sam to lead the way. Sam took a few tentative steps toward the woods and suddenly came to grips with the fact that he had not made very careful observation of the way in, much less the way out of the grassy peninsula. Though he realized he was a little vague on the way they got to their location he didn't dare let on to Jack that he was more than a little unsure of his way back to the trail.

Sam bent down under the vine maple and elderberry, and then headed into the brush with Jack following along. He showed Jack how to avoid entanglement by staying low as he moved through the thick brush that surrounded the opening to the lake. Every so often, he paused to reconnoiter his route back to the hillside trail, and led Jack on a veer to the right, moving gradually uphill as they went. He expected to intersect the trail at a right angle in a few minutes of travel time, but ten minutes later, they were still looking for the trail. They were now out of the thick brush and in the shade of the forest, standing at the base of an uphill incline that continued for a very long ways.

Sam stopped. "Hmm, I expected to be at the trail by now. It wasn't this far from the lake, was it?"

"I don't know, Dad. I was just following you."

"I know. I was really just kind of thinking out loud. But be sure and say something if you see anyplace that looks familiar. Let's go up this hill a little more and try to get a view of the situation."

They trudged up an increasingly steep, forested slope. Sam turned around a couple of times to see if he could get a view of the lake. No luck. He looked ahead up the slope and saw a flat spot he had not previously seen.

"Let's get up on that bench just ahead. I know we're too high to find the trail. It's gotta be below us. But let's see what things look like from up there." The pair continued their ascent until they reached a flat, circular area in the middle of the forested slope. Sam reached the flat bench on the tree-covered hillside, and then waited for Jack to catch up. While Jack was still scrambling up the slope, Sam paused and looked out over the forest below. He planned to look out over the forest for signs of the trail but the view surprised him. There was an opening in the forest canopy and the lake shone a brilliant blue in the distance. The view was as unexpected as it was spectacular. Then Sam turned around to inspect the hillside terrace on which he was standing. Again, there were some unexpected qualities about it. By now, Jack had reached the terrace, panting.

Knowing that they were lost, Sam also thought it best to downplay the situation by appreciating their surroundings. "Wow! This is neat up here. Check out this view of the lake! This flat place probably formed when a part of the hillside slid a long time ago. It usually happens where ground water comes out of the hill, loosening a chunk of earth and causing it to slide."

"Dad, are we lost?" Jack interrupted.

"I wouldn't say we're lost. We're just a little disoriented. We'll figure it out, but first I want to check out this little hillside bench up here. This is cool."

The teacher in Sam had a tendency to take over, especially at anxious moments like this when Sam was trying to cover for the fact that he *was* essentially lost. He turned around.

"Sure enough, there's the spring back there by those cedar trees. The slightly hilly surface tells you a landslide caused this scenic little bench. The trees look like they're about a hundred years old so that tells you how long ago the hillside slid and created this little bench here. Look at this view. This is great. Now we just gotta figure out where our trail went."

"Do you think that water is okay to drink, Dad? My water bottle is empty."

"I dunno. Let's go see." They walked back to the spring that was trickling out of the steep hillside.

"Wow, look at this tree, Dad!" Being a keen observer, Jack often noticed things that Sam overlooked. Such was the case with the mysterious pattern in the bark of the cedar trees by the hillside spring. "The bark is all peeled up the tree in strips."

Sam walked up to the cedar tree and stood in silent amazement. He lifted some of the ribbons of bark that encircled the tree then let them drape down against the trunk of the tree. The strips of bark had been peeled from the tree but they remained attached some ten feet up. It was as though the tree wore a hula skirt made of ribbons of its own bark.

"That's the darnedest thing I've ever seen. Somebody or something did that to the tree, but I have absolutely no idea how...or why."

They stood and looked at the tree for a while. Sam instinctively looked down to see if footprints or other disturbances in the ground could be used to suggest a culprit for this strange project. It was then that he noticed that the ground had the same packed down aspect to it as the trail that they followed around the lake. He began to study the ground more closely, and he noticed for the first time that most of the flat bench was compacted earth without much groundcover on it. Sword fern and low-growing salal covered the edges, though the center of the bench was barren and well compacted.

In the very center was a curious structure that Sam had initially overlooked. At first he thought it was a pile of earth. But on closer inspection, he saw that it was a large matt of moss.

"*Strange indeed,*" Sam thought. It occurred to him that moss generally grows on rock. He bent down, grasped a thick wad of moss and lifted. Sure enough, a bed of jagged, interlocking stones lay beneath the moss carpet. The rock pile had a rectangular base and sloped upward in the center, forming a mound that rose about three feet higher than the surrounding earth. Sam peeled back more of the moss and examined what appeared to be a rock cairn. He pulled at one of the stones. It wouldn't budge. It was interlocked with the other stones around it so tightly that raising one stone meant raising several at once. He replaced the moss and stepped back to examine the situation.

Here was a surprisingly intricate cairn placed in a remote, concealed location deep in the wood on a scenic bench high above Squaw Meadow. Sam puzzled over what this structure could be. It was so flat, elegant, yet inconspicuous that, more than anything, it had the look of a grave. The only question was, whose grave? Maybe it was a pioneer grave. Maybe it was an Indian grave, maybe even an Indian of some importance. The grave could be hundreds of years old, Sam thought, but the cedar tree with the peeled bark encircling the trunk wasn't done a hundred years ago. More like a hundred *days* ago. And yet it was all so remote and well concealed. Who would spend time hauling stones up or down the hill to make this monument, which clearly had an unnatural shape and appearance?

"What is this thing, Dad?"

"This whole place is starting to give me the creeps. I would swear we're looking at some kind of grave or monument. But I can't figure out why it would be out here in the middle of nowhere. It sure is a killer spot though. This whole place is amazing. I'm not sure what is going on here, but I think we just found a great place to leave our pie. If anybody or anything lives out in these woods that we don't know about, I just bet you that they know about this place." Sam had another thought, and smiled. He looked slowly around one more time. "It's perfect. They could be watching us right now. We'll leave the pie right here...and we're not going to tell anybody where this spot is. At least not right away, okay?"

"No problem, Dad. I couldn't find my way back here anyway. We're lost. Remember?"

Sam flushed with embarrassment. "Not lost, just disoriented," he corrected.

"Fine. So could we get un-disoriented, now?"

"Sure thing. Just give me a minute to place our little gift."

He took the pie out of the sack and placed it atop one end of the massive cairn. He paused to look it over for just a minute, then, rolled up the bag and stuffed it into his backpack. "This is perfect. This is so cool."

"Great," Jack insisted impatiently. "Now, let's find our way outta here."

"Okay." Sam paused again and looked out toward the lake, which was visible at the bottom of the hill, and a little bit to the right. That was the first time he noticed that the lake was not straight down the hill.

"I think we veered too far left as we avoided the devil's club by the peninsula. There's only one way to find out. When you're lost, the best thing you can do is to retrace your steps back to the last familiar location. First, let's see if we can find our way back to the peninsula. Looking at the lake down there, I can kind of see where it should be. Follow me." Sam headed downhill, but the he stopped abruptly and turned back toward Jack. "And whatever we do, let's stay together."

"You got it, Dad"

They headed down the hill, entering taller brush that soon obscured their view of the lake. Sam relocated the dense thicket of devil's club, worked his way around it, and then cut back to his right, leading Jack the entire way. In ten minutes of easy going, they were within sight of the peninsula in the familiar clearing just ahead. "This is it. C'mon. Now, I see what we did. We went too far north on our way out, in the direction of Squaw Butte. The trail we were following must end or veer away from the lake. I bet it heads up to the ridge top or even toward the bench we were just on. What do ya wanna bet? Anyway, we're back at the peninsula. Ready to try this again?"

They walked out onto the peninsula and into the midday sun once again. Jack couldn't resist looking down at the newts in the water one more time. Then he heard a rustling in the grass just a few feet from where he stood. Jack glanced at the spot. His eyes widened.

"Whoa. Look, a snake!"

He instinctively pounced on the snake with both hands open, palms flat toward the ground. The grass that the snake was moving through was pressed flat against the ground by his palms. The rustling of grass stopped. "I have him Dad. Help me. I can't see him, but I know he's trapped in the grass."

Sam jumped to Jack's side and got on his knees, pressing his own flat palms onto the grass on either side of Jack's hands.

"Good thing there's no poisonous snakes in western Oregon, Jack. Otherwise, this kind of move would be downright dangerous."

"Not 'poisonous', Dad. It's 'venomous'. And there *are* venomous snakes in the Cascades, just not around here. There's only timber rattlers, and they're on the east side of the Cascades. We're on the west side."

"Actually, we're pretty much at the summit of the Cascades, up here, so we could be within range of some east side species. But whatever we've got under here sounded small. Just remember, if I get bitten by a rattlesnake and die, I'll never speak to you again."

Jack reassured his father, "I'm sure it's just a garter snake."

Sam lifted a hand and parted some of the grass. "Okay, lift up just one hand." Jack lifted his hand and waited. An instant later a serpentine form weaved between stalks of grass. They both thrust their hands down at the same instant.

"There's his tail!" Jack shouted. Grab it!"

Sam took the tail between his thumb and forefinger. He held it tight. Slowly, he pulled backward on the tail. Pulling the tail gently upwards, the snake came free. He held it up in the air. The snake squirmed in the air as Sam held it up for Jack to see. Both Sam and Jack's eyes widened as they got their first good look at their catch. "Wow! This ain't no garter snake. What the heck is this thing?"

"I haven't a clue!" Jack replied.

"Whaddya mean? You're the snake expert. You're the one with posters all over his bedroom walls. You're Mister No-Poisonous-Slash-Venomous-Snake-This-Side-Of-The-Mountains Expert! You're supposed to know this stuff," Sam insisted.

"I have no idea what the heck this thing is! It doesn't look like anything I've seen before. It's bright green and blue. Look! It looks like it's changing colors!"

At a level beyond his years, Jack reflected for a moment, "That sure isn't some California red-sided garter snake, and that's most of what's around here. There's also bull snakes around here, but it's not that, either. It might be some kind of rubber boa. Those are supposed to be around here, but I don't think they look like that."

"Now, it's so green it's kind of iridescent. It's got a tiny head so I don't think it's poisonous...I mean venomous. You sure you have no idea what it is?" Sam asked.

"I really don't know," insisted Jack.

"Wow! In that case I think we have to take this back with us so we can figure out what it is. This is one cool snake. How can we get this back home?

"Dad, we can't take this home with us. It lives here," Jack protested.

"Normally, I'd agree with you, son, but this is different. This is a real find. Heck, I'll make a deal with you. We'll bring it back and release it after we find out what it is, but we absolutely have to take this puppy home. Otherwise, we'll never figure out what it is. It certainly isn't the usual Willamette Valley garter snake. I wonder how we can transport this thing." Sam thought for a minute. "I know, we can empty out the first aid kit and use the box. I'll poke a few holes in the lid so it can breathe."

"Dad, I really don't think we should take this with us..."

"Don't worry, Jack, we'll bring it back. I promise. But not until we find out what it is."

Sam emptied the pack and took out the first aid kit. He emptied its contents back into the grocery store sack that he used to carry the pie. He poked a few holes in the lid with his Swiss Army knife while Jack held onto the snake and looked it over. It slithered between Jack's fingers as he studied it. Soon the box was ready and Jack reluctantly dropped the snake inside. "Don't worry, snake, you'll be out of there soon," Jack said, as Sam snapped the lid shut.

Chapter 14

J ACK WAS SITTING on the sofa in the living room. Cartoons played on the television but the snake in his hands had Jack's undivided attention. Next to him on the sofa was a 'creature carrier,' a clear plastic, shoebox-sized container with a tightly fitting blue plastic lid and a carrying handle. A layer of grass and leaves covered the bottom of the box. Jack's mother, Grace, was across the room in the kitchen area slicing tomatoes. She looked up to see Jack handling the creature he'd brought home from Squaw Meadow a few hours ago. A look of concern registered on her face.

"Are you sure you should be handling that snake? You don't even know what it is. How do you know it isn't poisonous?"

"You mean 'venomous' Mom. They're called 'venomous' snakes, not 'poisonous,'" Jack corrected.

"Fine. Then, how do you know the snake isn't *venomous*?" she said in a slightly irritated tone.

"Because venomous snakes have a head that's wider than their body. That's where the venom glands are. Plus, venomous snakes almost always have eyes with slits for pupils. This guy's eyes are round. Look how small his head is. He couldn't be venomous. Besides, there are no venomous snakes on our side of the mountains. The closest venomous snake is the timber rattler. They're on the other side of the mountains."

"Okay, Mr. Smarty-pants, then what kind of snake is it?"

"I don't know. It's not in my snake book, but Dad says this book doesn't have all the kinds of snakes that live around here. I need to get a better book. Dad said he'd take me to the library tomorrow."

The golden retriever suddenly sat up and faced the door. Jack sat up and stretched his neck to see out the window in the front door. "Someone just drove in the driveway."

Feet sounded on the wooden steps that led to the front porch of the house, as Sam appeared in the room.

"Someone's here, Dad," Jack said as he turned toward the window.

"I know. It's Nick Rollo, the bigfoot man. I called him."

"Is he staying for dinner?" Grace inquired.

"I don't think so."

Sam headed out the door and down the three steps that led to the parking area in front of the house. "Hi, Nick! Thanks for coming by. I know you're in a hurry. I just wanted to get your opinion of something I found today. I was up around Squaw Meadow today with my son. We were having a look around, doing a little hiking, getting lost, and... trying a baiting experiment."

"Baiting for what?"

"Care to guess?"

"I know it's not bigfoot, because you don't believe in bigfoot," Nick said with a sarcastic smile.

"I guess I've become more open to the possibility for two reasons. First, I met an Indian who had a lot to say on the subject, and then we've had a few things happen around here lately that have me wondering."

"Like what?" Nick asked.

"Nothing very definite, but just some weird activity in the woods. My son gets the feeling he's being watched sometimes when he's back there hitting baseballs," Sam gestured toward the back of his property and the baseball diamond. He decided to leave out all the details of the baseballs that came flying back out of the woods. The whole thing seemed a bit too uncertain for him to label as mysterious. But he did see a benefit in bringing up his conversations with Iris's Uncle Henry.

"Like I said, I met this guy named Henry Threelynx who grew up on the Warm Springs Reservation. He's the uncle of a kid in my class. He was actually pleased that we did the sasquatch lesson, unlike my former neighbor Bart Foster, whose kid is also in my class. Bart complained about it to the school principal."

"That doesn't surprise me one bit," Nick sighed, shaking his head. "I know the guy. My daughter played with their kid when they were little. As they got older, they ran in separate circles for reasons that seemed to have everything to do with the Foster's income and social groups. My household is too 'blue collar.' About the same time, Bart decided I was a weirdo because he learned through his kid about my interest in 'Bigfoot'. In fact, I have an interesting story about that, but before I get into that, tell me about this guy from Warm Springs."

"Yeah, well, he stopped by my classroom one morning and said he thought it was neat that his niece got a chance to say what she knew about the subject. He never thought that would happen in a paleface place like Redland Middle School, and he actually thanked me. Then, he laid out what he described as the Native American 'take' on the situation. He told me that the Yakama Indians think of them as a separate tribe that they call "Ste-ye-ha-mah," which translates into "Stick Indians." Other tribes, like the Hoopa Indians in northern California, see them as spirit beings, which they call "Oh-mah," which translates into 'boss of the woods". The Chinook tribes, which lived around here, called them 'Skookums.' Every tribe has a name for them. There's lots of names, but no agreement on how they're spelled, since the Indian dialects were often spoken but seldom written.

"I didn't mention you by name but I said I knew someone who was putting out cameras and actively searching for tracks. Henry said they don't like being tracked and the cameras would never work, anyway. He advised me to just get friendly with them by leaving them what he called "offerings" or "gifts." He hated the word "bait." He felt that would insult them. Anyway, he says that if I wanted to get on their good side, I should skip the cameras and put out cooked food. He said they like cooked chicken, and apple pie and things like that."

"So he's saying you should provide catered meals?" Nick laughed. "Great. You can call yourself 'bigfoot Meals-on-Wheels.'

"Precisely," Sam agreed with a smile. "Which I thought was cute, though I didn't feel too inclined to actually do it until I learned that there are serious plans being floated to develop part, if not all, of the area. around Squaw Meadow. And, by the way, I bet you can't guess what local business-man is behind those plans."

"Let me guess. The same guy who complained to your principal about a bigfoot lesson in science class?"

It was now almost completely dark. A gibbous moon was high in the clear night sky as the two men stood talk-ing in the cool air. Sam leaned against Nick's dark blue pick-up truck that was raised with heavy springs and big tires. As they chatted, Sam looked inside the matching blue canopy.

Nick noticed. "Yup, I keep a lot of stuff in there ready-to-go, just in case the telephone call is good enough. I do get a lot of cranks, fools, and drunks calling me, though. I hardly ever answer the telephone anymore after 7:30."

Nodding sympathetically, Sam continued. "Anyway, back to our good buddy Bart Foster. Living on the road up to Squaw Meadow as I do, you can imagine how I feel about plans to put a big resort up there. Yet, as a class-room teacher who's living a hand-to-mouth existence, I'm also feeling rather powerless to do anything about it. Then, it dawned on me that if there really were such things as sasquatches, and if they did indeed live up there around Squaw Meadow, then we would be looking at the ultimate in endangered species. That would mean the Endangered Species Act could be invoked to stop the development and protect their critical habitat, namely Squaw Meadow."

"I see. I will say, as sasquatch habitat goes, the Squaw Meadow area would be as good a place as any. Lots of sight-ings happen up there. All we gotta do is *prove* that there are sasquatches living around there. That should be easy, eh Sam? We'll just cruise up there with a giant net and hide behind a tree. We nab the first one that comes along, tie it up and haul it back to town. If we get an early start, we can be home by lunchtime." Nick was pleased with his wry sense of humor. The moon illuminated his wide smile.

Sam responded with a little sarcasm of his own. "I was thinking of just digging a big hole and covering it with sticks. That way we wouldn't have to waste an entire morning hiding behind trees." They both laughed.

"I know it's too funny to resist but I must confess that, ever since I heard about the plans to develop the meadow, I've been trying to come up with an idea, any idea, on how to stop it. I know the idea of a sasquatch sanctuary is pretty far-fetched, but I'm fresh out of other ideas.

"I've been trying to prove the existence of these creatures for years. And, I'm not the only one. There are more people than you realize who are working the same plan. Let's see, I know of guys in Florida, Texas, Ohio, and Washington who are hunting these things very seriously. They all think they're going to be the one who gets it done first. Then, there's another hundred guys in northern California, alone.

"Don't get me wrong. Saying 'I want to see someone succeed' is putting it mildly. But when one considers how *many* people are working this program, and how *little* success they've had...well...if we're going to accomplish the impossible before the first bulldozer rolls up to Squaw Meadow, we'd better get going ... or come up with a better idea."

"I guess I've already started. After talking to Henry, I went up there yesterday with my son and left a 'gift.'

"What did you put out?"

"You'll probably laugh, but on Henry's advice, I left an apple pie."

"Oh, don't worry, I'm not laughing," Nick said. "Even though I favor the view that bigfoot is a species of North American great ape, I do know that there are other points of view. And I know that Indian mythology sees them as either a lost tribe or a group of spirit beings. Now, I have a reason for disagreeing with them, and that's built around the fact that gorillas were not known to science until the early 1900's.

"American Indians and settlers in this area didn't know there was such a thing as great apes until much later than that. Nor did anyone else, so if they saw such a creature around here, they had absolutely no idea what it was. The word 'ape' just didn't exist. My point is that the word ape doesn't appear in place names around here, but that may not mean they weren't seeing apes. They may have been seeing them though they had no idea what they were. The fact that they walked on two feet, at least most of the time, suggested to them that the creatures were human, since there was no other example of human-sized primates any-where in the world.

"But, I will admit that even though *I* see the bigfoot phenomenon as pointing to a population of apes, I haven't been able to prove that fact and no one else has either. And, I might add, it isn't because we aren't trying. But, with noth-ing major to show for all my work, I certainly know better than to ridicule someone else's approach."

"My point is that I'm totally okay with your need to test other points of view. I won't laugh. Hell, I hope you succeed. I will offer that, whatever you decide to do, I think you have to do it a lot. These things, whatever they are, seem to be very rare and they also seem to range quite widely. You'll probably need a lot of bait or gifts or offerings, or whatever you want to call them, before you get any results, and pies are just too expensive to leave around the woods whole-sale."

"I can see it now, a white 4-wheel drive delivery van with a bigfoot logo painted on the side with the words, "Sam's Sasquatch Good Eats!"

Sam laughed, "Anyway, that brings me to the reason why I asked you to come. You see, it's not what I left in the woods, but where I left it. Jack and I were wandering around in the timber up there...well, we were lost actually... and we found something."

"Tracks?" Nick interrupted eagerly.

"No. Better than that. We found what looks like some kind of hangout. And in that hangout, or whatever you want to call it, we stumbled upon what looks for all the world to be a grave."

"You found a grave at Squaw Meadow?" Nick repeated loudly.

"Shhh. Not so loud," Sam hissed. "I don't want my family to hear."

"Okay, sorry. I'll keep it down. You definitely have my attention. Let's hear it."

Just then Grace opened the log house door and called, "Supper's ready. Nick, would you like to stay and eat?" Nick shook his head to Sam.

Sam called back, "Go ahead and start. We'll still be a few minutes."

"Okay, just checking."

The two men could not see the slight look of disap-proval on Grace's face as she quietly closed the door. "This foolishness has gone on long enough," she thought to her-self as she called Jack and Elizabeth to dinner.

Sam took a deep breath and began again. "It was way up on the side of a hill above the upper lake, you know, the big lake to the north of Road 4610.

"You sure it's a grave? Was it marked?"

"No. It wasn't marked. It looked pretty old. I'm not totally sure what it was, but it did have the look of a grave. It's a very carefully laid pile of interlocking rocks about twelve feet long by about five feet wide."

"It seems that, if it is indeed a grave, there are a few possibilities. It could be someone's deceased pet."

"It's too big."

"Okay, it could be a pioneer grave, in which case Bart Foster would probably know about it since his family homesteaded up there until the late thirties."

"I'd think it would be marked."

"I tend to agree. It could be an Indian grave, although I thought Indians utilized burial grounds, in which case there should be more than one grave. If it's a lone grave, it could be some drug dealer who double-crossed his business partners and met an untimely end..."

"With all the meth traffic that goes on around Redland these days, I guess it wouldn't surprise me to find the body of some 'crack head' who got whacked by his buddies, but I would expect to find a guy like that face down in the ditch next to the road...or maybe in a shallow grave ten feet from the road. This thing I found is too elaborate. It's some kind of monument.

"Whatever it is, it's intricately built. Plus, it is way back in the woods, way up on this hillside, with a fantastic view to boot. There's a little spring nearby. Oh, and I forgot to tell you about a cedar tree ten yards away from the rocks that has carefully peeled strips of bark that go around the entire tree. The tree looks like it's wearing a hula skirt.

"A spring, rock, view, and one of the longest lasting trees in the world. I think, that maybe, it is a primitive shrine."

"Okay, so if you had to say, what would you say this thing is that you found?"

"I really don't know," Sam admitted, "but, I guess I want to rule out the possibility that it's a sasquatch grave. That's why I'm trying to get your opinion on this, as opposed to some Forest Service archeologist."

"That's ridiculous,"

"What's ridiculous?"

"Apes don't dig graves."

"Fine. What makes you so sure they're apes?"

"What else could they be? Spirits don't dig graves either,"

"Let's forget the lost tribe and spirit beings, for now. How about Neanderthals? Or *Homo erectus*, also known as Java Man. Personally, I think the idea that all of our human ancestors are extinct will someday be disproven. You're the one who told me about the Russian researchers who insist Neanderthals still exist in the Caucasus Mountains. Perhaps this whole bigfoot thing points to remnant populations of Neanderthals in North America."

"Well, my working hypothesis is they're apes, specifically *Gigantopithecus blackii*. All the experts on this subject that I respect are in agreement. That includes the late Dr. Krantz at Washington State, and Dr. Meldrum at Idaho State. All the serious scholars on the subject are of the same view."

"Well, you may be the bigfoot expert, but I am an expert on something too, and that's science. And this I know: If you're going be scientific, you have to look past your biases. You have to be willing to not just consider, but to investigate *all* of the possibilities, not just the possibilities that you like, or that put you with the "in" crowd. Maybe your pals, the experts, are right. But, maybe they're not. And even though they, and you, may be seen as 'rebels' for just suggesting that things like 'bigfoot' really exists, you could still be barking up the wrong tree.

"As you said, the 'ape' paradigm hasn't been shown to be true. So, until you succeed in proving its existence, you would be wise to at least remind yourself of the competing possibilities, and maybe even *investigate* them. I mean, just in case one of them ends up being *right*."

Nick stood silently staring at Sam and thinking of what to say next, for he was momentarily speechless. To himself, he thought, "How does this man know what he knows?" Then he found the words to say the only thing he could think to say.

"Okay, you win. But there's only one way to find out who is right. We're going to have to have a look at that grave, and by that I mean *in* the grave. Are you okay with that?"

"I guess so. I don't like the thought of opening a grave, but I guess it's 'yes' for now."

"Great. I don't suppose you can get free tomorrow. It's supposed to be a nice day."

"I can try. Weekends are pretty busy with baseball so if we're going to get up there any time soon, I guess I'll have to take a day off of work. I think I can do it. Let me work on it. Unless I call you tonight, let's just plan to meet here at, say, 9 a.m. tomorrow.

"Great," Nick said, looking at his watch.

"Oh, by the way, speaking of Bart Foster, his name came up at my house the other day. My daughter was looking for something on my shelf of bigfoot books, which is pretty rare for her. I suggested *Legend Meets Science* because it's the most scientific book on the subject. Then, she said she was actually looking for a certain book called *The Locals*. I asked her why. She said she learned on the internet that it had weird stories about folks who actually interact with sasquatches. That's what this friend of hers wanted to know about: whether there are people who see sasquatches on a regular basis. In the bigfoot biz, we call it 'habituation.'

"Here's the good part. I asked who this 'friend' was, and she said 'Ellie Foster!' I couldn't believe it. I thought she and my daughter were enemies. Ellie's queen of the popular jock girls and my daughter is the alternative, black outfits, artist-type. Of course, the fact that Ellie, the popular girl, was actually talking to her flattered Jenna, so she really wanted to find this book for her. I went along with it, especially since I never cared for that particular book, anyway. It's a little too far out for me. So, I said she could borrow it, but only for a couple weeks, but I wanted it back before school let out for the summer. I'm not really sure what it was all about, but when Bart Foster's name came up a few minutes ago, a light bulb went on in my head, and I thought you might be interested."

"Yikes! That *is* interesting! Bart's daughter Ellie wants to borrow a bigfoot book? You gotta wonder what's up with that. Especially since her parents were the ones who complained to the principal about the lesson we did. They thought the whole subject was inappropriate for the oh-so-fragile eighth grade minds, and now Ellie, of all people, is shopping for a little supplemental reading on the subject. I have a feeling I haven't heard the last of that one."

"That's why I'm not a teacher! No matter what you do or say, someone is always going to complain. I don't know how you put up with it." Nick looked at his wristwatch. "Now I really have to go. See you tomorrow. Nine o'clock."

"See you then," Sam said, as Nick moved for his car door. Though he didn't say anything more, he wondered, "What have I gotten myself into?" He spent much of the evening wondering whether he was poised on the brink of discovery or disaster. He recollected that he had agreed with Jack that they would keep the location of the monument a secret. Now, by challenging Nick's thinking as biased and unscientific, he had just agreed to help desecrate a grave.

Another thought fueled Sam's eagerness to revisit the site of the suspected grave: This might just be the answer to his prayers; an opportunity to stop the development of Squaw Meadow once and for all. It was beyond ironic that he was now a willing participant in a search for bigfoot evidence; something that he viewed as delusional only a few days ago. Although he wasn't eager to dig up a grave, Sam couldn't resist daydreaming about what might happen if he and Nick unearthed a set of huge hominid bones beneath the pile of carefully laid stones.

It would be a scientific blockbuster for the ages. Irrefutable evidence of living human relatives would be presented to the worldwide scientific community. Not only would world attention be brought upon Squaw Meadow and the population of hidden hominids that lived there, but also Sam's role in the find. He would no longer be a lowly science teacher toiling in obscurity. He would have a permanent place in scientific history. At certain moments, his head was positively swimming with delusions of grandeur that might begin to take shape as soon as tomorrow.

In nanoseconds, he was consumed with anxiety about negative consequences if it turned out they unearthed the grave of a Native American chieftain. He would be seen as a grave robber, almost the worst of criminals. Hated, despised, fired, unable to fend for his family or his homestead. Was the risk worth it, for something entirely new to science? He could go to jail. No, prison!

Sam knew that the Antiquities Act made it a federal offense and a felony to desecrate an Indian burial on government land. He was not sure, but he suspected the grave may not be on federal land, but even so, he would be in a great deal of trouble if things went in the wrong direction. It would be important to figure out who owned the land before any find was disclosed. To his knowledge, there had been no mention of Indian burial sites in that area, but if the remains looked human, he might be able to argue that it was an honest mistake.

Sam immediately decided if he and Nick unearthed anything, anything at all that suggested they were digging in an Indian or a pioneer burial site, they would restore the grave right then and there. It dawned on him that he and Nick would have to agree to that before they began any digging. Nick seemed like a straight shooter who wouldn't have any problem with establishing a few ground rules before they started.

It was a long night for Sam. He couldn't stop his mind from working through the multitude of possibilities. Like counting sheep, he kept thinking of what might or might not happen next. He finally fell asleep.

At 9 a.m., Sam was packing a lunch into his daypack and filling his water bottles when Nick rolled up the driveway. On the ground by the parking area lay a pick, a shovel, and a digging bar. Nick had a shovel and a fire-fighting tool called a 'Pulaski' in the truck. Having seen the site, Sam knew it would be more a matter of moving stones than digging dirt. A pick and a pry bar were going to be the useful tools.

"Since you have a shovel, I'm leaving mine here. Did you bring a pair of work gloves?" Sam asked. "We're going to have to move a lot of stone."

"Yeah, I brought gloves. Anything else?"

"No, we're just going to have to get up there and see how we do. We may not get the whole job done in one day. I just don't know. But let's just see what we need once we get started. I really don't think we're going to be doing any real digging. I think it's going to be a lot of moving rocks. It's one big pile of rocks from what I could tell."

"Okay then, I guess we're off." Nick got in the driver's seat. They headed out Sam's driveway and turned to the left, uphill toward Squaw Meadow. They rode in silence for the first ten minutes, both staring straight ahead and not sure what to say. Sam wondered again whether they were scientific pioneers or grave robbers. He didn't really want to bring up that whole concern by way of conversation but he felt that it was high time to develop their plan of attack.

"What are we going to do if we find something?" Sam asked.

"Good question. Say we find a bone or set of bones. I guess we would take them to the pre-eminent expert on all things bigfoot: Dr. Meldrum at Idaho State University in Pocatello. We would leave it up to him to either confirm or reject the fact that they are genuine bigfoot bones. If Dr. Meldrum didn't endorse the find, then I wouldn't be in favor of trying to take it any further than that."

"Okay, lemme ask you this first. What if they turned out to be bones from some sort of Indian grave, either a chief or something else."

"Then I'd say we would want to get them right back into the ground and restore the site to its original condition. Digging up Indian graves is a federal offense, you know."

"Great. So we agree on that?"

"Yes, we do. The thought kept me awake half the night last night." Silently, Sam agreed. He was not alone.

"Which also suggests," Nick continued, "that if we do find anything in this hypothetical grave, we just might want to collect one and only one bone, and leave everything else right where we find it. If there's any doubt about what it is, we get our assessment done as quickly as possible, ready to plant that bone right back in the ground if necessary. Then we're gonna cover our track on the way outta there, never to return. Does that sound about right to you?" Nick asked.

"Definitely. Although, I think that it's gonna be tricky to restore that grave to its original condition. You'll understand better when you see this thing. Meanwhile, let's explore the other possibility. I've been trying not to get my hopes up here, but let's just say, for the sake of preparation, that we unearth some kind of skull or leg bone that is huge. I assume we stay completely mum about the whole matter and we drive the dang thing to Idaho for the official determination. I assume that if it is determined to be a bigfoot bone, we can't be accused of desecrating Native American graves."

"That's just one of the million dollar questions. Not to bring up a sore subject, but if my view of the sasquatch phenomenon is correct and we find a bone from a *Pongidae* or ape lineage, then we have quite plainly done nothing more than unearthed some animal bones. There ain't no law against that. On the other hand, if your New Age take on bigfoot holds true and it turns out to be *Homonidae*, that is, human lineage, then it could go either way. It could be seen as caveman, Native American, or something entirely new and different than anything ever found before, in which case you're famous because you found the grave, but you're also to blame, because YOU found the grave. I'm just the adviser here. Either way, it's your ass that's on the line. Can you live with that?" Nick asked.

"I guess we'll cross that bridge when we come to it. But the reason I'm even doing this is not for fame and fortune. I'm trying to put a stop on a plan to develop most of that meadow into a destination resort. And that leads me to the whole Endangered Species Act. If it were possible to prove that these things live up here around Squaw Meadow, then it should be a cinch to get the place set aside as habitat."

"If that's what you want, then you'd better hope they're animals, not humans."

"Why's that?"

"Because endangered species protection applies only to animals, not to people. Humans aren't endangered. Last time I checked, there's more than enough people to go around."

"Hmm. Good point, although it may be more complicated than that. What if they turn out to be primitive humans. If they were found to be another species of the genus Hominidae, but not *Homo sapiens,* then they would certainly qualify for protection as a separate species. In fact, it would be a species like nothing ever before: a species that was somehow related to us. The interest would be huge... off the charts...absolutely unprecedented. It would be the anthropology blockbuster of all time. What would happen to everything else we thought to be true about humans if it were suddenly shown that *Homo neandertalensis*, say, or *Homo erectus,* 'Java man,' still walk the earth? We already know that many humans carry Neanderthal DNA. Two different genetic studies have agreed on that finding. But what if we also found that we actually have human relatives living right here on this continent with us. They might even be so genetically similar that they could interbreed with *Homo sapiens*. That would be a far bigger deal than the discovery of a species of ape in North America, even though that alone would be absolutely huge."

"The possibilities are so huge that one could never fully predict what might come of it," Nick said. "Either way, the place where it happened would be scientifically locked up for a long, long time. If Squaw Mountain were that place, then Squaw Meadow would become a household name. The scientific interest in the place might be so great that a golf course or a ski resort might be preferable. If it were shown that the creatures were of a human lineage, we would be obliged to provide them with a reservation at the very least. All of a sudden, even your homestead might be condemned by the government and swallowed up by the reservation. This whole thing could backfire on you and you could lose your place to the Stick Indians. Think about that!"

"Well, I guess we just have to take that chance. We might be running away with delusions of grandeur just a bit. We haven't even found anything yet. There certainly are some mind-boggling possibilities here, though. I guess we just have to keep our fingers crossed that we find something first. Then we'll have to decide what we want to do with it."

"If we find anything promising, we'll have to turn it over to somebody to make the official determination. And since there aren't many scientists who will even entertain bigfoot as one of the possibilities, I'd say we'd pretty much have to go through this Meldrum dude in Idaho. He's definitely our best bet. In fact, I think he's our only bet," Nick said.

"We'll be finding out soon enough. We're almost there. We park at the bottom of this hill."

A few moments later, the truck rolled to a stop. The pair stepped out without speaking a word as they shouldered their daypacks and grabbed their tools. Nick carried a shovel and digging bar. Sam carried a pick-mattock. Nick locked the truck as Sam walked up the road toward the opening in the brush that led to the trail. Nick caught up and Sam gestured silently toward an opening in the brush.

The pair ducked as they stepped into the thicket. Neither man spoke. There just wasn't anything else to say. Both of them felt their heart beats quicken with the anticipation of some remarkable events that might be about to unfold. There was an unspoken, but palpable, excitement that both men felt. They tried to contain it in order to maintain their focus. They didn't want to get their hopes too high.

Inwardly, Nick also felt a certain doubt about the whole matter, simply because he had been working the bigfoot-evidence-collection plan for not just years but decades. Nothing major had ever materialized from his countless other attempts. He told himself that the pattern was letdown after letdown. No point in getting too excited about this outing.

Sam found himself squelching his pangs of excitement with a different rationale. He knew that there was something mysterious about the cairn he found yesterday with his son, but he was steeped in years of skepticism as a science teacher. It just didn't seem possible that anyone could prove at this late date that apes, sasquatches, or Neanderthals actually existed. The very idea that he, no less, could somehow be the driving force behind such a monumental discovery seemed too incredible to even consider.

"Don't get too excited," both men simultaneously thought to themselves.

The first order of business was just finding the spot. They silently plodded along the vague trail that Sam and his son had traveled the day before. A few minutes into the woods, Sam paused and stepped off the trail. Nick came up alongside Sam, expecting him to say something.

"The first thing that had me wondering about this trail was the fact that there aren't any hoof or paw prints. It seems like a pretty well used trail, but there isn't any clear sign of what kind of critters are using it. I would expect to see lots of elk and deer tracks on a trail this wide, but there aren't any tracks from either one. I can't figure out who would be using this trail to make it this well-worn."

Nick said flatly, "Pot farmers."

Sam looked at Nick and smiled. "I suppose it's possible, but I'm not seeing people prints here either. Plus, we're up here at 4,500 feet elevation. I wouldn't think there would be much of a growing season at this elevation."

"Don't bet," Nick shrugged. "Anyway, lead on."

The two resumed their silent trek, finally reaching the patch of thorny devil's club. Sam peered through the woods to his right and could see the point of land where they had lunch the previous day. Then he carefully studied the ground to see why he had lost track of the trail the day before. It was then that he noticed that the trail actually took a turn up the hill, to the left. He had been so intent on finding his way to the lake's edge yesterday that he'd failed to notice that the trail he was following veered off in the opposite direction. He studied the trail some more. He saw that once it headed up the hill, it faded out altogether, as though the creatures using the trail took slightly different paths each time they used it.

"See how the trail kind of heads up hill right here then fades out? This is where we got messed up yesterday. It kinda seems like they're taking different courses up the hill so their path isn't so obvious."

"Bear are smart enough to do that. They're pretty good at hiding the approach to their den. Still, I don't see any sign of bear. Bear claws don't retract, so you'd see marks from their claws if bear were using this. So, where to, Magoo?"

"The spot is up there and around the corner of the hill, just out of sight."

Sam began to climb toward the spot, with Nick following behind. After ten minutes of steady climbing and perspiring, they took the last steps onto the elliptical flat bench and dropped their tools. Nick turned a full circle to take in the scene. They stood and stared, perched high on the side of the hill, with a view of the distant lake seen through an opening in the trees.

"This is the spot...and there's the cairn... or grave...or whatever it is." He gestured toward the rectangular rock pile that was situated in the very center of the bench. "Notice too, that you've got a spring over there against the hillside... and there's a cedar tree over there with bark stripped and left hanging in ribbons.... What kind of critter would do that?" Sam asked.

"Wow. Look at that. That's really is something..." Nick studied the tree, lifting a few of the ribbons of cedar bark then letting them fall back against the tree.

Sam continued with observations from the previous day. "Notice how the soil around the entire bench is pretty well compacted and there isn't much in the way of ground cover. It seems like this bench gets used but there's no sign of any particular critter. No tracks, no scat, no nothing." Sam paused, and his eyes widened. "You know what else? We left a pie up here yesterday! Right there on top of the rocks. It's gone. I don't see any sign of it, anywhere."

"I guess we know something's been up here, then. Speaking of rocks, it's time we looked at this grave of yours."

Nick took off his daypack and unzipped it. He produced a camera and took a picture of the rock pile. Sam took off his pack and got out his water bottle. He walked over to the rock pile and lifted part of the layer of moss that covered the rocks. "Look at the way these rocks are all laid in here so that they interlock. I'd have to say that this isn't some natural formation."

Nick snapped a close-up photo of the rocks. He let his camera hang around his neck as he studied them more closely. Nick pulled back more of the moss and surveyed the rocks beneath it. He pulled at one of the rocks but it refused to budge.

"Here, use this." Sam handed the pick to his partner in crime, who jammed the pointed end into a space between the interlocking stones. He pried on the wooden handle and a cluster of five stones popped loose. Sam picked up one of the stones and studied it.

"See, these are light gray. It's andesite, but everything we walked past on the way in was black basalt. These rocks had to have been hauled up here from somewhere else. Who would go to all that trouble, and why?"

"I must say, I'm at a loss to explain this myself. It does have the distinct look of some kind of grave, but I also think we can safely rule out the possibility that some Clackamas County drug dealer is under here."

Nick stared at the rock pile, and nodded. "Yeah, I think you've found something very interesting here, Sam. It's going to be a bit of work to loosen these stones, but maybe once we get past the first layer, things will be a little easier. But if I don't try to see what's inside this thing, it would bother me for a long time. Notice how long the pile of rocks is. It's about ten, maybe twelve feet long and four feet wide. The dimensions do seem a bit too large for a human grave."

"That's what I thought yesterday. Ready to start digging?" Sam asked as he put on a pair of work gloves.

"No time like the present. It's almost noon. I don't know if we're going to have enough time to do the whole job today. We'd better get going. One thing's for sure; this shovel I brought is useless."

Sam laughed and took hold of the pick, raised it, and let it fall on the pile of stone. A rock shattered and bits flew in several directions. "Yikes," Sam yelped, as bits of rock flew backward into his face. "I'd better wear some eye protection." He put down the pick, rummaged through his pack and found a pair of sunglasses. As he put them on, mosquitoes began to gather around the exposed flesh of his face and arms. He waved his hand feebly at the gathering bugs as he prepared to take another swing with the pick.

"Say, Nick, did you bring any bug repellent? I didn't think about mosquitoes when I was packing my things this morning."

Nick was now starting to wave off mosquitoes as well. "No, I didn't think about it either. I guess it is getting into a mosquito time of year."

Sam pulled at a couple of rocks and finally got them to dislodge. "You know, we should probably take a careful note of how this thing looks before we get too far into it.

If we do have to put it back together, it would be nice to have a sense of how it came apart. Why don't we start at this corner and pile the stones here as we take them off. It seems to me that we ought to work from a single corner rather than the center of the pile. That way we might be able to get fairly deep into the pile without disturbing the center of the cairn. We might even hit earth and dig under the rocks without disturbing it, and get right to the meat of the matter that much quicker."

"Yeah, that makes good sense." Nick agreed. "That seems a lot easier than trying to go right down the middle of this thing. Man, these bugs are getting intense!"

Nick was swatting at the ever-thickening cloud of mosquitoes that circled around his head. "You don't have any cigarettes, do you? Anything that made smoke might help keep these rascals at bay."

"I don't smoke, but right now, I'm wishing I did. These things are going to eat us alive if we don't find something to get rid of them."

The two men tried their best to keep working. They pulled stones away from the corner of the cairn and carefully laid them in a row as they went. They used the point of the pick to pry loose the stones, which raised the stones around it each time a stone was dislodged. The pick had to be pulled with great force, requiring the combined effort of both men to dislodge the stones. It was arduous work, and the harder they worked, the sweatier they got, and the more intense the mosquitoes became.

After only fifteen minutes of work the two were dropping their tools to brush off dozens of mosquitoes that were landing on the bare skin of their arms, face, and neck. It soon got to the point where they could only work for thirty seconds before the piercing of their skin by dozens of mosquito proboscis inflicted enough pain that they had to drop their tools and brush the blanket of insects from their exposed skin. At last, the irritation became intolerable. Sam threw down the pick, and stepped back from the rock pile, flailing at the mosquito hoard that surrounded him.

"I can't take this! If we stay here any longer I'm going to be one giant mosquito bite in the morning! I gotta get out of here before they drink all the blood I have!"

"I hate to give up so easily but this *is* getting ridiculous. There's no way we're going to get anything done before we get eaten alive. We obviously overlooked an important detail in our planning. You didn't say anything about mosquitoes when you described this place."

"I know. We were here yesterday and there weren't any bugs at all. There must have been a big mosquito hatch or something just today. I didn't know a situation could change so much in one day, but yesterday we weren't working and getting sweaty. Mosquitoes zero in on carbon dioxide sources to find the animal blood that they need to survive. The harder we work, the more mosquitoes are going to come running to the feeding frenzy we seem to have created. I think we're going to have to clear out of here and come back with head nets and bug repellent."

"Do you think we have time to go back to your place, get some bug repellent, then get back here in time to get this job finished?"

"I don't know, but we have to try. We're not going to get anything done this way! *This is hell!* I vote we get the hell outta here right now!" Sam said while swinging and swatting with his arms.

"I'm with you," Nick said grabbing his pack and shovel.

The two ran off the flat bench in the middle of the woods, down and around the side of the hill, until they reached the first discernible sign of the trail they followed in from the car. By the time they had reached the trail, they had left the cloud of bloodthirsty mosquitoes behind. They stopped to catch their breaths. There was no hope of returning to the site of their excavation without protection from the insect hoard.

"Let's head back to my place and regroup."

"Agreed."

The pair commenced the silent trudge back to the car. About half way down the trail to the car, Sam broke the silence.

"That was one heck of a mosquito onslaught. I don't think I've ever experienced an insect encounter quite that intense before. That must be what Alaska is like in the summer."

"I once went on a fishing trip to the Copper River and the mosquitoes were about that bad, but we were prepared for them. That situation up there caught us a bit off guard. I have my doubts about getting back here in time to get anything else done today."

"I won't have time to come up here tomorrow. If we don't get back here today, I won't have any time until next weekend. If we hurry, we might still have time to get back up here."

The pair quickened their pace, but upon emerging from out of the shady woods and into the intense sun on the unpaved forest road, a new and unexpected problem confronted them. One of the tires on Nick's pickup was flat.

A flurry of unscheduled activity ensued, beginning with emptying out half the contents of Nick's pick up in pursuit of the necessary tools. Nick finally produced a 'bottle jack' and proceeded to have considerable difficulty getting it into position. There just wasn't enough clearance to situate the jack beneath the axle when the tire was completely flat. Then the pair of men set about searching the woods for a limb sufficiently stout so it would serve as a lever to raise the car up enough to slide the jack under the axle. They broke several candidate sticks before they found one that was sufficiently robust to raise the truck even a small amount. The unscheduled repair took over an hour. At last, they were heading down the road, but it was now approaching four o'clock.

"I don't think we're going to make it back up here again today," Nick said, shaking his head.

"I think you're right. So I haven't had time to ask you, yet. What do you think of the situation up there? Does is seem like a grave to you?"

"I must say, it certainly has that look about it. If it didn't look good, I wouldn't have wanted to tear into it in the first place. I guess I can't be sure, as you said yourself, but I will say it looks good enough to justify a bit more poking around. We just have to figure out a time when we can get back up there to have another go at it."

They tentatively decided to try for Saturday, which was five days away. Nick dropped Sam off at the end of his driveway and kept going down the road back to town. Sam walked up the long driveway with the pick and the digging bar on one shoulder and a pack slung over the other. He itched everywhere. "Foul insect beasts," he thought. "What brought all that on?"

Chapter 15

I N THE MIDDLE of the night, a deafening crash woke Sam from a deep sleep. The entire log home shook violently. Sam and Grace's bed lurched up then slammed back down on the floor like a car going too fast over a speed bump. The crash of impact and the splintering of wood was deafening. It sounded like a plane hit the house. Then it was quiet.

Sam leaped from his bed wearing only a pair of boxer shorts. He had no idea what made the thunderous noise, what had happened to the house, or what was left of it. He raced out the bedroom door with only one thought on his mind: his children. He turned toward the kids' bedrooms and ran smack into a large piece of ceiling that sloped down toward the floor at a steep angle. The hallway that led to the kids' bedrooms had been obliterated. He fumbled for a light switch in the hallway. He found the switch on the wall and flipped it. It didn't work. Sam was now in a panic.

The house had been smashed in half and he couldn't get through the debris to the kids bedrooms. He listened for the noise of voices or screams. He heard absolutely nothing. Sam turned and ran back down the hallway toward the stairs. He stumbled down the stairs in the darkness, thinking he would have to go outside and around the house to reach whatever was left of the kids' bedrooms.

He got to the bottom of the stairs and flipped another light switch that didn't work. He peered across the darkened room toward the kitchen. A faint light from the moon outside illuminated the room just enough to allow Sam to see that the kitchen was not visible. All he could see was a smashed ceiling sloping downward at a steep angle and touching the floor. The entire house was smashed in half. Sam was trapped in one half and his kids in the other half, and Sam could not get to them. He didn't know whether they were dead or alive.

"This is the wrong time to panic," he told himself.

He ran toward the collapsed ceiling and grabbed the end of a large piece of wallboard that was hanging by an edge. He pulled it loose to expose the broken roof joists inside the destroyed ceiling. Behind the twisted joists Sam could make out a large tree trunk which was lying across the shattered remains of the house. At last, Sam understood what had suddenly demolished his house while they slept. A large tree had fallen across the house and smashed it. Now he had to get to the kids. Sam screamed as loud as he could.

"Can you hear me in there!" he yelled into the jumble of broken lumber and wallboard panels. "Are you kids alright?!"

Silence.

"Can you hear me?"

More silence.

"Somebody answer me!"

Sam had to fight back the urge to panic. He had to get to the kids, but he wasn't going to get through the broken lumber of the house, not to mention the immense tree trunk lying across the roof.

He turned around and ran to the front door. He threw open the bolt, yanked the door open, and threw his body out onto the porch. He stumbled down the three steps to the ground and froze in his tracks. There was somebody standing right in front of him. That somebody was tall and wide and huge. Then he saw two more upright profiles flanking the one directly in front of him.

Sam gasped. He could not believe what he was seeing: three immense, beings stood shoulder to shoulder across Sam's path.

Sasquatches? Not one, but three? And why were they just standing there? What did they have to do with the destruction of Sam's house? This was an emergency of the highest order and the lives of Sam's kids were at stake. But they blocked Sam's path. The whole scene was surreal. He wasn't the slightest bit concerned for his own safety, despite the fact that three monsters were challenging him.

All that Sam could think about was trying to rescue his children. He tried to run but his legs wouldn't move. He blurted out the only thing that occurred to him.

In a shrill voice, he screamed at the three immense beings. "Why are you just standing there? The KIDS! DO SOMETHING!!!"

The dark and monstrous beings said nothing, nor did they budge. They just stood there, silent, fearsome, and completely blocking Sam's path.

"Can't you understand me?! You have to do something!"

The middle of the three dark beings stepped forward. His eyes glowed red and he looked directly into Sam's eyes. Sam was inexplicably frozen. A loud low voice filled his head with four words: "Put my grave back!"

At first, it didn't even register in Sam's head what the menacing being meant. He shouted louder at the immense black silhouettes that blocked his path. "The kids! I have to get to the kids." Now he was shaking violently from side to side. He heard his wife shouting to him. "Sam! Sam!"

"The kids! The kids!" Sam yelled over and over.

"Sam! Wake up, Sam! Wake up! It's okay. Wake up!"

Sam's eyes popped open. He was lying in his bed. The light was on. He was drenched in sweat. His wife was shaking him. Sam gasped. His eyes were wide with fright. He put his palms on his forehead and held his head for a moment. Then he quickly sat up and frantically looked around the room. Everything was in order.

"Are you okay, dear? You were having a nightmare!"

"The kids! Are they okay?" he asked frantically.

"Everything's fine. You were having a nightmare."

Sam threw back the covers and lept from the bed. He was on his feet and heading for the kids' bedrooms. The hallway outside his bedroom was intact. He ran to the door of his daughter's room and pushed the door open. The nightlight by the closet illuminated her motionless form sleeping contentedly in her bed. Sam breathed a sigh of relief. He peered into his son's room where the light from the aquarium shone on the sleeping boy. He turned and went down the hall. The house was completely intact. The ceiling was not touching the floor as he had envisioned only a few moments before.

Then he flashed on the vivid image of three immense forms standing side by side in front of him on the lawn. The words he heard them say suddenly replayed in his head. "Put my grave back."

Sam felt the hair on the back of his neck raise, hard and fast. He went to the front door, flipped on the outside porch light and opened the door. There was no one on the lawn. Everything was as it should be. He began to shut the door then noticed something on the porch at the top of the steps. It was small and round. It looked like a rock. Sam opened the door wider and stepped out. He picked it up. It looked like a perfectly round ball of mud. It was dry cracked mud in the shape of a ball. Sam was thoroughly confused.

"Could it be?" he thought to himself. He dropped the round object onto the cement walk at the base of the steps. The mud cracked and fell off and the unmistakable stitching of a baseball seam was exposed in the yellow of the porch light. As he suspected, it was a mud-covered baseball. Sam felt his blood run cold. It somehow didn't seem to be just a mud-covered baseball. It was a calling card.

"Shit," he said to himself. Sam thought for a moment. He thought about the four words he heard from the immense dark form that blocked his path to the kids. Suddenly, he knew what he had done and what he had to do next. Sam looked at his watch. It was 4:30 a.m. He thought about calling Nick but then decided he should wait. Sam didn't want to go back to bed and try to sleep. He didn't think he could. He got his robe from the hook on the wall in the bathroom and put it on.

Sitting down in a chair in the dark living room, Sam closed his eyes and thought about pulling the stones away from the grave above the lake the previous afternoon. He suddenly recollected the hoard of mosquitoes that beset them as they pulled the tightly interlocked stones apart. He put his hands over his eyes and threw his head back.

"What an idiot I am!" Sam said to himself. He sat in the chair in the darkened room. He closed his eyes and thought about their escapades of the day. Sam's mind went blank. What seemed like a moment later, his eyes sprang open. The room was filled with daylight.

Sam looked at his watch. It was 6:30 a.m. He was never so happy to see daylight fill a room. His horrible night had passed, but he kept thinking about the menacing form that stood before him in the dream, and the phrase it repeated: "Put my grave back."

Sam picked up his cell phone and pushed the button that recalled recently dialed numbers. He spotted Nick's phone number in the list and highlighted it. He dialed it. In two rings, Nick answered.

"Sam?"

"How'd you know it was me?"

"My phone has 'caller I.D.' but this time I didn't even need to look at it. I just knew."

"Nick, we have to go put that grave back."

"I know," Nick said almost before Sam was finished with the sentence.

"What do you mean, 'You know'." There was silence from the other end of the phone. "Don't tell me." Sam asked, "Did *you* have a bad night, too."

Nick slowly said, "That's putting it mildly." Nick sounded traumatized, even over the telephone. There was a long silence, which Nick broke with a single, ominous sentence. "Last night was the worst night of my life."

"Are you thinking what I'm thinking?"

"I think so. We need to fix that grave right away. Like, today. I'm not going to sleep until we put it back like we found it."

"How soon can you get over here? I can be ready to go in an hour."

By 8:30 the two men were motoring up the road toward Squaw Meadow, bouncing on the bench seat of Nick's pick up; staring silently at the road ahead.

Nick broke the long silence. "I hate to ask what happened to you last night?"

"Nothing major," Sam replied with his usual sarcasm. "They basically made it clear that they would smash my house and my kids if I didn't put the grave back, *post haste.*"

"*They?*"

"Three of 'em. They were waiting for me on the lawn when I ran out of the house. One of them said, 'Put my grave back.' It was the scariest, most vivid dream I think I've ever had. To top it off, after my wife woke me up, I got up the courage to go outside. There on the front porch was this mud-covered baseball. It seemed like a calling card. The dog could have left it there, I suppose, but after that nightmare, I'm not taking any chances. I don't ever want to have another night like that. How about you?"

"I kept waking up to the sound of rocks hitting my roof. Then sticks were hitting the side of the house. Every time I'd go to sleep I would see this angry face saying, 'Fix my grave, fix my grave.' Then, I'd wake up and hear rocks on the roof. I'd fall asleep and hear the voice and see the angry face again. This went on all night. I didn't sleep more than a half hour. By four a.m. I knew I wasn't going to get a wink of sleep until we got up there and fixed the grave."

"Think they might be waiting for us when we get up there?" Sam asked.

"I hadn't even thought of that." Nick thought for a moment. "I suppose that after the night I spent, I'm willing to take that chance. I don't think I'm going to get any sleep until we fix that grave. I don't think my *roof* can take another night of that," Nick said a faint smile. Then he added, "I suppose if they're ready to kill us when we get there, then we won't be able to fix the grave."

With a smile, Sam said, "I suppose. Maybe they'll just wait until we put it all back, *then* finish us off."

Nick managed to crack a slight smile. Then Sam asked, "By the way, do ya still think they're just some damn apes?"

"That's what bugs me the most," Nick said without hesitation. "I'm absolutely floored by what happened and what it seems to imply about these things. I mean, I'm terrified of them now. It's really changed my way of looking at this whole thing. It's too early to tell, but right now I feel like I'm done with this whole out-of-control hobby of mine. I've been doing this stuff for the past fifteen years. Not only can't I believe how wrong I was. Now, for the first time, I'm really scared of these things.

"That face kept coming back whenever I closed my eyes. After a couple hours, I was afraid to even close my eyes again. I knew it was waiting for me. It was the longest night of my life. I couldn't wait to get up there and fix that grave. I almost called you at 4:30 this morning. I was pretty sure you were awake."

"Actually, I was," Sam replied.

"Yeah, well, I just hope we can do it right. I don't ever want to have another night like that. It seemed like they were right outside my house. That was a mighty spooky situation all the way around. In fact, it was more than spooky. It was terrifying. But worst of all, it seems to say, to me at least, that these guys are absolutely NOT to be messed with. Whoever or whatever they are, they can do us in if they so desire. I mean, I found myself wondering about everything else that happened to us yesterday: the mosquitoes, the flat tire. Doesn't it make you wonder whether they somehow managed to send all that messed up stuff our way?"

"I must admit," Sam added, "I had that exact same thought as I sat in my living room: afraid to go back to sleep. It reminded me of the word that the Hoopa Indians in northwest California use to describe the sasquatch: "Oh-mah." That roughly translates into 'boss of the woods.' I think I'm starting to get it, now."

"Yeah, and that's the part of this whole situation that bugs me the most. Not just that I found out that there's more to this phenomenon than I ever expected, but that I spent the last fifteen years hunting for sasquatch, and thinking I would someday maybe get the chance to sneak up on one. Then, yesterday I move a few rocks off of a pile in the woods, and *bam-o*, they come find me...at home... and they're really pissed off!

"Do you know what that means? They know where I live! There's no hiding from them. *They* can come find *you* whenever they want! Maybe we're better off just leaving them alone! I mean, do you really *want* them coming around your house? I know I don't."

"Not if they're pissed, that's for sure. They seem to have made that much perfectly clear. Plus, it seems worse than that. I mean it may have only been a nightmare but it seemed like they were saying they could wipe out my entire family. It's like we just pissed off the bigfoot Mafia!

My wife thinks I'm a bit strange because I'm out looking for an imaginary ape. She doesn't know the half of it. If she finds out that they're not only real, but they're *real mad*... at *us*, no less...I mean, how am I going to explain all of this. I wouldn't even know how to begin. Who's gonna believe that bigfoot can control hoards of mosquitoes, flatten your tires, threaten to wipe out your house and family *from their graves!*"

He took a deep breath, "These guys are worse than the Mafia. At least the Mafia is human! We've got something even worse. We've got the 'Oh-Mah-fia' here! They're not just the 'boss of the woods' we're talkin' the *'mob* of the woods!'" Sam was doing his best to add humor to the situation, but underneath his exaggerations, he was genuinely unnerved.

"It is kind of funny when you step back and think about it," Nick said. "How is Mr. Science Teacher here going to tell people about all this paranormal shit that's gone on in the past few days?" Taking a cue from Sam, Nick was showing the first smile he'd been able to muster all morning.

"First we have to survive it, and we haven't done that yet. If we do, I know exactly what I'm going to say. Nothing."

"Whaddaya mean, 'nothing'?"

"I mean I don't plan to say a damn thing, because I know I can't convince anyone that any of this is true. I would end up looking crazy if I were stupid enough to try. It's just like the Mafia. The 'Oh-Mah-fia' has me too scared to go public! They know where we live, and they don't answer to 'the law.' Why do I suddenly feel like I'm Marlon Brando, and we're living in a remake of *On the Waterfront*?

The two men were still motoring up the road to Squaw Meadow. They were both staring straight ahead at the road that wound up the side of the ancient lava flow.

Nick swallowed his urge to raise his voice. "You're not even going to try?"

"Like I said, I know I can't explain it, so I'm not even going to try. I'm going to say nothing at all. Is that so hard to understand?" insisted Sam who was by now sensing the combativeness in Nick's tone.

"So you're trying to tell me that you don't mind the fact that you've stumbled upon the scientific bombshell of the century, and you're okay with just sitting there with your mouth shut?"

"I didn't say I was okay with it. I just said that's what I plan to do, because I know I don't have a choice, since I have no way to disseminate this earth-shattering information of ours. There is no proof. None. I mean, what do you suggest we do? Stand on top of the highest mountain and scream to the world the fact that cavemen with supernatural powers inhabit the earth?

Sam paused and took a breath, but also waited for that much to sink in before he said any more. "Don't you see? You know too much...more than anybody wants to know. So, you have no real choice other than to keep your mouth shut. I think there are some things that people have to figure out for themselves."

"If you just told them that there are beings on earth that can meddle in our affairs yet who also can rebuff our efforts to gather evidence on them, who is going to believe you? Nobody, that's who. Absolutely nobody. In fact, it's even worse than that. If you were so foolish as to stand up and tell the world what you thought you knew, they would assume you're crazy and have you put away. I guarantee nobody is going to buy anything that you or I say, so why waste our time?"

The hapless adventurers arrived at Squaw Meadow and found their way down the trail in record time. They carried no tools this time, just light packs. They walked the trail without words. They both knew exactly where they were going and what they were going to do when they got there. Both men took long strides and moved with silent determination. Both were alert for noises and motions in the forest around them. Nothing ominous occurred. No strange noises, no strange silences.

They arrived at the end of the trail and prepared to climb the hill. Both pulled out bug repellent and began rubbing the lotion onto their arms and faces. The pair then began a silent trudge up the steep hillside, eventually arriving at the flat terrace high above the lake. They dropped their packs, looked around, and listened. The sky was beginning to cloud up. The breeze had been blowing since they got out of the car, but now it was getting gusty.

"He-who-makes-the-wind-blow" muttered Sam, but loudly enough so Nick could hear him.

Nick paused and stared at Sam, but had nothing to say. Sam's short but pointed statement humbled Nick. Since last night, they were both very aware that there was much more to this whole sasquatch thing than they had ever imagined. Nick's view in particular, of the sasquatch as North America's great ape, had been demolished.

As they studied their surroundings, they braced for the expected onslaught of mosquitoes. They looked at each other as if searching for confirmation that they were taking the correct course of action. With the wind blowing, perhaps the mosquitoes were not going to be the problem that they had been yesterday.

They got on their knees and began the process of returning the stones to the big rectangular mound. Like a three dimensional puzzle, they pieced the stones together. For the most part, the two men attempted to recollect and reconstruct the exact configuration of stones. They tried to rebuild an interlocking fit and push them into place so that they nestled together. Thankfully, on the previous day before the mosquitoes repelled them, they had only unearthed about twenty stones.

It took them half-an-hour to replace the stones in a way that looked tidy and utilized almost every stone. Sam was inwardly glad that he suggested they disassemble the stones in an organized fashion yesterday. It made the process of reassembling the stone immensely easier. When the pair had restored the rock cairn to its rectangular shape, they had three stones left over which they laid at the base of the corner they disturbed. Then they both stood up and stepped back to survey their work. So far, the mosquitoes were a no show. Due to the cooler weather, they had not perspired as profusely as they had the day before, but they were still bewildered by the absolute absence of attacking insects.

Now that they were done, Sam reached into his pack and pulled out a bunch of flowers from his garden that were wrapped in a sheet of newspaper. He carefully laid the flowers at the high point of the rock mound. Nick watched Sam as he laid the flowers. Sam stepped back and kept his head bowed. Then he said in a low voice, "We're sorry. We put it back to the best of our ability. May you rest in peace."

Nick felt a bit sheepish about standing there as Sam delivered his combination of apology and devotion, but felt compelled to add finality to the matter himself. When Sam stopped speaking, he said, simply, "Amen." Upon those words, the winds quieted to a soft breeze.

Sam looked over at Nick and said to him, "I think we should also make a promise to each other, and to whomever else is listening, to keep this location a secret. We tell no one, ever. Agreed?"

"Agreed," said Nick.

They both picked up their packs and took one final look around. Nothing moved and nothing about the place seemed spooky or strange. It was just a normal, overcast June day. Without speaking another word, the two men headed down the hill, found the trail that followed along the edge of the lake and hiked back to the truck. Once they were at the truck, they got in, started it, and did a u-turn in the road. They headed up the hill out of the Squaw Meadow, and as they got to the top of the hill, Sam said to Nick, "I hope that makes everybody's spirit happy. I don't need another night like last night."

"Amen to that. If they don't like the job we did of replacing the stones, I guess we're going to hear about it soon enough. By the way, did you notice? No bugs. What do you make of that?"

"I haven't a clue," Sam admitted. "The whole thing is just too messed up for words, but I think that's the thing that bothers me the most. How the heck does someone or something manage to direct a horde of mosquitoes? The whole thing defies logic."

"And that's not the worst thing they seem capable of doing," Sam continued. "How do you direct vivid nightmares at two different people in two different places on the same night? Did you notice the wind was blowing the whole time we were there today?"

"Mere coincidence," Nick said dismissively.

"I find myself suddenly wondering whether *anything* in our world is truly a coincidence. Coincidence may just be an interplay of personalities and events that is being steered by forces we don't understand and probably never will. I know coincidences happen in the world, but I don't think one can attribute all of the events of yesterday and last night to coincidence."

"I guess I would have to agree, though I can't help but hope there's a scientific explanation for everything that happened." Sam stared at Nick with a look of amazement. "Of course, I have absolutely no idea what it might be."

"Yeah, well, let me know when you come up with one. I sure want to know what it is."

"You'll be the first to know."

There was a minute of silence as they rumbled down the dusty road. Then, Sam said, "You know, yesterday on our way up here, I was wondering about coincidences, too. It occurred to me that I was being guided up here, and so I thought that finding the grave was something that was maybe supposed to happen. I was, after all, coming up here in hopes of finding a way of stopping the whole place from getting developed. I thought that maybe something wanted me to find the grave so that we could find the bones, get the species recognized, and then get the area around that meadow protected forever.

"I really thought we might be pawns in some grand plan, or at least that I was being given an opportunity as a sort of answer to my prayers. I mean, my intentions were noble enough. It's not like I wanted the fame and fortune that would come from finding the first sasquatch bones. All I wanted was to protect the meadow. It just seemed like we were being handed the means to get that done.

"Now, I don't know what to think, but I'm pretty sure that if finding bones in that grave was the key to saving the meadow, it's just not going to happen. I was so hopeful that I was going to stop the land deal. If there is a conscious entity watching our moves, it obviously doesn't want it to happen that way. I thought yesterday maybe we were being offered some help with a noble undertaking that we were a part of. I guess not. Just wishful thinking, I guess. Now it's back to square one on the whole idea of stopping the development. See ya later, Squaw Meadow..." Sam said sullenly.

The wind was really starting to whip up and the sky was getting darker as storm clouds moved in from the Pacific over the Coastal Range, across the Willamette Valley, and into the Cascades. Just then, a very strong gust swirled overhead. Needles from the fir trees fell like green snow on either side of the road. About a hundred yards ahead of Nick's truck a large limb from one of the fir trees snapped and fell onto the road. Nick slowed his truck to a stop. The limb was about fifty yards ahead of them, but it effectively blocked the road. The pair in the car looked at each other. Sam smiled. "I think the 'The Boss of the Woods' just left us a calling card."

"Great," Nick said. "Either that or he's still trying to finish us off for messing with that grave. Did it ever occur to you he might be trying to bomb us before we get away?"

"Hmm. That thought doesn't make me eager to get out of the truck and move that limb. I'd be a sitting duck out there. Of course, I suppose we're a sitting duck right here. Watch a tree fall and smash the truck with you in it while

I'm out there moving the limb," Sam said, smiling, while also opening the car door.

"Damned if you do, damned if you don't. Okay, go move the limb."

Sam didn't waste any time jumping from the car and moving the limb while Nick eased the vehicle as close to the blockade as possible. Sam picked up the butt end of the limb and walked it to the edge of the road so that it was now lying parallel to the road but off to one side. He jumped back into the truck and Nick hit the gas. Gravel and dust blew from Nick's tires. The two held their breath for a few seconds until they were back up to a reasonable cruising speed, given the roughness of the road. The wind kept blowing but the rest of the trip down the mountain to Sam's house was uneventful. By the time they were in Sam's driveway, a windy rain was falling. Large drops were hitting the windshield. Sam gathered his pack as they pulled into the driveway. He put his hand on the latch but before he opened it, he looked at Nick and said, "If I don't hear from you tomorrow morning, I'll assume the night passed uneventfully."

"Likewise."

Sam lifted the latch and ducked out of the car as the downpour continued. Nick did a U-turn and headed out the driveway in his pick-up.

"Yeah, it'll be interesting to see what tonight brings, all right," Sam thought to himself as he headed up the steps to his house.

Chapter 16

S AM SAT IN somber silence on the sofa. He couldn't hide his dejection. He had done his best to restore the grave yesterday, but now he regretted it. Now, it was Sunday night and he had been moping around all day. He slept well last night. The nightmares did not return. He had not heard from Nick, so it was safe to assume that he'd gotten a good night's sleep as well.

It had been only a day and a half since he returned from the meadow but it all seemed like a distant memory. He no longer felt threatened by the menacing nightmare, but he was still having serious doubts that he actually did the right thing. He wondered whether he might have passed up the opportunity of a lifetime.

He had played it safe for the sake of his family, but his plan to save the meadow and avoid the increased traffic on his road, was now foiled. This left him bitterly disappointed and wondering whether it was really necessary to abandon the plans to search the grave just because they were confronted by of a bunch of mosquitoes and a bad dream...well...actually, two simultaneous bad dreams... in fact...two very bad dreams.

Still, maybe he was too easily discouraged. "Discoveries," he thought, "aren't made by the faint of heart." Maybe he should have stuck to the plan and not been so easily swayed by a dream. Perhaps it was the fact that the dream seemed to imply dire threat to not just him, but his entire family that forced Sam to see the ominous message that the dream contained. Truth be told, he wasn't so interested in ignoring what seemed like a clear warning. Until he had a better understanding of the forces he was dealing with, it didn't seem wise to take any chances with the welfare of his family.

"Never gamble with more than you can afford to lose," Sam thought. That thought seemed to close the door of any further debate. Right then and there, he resolved to have no further regret about the course of action he ultimately chose. He reaffirmed his commitment to leave the grave, or whatever it was, alone and never tell anyone of its whereabouts. Further, he resolved to have no further regrets about the matter, regardless of whatever ended up happening to Squaw Meadow.

His "no regrets" resolution didn't help him feel any better, though. He tried to relax on Sunday night before beginning another long work week. Yet, he kept going over the events of the past few days in his mind and it only depressed him. His dejection stemmed from the disappointment he now felt that his big plan to stop the land swap and development of Squaw Meadow had evaporated. In the space of little more than twenty-four hours, he went from excitement and optimism about his chances of stopping the development to a sense of resignation that one small guy could not stop a development that took its momentum from those who stood to profit from the exploitation of a public resource.

Sam found himself wondering about the mind behind the message that he and Nick were sent. "I guess the meadow isn't a priority in their mind," 'they' being the Skookums, the wood spirits that he was gradually becoming convinced actually lived in the area around Squaw Meadow. He sat on the sofa, with his hands clasped behind his neck and stared at the hemlock boards that made up the ceiling of his living room. "Okay guys," Sam said, "better move over up there in Squaw Meadow, because progress is coming your way. Unless, of course, you want to send me some kind of message about how we can keep that from happening."

"What did you say, Dad?" Jack asked from across the room.

Sam snapped out of his train of thought. "Oh, nothing. I was just thinking out loud..." he mumbled. He suddenly had a very strong thought that he wasn't doing a very good job of attending to the needs of his own family. The school week was about to unfold for his kids as well as himself. Maybe his wife was right. After the events of the past couple days, it was painfully obvious that he was spending too time on big projects that got him nowhere. It was time to shift the focus. He needed to put aside his desire to stop the development of Squaw Meadow. After all, he couldn't save the whole forest single-handedly. He tried that, and he failed. This seemed like a good time to put the focus back where it should have been all along: on his family. Suddenly, he felt a lot better.

Sam looked around the room. His daughter Elizabeth was sitting at the kitchen table with markers and crayons. She was coloring a poster involving the branches of the federal government. His son Jack was sitting on the floor with his creature carrier next to him and a field guide to reptiles and amphibians in his hand. He was flipping through pages and looking puzzled.

"No time like the present to involve yourself in your kids' life," Sam thought. He got up from the sofa. "Hey, Jack what are ya working on?"

"I'm still trying to figure out what kind of snake this is. You said you would help me figure out what it was so we could let it go again."

"You're right, I did. Okay, this shouldn't take too long. Let's see that field guide. Bring that snake over here."

Sam and Jack sat down on the sofa with the snake between them, flipping pages in *The Peterson Guide to North American Reptiles and Amphibians*. They spent the next hour poring through its pages. It was a sublime parenting experience: turning pages, reading, and studying the pictures, reading the passages, searching zoological websites, and studying the intricate details of the serpent in the plastic container. To Sam's surprise, the process was also very frustrating and even a little embarrassing, since he, an experienced science teacher, was having a lot of difficulty finding any kind of definite match.

"Something's wrong here," Sam finally concluded. "Maybe this book is too general. This snake is definitely not in this book but this book tries to cover the whole continent. I think we need a book that is specific to this region. I think we have one around here somewhere. Hold on."

Sam got up and went upstairs to search the bookcase in the hallway. He knelt in front of the bookshelf and sat back on his haunches while he scanned the titles on the shelves in front of him. As he searched, he flashed on the thought that he was now in the exact location that had been demolished by the immense tree in his dream.

That gave Sam a strange notion. He stood up and turned around to look out the window. The nearest tree was a large maple and it did have a bit of a lean in the direction of the house. If that tree were to fall in the right wind, it would indeed land exactly where it fell in his dream. How could his mind have known that? And how could his mind have woven a nightmare around this fact that he was not even consciously aware of until this very moment.

"I'm going to have to do something about that tree," Sam thought, "before it does something to me."

He went back to looking for the field guide to snakes of the Pacific Northwest. At last he found it and took it downstairs to show his son. He returned to the sofa and sat next to his son and put his arm around him. Having just recalled the horror of his nightmare and threat posed by the leaning tree, Sam felt a sudden appreciation of his family and his modest but cozy log home.

He felt something he couldn't recall feeling at any time in the recent past: a strong appreciation of all the good and right things about his life at that moment, and especially the steady success he and Grace were experiencing in the never-ending job of raising their kids. One vivid thought entered Sam's head, and that was the need to recommit himself to keeping things in his household going smoothly. It *had* to be his top priority in life. He resolved not to let any development, preservation, politics, work, and certainly not sasquatch mysteries, interfere with his commitment to family.

While Sam was having these thoughts, Jack was completely focused on the book that his father had brought down from the upstairs shelf. Jack flipped the pages with a deftness that demonstrated the boy's keen knowledge of the subject. After only a few minutes of flipping pages, Jack closed the book and handed it back to Sam.

"It's not in here," Jack announced with a quiet confidence.

"It's gotta be."

Sam took the book and began flipping the pages himself. He searched the garter snakes, bull snakes, and rubber boas that were the familiar species of the area. He looked for mention of species that were common to higher elevations, which were primarily garter snakes. The California red-sided garter snake was known to sport a variety of colorations but nothing matched the short smooth body of the snake that rested peacefully on the piece of bark inside the clear plastic 'critter carrier'.

Sam bent over and picked up the *Reptiles and Amphibians* book from the floor.

"Maybe we have something new that's never been found before," Jack suggested.

"I doubt it," Sam replied without hesitation. "There are zillions of biologists and herpetologists out there beating the bushes every day in hopes of finding some new critter that they can be the first to identify. They've been at this since the first biologists like Archibald Menzies and

David Douglas came out here in the early 1800's with the first wave of European explorers. I can't imagine that in 200 years of combing the woods, biologists would have missed something like this right here in our own back yard."

Now they were both looking a lot more carefully at the creature in the large clear container. Sam's daughter Elizabeth put down her colored pencil set and came over to see what everyone was so interested in. She casually looked at the snake creature for the first time. Then she matter-of-factly stated, "We've seen those before. Remember the day when we were catching newts at Squaw Meadow? We saw an eagle drop a snake into the water, then it swam right toward us. You grabbed it to see if had been hurt by the eagle. Then you let it go. It looked just like that. Remember?"

"Oh, yeah. I forgot about that. I guess it did look the same," Jack agreed.

"Okay, folks, this is what we're going to do. We're going to hang on to this critter for a few more days. Jack, you're going to catch some flies, some worms, or whatever you think it might like, and do your best to keep it fed. I'll make a call tomorrow to Oregon State University. I'm sure they have some big herpetology expert down there that will be able to identify this thing. I'll find out exactly who the big cheese for snakes is and I'll get his or her e-mail address. We'll take a digital picture of this guy and send it to him," and with a flash of political correctness, Sam added, "or her."

Sam's wife was sitting at the computer terminal in the next room. She joined the conversation without getting out of her chair.

"I bet I can find out the big name right now," she said.

A few minutes later, they had a name of biology professor Russell Wertz whose Ph. D. dissertation was on reptiles of the Cascade Mountains. Jack watched as his dad wrote the e-mail message in which they requested assistance with the identification of an unusual snake from their local area. With a digital camera, Sam and Jack took a few pictures and loaded them onto the computer. They attached their digital pictures of the snake to the message and sent it on its way.

By lunchtime the next day Sam received an e-mail reply in which Dr. Wertz stated that he was not at all sure what the creature was in the pictures and would they mind bringing the creature in to his office in Corvallis. Sam was a little surprised at the quick response, not to mention the fact that the professor did not have an immediate answer.

Still, Sam wasn't really surprised or particularly excited about getting the critter in front of the professor. Their pictures didn't provide a ruler for scale and the lighting was not so good, so it was not the best photograph. He was certain that the question as to the serpent's identity would be resolve as soon as the professor got one good look at it.

What concerned Sam was not the identity of the creature but how he was going to arrange for an afternoon off so he could get the snake to Oregon State University. He did not really want to take a half-day off work and travel the distance to Corvallis just to find out that it was a locally common creature that was not listed in field guides with a continent-wide focus. Still, Sam made a promise that he would follow through on this question so Jack could get the snake back to the wild where he felt it belonged. After reflecting on the matter, Sam decided that the best way to make the wild goose chase worthwhile was to make it an educational outing for his son. He would involve Jack in the process so he could meet an expert and see a little of the zoology department at the state land-grant college. That alone would be a memorable enough experience for his son to justify making the trip.

Two days later Jack and Sam were heading down I-5 toward the college town of Corvallis. Jack sat calmly in the passenger seat of Sam's Land Rover with the critter carrier on his lap. Sam thought it was such a charming sight that he took a picture of Jack with the big clear box on his lap.

"Don't get your hopes up," was the advice Sam kept offering to his son when he asked his dad what he thought would happen at the meeting with the professor. "He can't have it even if it *is* rare," Jack kept saying. "It lives by the lake and I'm *going* to put it back. You promised."

Sam had no trouble reassuring Jack on that point. "Don't worry Jack; he'll know what it is right away. We won't be there long, and with any luck we can have it back at the meadow by nightfall."

Sam did his best to prepare his son for a letdown. He didn't want him to get too hopeful about the possibility that he had some new discovery. It was Sam's suspicion that the inability to identify the creature resulted from the fact that it was immature. Juvenile reptiles, and especially amphibians, can look much different than the adult creatures.

Ironically, it was Sam who needed to be prepared for the outcome of the meeting with the reptile expert. After exchanging pleasantries with the professor, they handed him the critter carrier and the professor immediately fell silent. He stared for a long minute or two at the creature inside. He opened the lid, reached in, and gently scooped up the serpent. He examined its underside, its head, and its markings.

He finally looked up and spoke. "Where did you find this?"

Sam anticipated this question and produced a forest service map of the Mt. Hood National Forest. He handed the map to the professor and pointed to Squaw Meadow. The professor examined the map through glasses that rested well down on his nose. He raised his eyes to meet Sam's gaze, looking over the top of the glasses. His expression was blank as he said the last words Sam ever expected to hear.

"I have never seen a snake like this before. I have no idea what it is."

Sam was speechless. He felt a sudden wave of emotion crash over him. Tears welled up in his eyes. He turned and looked at his son. Jack looked at Sam, then back at the professor. "You're serious?" were the only words Sam could manage to speak.

"Completely," the professor said, still looking at them over the top of his glasses. The professor sensed the confusion that existed in the mind of Sam and his son.

"It looks like it is a member of the *Enhydris* genus, or what are called mud snakes. No one's ever found one around here before so it's thought that we don't have any representatives of the *Enhydris* genus in the Pacific Northwest. They're found in jungle environments like Indonesia.

"The reason I know this is, I spent a summer at the Koenig Museum in Germany. A fellow I studied under, Mark Auliya was doing work in Borneo. Last year he found a new species of mud snake on the Kapuas River. It was a chameleon snake, no less, which really blew everyone's mind because snakes that can change color are extremely rare.

The thing about the *Enhydris* genus is that they usually have a very limited range when they do occur."

"So, you think we have a new species of snake here?"

"It's beginning to look that way," the professor said. "But, in order to be certain, we need to thoroughly survey the place where this one was found and see if we can find any more. If we cannot find at least one more, then that raises the possibility that someone put it there but that it really comes from somewhere else. It certainly seems unlikely, since I personally have no idea where this snake could have come from.

"Whatever it is, we have to verify that there is a viable breeding population of them before we get excited. There are other ways that a single snake or any creature that small, can end up somewhere. If we do find one or two more, then you can get excited. At that point, we would publish a monograph to the effect that we've found a new species."

"You're saying we have to go back to the place where this snake came from and see if we can find at least one more. If we are successful, then we can say it's a new species."

"Precisely," Dr. Wertz said.

"What about this snake. I promised Jack, here, that we would put it back where we found it. It's very important to him that the snake be returned to its home environment. I assured him that this particular snake wouldn't be killed or put into a scientific collection. Are you OK with that?"

Dr. Wertz paused before he answered and looked at Jack. "Son, you've done an amazing thing here. You must care an awful lot about snakes."

"I do," Jack replied without hesitation.

"Do you think you might study reptiles here at Oregon State someday?"

"Actually, I'm hoping to go to the University of Oregon."

"He's a big Duck fan," Sam confessed, referring to the University of Oregon's team mascot. "He's been brainwashed by my wife's family from an early age. They're all big U of O alums."

"I see," Dr. Wertz smiled. "Well, think about Oregon State, too, because we do more research into wildlife stuff than the U of O. We're the land grant college established under the Lincoln-Merrill act of 1865, so most of the wildlife research in the state happens here. And, of all the researchers that study and work here, very few of them have ever done what you, young man, may have done here, which is to *possibly*, and I must emphasize *possibly*, discover a new species. The fact that this all seems to have come from a person as young as you is, well, stunning. Just stunning. How did you become so interested in snakes?"

"We have them in our yard. I just like to catch them," Jack shrugged. The professor looked up at Sam. Sam shrugged, too.

"Can I take the snake back to the lake today?" Jack asked.

"You found it. I guess it's your call. But we don't want to find the same snake a second time. We need to be able to identify this snake. We'll make some photos, weight it, and measure it, and then we'll mark it with a non-toxic dye before you take it back to its habitat. I would very much like to see this area. I'll bring along a couple of graduate students, and you can show us where you found it. We'll do our best to find another one. We definitely need a type specimen for scientific scrutiny. If you don't want to let us have that one, we'll respect your wishes. We need to verify that there are more of them, anyway, so we need to collect at least one more. I hope you're okay with us trying to find one of our own, though," Dr. Wertz said.

"I guess so, as long as I can put this one back where it lives."

"Absolutely," the professor agreed. "We need to see where it lives, anyway, and since you know, I'm counting on you to show us."

Jack smiled.

Dr. Wertz picked up the phone and began the process of taking the measurements on the snake. He spoke a few words into the phone then hung up. He looked at Sam and said, "This whole process could take an hour. Do you fellows want to get some lunch and then come back?"

"Well, what we'd really like to do is look at some of the other snakes in your collection. I bet you have a museum or something like that around here."

"Indeed we do. It's downstairs in the basement. It's across the hall from the lab where we'll be measuring the snake. C'mon, I'll walk you down there. Jack, would you bring the snake. Maybe you would be interested in watching as we measure it."

"We both would," Sam said.

They descended the stairs and met a graduate student who was on his way up. The graduate student did an about face and followed them into the laboratory area. The lab was a large, brightly lit room with dozens of aquarium tanks lined up in three long rows against the back. A large counter filled the center of the room, which supported an array of instruments and tools. They began the measurement process at the center counter as Sam and Jack watched. Sam looked at the posters on the walls in the lab.

Sam was amused to see the same "Snakes of North America" poster that was on the wall in Jack's bedroom. Sam surveyed the other posters for ideas that he could use when Jack's birthday came up in another month and a half. There was a poster that featured endangered species, which displayed a slogan beneath the illustration: "Before it's too late."

Sam wondered where he might find a copy of that poster. He thought he might ask the professor or the graduate student where they got the posters. Suddenly, the posters on the wall sparked an entirely different question in Sam's mind. And he was in the perfect place to get an immediate answer to his question.

"Dr. Wertz, there's something else I need to ask you when you get a second."

The professor watched over the graduate student's shoulder for a moment longer until he was satisfied that he knew what he was doing. Then he stepped back and leaned against the counter next to Sam. He looked at Sam in anticipation but didn't say anything.

"What if we do find more of these snakes where this one came from? What happens then? I mean, wouldn't this snake be an endangered species?"

Wertz became professorial, "There's a long answer and a short answer to that question. The short answer is: yes, that's the way these kinds of discoveries have generally gone in the past. If this follows the pattern, then it would be a very sensitive, very vulnerable species.

The long answer begins with: That depends. It depends on how widespread the species turns out to be. If we find that this snake only lives in a single place or a single kind of place, then those locations would be considered 'critical habitat' for this particular species and that habitat would definitely qualify for protection. Remember the snail darter? It was this minnow-sized fish that was discovered in the Little Tennessee River and it was the first time the Endangered Species Act was used to stop a big development project. Once it was shown that the snail darter was a rare and therefore endangered species, the U.S. Supreme Court ruled that construction of the Tellico Dam had to stop because the reservoir created by the dam would destroy critical habitat for just one species of small endangered fish.

"So, take this snake you brought in as an example. If it only lives in one place, then no one would ever be allowed to alter that particular habitat. It could be found that the species lives all over the Cascades, just like they eventually found in the case of the snail darter. In that case, as with the snail darter, it would be reclassified as 'threatened' not 'endangered.' I seriously doubt this would happen in the case of this snake, though. If this snake lived all over the place, one would rightfully expect that it would have been identified and classified by now. But, we mustn't forget the third possibility, and that is that the thing belongs somewhere else."

"How would it end up at Squaw Meadow?"

"The same way alligators end up in New York City sewers and leopards in the British countryside," Dr. Wertz explained. "People put them there. It's usually a pet that somebody no longer wants. Other times, a pet escapes into the wild. It's even possible that, in the case of a snake, it could have been carried there from some place fifty miles away by a hawk or eagle then somehow dropped. Birds can get blown into unlikely places by big storms. Stuff like that does happen, which is why we have to find a breeding population before we're allowed to make any bold claims."

Sam paused to think before he said any more. He wanted to smile. He wanted to laugh out loud. He couldn't help but let a little smile cross his face as he had one overwhelmingly positive thought: The tables had just turned again on Squaw Meadow!

He did his best to keep a straight face and a serious demeanor. Sam flashed on the thought that he should be writing some of this down. He reminded himself that this was an important chance to get useful information from a leading expert.

"So, it's possible there could be a species of snake that lives around here but hasn't yet been identified?"

"Oh, definitely. It's true that the bigger an animal, the harder it is to overlook, but the more we carefully look, the more frequently we're finding overlooked species right under our noses.

"Currently, they're doing a first-ever organized inventory of all living things in the Great Smoky Mountain National Park. It's called the ATBI, which stands for the 'All Taxa Biodiversity Inventory.' They're not even done yet, but as of 2011, they've cataloged almost 17, 000 species, and almost nine hundred of them are completely new to science. Granted, most of them are bacteria, algae, and things like that, but they also have dozens of spiders, butterflies, insects, and beetles that have never before been identified. Remember, this is in the national park that has more visitors than any other, and it isn't all that big. It's only half a million acres."

Wertz thought a moment, and said, "By comparison, the Mount Hood National Forest covers about a thousand square miles. That's about a million acres. I guarantee that there are more than a few undiscovered species in a forest that size. No one has ever done an organized inventory like the ATBI around Mount Hood. There's probably quite a bit of undocumented biodiversity in any area that size. It's a bit of a surprise to find a creature as large as a snake, but it does happen from time to time."

Sam thought a minute, then paraphrased what the professor just said, "So, it is possible that there could be a unique species of snake that only lives in Squaw Meadow?"

"Absolutely. There's a species of salamander called the Larch Mountain Salamander that is found only on rocky slopes in certain areas around the Columbia River Gorge. If there's a species of snake that is unique to a certain area around here, they probably wouldn't be limited to just a certain meadow, but they might be limited to a certain habitat type within this region. Snakes are found in more habitat types than any other vertebrates on earth. You often find creatures, particularly snakes, that are endemic to very specific habitat types, especially if there is something unusual going on like hot springs, a cave system, or some unique type of bedrock or plant associations. Like the snail darter, there are many examples of fish, amphibians, and reptiles which are limited to specific river drainages or specific alpine locations."

"You actually see it a lot in the Pacific Northwest," the professor continued, "because we have so many chunks of mountain real estate that came from somewhere else. They may be part of the North American continent now, but they were once separate landmasses located somewhere off the Pacific Coast. They supported unique plant and animal communities when they were distant island volcanoes. Due to plate tectonics and the movement of the ocean crust, they became accreted, that is, added onto the North American continent after existing for millions of years as separate landmasses."

Wertz paused to let his words sink in with his visitors. "In geology they are known as Wrangelias, or displaced *terranes*. It's a technical term which is spelled differently than the familiar word 'terrain'. The first one of these to be identified in North America was the Wrangell Mountains in Alaska. There are many others that have been identified since then, including the Tillamook Highlands here in Oregon, the Willapa Hills and the Crazy Hills in Southwest Washington, the San Juan Islands in Puget Sound, the Olympic Peninsula, Vancouver Island, the list goes on and on. The most impressive displaced terrane in the region is probably the Siskiyou Mountains in Southern Oregon and Northern California. That displaced terrane is quite large and it has some very distinct rock types, so you find plant and animal associations that aren't found anywhere else. Squaw Butte and Goat Mountain are thought by some to be other examples of displaced terranes.

"At one time, we thought that about fifteen million years ago the entire Pacific Northwest was covered by lava flows. Now the thinking has changed and we're finding that everything wasn't covered by those enormous eruptions. More recently, we've found evidence that higher points of land like Squaw Butte are actually part of the ancient terrane that wasn't covered up. That would mean the plants and animals might have survived the eruption and even been free to spread out onto the barren landscape once the lava cooled and soil layers began to reform in the humid climate.

"It's a hard thing to be sure of since there are so few good rock exposures to study on those highlands. The climate is so wet around here that soil and vegetation effectively covers all the bedrock. Road cuts created during road construction are the only way to get fresh exposures of rock to study, but when an area is high elevation and essentially roadless, we never get to study fresh outcrops."

While digesting this information, Sam's mind continued to connect this new-found knowledge to his Squaw Meadow predicament. "Well, that brings us to the next question. Every pristine and unique area faces some kind of threat from exploitation and development. Where this snake came from on Squaw Meadow is no exception. Is it safe to assume that, if some unique creature were found up there, even something such as a lowly snake, then the area would be seen as critical habitat and therefore entitled to some kind of protection?"

"Oh, definitely. If word got out that Squaw Mountain was critical habitat for some rare species, it would essentially remove the place from consideration for just about every kind of development or use that might alter that critical habitat.

"Logging, road building, any of that stuff, forget it. The Endangered Species Act is one of the most powerful pieces of legislation ever enacted. Some tiny little creature can bring almost all forms of development to a screeching halt. The ESA is the most important weapon in the arsenal of those who oppose various types of development and resource extraction. Remember the spotted owl a few years back? That brought most logging in the national forests to a halt, at least temporarily. But, if you're concerned about what this snake would do to the area in which you found it, I wouldn't get too concerned until we actually verify that there is indeed a population of these guys up there."

"Oh, no," Sam said quickly. "I'm more on the other side of the fence. I'm the last house on the road that leads to the meadow, and I have recently learned of plans to turn the meadow into a golf course and resort. But, truth be told, I didn't come down here with the thought that this snake had anything to do with my concern about these plans for the area."

Sam wondered whether his presence at the college was now going to be interpreted by the professor as an attempt to build a case for stopping a certain development.

"This is all a very weird and unexpected thing to be happening," confessed Sam. "I was absolutely certain that you would identify this snake at first glance and that would be that. The last thing I ever expected is that you would be telling me that we might have found a new species of snake. It just didn't seem possible. I was only bringing this down here because I thought it would be a good experience for Jack to meet the experts and learn a few things about snakes. Snakes have always been his passion. Ever since he could walk, all he wanted to do is catch snakes around our property, look at them, and release them. We were up at the meadow looking around a few days ago when my boy found this snake.

"It never occurred to me that it was anything out of the ordinary. I'm astounded."

Chapter 17

I T WASN'T FUN but it had to be done. Mowing the ball field on his property was a monotonous job. The late spring rains were winding down and the grass was long enough to hide errant baseballs. As Sam carved concentric circles with the mower, a loud thump came from the mower deck, then it stopped. Without hesitating, Sam shut the tractor engine off. He jumped off the tractor and reached into the mower deck in search of the baseball that jammed the mower blades. In a few minutes, the tattered baseball was pulled from the mower. As Sam threw it toward the backstop, he noticed his wife was walking purposefully in his direction. He sat down on the seat of the riding mower and waited for her arrival. Sam could tell from the deliberate nature of her walk that something was on her mind.

"We need to talk."

"I could tell," Sam thought to himself, though he didn't say anything. He just raised his eyebrows and prepared himself to do some listening.

"This whole bigfoot thing you're into is getting embarrassing. You know as well as I do that there are no secrets in a town this small. Well, today at the grocery store, I ran into Judy Foster and she told me you had created some problems for them with a certain lesson you ran a week ago. According to Judy, they're not the only family that is outraged by what you did in class—"

"The Fosters are pursuing a hidden agenda," he interrupted, "and character assassination appears to be one of their tactics. You know as well as I do what they're up to. They're trying to sell the community on their little money-making scheme, and it doesn't take a genius to figure out that we're a source of opposition. They want to marginalize us and they think they have a way to do it. It sounds like they're trying to portray us as kooks."

"Well, I'm not going to let *my* reputation in this community get dragged through the mud because of some agenda *you're* pursuing."

"Wait a minute! I thought *we* were opposed to the whole Squaw Meadow resort thing. I thought we were in this together."

"I've changed my mind. It's just not worth it. I don't have the stomach for a battle with the Fosters and all the other people who see this development as a good thing for the Redland community. We're certainly not in any position to single-handedly try and stop a major development that's orchestrated by the U.S. Forest Service and the area's leading citizen. Have you lost your mind?"

"Sound like you think I have. I thought I was trying to protect the public interest, not to mention our happy little home."

"What's more important?" The forcefulness of her tone was rising. It was starting to sound more like a fight than a discussion. "Forty fewer cars driving up our road every day, or supporting the economic development of our community? Has it occurred to you that the road will be a two lane, oil road, not the gravel trail we have now? Has it occurred to you that our land and our house will soar in value? We could sell this place for three times its current value."

"Whoa! Sounds like Judy Foster has really won you over. Did she convince you to join the Redland Chamber of Commerce, too? I don't know about you, but I don't want to see this place increase in value because I don't want to sell it. I thought the whole idea was to keep things like they are now, and stay right here, hopefully forever."

"Do you really expect me to live out here in the sticks for the rest of my life? Maybe to you it's some romantic forest, but to me it's the goddam sticks! I didn't want to move out here! It was you. Don't you remember?"

"I thought I did. I remember you saying that it didn't matter where we lived as long as we have each other, but now I'm hearing you say you don't want to live here anymore. Is this confrontation about my opposition to a development or your decision to make a new lifestyle choice? I like living here. I don't want to live anywhere else. When we moved out here, you said the same thing. It sounds like you don't feel that way, anymore."

"I'm tired of trying to live on a teacher's salary and a garden! You need a real job. A job that pays something. I want a new car. I want to travel. All we do is mow the stupid ball diamond, hoe weeds, and fix fences so the deer don't eat everything we raise. Not only doesn't it look like you'll never get a better job, but you're half way to getting fired from the job you have now because you had to bring up imaginary bigfoot tales in a middle school science class. Sam, it's just an Indian legend. There are no bodies, no bones, and no photographs that are worth a damn. When will you get it through your thick head that bigfoot is no more real than flying saucers and ghosts?"

"Even if it is imaginary, it's still a valid science lesson," he replied.

"That's where you're wrong," Grace shot back. "Don't you understand anything? Your job is on the line. Introducing a legend as science was crazy! It was stupid. No wonder the principal is so upset with you. You're teaching thirteen-year-olds, for God's sake. They don't know a pollywog from a newt, and you're bringing in a boogie man and calling it 'science.' I can't even go in the grocery store without being humiliated when people tell me what you did in class. Now, you have Jack believing that some slimy little snake is some big discovery. Who are you kidding? They've been living here for centuries and you think no one knows about them! What a joke."

Sam opened his mouth to defend himself, but then thought the better of it. Grace was fighting back tears. Anything Sam said would only make matters worse. Sam bit his lip. Grace tried to collect herself. Sam sat silently on the seat of the lawn tractor; shoulders slumped over and head down. Grace took a deep breath, and wiped her eyes with the back of her hand.

"Sam, this is about it for me. The way I'm treated in this community has become intolerable. I can't take it anymore. I'm about ready to get a divorce. You can sell this place to the Fosters for all I care. I want to live somewhere where I can raise the kids like kids, not like lab assistants to a mad man."

"We've had this discussion before. If you want to go, then take the kids and go. No, wait. Let them decide whether they want to go or stay. I'm not going anywhere, and I bet you Jack wants to stay here, too. He likes nature and he likes baseball, and that's what we have here. I'll figure out a way to keep the place. And as far as the whole Squaw Meadow deal, someone has to fight the Forest Service and Bart Foster. If no one else wants to, I will.

"Look," Sam continued. "They *want* to drive a wedge between you and me. You know the saying: Divide and conquer. They have us figured for chumps that they can eliminate. I'm not against all development, but the more I look at the specifics of their plan, the screwier it begins to look. You think I haven't thought of how it might affect our property value?"

"If I thought for a minute that Bart's plan for the meadow could work, I'd be for it, too. But every time I think about the details, it looks more short-sighted, if not completely unworkable. How are they going to get power up there? How will they get rid of the sewage? How are they going to build on the steep, unstable hillsides? How are they going to get people in and out of there in the winter? Their plan won't work, but the Forest Service doesn't care, because it's Bart's money, not theirs, that will be lost. Meanwhile, they just want the timber off that land. And to get it, all they have to do is make the opposition, namely me, look crazy, and it appears they're succeeding. Heck, maybe I'm even helping 'em. But I'm the only one who can see all the problems that they don't want the community to look at, because if they did, they would see that this whole plan *cannot* work.

"Now, as far as '*us*', all I can do is ask you to calm down. Give it a little more time before you decide to throw it all away. And, try not to let the gossip mill work on you. They're trying to get you excited. They're using you."

"I might win or I might lose," Sam concluded. "Either way, I'm okay with it, but I have to try. Meanwhile, all I can say is: don't panic. We'll get through this."

"You've already lost, but you're not taking the rest of us with you." Grace spat.

She turned around and stomped off in the direction of the house. Sam sat silently in the seat of the lawn tractor. He stared off in the direction of the woods. He shook his head, reached forward, turned the key, started the tractor, and kept mowing.

Chapter 18

HE COULDN'T SLEEP. It was 1:30 a.m. but his mind raced like it was the middle of the work day. Floods of thought often afflicted him and, rather than toss and turn in bed for hours, he would take nighttime walks around his five-acre property. He had created a system of trails over the years that made these midnight walks quite pleasant.

If the Zodiac glow and the urban halo from Portland were bright, he would wander trails in the neighboring National Forest. He never used a flashlight. He didn't even carry one. He knew the trails well enough that he didn't need one, and he observed many times in the past that the beam of a flashlight seemed to make the nocturnal woods go quiet.

The walks in the dark forest gave Sam a chance to not only collect his thoughts, but also to get some exercise after a day's work. He had come to enjoy and appreciate the peacefulness of his woods at night. Nighttime walks were one enjoyable aspect of living in the country, and Sam made a point to appreciate such things lest he forget why he moved to the country in the first place.

On this particular occasion, Sam had more thoughts and concerns than usual racing through his mind. He was thrilled with the unexpected outcome of the trip he and Jack had taken to Oregon State. He was trying to follow Dr. Wertz's advice and not get too excited about the snake they found. He kept reminding himself that it may not really be a brand new species.

The return to the meadow a few days later with the professor was also a disappointment. They spent a full day searching the most accessible edges of both lakes. They didn't see any snakes at all, but the weather was cool and they didn't have a boat to get to the more inaccessible places. Sam didn't mention anything about the grave up on the bench but he did show the professor how to navigate the trails that he and Nick used to get to and from the grassy point.

With the professor present, Jack released his snake at the spot on the grassy point where they found it. As soon as they released it, it made a beeline swim across the lake toward a large talus slope on the other side. They watched it and wondered if the snake was providing a clue as to its preferred habitat. But, having no boat, they were unable to follow it or take a closer look at the place where the talus slope met the lake's edge.

The professor observed that it was just the kind of rocky outcrop that was preferred by the Larch Mountain salamanders and they were a good example of a creature that had become adapted to a very specific habitat type.

According to the professor, large expanses of bare rock adjacent to alpine lakes provided a unique habitat type that was home to a number of equally unique creatures. The professor resolved to dispatch a couple of graduate students to conduct a very thorough search of the most inaccessible portions of the lake margin.

As Sam walked the trail around his homestead in the dark, he wondered what would happen if they did indeed find more snakes, thus verifying the existence of a new species. What would they name the new snake? That would be the fun part. What wouldn't be fun would be enduring the community's reaction to the news that some new spotted-owl style creature existed up there at Squaw Meadow, and maybe other places around the Clackamas River drainage.

What would happen to his remaining friendship with Bart Foster when Bart learned that Jack found the latest version of the snail darter that would ultimately be used to block his Squaw Mountain development? Would it be wise to let it be known that Jack was even involved in finding the new species of snake? Might there be some unforeseen negative repercussions that his son would have to endure? Making a new discovery might not be a positive thing, especially if the discovery had negative economic consequences for an already depressed timber town like Redland.

But it didn't seem fair to deny Jack the chance to feel some well-deserved pride for his scientific achievement. It was hardly a thing to keep under wraps. Sam's brain reeled with conflicts and concerns as he quietly strolled the trail that encircled the perimeter of his property.

The sky was heavily overcast but the light of the gibbous moon penetrated the cloud cover, enabling Sam to see the trail and find his footing without a flashlight. Regardless, he was very familiar with the trails so he could easily stay on the path, despite the dark, simply by feeling for the firmer ground with his feet. Whenever the ground felt spongy or littered with sticks, he redirected his steps until he could again feel the firmer ground of the trail.

Soon, Sam could make out the faint outline of the small bridge over the creek ahead. The bridge was really just a long plank deck over a spring creek, so he walked very slowly, feeling with his feet as he went so he didn't step off the side into the water.

He successfully negotiated the bridge with the help of the moon's faint light. Once he got to the other side of the bridge, he was in the darkest, thickest, favorite part of his woods. It was this primeval patch of woods that impressed Sam when he and Grace were looking at this property ten years ago. It was dense and lush to the point of being jungle-like. The maples and cedars that managed to stay rooted on the steep, unstable slope were draped with curtains of moss that hung from their branches like leather fringe on the sleeves of a Davy Crockett-style jacket. The trail Sam built followed the base of a steep slope that led to the mountainous highlands around Squaw Meadow. If one were to head up the hill and keep going, one could travel for many days before crossing another road. The slope faced north, preventing the sun from ever penetrating to the forest floor.

As Sam crept along the trail at the base of the hill, he was suddenly surprised by the sound of breaking sticks from high up on the hill above him. He froze and strained to hear. Deer were a constant presence on his property, especially during the summer when his garden and his apple orchard presented an irresistible feeding opportunity for these nighttime fruit and vegetable bandits. Sam assumed that he was hearing the cautious approach of his deer herd as it worked its way toward his garden under cover of darkness.

He strained to hear more. The cracking of sticks grew closer, and as it did, it took on the distinct sound of walking. More surprising to Sam, it seemed like a single creature, and it seemed to display the 'crash-crash' cadence of a two-footed creature, not the 'clippitty-clop' of four legs. Still more surprising, the moving creature was heading directly toward Sam's position. He had surprised deer in the woods countless times before and when he had, they invariably fled the scene.

But this time Sam sensed things were different. As he silently stood on the darkened trail, the footfalls continued to grow louder and nearer. Still thinking it must be a deer that had not noticed him, Sam decided he should step off the trail so the deer didn't walk right into him. The thought that it might be a buck with a large set of sharp antlers concerned Sam. He knew that such a beast could use its antlers to gore him against a tree.

He wasn't going to take any chances. He stepped off the trail for the protection of the nearest tree. Clumsily, he stumbled over a large sword fern. As he fell forward, he hugged the darkened form of a maple tree beside the trail. There, Sam stood and waited for the deer, or whatever it was, to walk on past him on the trail that he just vacated.

Sam couldn't help making noise as he stepped off of the trail into the leaves and fern, but now that he was behind the tree, he could silently wait and listen. The woods had fallen completely silent. Sam waited patiently for the creature to make the next move. Nothing stirred. He stood against the tree and listened for what seemed like a very long time, but was probably less than ten minutes. He became impatient, wondering whether the motion and whatever caused it, was really as close to him as it sounded. Sam waited a few more minutes and finally decided that whatever it was, had left.

He cautiously stepped back on the trail. He paused and listened again for stirrings and heard none. He regained his confidence and began to once again make his way along the trail in the dark. He crept ahead another fifty yards and came to a bench that he had long ago placed in this charming spot beneath a cedar tree where the two trails converged. Sam was fond of the spot because it was in the coolest, shadiest part of the forest surrounding his house. It was also directly beneath a gracefully curved cedar tree, right next to a small spring that seeped fresh water from the base of the steep hillside.

As he approached the bench, he again heard the unmistakable sound of footfalls that were making no attempt to be stealthy. Whatever it was, it crashed loudly through the underbrush, once again moving precisely in the direction of his new position. What surprised him the most was all the noise that the creature was making. It almost seemed too loud. It was moving along a trail that was generally free of sticks and leaves but it still managed to make a considerable racket as it moved closer. It also sounded very close; now only twenty-five feet or less from him.

Still half convinced that it was a deer from the sounds it made, Sam again tried to get out of the creature's way. He stepped up onto the split-log bench beside the trail.

He stood on the bench, doing his best to crouch close to the cedar tree that grew out of the steep hillside. As he tried to conceal himself behind the tree, the footfalls continued to approach closer and closer. Sam grew tense and instinctively hugged the tree. It seemed from the approaching noise that whatever it was out there was heading right for him! A collision seemed imminent. From the sound of the approaching footfalls, it was now terrifyingly close... less than ten feet from where Sam was perched, standing on the bench, hugging the smooth bark of the cedar tree. Just when it sounded like it was close enough to touch it, the approaching noises of footfalls came to an abrupt halt. Sam was frozen, petrified with fear. He peered into the night, trying to distinguish at least an outline of the form that was now right in front of him.

Strangely, Sam couldn't see a thing. The forest seemed to be impossibly dark, so dark that Sam couldn't make out the outline of a tree or even the sky, much less the outline of whatever creature was just out of arms reach and apparently standing silently in front of him, watching him.

The sudden deepening of darkness was perplexing. A few minutes ago he could see the outline of trees and the sky at the top of the steep hillside behind him. Now, he couldn't see anything, not even his own hand in front of his face. At this point, he was wishing he had a flashlight, not only to see what this thing was, but also because he was terrified and hoped to just scare it away.

Then it occurred to him that he did have with him a means of making light, although a very faint one. His digital wristwatch had a tiny light on the face of it. Sam slowly raised his left arm and pointed the face of his wristwatch at the invisible form that seemed to be standing silently in the middle of the trail only a few feet from the bench on which he was standing.

He pushed the button while aiming the watch face in the direction of the silent form. His plan was a failure. The light wasn't helping. He wasn't even sure the light was on. In any event, it didn't throw out the light he was hoping for. He continued peering intently into the inky blackness, trying to make out any shape at all in the woods in front of him. Silence prevailed, but suddenly Sam was aware of a noise within. It was his pounding heart.

At that point, he didn't really feel fear, just confusion. Somehow, he calmed himself a little. He was certain something was right in front of him but he couldn't see a thing. He was squinting as hard as he could to distinguish any kind of form or motion. There was absolutely no noise or motion to suggest that something was even there. Sam found himself questioning his perceptions. Maybe nothing was there and he was somehow mistaken about the nearness of the noises he was hearing.

Suddenly, everything changed. From directly behind his left ear came the sound of a sneeze! Sam jumped out of his skin! He whirled around, still holding his hand on the button of his wristwatch. Sam was now pointing the wristwatch behind him, as if to illuminate the surroundings enough to see what it was that was now behind him.

There he stood, frozen, on a bench in a darkened forest pointing his wristwatch at unseen animals that were making perplexing noises. He didn't budge until he was suddenly struck by the absolute absurdity of his situation: surrounded by unseen creatures in the midnight forest, the only move he could muster to defend himself is to raise his twelve dollar Casio wristwatch and point its feeble light at the unseen form like it was some sort of ray gun. At that moment, all Sam could think about was how silly he must look, standing on a bench, cowering behind a tree and pointing his wrist watch first at one unseen creature in front of him, and yet another one behind him.

No matter where Sam looked, he saw nothing. He felt surrounded. He'd had enough. He jumped off the bench and ran from both noises, down the trail, over the creek and back toward his house. In the black of night, he stumbled but caught himself before he fell flat.

It was too dark to run. Sam forced himself to gingerly feel his way along with his feet. Although he had found his way through these woods countless times in the past, Sam now had great difficulty seeing the plank bridge and portion of the trail that led out of the woods, across the ball field and back to his house; his safe log home.

After slow, careful, feeling and stepping, Sam finally arrived at the house, panting. He sat down on the deck chair outside the side door to unlace his boots. As he did so, a cackling, shrieking, almost laughter-like sound arose from the woods from whence he had come. It was loud and penetrating; so loud that it was heard inside the house. Sam looked up and saw a light go on in the bedroom window. Sam hurried into the house to see if his wife was alarmed by the sudden noise.

Despite the late hour, Sam was surprised to find Grace sitting up in bed. Her eyes were wide with surprise and even a bit of fright. She sighed with relief at the sight of Sam.

"What the heck is that noise?" she asked sharply as soon as he walked into the room. Long, sharp cackles at regular intervals could be clearly heard through the open window.

"I have absolutely no idea, but it just chased me out of the woods. Whatever it is, it isn't a coyote, or anything else we've ever heard before."

"Yes," was the only reply Grace could manage.

Sam didn't know what to say. He was completely bewildered by the noise they were hearing, not to mention his entire experience of the last twenty minutes. The concern showing in his wife's plaintive eyes suggested that she looked to Sam for some kind of explanation. He had none. He just shrugged and silently turned around, then went back outside to finish taking off his boots.

Sam stepped out the door, back onto the deck outside the washroom, and sat on the chair to finish unlacing his boots. Just as suddenly as it began, the warm, summer night returned to silence. The cackling laughter, or whatever it was, suddenly stopped. Sam briefly considered going back to the bench in the woods with a flashlight to see what he could make of it, but fear was still the overriding emotion that swirled through his tired brain. It was now close to 2:30 a.m. He'd had enough excitement for one night. He decided to just finish taking off his boots and go to bed.

Chapter 19

HENRY STRODE INTO Sam's classroom smiling. Sam jumped up from his desk to greet him.

"Hi, Henry, I really appreciate you coming by."

"Happy to help out, Mr. Ward. Iris told me that you had some questions you wanted to ask me. She said you had something happen to you that might be sasquatch-related."

"Yes, I did. In fact, I've had lots of things happen. You see, I've been looking into this whole sasquatch thing and I've run into some weird circumstances that I thought you might be able to help me sort out."

"Go on."

"Well, for one thing, I think it's possible that I found a grave. Have you ever heard of anything like that before?"

"Not really, but they have to die somewhere, I suppose. Is it somewhere around here?"

"Yes, it's up by Squaw Meadow."

"I wouldn't mess with it if I were you. They're very powerful beings. My people also say they live for a very long time, but they do die, and when they do, I trust that their brethren dispose of the remains in some respectful manner.

"How long do they live?"

"At least as long as we do. Probably a lot longer."

"Okay, here's the weirdest part. I went back to this place I found with another guy. We dug into it—"

"Uh-oh."

"...It was tightly stacked rocks and we tried to uncover whatever we thought was in it. We didn't get far. First, mosquitoes drove us off, then we got a flat tire. We planned to go back and probe the rock stack some more the next day, but that night both of us had these nightmares that were so horrible that it changed our plans. Instead of going back to dig some more, we put back every one of those stones exactly as we found them. The funny thing is that there weren't any mosquitoes the next day when we returned. I can't tell anybody else all of this because they think I'm crazy already. I need somebody to tell me that I'm not imagining this stuff."

"Like I said, they're very powerful beings."

"So you're saying they can control insects, and people's dreams?"

"And a whole lot more," came the answer. "But you don't need *me* to tell *you* that these things can happen. Sounds like you found that out for yourself or we wouldn't be talking right now."

"So, I'm not crazy?"

"You're crazy for messing with that grave, but are you imagining things by way of the repercussions for messing with the grave? No, you're not. But you are also lucky, because they're not always nice. If you had asked me what to do when you found the grave, I would have told you to leave it alone. But you would have always wondered whether I was telling the truth. If you ask me, you're lucky to be alive, Mr. Ward. They could have easily killed a couple of dumb asses like you two. I wonder why they didn't. They must have plans for you…" His voice trailed off, and then he looked Mr. Ward right in the eyes with a penetrating stare.

The teacher felt slightly uncomfortable. He looked down at the floor and shrugged sheepishly. He felt foolish about the escapades he just confessed to.

The elderly Indian sensed the awkwardness. He shrugged, then continued, "Just as well, because now you got what I would call a gentle reminder to not defile their sacred locations. Putting back that grave was the smartest move you ever made. Don't ever go back and disturb that spot again. They seem to have the ability to enter our lives, if they see fit. They can cause very positive things to happen in your life, or very negative ones. I would not give them a reason to cause negative things to happen. Remember what I said last time I was here. To use a baseball analogy, they can throw you a fat pitch or they can throw the ball right at your head and put you face down in the dirt.

"To put it another way, they don't drop money in your path but they will lead you down a beneficial trail, or they can lead you right off a cliff. My people are taught to treat them with great respect. We acknowledge their unseen presence. We leave them offerings and recognize their power. And whatever one does, one must not do something that would make such powerful beings angry. It isn't an easy thing to do, but I think that stunt with the grave would certainly do it."

Chapter 20

AN UNFAMILIAR, DUST-COVERED sedan rolled to a stop in Sam's driveway. Sam and Jack stopped their batting practice to see who it was. The driver's side door opened and Dr. Wertz, the Oregon State reptile expert stepped out. He looked around and saw the pair playing baseball at the far end of the property. He waved. Satisfied that he was in the right place, Dr. Wertz re-entered his car and shut of the engine as Sam and Jack walked across the field to greet their unexpected guest.

Sam extended his hand as he approached Dr. Wertz.

"Hi, Sam. Hope it's okay that I showed up uninvited. I was on my way back from Squaw Meadow and I saw your driveway. I took a chance on catching you at home."

"I'm glad you did. I've been meaning to call you and see whether you had a chance to go back up there and scout around some more for snakes. I didn't want to bug you but

I've been dying to hear whether you've been up there since the day we went together.

"Yeah, I just took a graduate student up there this morning. His name is Jim Marshall. He's still up there. He plans to look around for anywhere from a few hours to a few days."

"Does he have a boat?"

"Yeah, he has a canoe, so he can get around the lakes as much as he needs to."

"That'll really help him. Did you show him that huge talus slope on the other side of the lake? I would encourage him to paddle over there and look around where the big rocks at the base of the slope sit in the water. That seems like the best snake habitat to me. Plus, it's on the far side of the lake where people don't generally go, so I would expect things to be a little less disturbed over there."

"Good point. We didn't really get a chance to do too much exploring before it was time for me to leave. It took us a little longer than I expected just to get up there and find the meadows. We took a wrong turn at the sign that said Raccoon Ridge. We ended up at Grouse Point before I realized that we'd taken a wrong turn."

"Yeah, you have to stay right. There used to be a sign saying Squaw Meadow to the left. The sign's been gone for a few years now. Someone stole it, just like they steal most of the other signs up there. You wish they would just shoot holes in them and leave 'em there, like they did in the old days."

"Well, we finally figured it out. Anyway, Jim is up there now. I told him about you and your son, and we saw your driveway on our way up there this morning, so he knows where you are. I just wanted him to know somebody in the area in case he has a car problem or something. I showed him where you live. Was that okay? I'm hoping we can rely on you as resource... a local contact in case we need one."

"Oh, absolutely. If there's anything at all I can do to support the project, just let me know. Obviously, I want to see you guys succeed, but I also understand that you have to do things a certain way. Just let me know if you need anything. Otherwise, I'll leave you alone."

"Thanks, we really appreciate that. Jim will be coming and going for the next few weeks."

"No problem. Have him stop in and say hello. We'll be glad to meet him. So no sign of any snakes yet, I assume?"

"Nope, but we just turned him loose today. He'll be joined by two more grad students when they get into town for the summer term. Generally, reptiles are most active in early summer around here because that's the mating season. If we don't find anything by the fourth of July, then our chances of success diminish. Mating season is usually over by early July, at which point daylight, and diurnal activity, falls off markedly. That's why we got up here as soon as we could. Anyway, I have to be back in Corvallis by three o'clock, so I have to get going."

"If there's anything I can do to help, just ask."

"You know, if you happen to get a chance to show the grad students around the meadow up there, it would be a big help. The two gals that have yet to arrive are not from this area. They could use a little help getting familiar with their new surroundings."

"I'll keep my eye out for them."

"Thanks, I appreciate it." Dr. Wertz got back in his car and started the engine, backed out of the parking area, turned around on the grass and drove off. Sam and Jack waved good-bye. Then they went back to their baseball practice.

As they walked back to the baseball diamond, Sam looked down at Jack and said, "It'll be interesting to see what happens if that grad student Wertz took up there decides to spend the night. Bigfoot or no bigfoot, Squaw Meadow is a spooky place to be camping all alone."

The next morning was a sunny Saturday. The Wards were eating breakfast. Jack was wearing his baseball uniform. His baseball mitt and cleats were neatly placed on the bench outside the door. A van rolled in the driveway with a big green fiberglass canoe on top of it. Sam turned and looked out the window without getting up. One glance at the car was all he needed. "That must be the graduate student Dr. Wertz mentioned."

"How can you tell?" his wife wondered.

"Dr. Wertz said he had a canoe. I wonder what he wants."

Sam took his coffee cup with him as he got up from the table. He went outside the door and waited on the porch as the man slowly got out of his van. He was a tall, lanky fellow with chin whiskers, a thin mustache, and a ponytail holding back shoulder-length mane of straight brown hair. His eyes were red and he had faint circles under his eyes. He smiled and waved at Sam once he noticed him standing on the porch sipping his coffee.

The man spoke in a tired, yet cheerful voice. "Hello, you must be Sam Ward."

"Yeah. Jim, right? I talked to Russell Wertz yesterday. He said you were up at Squaw Meadow. I take it you stayed the night. How were the mosquitoes up there?"

"Pretty bad," Jim replied as he extended a hand toward Sam. "I tried to sleep out, but I had to move into the van before long. It's nice to meet you. Are you the one who found the snake up there?"

"Well, actually, it was my son who found the snake, but yes, I brought it to Russell Wertz once we realized it wasn't in any of the field guides. Any luck so far?"

"No. I was hoping you could show me where you guys found it so that I can narrow the search."

"I'd be happy to, but we have a baseball game to go to in an hour. If I were to go up there with you, it'll have to be either this afternoon or tomorrow. I could show you on a map and get you pretty close. I don't suppose you have a map of the area."

"Yeah, I have a map. Hold on."

He returned to his van and reached in the open window on the driver's side. He pulled a folded small scale topographical map from behind the sun visor. He carried the map back to the porch and handed it to Sam.

Sam unfolded the map and pointed. "We were picnicking on this point of land right here on the west side of the big lake. We were on foot so we made our way along the edge of the lake. Since you have a boat, you could just paddle right to the spot and save yourself a lot of trouble. Anyway, it was this point of land right here. If you don't have any luck, you might paddle across the lake and look on this opposite shore. These are rock cliffs and big boulders that go right to the water's edge. Not only is this area good habitat, but people can't get to it on foot, so it's the most undisturbed part of this lakeshore."

"That's great. That helps a lot," Jim said.

"Are you going back up there today? I might be able to meet you up there after our baseball game," Sam offered.

"I have to go home and check on my cats and take care of some stuff, but I was hoping to go back tomorrow for a couple of days. It's a pretty area up there. I like it a lot, but I didn't get much sleep last night."

"Oh, really?"

"Yeah, um, it's kind of embarrassing. See, it wasn't really the mosquitoes that drove me into the van last night. There was somebody prowling around my camp."

"Indeed," Sam said.

"Yeah. At first I heard some stirring in the bushes while I was organizing my camp after dinner. I figured it was just squirrels or chipmunks. But later, when I was in my sleeping bag, I heard lots of crashing around in the bushes. Whatever it was, it sounded pretty big. It almost seemed like it was making more noise than it needed to, like it was trying to scare me. I thought it might be a bear, so I decided to sleep in the van. I moved to the van so fast I left one of my coolers outside."

"So, I'm lying there in my sleeping bag with the window open on the passenger side, and I hear something come right up to the van. I could hear the crunching of footsteps. It came in really close. It sounded like it was right outside the van. That's when I remembered that I left a cooler out there. Well, I wasn't about to go get it. No way. It was really spooky. I could hear something moving around out there and it sounded like it was walking on two feet. I could hear the crunch-crunch of footsteps. Every time I moved a little bit inside the van, it would stop for a moment, then it would move again. At one point, I felt the van wiggle like it touched the van or it leaned against it. When that happened, I was really freaked! I laid there for hours, listening. I think I finally fell asleep around 3:30 or 4.

"Then, this morning, when I got up, I noticed the cooler was open, but everything was still inside the cooler. The only things that were missing from the cooler were two chocolate bars. They were right on top when I went to bed. I'm sure of it, because I had three of them, and I ate one last night after dinner. I left the other two in the cooler. In the morning, they were gone. Everything else was untouched."

"Interesting. Anything else happen that was out of the ordinary?"

"Well, maybe just one other thing. While I was looking around the smaller lake, I walked into this one area where I was suddenly overwhelmed by the most powerfully bad smell you can imagine. I thought maybe there was a dead animal around but I couldn't find anything. The smell was so bad I had to get the hell outta there. It made me a little sick to my stomach. It was right before I was going to make dinner and I totally lost my appetite. I had to go lie down for a while before I felt well again. I never did see what made the smell, but I wasn't going to hang around and keep looking. It was so strong it was almost incapacitating. I never smelled anything quite that bad before."

"So, what do you make of it?" Sam inquired.

"I really don't know. Do you think maybe the place is haunted?"

"Maybe. I guess you might see if it happens again."

"I'm not sure I want to. I was wondering when I come back if I might park my van in your field and sleep there the first night. I didn't get much sleep up there last night."

"Well, sure. If it helps any, you're certainly free to camp right over there." Sam gestured toward the open area between the woods and the backstop. There's a water spigot right there behind the backstop and you can use that picnic table for cooking and eating."

"Thanks. I suppose I'll try and sleep up there tomorrow night, but if you look out and see me parked in your field when you get up in the morning, you'll know what happened."

Chapter 21

≈

FOUR DAYS LATER, Jim Marshall's blue van rolled to a stop in the noon day sun at the Squaw Meadow parking area, overtaken an instant later by the dust-cloud that the van spewed as it rumbled up the unpaved Squaw Mountain Road. The engine stopped and the driver's side door opened. Jim stepped from the vehicle and stretched. He turned around and looked up the hill that he had just descended. The dust that followed his vehicle's path began to clear just as another dust-plume appeared at the top of the hill. Jim stood staring in the direction of the approaching dust plume, which turned into another vehicle that approached the parking area. An older, white Porsche 911 sports car with an open roof rolled to a stop behind Jim's van. Another plume of dust engulfed the parking area as the engine of the Porsche stopped. Two young women in sunglasses smiled at Jim as he waved a hand in front of his face in mock objection to the cloud of that dust settled around him. A black dog with a small body and tall pointed ears sat in the center of the small back seat of the Porsche, tongue hanging out and panting rapidly.

The doors of the Porsche opened; the dog jumped out and ran a circle around both cars, stopping to lift a leg on the front tire of Jim's van. Then the dog paused, stuck its nose in the air, sniffed, and then sprinted over to the water's edge where it lapped up large gulps of water. As the dog drank from the pond, an attractive young lady with a thick head of very black, shoulder-length hair disembarked from the driver's side of the Porsche. She watched the dog carefully as it stopped drinking and dashed off along the shore of the lake, disappearing in the undergrowth that occupied the shoreline.

"Elvis! Come!" shouted the young lady in the direction of the departing dog. A moment later, the energetic dog reappeared and dashed up to the young lady who stood next to her open car door, wearing shorts that flattered her slender legs. Her sandals revealed brightly painted red toenails.

"Good dog, Elvis. You stay!" she commanded. The dog, ignoring her command, trotted off with its nose low to the ground, following a scent into the brush on the other side of the road. The dog again vanished into the brush.

"Elvis! Come!" shouted the slender woman as she tipped her sunglasses up on top of her head. There was no sign of the dog. She looked in Jim's direction and saw a look of concern behind his sunglasses. She flashed a nervous smile at him, showing a set of bright white teeth that seemed to glisten in the bright noonday sun.

"Sorry about the dog. I'm Molly. Molly McKay. I assume you're Jim. Dr. Wertz said you'd be here. This is my friend

Emily," Molly said, gesturing toward the passenger seat of the car. A long bare arm waved through the open roof of the dusty Porsche.

"I heard. I mean, I know... I mean, Hi, I'm Jim," he stammered.

Jim was thoroughly taken aback. In the middle of this hot, barren patch of dust appear two pretty girls, a hyperactive black Labrador puppy, and a white Porsche. Jim thought to himself that he'd never before seen such straight, even teeth. Molly's appearance stood in stark contrast to the roadway. Her eyebrows were perfectly plucked and highlighted with eyebrow pencil. Her teeth were bright, big, and perfectly straight. Her lips shone of bright red lipstick. Her toenails were the same shade of red as her lipstick. Her tank top was a paler red, which contrasted neatly with her white shorts. A gray, rolled up sweatshirt was draped casually around her neck and her sunglasses were perched atop her head where they held back her straight black, shoulder-length hair.

While Molly looked like she stepped off a page of a fashion magazine, she certainly didn't look like she was ready to go tearing through the brush in search of elusive snakes. It was a bit of a shock for Jim to see a woman wearing any make up at all in such a remote and dusty place. Then there was the dog...the now missing dog. Molly let out a shrill whistle in the direction that the dog had disappeared, then strode over to the edge of the road where she peered intently into the thick brush. She pondered the situation for a moment before carefully stepping into the thicket and disappearing. Jim winced at the thought of what was about to happen as tender, bare skin met the thorny thicket. He decided to say nothing and let natural consequences play out.

Meanwhile, the other female, Emily, began to budge from the passenger side of the white sports car. Her door opened and she stepped slowly out of the car and stretched. She was taller and thinner than Molly, with exceptionally long legs. Her skin was pale and freckles dotted her small, curled nose. Her wavy brown hair was tied back in a high ponytail that accentuated her long, slender neck. She wasn't wearing any make up, but her high cheekbones and upturned nose were eye-catching enough. She wore khaki shorts and a white, short-sleeve canvas shirt with epaulets on the shoulders. Contrasting Molly's flip-flops, Emily wore low hiking boots and thick socks.

Although she was no less fashionable than her friend, Jim was relieved to see that Emily's outfit looked a lot more appropriate for camping, although Molly certainly did an expert job of looking good. Jim wasn't sure whether he should be grateful or outraged at the grad-students Dr. Wertz found to send him. When he told Dr. Wertz he'd appreciate the help surveying Squaw Meadow, he never expected a pair like this.

After overcoming his initial surprise, Jim was able to see a positive side to this situation. "This might work out well after all," Jim thought to himself. "I might not find a new snake species, but camping out with this Molly and Emily pair will be a welcome change."

Despite their good looks, these undeniably attractive women didn't really look like experienced campers. On the bright side, the weather was warm and clear, and Jim had a van full of camping gear. At least the company in camp would be more interesting than it was last week when he was up here all alone.

Jim thought of himself as a tough, experienced, and knowledgeable scientist. He sometimes fancied himself as the zoological equivalent of Indiana Jones. But now, with two poorly prepared, overdressed young ladies, the picture suddenly changed to something closer to an episode of 'Dukes of Hazard.'

As Jim pondered where to begin, Molly miraculously reappeared from the brush, dragging Elvis, the gangly-legged black Lab puppy, by the collar. She was remarkably unscathed after her foray into the underbrush. She dragged the dog over to the Porsche and reached in the back seat and produced a leather leash. She clipped the leash onto the dog's collar and breathed a sigh of relief as she leaned against the dusty car.

"Quite the energetic puppy you got there. I take it he's not used to being in the woods," Jim said, trying to be polite but expressing his concern.

"I know. It's my boyfriend's dog. He's out of town all week, and when I agreed to watch his dog, there was no camping in the plan. This all came together quite suddenly. Yesterday, Dr. Wertz told me another graduate student had to drop out of summer quarter for health reasons. He said he needed a replacement to help survey some meadows for reptiles. He offered to give me four hours of practicum credit, which I really need if I'm going to finish my degree program on time. I didn't know it was going to be way out here. I told Dr. Wertz about the dog. He said I should let you decide...Do you think Elvis will be okay if I keep him tied up in camp all day?" Molly smiled a sweet but slightly nervous smile as she held the dog firmly by the leash.

Jim didn't appreciate being put on the spot and his immediate reaction was that this was a bad idea, although it certainly was difficult to say 'no' to a woman with such a pretty smile. He had no stomach for being hard-nosed and, except for the dog, he thought that these two would be an amusing change from the usual earthy grad students.

"I guess we can give it a try," Jim decided. "But, I can't be responsible if the dog gets lost or gets into a tangle with a wild animal. Whatever happens, it's up to you to manage the dog. Agreed?"

"Agreed," Molly said, with a look of relief.

"What kind of wild animals are up here?" Emily asked in a concerned tone.

"All kinds. This is the national forest."

"I'm really afraid of bears."

Now Jim was beginning to feel a bit overwhelmed. "Who in God's name," he wondered, "would come into to the wilds of the Cascade Mountains if they were afraid of bears?" He paused long enough to conceal his impatience with the question. Then he shrugged.

"I've only been up here for a few days, myself. I haven't seen any bears, but I know they are up here. But what's the big deal? There's bear almost everywhere. They're just black bears. They're no real threat. Black bears are big chickens. They won't mess with you unless you start feeding them. Mountain lions are a lot more dangerous than bears."

"That was my next question."

"Well, if you're worried about cougars OR bears, maybe that dog is a good idea after all. If anything comes around, he should be the first to know it. I think the local wildlife is a bit more likely to steer clear of our camp as long as he's around. He turned to Molly. "Did I hear you say his name was 'Elvis'?"

"That's right, Elvis the Dog. That's his name, not that he answers to it. But don't worry; I'll keep an eye on him. He's actually a good dog once he gets used to his surroundings. Do you know where you want to camp?" Molly asked.

"Yeah, just around that bend up ahead is a road that takes off to the left. It dead-ends at a camp spot just a short way in. It's right by the lake. It's great, as long as the mosquitoes aren't too bad."

"What about bears," Emily asked again. "Do you think there are any bears there, next to the lake?"

"Like I said before, I only camped here last week, but I didn't see any bears or bear sign." Jim flashed on the disturbing night he spent, wondering what was outside his tent and going through his cooler after he retreated to the safety of his van. He wasn't about to bring that up, but he did feel a sudden pang of pity for the fearful female he was attempting to reassure. "If they only knew…" he thought to himself.

"I brought some bear spray just in case," Emily said. "Do you think this will be enough?" Emily held up a quart-sized aerosol can of bear repellant.

"Wow! I didn't know they put that stuff in such a big can. That looks like a lifetime supply. Yeah, I'd say we're okay on bear repellent. Man, I gotta admit, you two crack me up. This situation is getting comical. Here I am in the wilderness with two girls with red toe nail polish; a Porsche, a dog named Elvis, and a quart can of bear spray. This is starting to feel like I'm in a Fellini movie."

"My toe nails aren't red," Emily objected, pointing to her hiking boots. Molly flashed her bright white teeth and blushed.

"You two *do* know we're supposed to be up here looking for some kind of snake, don't you?" Jim asked.

"Yeah we know that," Emily said. "Snakes are fine. I know there aren't any venomous snakes in western Oregon. It's only the bears that I'm afraid of."

"Black bears don't eat people. They're not even aggressive. They're basically cowards around people. Grizzly bears are a different story, but they aren't even found in Oregon." Jim explained.

"I know. I just have this phobia about bears. When I was a kid we went camping in Glacier National Park once and my dad sat around the campfire all evening reading us stories of grizzly bear attacks. He scared us to death. Ever since then, whenever I go camping, all I can think about is bears," Emily said.

"Your dad should be fed to the grizzly bears for doing that to you. What was the guy thinking? Taking the kids to Glacier National Park of all places, then scaring them to death with stories of bear mutilations? That's cruel. Anyway, I should think you have nothing to fear around here by way of bears as long as we keep our food put away at night. Bigfoot, maybe, but no bears."

"Very funny," Emily smiled. "There's no such thing as a bigfoot."

"You shouldda been here last week," Jim said.

"Now you're just trying to scare me," Emily said.

"And it's not gonna work. We're not falling for any bigfoot crap. We're not that stupid." Molly scolded playfully.

Jim only smiled. "If they only knew..." he thought to himself.

He began untying the canoe from the top of his van. "Well, gang, as you know, we have a job to do here. We're supposed to try and work our way around the lake in search of snakes. Maybe we should get our camp set up first, have some lunch, then spend the afternoon surveying the lake margins from the canoe. We might need to leave one person in camp, especially since you have a dog."

"I think we could leave the dog tied up in camp if we're not gone too long," Molly said. "Then maybe one of us could survey on foot."

"I'm not going to survey alone on foot. I'll help in the canoe," Emily volunteered.

"Me, too!" Molly said. Then she looked at Jim and smiled. "Whaddya say, Jim. You willing to trust us with your canoe?"

"My God! What a bunch of chickens! Do you even know how to paddle a canoe?"

"Sure," Molly insisted. "What's to know?"

"Oh, great. Instant experts. Just add water," Jim said in an amused way. He was beginning to warm up to his inexperienced but lively graduate students.

"C'mon Jimbo," Emily said. "You're the big outdoorsman. You'd do a better job getting around the lake on foot. We'd be better off in the boat where you can keep an eye on us from shore. We can't get lost in the canoe, and we'll be safe from bears out there."

"Ever get the feeling you're being manipulated?" Jim asked sarcastically.

"I suppose it makes sense to put you two in the boat. But, we set up camp, first." As he worked to untie the ropes he muttered loud enough for them to hear, "The way I see it, I'll be protecting *the bears* from *you two*."

The girls giggled. Then Jim added, "Promise me you'll keep your lifejackets on and stay out of the middle of the lake."

"You got a deal, Jimbo," Molly said in a playful tone, flashing another big smile.

Again, Jim marveled at the radiance of her smile. He thought to himself, "It's worth it to let them have the canoe, just to see that smile."

Warming up to his company, he thought, "I might even enjoy the next couple days."

After an hour of steady work, the crew had their camp set up. They had lawn chairs and a folding table, a camp stove, a lantern, two tents, and a pile of firewood. They were ready to start surveying for snakes. It was a big job and Jim wasn't entirely sure how to go about it. If the girls could accomplish anything by way of surveying, it would be a bonus, but Jim decided he wouldn't count on a meaningful contribution from them: one with painted toe nails, perfect hair, and a pretty smile, and the other one looking gorgeously outdoorsy but harboring an exaggerated fear of bears.

The more he thought about it, the better off they seemed in the canoe. They couldn't get lost and most of the lake was too shallow to drown in. He was looking forward to the company at camp just in the event things got spooky again like they did last week. The more he thought about it, the more the dog seemed like a godsend.

Elvis the Dog was tied to a small tree in the center of camp, well away from the Tupperware bins that contained their food. Then Jim escorted the girls to the canoe that he portaged beside the lake. Jim helped the girls properly fit their lifejackets and get situated in the canoe. He explained that the steering would be Molly's responsibility since she was sitting in the stern. Emily would generally provide forward propulsion, paddling on the opposite side of the canoe from the side that Molly favored. This would allow the canoe to go straight, or 'track' across the water.

Jim warned them that if they both paddle on the same side of the canoe, they would only go in circles. The girls laughed as Jim pushed the canoe away from shore and they began to paddle. Sure enough, the canoe immediately began to travel in a large circle. The girls giggled as they struggled to coax the boat into taking a straight path. Jim reminded Molly that it was up to her to steer the boat by trailing her paddle, using it as a rudder. Molly reached back with her paddle and put it in the water, then looked at Jim over her shoulder.

"Like this?" she shouted.

A bit anxiously, Jim called back, "Yeah, now just hold it there and wait. It takes a second or two for the canoe to respond."

A moment later the canoe was traveling a straight-line course.

"Hey, I think I got it!" Molly announced proudly, and off they voyaged across the lake. Jim stood on the shore, watching in silence, as the pair in the canoe got smaller in his field of vision. The two ladies in the canoe didn't look back. Jim never took his eyes off them, but he breathed a sigh of relief as he watched them glide across the center of the lake that comprised the center of Squaw Meadow.

Amidst laughter and splashing, Jim could still discern that Molly was indeed holding her paddle steady in rudder-like fashion as Emily's shallow strokes splashed up water by the bucketful. Jim couldn't help but be impressed at how quickly Molly grasped the skill of holding the canoe on a steady course. He wondered if he had underestimated her when, on the basis of first impressions, he assumed she was an incompetent female with red toe nail polish and a spiffy Porsche.

Then, it dawned on Jim that he was so concerned with getting them up to speed in the canoe that he never discussed a strategy for surveying the lake for the snakes that Dr. Wertz was so interested in finding. "Too late, now," Jim thought. They were cruising steadily up the narrow lake and way out of earshot.

"I guess I've done all I can do for those two," Jim shrugged and tromped back to his van, which was parked at the roadside behind him. He opened the passenger door and grabbed his field pack off the floor. He threw one arm through the strap and slung the pack over his left shoulder. In the same move he thrust his right hand into his pants pocket and produced his car keys. He locked the doors of the van then returned to the edge of the lake. The girls in the canoe were now a small speck, far away in the long, narrow lake. A long wake of spreading ripples trailed off the canoe toward the nearly parallel shores of Squaw Lake.

Chapter 22

JIM WAS STEADILY making his way up the west shore of Squaw Lake. All around the lake, steep slopes of thick timber kept the noonday sun from finding the forest floor. A thousand feet above him, the steep mountain slopes, gave way to barren rock sentinels; towers of crumbling basalt which presided over the lush greenery and open blue lake water on the valley floor.

Squaw Lake sat at the upper end of a narrow forested valley that hooked around three sides of Squaw Butte. It descended steeply through a narrow mountain gorge before the valley widened out in the vicinity of the Ward homestead, a few miles upstream of the confluence with the Clackamas River. Squaw Butte was the highest of several jagged ridge tops of crumbling basalt that surrounded Squaw Meadow.

Jim paused to consult his yellow field notebook and reread the description Sam Ward had given him of the beach where he and his son Jack had found the first snake. He looked again at the photograph of the snake that was taped to the page of his notebook. He carefully studied the photograph. He closed his eyes and memorized the field markings of the bright green snake that was displayed in the photograph Dr. Wertz had given him.

Jim put his field notebook back into his pack and began his trek around the margin of the lake. He did his best to study the ground for signs of movement as he walked along. Every once in a while he lifted a log or stick in hopes of disturbing a snake that would then slither out into the open and across his path. Jim proceeded in this fashion for three and a half hours. During that time, he saw a few garter snakes and one bull snake, but nothing unfamiliar and certainly no new species.

Eventually, Jim found the grassy point that Sam Ward described as the place where his son first found the unclassified specimen. It looked exactly like the place that Sam described: a sunny, scenic and inviting spot with a commanding view of the lake. Jim scanned the lake for sign of the girls and the canoe. He spotted it at the upper end of the long, narrow lake. It was beached on shore and the girls were nowhere in sight.

"At least they're on shore," Jim thought, "that's a good thing." Then Jim wondered whether the pair might not find more trouble on shore than they would in the canoe. "Too late now," he shrugged. Jim dropped his head and began looking around. At the edge of the grassy clearing he spotted an uncommonly large scat. Jim had studied scat identification in his undergraduate program. He thought he'd see what he could make of the unfamiliar scat. He assumed from its size it was dropped by a bear, but when he examined it closely, he couldn't help but feel that it wasn't bear scat, or at least not like any bear he'd ever seen before. Whatever dropped the scat had done so recently. It looked very fresh, uncomfortably fresh.

He measured the diameter, but not too closely. It was three inches, which was huge. Only a grizzly bear could leave a scat with that diameter. "Indeed," he thought with a bit of a smile, "this is the mother-of-all-turds."

Jim's thoughts immediately turned to Emily and her extreme fear of bears. He wasn't about to mention it to her, but something large had left a conspicuous calling card.

His interest returned to studying the lake edge for signs of snakes. He wandered back into the shade away from the grassy point. When he got to the thick tangle of devil's club he decided that it was futile to look any further in that direction. He turned back toward the point and started to work his way further up the shore of the lake. In another hour, Jim was still intently searching his way up the one side of the lake when he heard a splashing noise. He looked up to see the two girls gliding along in the canoe heading back toward camp at the lower end of the lake. They hadn't seen him, so he shouted "Hey!" They stopped paddling and looked in his direction. From the stern of the canoe, Molly changed the direction of the travel and headed for Jim standing on the shore. When the canoe got within fifteen yards of his position, the paddlers greeted the lone hiker.

"Hey there, Jimbo, any luck?" called Molly from the back of the canoe.

"Not a thing! How about you guys?"

They both shook their heads. Jim looked at his watch. It was already 4:30. It would take him the better part of an hour to retrace his steps back down the lake to the van.

"Why don't you two give me a ride back to camp and save me a whole lot of hiking."

"Think this thing will carry three people?" Molly said. "There's only two seats and we don't have another life jacket."

"It'll have to. Don't worry about a life jacket for me. We'll stay close to shore and I'll take off my shoes if I take a bath." The girls laughed. Jim smiled and pointed, "Pull up to that grassy spot down there. It's a better spot to land than where I am right now."

Jim ducked back into the brush and headed down the bank toward the grassy point. When he got there, the girls were out of the boat. Molly was admiring the view from the grassy point. Emily was standing at the edge of the brush, looking down at the ground. When Jim emerged from the brush, the first thing Emily said was, "What left that?"

Jim looked down and saw the very large, cylindrical scat that he had found earlier in his survey. "Oops!" he thought to himself. That was one thing he didn't want Emily to see for fear of adding to her anxiety about bears.

Jim decided he would do his best to minimize it, if possible. "I don't know. I saw that when I came through here about an hour ago. I think it's probably bull elk a couple days old."

"It's a bear, isn't it?" Emily insisted.

"I don't think so. Bear scat is usually a big pile of individual black dollops. That cylindrical shape looks more like a human turd, but occasionally, a bull elk with a digestive problem will leave a pile like that."

"I don't know much, but that looks way too big to be human, and I don't think it looks like elk," Emily said. "That thing is huge. It's like three inches in diameter. I've never seen anything that big!" Both girls giggled.

Jim thought a second, then said, "Let's just get going, shall we. We're looking for snakes, not animal scat."

The three graduate students piled into the canoe. Molly was still in the rear and, like a good voyager, she shoved off the bank with the tip of her paddle. She expertly reached back with her paddle to rudder the canoe through a curving arc that aimed the canoe down the lake toward their camp. Jim was surprised at how smooth she'd become at guiding the canoe. They were back in camp fifteen minutes later, just as the sun began to disappear behind Squaw Butte to the west, and shadows began to migrate across the lake.

The van with a still-dripping canoe on top pulled into the campsite behind the white Porsche. Elvis the Dog was standing at the end of a taut length of rope, barking at the van as Jim shut the engine off. The trio clambered out of the van and Molly rushed to reassure the dog and release it from its tether. With Elvis the Dog now free to roam, the three sat down in the lawn chairs that encircled the fire ring filled with broken glass and fire ashes from past "visitors."

"I was going to have a beer, but why don't we all sit down and make some notes before we forget anything? I need to know what, if anything, you ladies found up there at the top of the lake."

"We didn't find any snakes but we saw a ton of newts; rough-skinned newts, to be exact. We must have counted thirty in one spot at the top end where the creek enters the lake," Molly began.

Jim held up his hand. "Whoa, hold on. Let me get out my field notebook."

"Don't bother, we wrote everything down in my notebook. I'm just giving you the greatest hits," Molly reassured him. "We found a Pacific giant salamander under a log. When was the last time you saw one of those, eh? Thing was huge. Then we also found an Oregon *ensatina* salamander in the duff layer near that same spot we saw all the newts.

"Have you been to the very top of the lake where the creek empties into the lake?" Molly asked.

"No. Today's the first time I ever put the canoe in this lake. I was up here for a couple days last week but I did all my surveying on foot. I never launched the boat so I never made it very far up the lake."

"Oh, well it's real boggy all around the mouth of the creek. There's skunk cabbage all over the place. You have to be careful where you step or else you'll sink in the mud. It's almost like quick mud in places. Anyway, we looked all around and saw lots of wetland habitat that looked great for frogs and salamanders. We found Pacific tree frogs, spring peepers, and even a few red-legged frogs."

"Like I said, lots of amphibians but no snakes. In fact the habitat didn't even look good for reptiles. It was wet everywhere. I would think that snakes would prefer a drier, sunnier site. Did you see that huge jumble of rocks that extends all the way down the ridge and right into the lake across from where we picked you up on the way back?"

"Sure did. I was looking at that talus slope and thinking the same exact thing. You know, you're pretty good. A lot of grad students don't know what a Pacific giant salamander is, much less where to find one. I guess I owe you ladies an apology. I must confess that when you two pulled up in the sports car with a dog, I had serious doubts about you."

Emily stopped in the middle of a sip of wine and sat forward in her chair and looked intently at Jim. "Why? Because girls aren't tough enough to do field work?"

Jim sensed the hostility in her tone. "Well, you know... the dog...the sports car...two females...It's not how field biology usually goes. Mind you, I find it a refreshing change. Eager to change the subject, Jim asked, "Whose dog did you say that was?"

"Well, Elvis is actually my boyfriend's dog but I'm watching it for him while he's out of town. He went back to visit his family in Toledo, Ohio. He was going to put Elvis in a kennel. I didn't know I would be coming up here when I agreed to watch him or I would have gone along with the kennel plan. This whole Squaw Meadow survey came up rather suddenly. What brought all this about?" Molly asked.

"Apparently, a guy and his kid who live down toward Redland found the snake up here just a couple weeks ago. They brought it to Dr. Wertz, who thought it was a big enough deal that it should be pursued immediately. I did some herpetology surveys for Dr. Wertz last summer so he asked me if I would take this on. It seemed like a good idea until I got up here and saw how much area there was to cover."

Jim took a swig of beer and went on, "I told Dr. Wertz that there was no way I could get the whole thing done in two weeks, and that's all the time I had until I began my summer term classes, plus I have oral exams to prepare for at the end of summer term. I have a pretty full plate. Anyway, I told him I needed some help and he said he'd do what he could. Next thing I know, you two show up. I gotta tell ya, I really appreciate the help. You're getting credit for doing this too, I hope." Jim asked.

"Oh, yeah," Emily said. "Wertz promised us four practicum credits if we put in five days up here over the next month. He wants us to work with you for a couple days so we learn the area, then we can put in time whenever we want, as long as it's within the next month. As you know, it's thought to be breeding month for high elevation snakes, which puts them out and about, which in turn, greatly improves our chances of catching one."

"Yeah, that's the thinking," Jim said, "but when an entirely new species is involved, I don't know how anybody can say when they're most likely to be active."

"I think you just have to assume it behaves like the other snakes that live around it until you learn otherwise," Emily said.

"Well, that's what we tend to do alright, but that assumption may actually prevent us from finding what we're looking for if it has developed behaviors that speak to a very different biological clock. Remember, we are talking about a new species. Similar species that live in close proximity to each other develop a means of reproductively isolating themselves from the other nearby species in the same genus. So, if we do find that this really is a new species of snake, it will probably not end up following the reproductive calendar of any of the other species that share its habitat."

Emily drained her wine glass then vigorously slammed it down on the inverted milk crate next to her chair. "OK, Mr. Smartypants, then what are we doing up here now?" she demanded. "If what you say is true, then we're wasting our time." Again, Jim felt a bit of challenge in Emily's tone, so again he decided it was a good time to change the subject.

"Speaking of wasting time, I think we're wasting time sitting around when we could be getting our dinner going. I brought enough spaghetti for three. Would you ladies care to share a spaghetti dinner with me?"

Molly smiled at Jim. "We have all the stuff for tacos but it'll keep until tomorrow night. If you think there's enough spaghetti for all of us, then we'll make tacos for you tomorrow."

Molly couldn't help but be impressed with the graceful manner in which Jim avoided Emily's verbal challenge by shifting the subject of conversation to the dinner menu. She saw the value in keeping the discussion focused on dinner for the moment, but Emily was on her second glass of wine and feeling a bit feisty.

"There are other ways a species could reproductively isolate itself, you know," Emily said. "It could have a courtship ritual that takes place under very unique circumstances, such as night, or under water, or some other weird circumstances. Did you guys know that bald eagles mate while freefalling through the air. That must add a certain sense of urgency to the whole affair, eh?"

Jim, who was unwrapping raw hamburger, looked up and smiled. "I guess so! Sex while free-falling! What a hoot! That'll sure limit foreplay."

Molly shook her head and smiled as she rummaged through a bin of utensils. Emily poured herself another glass of wine and picked up the field guide to snakes that was lying on the milk crate between their camp chairs. She thumbed through it while Molly and Jim got the spaghetti dinner going. Once the sauce was simmering and the pasta water was boiling they sat around the fire pit and discussed their plan for the next day.

"The canoe will really speed up our survey," Emily said. "We can get the whole shoreline covered tomorrow if we work from the canoe."

"Well, yeah", Jim, agreed, "but the boat can't do the whole job for us. We have to cover the shoreline on foot if we are going to cover it thoroughly. As much as I like working from the boat, we have to get out of it if we're going to do any good. There's a lot of brushy areas to survey in back of the shoreline."

Emily's glass was empty again. She reached for the wine bottle, as Jim and Molly looked at each other. Jim winked at Molly and smiled. Molly shrugged to herself and picked up her glass and thrust it in Emily's direction. "While you're at it, I could use a refill."

By the time dinner was over and the dishes washed, it was almost dark. Jim packed camp gear into the Tupperware boxes while Molly and Emily played cards, using the upside-down milk crate as a table between their camp chairs. Molly was staring intently at her cards while Emily talked to the dog that was sitting next to her.

"Elvis, she's worried. She needs a jack and she's not going to get it, because I have it right here," Emily said as she waved a card in front of the dog's snout. Emily giggled and sipped her wine. Her eyes were glazed and her cheeks were ruddy. She rocked back in her chair, laughed, and then raised her eyebrows in a look of playful helplessness.

"Jimbo, will you be a good woodsman guy and build us a campfire?" Her speech was a bit slurred and Jim was amused by her jovial manner.

"I was just thinking the same thing myself," Jim said, springing from his lawn chair. He opened the rear doors of his van and began tossing pieces of firewood out and onto the ground near the fire circle.

"I didn't know you had wood right there in the van," Emily said. "I could have gotten that."

"Did you bring it with you from town?" Molly questioned.

"Sure did."

"You hauled firewood up to the national forest?" Molly asked incredulously. "Talk about 'hauling coal to Newcastle'!"

"It's a lot easier than gathering it, especially around here," Jim said with a smile. "And I don't see very much coal lying around in this particular part of Newcastle. Remember, even in Newcastle, you have to dig for coal. It isn't just lying around for the taking."

Emily resumed staring at her cards as Jim stacked wood in a loose teepee in the fire ring. She rocked back on her camp chair. One of the legs suddenly pushed through the soft earth, penetrating a mole tunnel. The chair lurched to one side and Emily's feet flew up in the air.

"Gaaak!" she exclaimed while falling over backwards in her camp chair, playing cards flying into the air, then fluttering back to earth. Meanwhile, she hit the earth with a soft thud and the squeak of the chair. She remained motionless, her feet in the air. Jim and Molly jumped up.

"Are you okay?" they asked in unison. Emily remained motionless and began to laugh. "I'm fine. It was a soft landing. This is kinda comfortable, really."

Jim smiled and extended a hand. She didn't reach for his hand, but drew her knees to her chest and gracefully rolled to one side, got onto her knees, stood up, and dusted herself off. Her complexion was flush. She staggered then regained her balance, stood up, then plopped back down in her chair.

"I spilled my wine on re-entry," she declared, then picked up her glass and held it out in the direction of Molly. Molly smiled and took it from her and refilled it with wine. They gathered the scattered playing cards and resumed their card game as Jim went back to building a campfire.

As the campfire gained life and illuminated the underside of the tree canopy, the two girls kept up a lively round of chatter and occasional laughter. Jim studied a topo map of the landscape surrounding the lake. The jug of wine got lower as the girls laughed louder and more often. Jim heard Emily shout "Whoa!" and over went her chair for the second time. Molly sat and laughed, as Emily repeated her tuck and roll to the side, before regaining her feet again. "I swear I'm not drunk. It's these mole tunnels that my chair leg keeps falling into," Emily insisted, her speech slurred.

"We believe you," Molly said between peels of laughter. Jim smiled and shook his head as he put away his map. He walked over to the campfire, took up a chair. It was time to join the fun. Molly gathered up the cards and began to shuffle them.

"You gonna join us for cards, Jimbo?"

"I'm tired of cards," Emily interjected before Jim had time to answer.

"Okay, I'll just have a glass of wine, before you two polish it all off."

Jim had paused to think long and hard about his next card play. His mind strayed and he let himself appreciate his surroundings at that moment. Molly was petting Elvis the Dog who sat contentedly under her folding chair. She smiled a broad smile as she reached for the wine bottle and refilled her glass. Jim was again struck by her smile, and the glow of her wide brown eyes in the yellow firelight. He let his gaze linger on her radiant countenance, which was accentuated by the warm glow of the flickering yellow and orange of the campfire light. It occurred to Jim that he was having a delightful time as leader of this hastily assembled field team.

"C'mon, Jimbo, it's your play," Molly said.

"I know. I just can't make up my mind…"

Molly kicked Jim on the foot, causing him to look up in her direction. Elvis sat up and sniffed the air. Molly was again flashing her smile but this time she was pointing with her hand of cards in the direction of Emily, who had nodded off to sleep. At that moment, Emily's camp chair toppled over backwards a third time. Emily landed with a thud on the soft ground as her playing cards flew up then fluttered down to earth. Jim and Molly burst into simultaneous laughter. Emily lifted her head up, mumbled something unintelligible, and let her head drop.

"Are you alright, Emily?" Molly inquired.

"Fine…just fine…this is really rather comfortable…" Emily mumbled.

"Safer, too," Jim added. "Now that you're on the ground, you can't fall anywhere."

Jim and Molly laughed anew. Then Molly said, "We should help her up."

"I suppose," Jim said, and began to get up. He paused to assess the situation. There lay Emily, tipped over backwards but still in her chair. Her feet were in the air with the soles of her feet facing the campfire. Her playing cards were strewn about the ground. Emily was motionless.

"She does look comfortable lying there. She looks like an astronaut in the capsule awaiting lift-off," Molly playfully observed.

"I think she lifted off a half hour ago. Right now I think she's somewhere between Mars and Jupiter," Jim quietly laughed, "Wonder what's gotten into her tonight?"

"She's had a long day."

"Don't you think we should put her to bed?"

"Okay, but she looks happy. Let's give her a few minutes."

290

Chapter 23

SUDDENLY, ELVIS BEGAN to bark steadily. Emily didn't budge. Molly and Jim peered out into the inky blackness of the nocturnal forest. Their eyes were accustomed to the light of the fire and they could not distinguish anything beyond the sphere of illumination created by the firelight.

"Listen!" Jim whispered. The faint sound of sticks snapping emerged from the darkened woods. "Do you hear that?"

"What do you think that is?" Molly inquired nervously.

"Hard to say," Jim said, trying to sound unconcerned for Molly's benefit. "I suppose I could go check it out. I have to go to the bathroom, anyway. Can I borrow your flashlight?"

Elvis continued his cacophony of barking as Molly handed Jim her flashlight. He stood and faced the darkness, wobbling slightly. The wine was having its effect but his curiosity was also aroused. He wondered what might be lurking on the margins of their camp. Jim stepped toward the dog and petted him on the head.

"It's okay, Elvis. Lie Down!"

Elvis stopped barking but growled as he stared in the direction of the snapping sticks. Jim turned on the flashlight and illuminated the foliage at ground level. He walked into the woods, and scanned his surroundings again. He stepped behind a tree and began to urinate. Suddenly, he smelled a very strong, putrid smell as if there was some rotting garbage nearby. Jim finished urinating and stood silently, listening to the nighttime woods.

The putrid smell lingered, making Jim feel slightly nauseous. He walked several steps farther into the woods, stood still and listened some more. The putrid smell was now stronger. Jim decided he could not bear the smell anymore. He worked his way back through the woods in the direction of the campfire glow. As he got to the edge of the camp clearing he appreciated the beauty of the scene: the glow of the campfire illuminated the forest canopy in broad orange hemisphere. The fire was burning brighter than when he left. Facing him, Molly sat poised and alert, with one arm around the neck of Elvis the Dog sitting at her side, also gazing intently in Jim's direction.

Molly's jet-black hair had a glossy sheen, which contrasted sharply with the white cable-knit turtleneck sweater she wore. Comically, two sneaker-clad feet dangled in the air next to Molly, identifying the spot where Emily slept soundly in her up-ended lawn chair. As he stepped into the firelight, Elvis sprang to his feet, Molly smiled, and Emily snored.

Jim didn't wait for Molly to ask. "I didn't see anything, but something out there sure stinks. It could be some garbage somebody dumped out there, but I didn't see any-thing like that. But the farther I went into woods, the stron-ger the smell got. It started to make me nauseous. I didn't hear anything moving, though, and I certainly didn't see anything out there. I think something is around, but there's no way to tell what. There's a lot of elk around here, not to mention the deer and bear, but they won't come in around our fire.

Molly reminded Jim, "Don't mention the 'b' word around Emily."

"I know. Look, she's got that big can of pepper spray clipped to her belt." Jim said. Is it for repelling bears or horny field biologists?" Jim kidded.

Molly smiled and looked at Emily, still sleeping in the up-ended lawn chair. "Probably both. That's why she brought the economy size."

They both laughed. "Yeah, grad students are a rough bunch," Jim said. "Anyway, this grad student can't stand to see that kid lying there with her feet in the air and her head in the dirt. Whaddaya say we put her to bed before I pass out, too." Jim grabbed the arms of his camp chair and rose. Once he was on his feet, he paused, wobbled, and then fell back into his chair with a muffled thump. "Whoa, I think it's already too late! I guess Emily's not the only one who overdid the wine.

Molly giggled. "You stood up too fast!"

"Okay, let's try again." Jim stood up slowly and licked his finger, held it in the air with mock seriousness, and tested the breeze.

"Yep. The air's definitely thinner up here, but I'm get-ting used to it. Me thinks I'll make it this time." He reached over and extended a hand to Molly. She took it and rose from her chair. Then she grabbed Jim's arm and held it as she took the few steps toward her unconscious friend. Jim caught a whiff of some delightful apricot fragrance Molly was wearing as she unexpectedly clung to his arm. He felt his heartbeat quicken.

Together they hoisted Emily up from the ground and guided her toward the tent. Once she was inside, Jim stepped back. "In the name of decency, I'm going to let you get her tucked in."

"Will do," Molly agreed.

Jim returned to his chair and stoked the fire. He heard a stirring by his side, which startled him. A dark, four-legged form moved out of the shadows toward the fire. Jim gasped, then caught himself as he realized it was Elvis the Dog.

"Elvis! I forgot you were here," Jim whispered. A flashlight beam moved back and forth inside the tent. A sleeping bag zipper made a loud "zip!" Elvis walked a circle around the fading campfire, thrusting his nose in the air and sniffing it.

"I guess it's you and me, pooch. Whatcha smelling?"

Jim studied the dog, as it continued to walk around the campsite, intently sniffing. Another loud "zzziiippp" came from the tent and Molly emerged, feet first. She stood up, wobbled, dusted herself off, and returned to the fire. She stood in the firelight opposite Jim.

Her black, shiny, shoulder length hair was perfectly combed. The warm yellow light of the campfire cast a warm yellow glow upon her countenance.

Meanwhile, Elvis the Dog, now standing with his little hind end toward the fire, stared into the darkness beyond the fire. He growled quietly into the night. Molly, went over patted him on the head. "It's okay, puppy. This is your first campout isn't it?" Elvis quit growling but kept staring into the inky black beyond the fire.

"That must be why he's so nervous. He must have been out somewhere checking things out. I'd forgotten he was even here until, all of a sudden, he came charging back into camp."

"I'd just been thinking about Emily and her bear repellent, and here comes the dog, sprinting in out of the dark. He scared the hell out of me. I thought, 'Great, here comes a bear, just after I put the bear spray to bed with Emily.' I almost came diving into that tent with you. I did a classic double take. Fortunately, I recognized ole' Elvis just before I jumped up and made a mad dash for your tent. I felt kinda stupid."

Molly smiled broadly as Jim related his story. Her eyes twinkled in the firelight. She walked over to Jim, and to his surprise, she reached out to him, took both of his hands, and gently pulled him up out of the chair. When he was on his feet, she looked up into his eyes and said, "Thank you for helping me get Emily to bed. I wasn't sure what I was going to do with her. That was very gentlemanly of you."

"My pleasure, ma'am," he replied with smile and an imitation cowboy drawl. "We couldn't very well just let her lay there." Jim stepped closer to Molly and put her hands around his neck. He put his hand to the small of her back and gently pressed her body against his. He put his other hand behind her head and brought his mouth down to meet hers. They kissed. Her smell, her touch, and her lips were all more intoxicating than the wine.

Jim felt a flood of passion, which was interrupted as quickly and unexpectedly as it began by the intense barking of Elvis. Molly pulled her head back, folded her hair behind her ear with her index finger and turned her head toward the frantically barking dog. To Molly's surprise, Elvis was not barking at the two campers in their moment of inebriated passion. Elvis was barking madly into the night.

"It's okay, Elvis. It's okay," she said, but Elvis would have no part of her attempts to reassure him. Molly was both embarrassed and perturbed by the dog's untimely outburst. She looked into Jim's eyes and expected to see annoyance. Instead, she saw amusement as Jim eyed the agitated canine.

"I thought he was objecting to us, this, but it appears he's more concerned with what's out there," Jim said, gesturing with his head toward the darkened woods. "Does he do that whenever you kiss a boy?"

Molly smiled. "Maybe he's not used to being out at night. He's still just a puppy. What is it, Elvis?"

Elvis was inconsolable. The two stood together, staring. They were unwilling to surrender their embrace, but unable to ignore the barking dog.

Molly looked up at Jim with uncertainty in her eyes. "Do you think something's out there?"

"I don't know, but if the pooch knows what's good for him, he'll stay here."

At that very instant Elvis the Dog darted off into the inky black of the Mount Hood National Forest.

Molly gasped. Their embrace dissolved. "ELVIS! ELVIS!! COME BACK HERE," she shrieked.

The barking continued but got noticeably more distant as the stressed puppy pursued some unknown purpose. Molly called again, "ELVIS!!"

A stick was heard to snap, then a loud, "Yelp" that Jim assumed was coming from Elvis. Then total silence. No one moved. Nothing else stirred anywhere around the campsite.

Jim and Molly stared at each other in shock. Molly called again. "ELLLVIIIS!"

Nothing but silence came from the forest that surrounded them.

"I hope I'm wrong but it sounded like Elvis just left the building."

"Is that supposed to be a joke?" Molly glared.

"Sorry."

"We have got to find him, get him back here, with us—" Her voice trailed off.

Jim grabbed a large flashlight from beside his chair and shone it into the woods where the dog was last heard. Nothing. The surrounding woods were absolutely silent. He whistled a couple of long whistles. No reply. They faced the woods in silence. Not even a cricket or tree frog could be heard. Only the hissing and crackle of the campfire challenged the stillness of the forest.

"Alright, I guess I'm going out there. Suddenly that bear repellent of Emily's doesn't seem like a bad idea."

"Want me to get it?"

"Well, she's not using it...Better yet, you get it and keep it handy. And keep the fire burning real bright so I can see you from out there.

"I'm going to head out that way about a hundred yards, then if I don't find anything I'll circle all the way around the campfire, so don't panic if you hear crashing out in the woods. That'll be me. I'll go out as far as I dare, but keep that fire going so I don't get lost. Okay?

"Yes. Thanks, Jim. Be careful."

"You can count on it."

A dozen steps further into the woods, Jim was again confronted by the same acrid stench. He turned to see

Molly's darkened profile, backlit by the campfire behind her, standing motionless and facing his direction. "Ugh! Do you smell that?" The putrid smell hit Jim like a wall and made him feel queasy.

"Smell what?"

"I smell the garbage again," Jim whispered. He thought it might not be a good idea to elaborate, lest it was the remains of Elvis that was the source of the awful odor, but he knew the dog's remains wouldn't smell yet.

"It's probably some campers' trash…"

He kept scanning with his flashlight but saw nothing that could be the source of the smell. It was all Jim could do to advance in the face of the overpowering stench. The hair on his forearms and the back of his neck was now standing up. He felt fear. A sudden sense of deadly peril overtook him. It stopped him in his tracks. He could not take another step forward but he did not know why. The intensely bad smell was making his eyes water, and even sting. It was too much. He had to back off. The horrible odor instantly disappeared. He stepped forward again. The stink returned just as sharply as it had vanished. His heart rate quickened and he gasped for fresh air. He retreated yet again.

Jim tried to calm himself and considered the possibilities: abandoned deer carcass, dumped garbage, an open pit toilet, or discarded spoiled meat. But, why hadn't they noticed the smell before since they had been there all evening? Jim took a few more steps back. He turned and looked back to find the firelight. The soft flames illuminated the forest canopy like a golden umbrella of light over the camp.

A flood of negative thought suddenly overtook Jim. "Great," He thought to himself. "What a messed up deal! Three minutes ago I was at the gates of Heaven, now I'm on the threshold of Hell! Seconds ago, I was kissing a beautiful girl. Now I'm terrified and groping my way around a pitch-black forest amidst an eye-watering stench. How quickly can a guy's fortune change? And what could possibly go wrong next?"

An instant later he got his answer. A stick snapped loudly to his right and he froze. The hackles on his neck were up again. He listened. Nothing. He whistled twice. Silence. He turned and moved in the direction of the noise, scanning the forest with his flashlight. Jim looked for the glow of the campfire to get his bearing then moved about a quarter of the way around the fire and paused to listen again, then he let out two quick whistles. Two soft whistles of the same cadence pierced the night, coming squarely from the place that Jim just left!

"This is too weird," Jim thought to himself. He did an about face and began heading back from where he just came. Then he froze. It suddenly dawned on Jim that somebody *else* was out there!

"Who's out there? Molly, is that you?" Jim whispered.

Silence.

Suddenly the situation seemed very menacing. Jim had to fight back a wave of panic as he recollected the events of the last few minutes: the dog disappears, the terrible stench, the snapping noises, the sudden quiet of the woods, the whistles …something was very wrong…and someone or something seemed to be out there, concealed by the darkness but in the immediate vicinity of their camp!

But how could that be? Where did they come from? There were no other cars, and no other campers anywhere around. "Were they being stalked by someone?" Jim wondered. Suddenly, he got the sick feeling that he had just made a really stupid move. He suddenly surmised that his field team was in an incredibly vulnerable position: one guy and two girls, one of whom was drunk and asleep, deep in the national forest with no means of defense except for a can of pepper spray.

Someone or something just nabbed the dog and now "It" was stalking their location. Worst of all, he had been lured away from the rest of his group. He was alone in the woods and the two girls were alone in the camp. This was not good. Elvis the Dog was now the least of Jim's worries.

"What am I doing? Elvis, ain't nuthin' but a hound dog. I need to get back to that camp and keep an eye on those girls." he wheeled around and headed toward the distant firelight. As he worked his way back to camp, an even worse thought crossed Jim's mind: He might have been tricked into leaving the camp to look for the missing dog.

He broke into a run and took only three long steps before a branch caught him in the shins. He went down with a thud. Sticks snapped and branches crashed as Jim hit the ground face first. He tried to put out his hands to break his fall, letting go of his flashlight as he fell. His forehead struck a branch lying across his path. He let out a muffled moan as stars momentarily appeared behind his eyes. He paused to collect himself, face down in the ferns. He felt a piercing pain in his hand.

"Owww!" he said aloud as he put a hand to his forehead. He felt something warm running from his forehead down his face. "Blood, damn." Then he felt drips from his fingers. "Punctured hand! Double DAMN."

"Jim, are you O.K.?" Molly called out.

Inwardly, Jim was relieved to at least hear Molly's voice, indicating that everything was still all right in camp, at least for the moment. "I think so!" he called back. "I fell. Just give me a moment." Jim was holding his hurt hand. Again, he caught his breath. "At least it's not spurting," he thought to himself.

He lifted his head and searched for the beam of his flashlight. It was nowhere to be seen. The bulb must have broken when he fell. He felt with his hands and found it just ahead of his right hand. He clicked the switch repeatedly but the light didn't work.

"I guess Emily isn't the only one who's sideways." He got up slowly, and groped his way through the branches and ferns, carefully working his way through the underbrush toward the firelight, carrying his now-broken flashlight. Jim stumbled one last time as he entered the clearing and the warmth of the fire.

"Jesus, your head is bleeding!" Molly exclaimed. "And your hand! What happened?"

Jim put his hand to his forehead as he stumbled toward the nearest camp chair. His hands were trembling. He looked at his palm. His head was spinning and he felt dizzy. Molly ripped off a paper towel and handed it to Jim.

He tipped his head back in the chair and thrust his legs out straight, digging his heels into the dirt. He held the towel to his forehead, and applied steady pressure.

"What happened? Any sign of Elvis?"

"No sign of the dog...I think something's out there... could be a person...it whistled...I got worried about you... stupidly tried to run back to camp...I fell...gimme a minute...I think I'll be okay,...would you please get the first-aid kit? It's in a box behind the driver's seat of my van."

"Okay." Molly rushed the few feet, flung open the door and found the pouch.

Finally, Jim lifted his head and slowly sat upright, raising his knees and putting his feet flat on the ground.

"Pepper spray...where's the pepper spray?"

"Right here," Molly said, pulling it out of the pocket of her down vest.

"Good. Keep it handy." Jim busied himself with alcohol to cleanse his wounds, some anti-bacterial ointment and bandages. It wasn't hard to feel where all the stuff needed to go. He knew he'd be hurting in the morning.

"What about Elvis?"

Jim ignored her question. "Did I get it all covered?"

She looked him over. "Yes, but it's still bleeding."

"I'll keep pressure on it. No sign of Elvis, but right now we have to take care of ourselves. There's nothing we can do for the dog. I broke my flashlight when I fell. We'll have to wait until it's light to look for him. I'm not sure what's going on out there but I don't like it, and since all we have is a can of pepper spray, I think we'd better all sleep in the van...with the doors locked."

"What do you think it is?"

"Out there? I really don't know. It could be a person. The dog disappearing is what makes me think it's not just some prankster." Jim took a breath, "Should I say this?" he thought to himself. "Yes, she needs to know what's going on," he decided.

"I thought I heard something moving out there and decided I shouldn't be wandering around out there looking for a dog with you and Emily by yourselves back here in camp. So I quit searching for the run-a-way dog and started to high-tail it back to camp. That's when I fell."

"I guess I see your point. Thanks for thinking of us. I guess, under the circumstances, I'll have to hope and pray that Elvis can find his way back."

"Yeah, would you fish me out three or four aspirin from the kit? Just set the bottle on the table where I can see it.

"We have to wake Emily up and get her into the van. You go try to rouse her while I make some room in the van. I'd be inclined to drive out of here tonight if the dog wasn't still out there somewhere. If we left, and he came back, Lord only knows where Elvis would wander next."

"No, we can't leave with Elvis out there. Please. We can lock ourselves in the van. We have the pepper spray. We can't leave Elvis up here."

"Fair enough. Now let's get busy."

Fifteen minutes later, Emily was snoozing soundly on the floor in the back of the van. Jim and Molly were trying to get comfortable in the reclining bucket seats in the front. The doors were locked, the windows were open very slightly for ventilation, and they stared at the campsite through the windshield. The campfire was dying down but a small flame still flickered.

"I slept in this seat only once before, and it was one of the most uncomfortable nights ever. Why don't you lie down in the back with Emily?"

"I want to keep watching for Elvis"

"My hand is throbbing but the bleeding has stopped. I feel like I've been beat up. We should sleep if we can."

Chapter 24

SAM WAS SITTING at the kitchen table reading the newspaper, and sipping a cup of coffee on a sunny Saturday morning. The kitchen door was open to let in the fresh morning air. Through the closed screen door behind Sam's chair, he could see his son was walking along in the tall grass at the edge of the yard. Jack walked very slowly, and peering intently at the ground as he stepped with careful, measured strides.

Suddenly, Jack stopped walking and stared even more intently at a single spot just ahead of his feet. He reached in his pocket and pulled out a pair of gloves and put them on, then pounced, hands first, upon the very spot of ground that had captured his undivided attention.

He brought his hands together and stood up, now holding a brightly colored red, yellow, and black snake that squirmed and writhed in his hands. The snake was impressively large for a garter snake, being almost three feet long. Jack stood upright, held the snake out at arm's length and smiled. Then he turned and ran up the steps of the house and stepped up to the screen door.

"Look, Dad! This one's huge!" Jack announced through the screen.

Sam put down his coffee cup. "Wow. That IS a huge one. Is that a bull snake?"

"No, it's just a really big red-sided garter snake. See the red lines on the sides!"

"Crikey! She's a beaut!" Sam exclaimed in his best imitation of crocodile hunter Steve Irwin. "That may be the biggest garter snake you've ever caught around here. What are you gonna do with that thing?"

"Just let it go. I think I've caught this one before."

"Good deal, boy!"

The sound of car wheels on the gravel driveway caused both Sam and Jack to turn around and look. Their old retriever dog began barking at the sound of the approaching vehicle crackling up the gravel. A white convertible Porsche with two young ladies rolled to a stop. The dog walked circles around the idling vehicle, still barking, as the cloud of dust from the driveway drifted over the lawn.

Sam was leaning back in his chair so he could see out the back door through the screen door. "Whoa!" Sam said, when he observed the sports car and its female occupants.

"Who's that, Dad?" Jack asked, also looking toward the driveway. He was still holding the snake in his gloved hands.

"No idea...," Sam said, jumping up from the table and moving toward the kitchen window over the sink where he could get a better look. "...no idea at all."

Sam swung into house-husband mode. He hastily opened the dishwasher and began loading the pile of dirty dishes next to the sink into it. Jack stood on the porch, clutching the snake, staring at the white sports car.

The driver's side door opened and Molly extended a hand toward the dog, which sniffed it and immediately ceased barking. Slowly, the passenger side door opened but the dog showed no interest, instead eagerly accepting Molly's friendly gesture of scratching behind his floppy ears. The two young women, both wearing shorts, tank tops, and hiking boots, stepped away from the Porsche, unsure of where they should go, or do next. Emily moved unsteadily, feeling a little ill from her over-indulgence the night before.

The Ward's golden retriever now sniffed Molly's bare legs. The women gazed at the house and the young boy with a long serpent standing on the porch. Molly waved as she and Emily approached Jack, who remained standing silently on the porch. He was clutching the robust garter snake with both hands making it squirm mightily.

Molly stopped at the foot of the porch steps and smiled her sweetest smile. She removed her sun glasses, and said, "Hi there, young man. Is this the Ward place?"

Jack nodded, without saying anything. Sam could see the two grad students through the kitchen window, though he continued loading the last of the dishes in the dishwasher while staying out of sight.

"Are your parents around?"

"In here!" Sam shouted from inside the open kitchen door as he slammed the door of the dishwasher and stabbed the button with his finger to turn it on. Molly stepped up onto the back porch, bent down and rested on her haunches, and met Jack at eye level.

"Wow, look at the size of that snake! Where'd you get that?" Molly asked in her friendliest tone.

"I caught it right over there," Jack offered, gesturing toward the edge of the lawn.

"I bet you don't know what kind it is," Molly challenged, flashing a smile at the boy.

"It's a California red-sided garter snake."

"That's very good, young man. How did you know that?"

"I just know."

"You know, I study snakes at Oregon State, and I learned the name of that kind of snake only last year. How old are you, twelve?" Molly asked, still smiling her warmest smile.

"Eleven," Jack replied.

"You're pretty smart for an eleven year old. Do those snakes reproduce by laying eggs of do they have live young?"

Jack, now feeling a bit more relaxed around the two pretty strangers, said, "All garter snakes have live young. Only the big snakes like pythons and cobras lay eggs. The only snakes around here that lay eggs are gopher snakes."

"Why you're one amazing young man. My name is Molly. I'd offer to shake your hand if you weren't holding that snake. What's your name?"

"Jack."

By now, Sam was standing at the screen door, holding his coffee cup and smiling. Molly looked up and smiled, too. "You must be Mr. Ward."

"Call me Sam. Please let me guess, you two are Oregon State grad student," he said as he opened the screen door to let the two ladies into the kitchen.

"That's right! How'd you know?"

"Russell Wertz said I might see a couple of young ladies going up to join Jim at the meadow."

"That's us! I'm Molly and this is Emily," Molly said, gesturing her friend.

"Can I offer you ladies a cup of coffee?"

Molly attempted to refuse the gesture of hospitality with a shake of her head, but Emily quickly overruled her. "I'd love one. Please."

Sam reached for two cups from the shelf.

"We're sorry to intrude, Mr. Ward, er, Sam."

"No trouble." Sam said. "Sit down, ladies. Either of you take cream in your coffee?"

"We both do," Emily said as they sat down next to each other at the kitchen table.

"Here you go," Sam said, placing the full coffee mugs in front of them and turning around to refill his own from the coffee maker on the counter. "Have you been up to the meadow yet?"

"We just came from there. Jim sent us down here to find you," Molly said.

"Really?"

"Yes, we surveyed the west side of the lake yesterday. We were hoping to do the east side today, but we ran into a little problem. Actually, we ran into a big problem. That's why we're here. Jim was hoping we might catch you at home. We need some reinforcements."

"Uh-oh. What kind of problem? Is Jim hurt?"

"A little banged up, but I think he'll be alright. To make a long story short, my dog ran away last night. Under slightly mysterious circumstances, I might add. We could use some help trying to find him. We need to borrow another canoe. We have one, but it's just not enough. Anyway, Jim said you also know the area really well and might be able to help us look for him. I realize it's a lot to ask. I understand if you're too busy."

"As you can see, I'm not terribly busy. Hell, I'm taking it easy! But I do have a youngster to watch and my wife is at a horse show with my daughter. Maybe I could bring my boy with me. He's a keen observer. He might be just the guy we need. So tell me what happened."

"Well, we were camped at that one spot just off the main road. We were sitting around the fire talking. It was late. We were about to go to bed. All of a sudden, Elvis, that's my dog, started barking furiously at something in the woods. Next thing we know, he takes off. We hear a couple of yelps, and that's it. He's gone..." Molly's voice cracked with emotion. She wiped her eyes.

Sam looks down in silence at his coffee cup and wrapped both hands around it. A long, awkward pause ensued.

Molly raised her head. "I'm sorry..."

"Quite alright. Did you say the dog's name was Elvis?"

Molly nodded, still looking down.

Sam broke the silence. "Great name. What kind of dog is it?"

"It's a black lab...a puppy, really. Less than a year old, so he's not very experienced in the ways of the woods. I probably shouldn't have taken him up there in the first place, but I wanted to get him used to camping. I kept him tied up all day. I thought it would be okay to let him off the leash when we were all right there in camp. He was fine all evening, until he heard something in the woods."

"I probably would have done the same thing. I think it's a particularly bad place to take a dog, but you couldn't have known that. Hey, they have to get used to the woods somehow. If he's a year old, he's almost fully grown, right?" Sam said, trying to be positive.

Molly nodded.

"Any idea what he was barking at?"

"Not really. I thought you might have some idea what's up there. That's one reason I wanted to talk to you,"

"Jeez, I hate to say it, but it could be anything. It's wild country up there. Did you see anything, hear anything, or find any tracks?"

"Jim did his best to look around in the woods after Elvis took off. That's when things got a little strange. He couldn't go too far in the dark, but he said he heard something moving around. Then he smelled something. He whistled for the dog a few times...."

"What did he smell?"

"I'm not sure. He just said he smelled something really bad, 'like rotting garbage,' is what I think he said."

"Then what?"

"Then he got really scared. He heard whistles in the woods and he thought maybe there were people around. Being concerned about our safety at that point, he decided to stop looking and get back to camp."

"Were there any other campers up there last night?"

"There wasn't a soul. There were no other cars. We were the only campers, as far as I could tell. That's the other thing I thought you might know about. Are there other camp spots up there where people could have been camping nearby?"

"Not really. The only good spots are right by the lake. There's a private holding back in there to the north of the lake but I know the guy who has that and he wasn't up there last night. That much I know. Besides, there's only the one road in and out of there, and it goes right past the lake, so if anyone else was up there last night, you would have seen a car. Did you see any cars at all last night, or other fires, or anything?"

"Nothing. It was real quiet all night. In fact, that was the other weird thing. Those lakes are full of frogs and they were croaking and peeping and there were lots of crickets. Then, just before Elvis started barking, the whole woods got real quiet. All the frogs and crickets just stopped. It was creepy. Nothing made any noise after that. After we gave up looking for the dog, we were kinda scared and we all slept in the van, so I don't know what happened after that."

Sam was silent. He lifted his coffee cup and took a long sip. He kept looking down at the table.

"What do you think, Mr. Ward?" Molly asked.

Sam looked up at Molly as he pushed his chair back and stood up. "I think you can quit calling me 'Mr. Ward.' Only eighth graders call me 'Mr. Ward.' Also, I think we're going to Squaw Meadow. Will you ladies help me load the canoe onto the car?"

Chapter 25

ACOOL BREEZE SCUTTLED the last wisp of morning fog off of Squaw Lake as the sun made its first appearance of the day. Jim Marshall felt a pang of hunger as he paddled his canoe solo down the long narrow expanse of open water in the center of Squaw Meadow. As long as he held the paddle with his fingertips and not his palm, he could use his injured hand to propel his boat without feeling any pain. His eyes were heavy with exhaustion from having slept so little last night.

As he approached the beach at the south end of the lake, Jim could see his van come into view, parked beside the road. He was disappointed to see that there were no other cars in sight. That meant girls hadn't returned from their trip to Sam Ward's homestead.

He glanced at his watch as the canoe's hull skidded to a stop on the coarse rock beach of the boat landing. He had just completed a trip around the entire shoreline of Squaw Lake: up the forested west side then back down the steep, rocky, exposed east side of the lake. As he carefully stepped out of his canoe, he heard the distant crackle of car wheels on the one and only gravel road that led into the high elevation meadows including Squaw Lake at the north end. Hopefully, help was arriving.

He dragged the canoe well up on shore, rocks screeching against the hull. Jim stepped into the beached canoe and plopped down to rest on a seat. He spun around to face the middle of the boat and raised the lid of a cooler in the center, then lifted out a bag of apples. He chose one and returned the rest to the cooler. He sat in the canoe eating the apple as first the Porsche, then an old, brown Land Rover with a red canoe on top appeared at the top of the short driveway leading down to the water's edge. The familiar cloud of dust wafted over the arriving autos as the engine of the Land Rover revved. The Rover turned hard, then backed down the sloping driveway to the boat launch. Jim couldn't see the driver, but whoever it was seemed very familiar with the process of approaching the water to launch a boat on the lake.

"That could only be Sam Ward," Jim thought, with a feeling of relief. Jim stood up and stepped out of his canoe and took a few steps to one side as the Land Rover rolled to a stop just a few feet from the end of his canoe.

Jim chewed his apple and smiled as the car engine died. Doors on both sides of the vehicle opened and Sam emerged from the driver's side. Instead of looking up at Jim, he searched the ground. He seized upon a football-sized rock and jammed it behind the front wheel of his car on the driver's side. With his vehicle well secured on the inclined boat ramp, Sam looked up and smiled at Jim. His son Jack stepped out of the passenger side, holding a green dip net with a long handle on it.

"Yeah! Reinforcements!" Jim smiled, raising his half eaten apple into the air in mock salute.

"At ease, soldier. Howdy, Jim. Word on the street is you had an interesting time up here last night."

"You can say that again. I see you brought a helper."

"Yeah, I don't think you've met Jack yet. Jim, meet Jack."

Jack smiled silently and looked at his dad. No one spoke.

Sam broke the awkward silence. "Any Elvis sightings?"

"Elvis?" Jack asked his dad.

"The dog. Elvis the Dog."

Understanding flashed across Jack's face and he nodded.

Sam spoke up. "Jack here has the sharpest set of eyes I've ever seen. If something's lost, Jack is your best bet for finding it. As a young 'un, I'd take Jack for a walk in the woods in the evening, just to wear him out before bedtime. It became a nightly ritual. He would insist on finding at least one newt or frog before he would agree to going inside. It often took several trips around the property but he always found one. Little did I realize we were programming his mind with wildlife 'X-ray vision.' Ever since then, he's had a very keen eye for wildlife of all kinds; birds, snakes, salamanders, you name it. This is one of his favorite places to come because this big pond is loaded with newts. You watch, he'll have a newt or a snake in no time."

Jack was already moving toward the edge of the lake and peering into the clear, shallow water for signs of motion. "Great. We can definitely use another set of sharp eyes."

The two ladies came down the path past the Land Rover where Sam was beginning to untie the ropes that secured the canoe on the roof. "Hi there, Jim. Any luck?"

"Well, the bad news is I haven't found the dog, but the good news is, I haven't found a dead dog. I hate to say it, but I expected to find his body somewhere around camp. I combed the woods all around but I didn't find anything. That's good. On the other hand, there's a lot of places he could have gone since he doesn't know his way around up here."

Sam interrupted, "That's bad."

Jim nodded.

"Anyway, it's great to have another boat and some extra help. It gets so steep away from the meadow that I really think he has to be somewhere around the meadow. And since most of the meadow is still flooded from spring snow-melt, a canoe is definitely the easiest way to get around. You can get to almost every part of the meadow by boat. I paddled up the west side this morning, whistling and call-ing the whole way. I haven't covered the east side yet. I ran out of time so I just kinda eyeballed it on my way back. There's just a lot more shoreline to cover over there, with all those inlets. It'll help to have two boats."

Molly said, "I shouldn't have brought the dog with me. It's stopping us from doing what we came to up here to do." She turned to face Sam. "I'm really sorry to put you all through this."

"Hey, look at the bright side," Sam said. "The dog has gotten more people up here to search. After all, we can look for the dog while we look for snakes. It's all just look-ing, right?"

"It's nice of you guys to do this. I really appreciate your coming up here," Molly said, showing a faint smile.

"It's a great day to take my kid for a paddle. We love it up here. But it never would have occurred to me to drive up here today if you guys didn't send out the call for help. More and more, I'm learning that there's wisdom in going along with a course of action that just kind of falls in your lap. You know what they say, 'Go with the flow.' Of course, when two babes show up in your driveway in a sports car and say, 'Let's go to Squaw Meadow,' it doesn't take Einstein to know it's a good day to go to Squaw Meadow."

Everyone laughed. Sam looked at Jim and added, "I bet you sent those two down to my place because you knew it would be more persuasive that if some homely guy showed up in a beat up van." Everyone laughed again.

Jim said, "I have to confess, that thought did occur to me. In fact, it worked out even better than I'd hoped. I sent the ladies after one more person, and they came back with *two*! And one of them ends up being Eagle Eye Jack. It's like they went out in search of a scout and came back with Daniel Boone!" Everyone was smiling and the mood became considerably more relaxed.

All the anxiety that Jim, Molly and Emily felt about menacing events of the previous night evaporated with a few humorous remarks. Jim felt particularly reassured for the first time all morning. He felt like the cavalry just rode into town at their moment of greatest need, and that 'the cavalry' saw their predicament as a simple matter to resolve.

Sam exuded a certain calm, confident, can-do attitude that was reassuring. The presence of Sam's young son, who seemed to regard this remote and slightly forbidding area as a giant playground, further bolstered Jim's hope that this whole mess would have a happy ending.

"Check it out!" Sam said, pointing toward his son. Jack was standing at water's edge, lifting his dip net out of the water. Unaware of the attention he was getting, he reached into the dripping net and grabbed a slippery brown newt. Jack looked up from what he was doing and noticed everyone looking at him. He grinned as he held the newt up in the air for all to see.

Sam smiled and shook his head. "See what I mean," Sam said to Molly.

"I guess I do." Molly turned toward Emily and Jim. "And I appreciate you guys, too."

Jim shrugged, threw his apple core into the woods, and said, "Okay, team, I'm open to suggestions."

Sam was the first to speak. "I think we ought to use both boats and head up the east side of the lake." He gestured with his paddle toward the rocky east shore. "Sounds like Jim already hit the other shore pretty good this morning, but there's a lot of little inlets in the rocks you can't see from here. Plus, the east side is much more difficult to access by land. It doesn't seem like the puppy could get very far along that east shore but we have to rule out that possibility before we search any more on the west side.

"We have two boats, so we should use them to our best advantage by spreading out and covering as much of the east side as we can. Obviously, we'll keep our ears and eyes open for signs of Elvis in all directions as we work our way up the lake. If we get to the far end of the lake and haven't had any Elvis sightings, then we'll divide up and try to cover the west shore on the way back. Sound good, everyone?"

Everyone nodded in agreement, and while no one spoke, the same thought existed in the minds of all three graduate students: Sam's confidence and knowledge of the area greatly increased their chances of success.

"Oh, and in case anyone forgot," Sam added, "we're also keeping an eye out for any and all snakes!"

In Sam's own mind, he was not optimistic about finding the missing pooch. In fact, he had to squelch the feelings that he had absolutely no idea what he was going to do next. Still worse, Sam felt that Elvis, inexperienced about the ways of the woods, had probably fallen prey to the local carnivores. He wasn't about to let his pessimism show, so he was making an effort to keep the mood light and positive.

Sam drove his car up to the road and parked it. He was gone from view for a couple minutes and when he returned, he was carrying a stout stick that was dead, dry, and stripped of bark. He hustled back down the inclined boat ramp to the waiting canoes. Everyone had situated themselves in the canoes and was patiently waiting in silence when he returned. As he approached the canoe, everyone looked in his direction, half-expecting him to say something.

"Folks, I was reading about cryptozoology on the Internet this morning. Cryptozoology is the search for hidden or undiscovered creatures. I guess that makes us all cryptozoologists. Anyway, I saw a message from a Russian guy named Dmitri Bayanov. He was saying that the superstition about "knocking on wood" to bring you good luck comes from the Celts in the British Isles. They believed that forests were inhabited by 'wood spirits'. If you rap on a tree with a stout stick, you would awaken the spirit living in that tree, who would then be awake to hear your prayer."

Sam looked around at the lake and mountain. "We have a huge area to search here and we're going to need all the luck we can get. So, before we leave, I'm going to try and wake up any nearby wood spirits that might be willing to listen to our prayers. I'll rap, and you all pray." With that, he rapped strongly, slowly, three times on a nearby cedar tree. The echo of the knock carried across the lake then returned a few seconds later. Sam smiled in satisfaction and tossed the stick back into the woods. "That should do it."

"Amen to that," Molly said.

Sam favored dividing the search party as equally as possible for the two canoes. Jack's seat was a low folding lawn chair that he was accustomed to occupying in the center of the canoe when boating with both his parents. That made room for Molly in the bow. Jim and Emily shared the green canoe.

Sam pushed his canoe off the beach and boarded it in one graceful motion. Jim followed. The canoes departed the beach and veered left along the east bank of the lake. So, off they paddled, Sam leading the charge.

"Stay positive," Sam thought to himself. "We can do this, we can do this. I wasn't doing anything today. I might as well take my kid canoeing at Squaw Meadow with some college kids."

They paddled for ten minutes up the widening lake. Sam reached down to get a water bottle out of the lunch cooler. Fumbling with the lid of the cooler he dropped his paddle in the bottom of the boat with a resonating thud. A moment later, a knock on wood emanated from the forest on the east side of the lake ahead of the boats. Molly turned around and glanced at Sam with a look of surprise. Sam raised his eyebrows and looked back at Molly. "I guess the spirits are awake. Care to answer it, Jack?" he said.

"Yep," Jack agreed matter-of-factly.

Jack turned his paddle upside down and thudded against the bottom of the boat with the t-grip on the end of his paddle. Paddling ceased. The canoes drifted to a stop. Everyone craned their necks and listened. A silent minute elapsed. Sam opened his mouth to say something but just before any words came out, a reply emanated from the woods, "Thud!"

"Hikers?" Jim said.

"Possible, but I doubt it," Sam whispered. "There's no trail over there."

"Then, what is it?" Molly asked.

"The locals." Sam whispered.

"The who?"

"Who cares? Follow that noise. When you're looking for a needle in a haystack, it's okay to grasp at straws."

"...and mix our metaphors," Molly muttered.

"Where'd it come from," Sam asked.

"Right about there," Molly pointed toward a cluster of dense brush on the east bank of the lake.

"Sound about right, Jack?" Sam asked.

"Yep, right there."

"Let's get a closer look, unless someone has a better idea."

They paddled closer to the east side of the lake.

Jack piped up, "Listen! Did you hear that?"

"Hear what?" Sam replied.

They paused again. "I don't hear anything, but then again, I've been to a few too many concerts by *The Who*. My hearing's not the best, anymore."

After a few seconds, Sam put his paddle in the water and began to paddle again. As soon as his paddle began to make a splashing sound, Jack spoke up again. "There it is. Did you hear that?"

"No," Sam said. "What was it?"

"Barking." Jack said. "It sounded like barking."

Molly gasped. "Elvis!"

"Shush!"

Sam held a hand high in the air, and then held his index finger to his mouth. The second boat drifted to a stop. Both canoes veered slowly sideways in the light breeze coming off the mountain. Everyone sat still. Ripples of wake stopped emanating from the motionless watercraft. The occupants of the canoes simultaneously strained to hear any sounds from the forested shore. The sun shone down on the warm June morning. A fish lept from the water then splashed. No one moved. Jack sat upright and shifted his head to one side, listening more intently than ever.

"There it is again. Over there!" Jack pointed toward the rocky east shore where a huge pile of boulders protruded from the still water of the lake and projected hundreds of feet up the steep slope of Squaw Butte.

"Good golly, Miss Molly, we're in business!"

Sam turned around and gestured once again toward Emily and Jim in the other boat. "Thattaway!" Then they began paddling toward the rock outcropping on the east shore of the lake.

"Can you believe this?" Sam said to no one in particular. "Jack, I don't know how you do it, but you do it every time. You're our lucky charm."

They drew nearer to the large jumble of boulders on the bank. Jack stopped paddling and listened. Everyone else followed suit.

"There it is, again," Jack said, pointing to his right side. "It's over there."

"I heard it that time," said Sam.

"Me, too. A dog. It's a dog!" Molly said, barely able to contain her excitement.

They paddled vigorously now, creating a chevron-shaped wake trailing outward from the stern of their craft. The second canoe began to fall behind as the powerful strokes from three paddlers in Sam's boat lunged it toward the rocky bank. As they drew closer to the shore, the enormity of the boulders became clear. Parts of the bank that weren't covered by huge boulders were thick with devil's club and mountain laurel. There was no obvious landing. They veered right and paddled parallel to the bank, looking for a flat spot or inlet where they could pull in to shore.

"Over there, right next to the rocks," Sam said.

Tall grass concealed a small sand bar. The canoe skidded to a stop beneath a huge ancient cedar tree.

"Elvis!" Molly called into the trees from her seat in the canoe. Barking immediately answered her call. Snapping and crashing could be heard from within the woods. "Here, boy!" she called. More sticks snapped. Jack stood up and stepped from the canoe onto tall grass. As he sunk in the morass to the middle of his ankles, he managed to steady himself with his paddle. Molly dropped her paddle and disembarked. She splashed through the ankle deep watercress up onto the rocks where she ducked beneath a low hanging branch and disappeared into the ferns.

Her voice continued to filter out of the dense brush, calling, "Here, Boy! Here Boy!"

Less than a minute later, Molly returned to the sand bar, guiding her Labrador puppy by the collar and a broad smile on her face. Sam was out of the boat, high-fiving with Jack as the second canoe pulled up to the sand bar.

"Elvis!" Emily called as Jim beached the second canoe. "Are we ever glad to see you!"

The dog was wagging his tail vigorously and moving energetically from person to person, splashing and sniffing everyone and yipping with excitement. Everyone was out of the canoes, standing in shallow water and smiling. Sam sat on a boulder at the edge of the grass, and Jack began working his way out the boulders to the point that they formed, protruding out into the lake.

"Be careful buddy, those rocks could dislodge and roll. They may not be as solid as they look."

Jack didn't look up or acknowledge his dad's warning. He just continued to scramble until he reached the scenic point of the rocks. Sam kept his eyes on Jack. The girls gathered around the dog and looked him over, deciding Elvis didn't look any the worse for spending the night out in the woods, in fact he was surprisingly free of cuts, scratches or other sign of injury. Jim stamped down tall grass with each step, working his way over to Sam.

"Amazing! That was easy!" he said to Sam.

"I know. I can't figure it out. How the hell did that dog find his way out here? Doesn't make sense. Don't get me wrong. I'm pleased we found it, but I never thought we'd see that dog again. Then, ten minutes after launching, he shows up on the inaccessible side of the lake. I just don't get it."

As Sam was talking, Jack was peering intently between the rocks at water's edge. Then he was leaning over, and reaching his arm between the rocks. Sam was still watching him, his parental instincts keeping him alert.

"Whatcha got there, Jack? More newts?"

Jack didn't reply. Instead, he stood straight up from his squatting position on the boulder, still staring intently at a water-filled crevice between the boulders at the edge of the lake. Jack's next move caught everyone by surprise, none more so than his father. Jack spun around to face the lake and jumped into the lake with both feet. He landed with a splash in knee-deep water, then lunged into the water with arms out in front of him and palms open. "JACK! What the hell are you doing?" Sam screamed, dropping his paddle and scrambling toward the boy who was now on his knees in water up to his waist.

In unison, Jim and the two girls stopped attending to the dog and looked toward the splashing boy. Jack didn't look up, nor did he acknowledge the outburst of parental alarm. If his last move was surprising to the group, his next move was about to positively astonish his spectators; Jack stood straight up, dripping wet, and lifted his arms out of the water to display a snake.

Sam froze in his tracks. Jack was at it again. He nonchalantly held the snake up for all to see, then looked over at his father, and smiled.

Seeing Jack standing calmly in the water, Sam surmised his partially submerged son was in no immediate danger. He slowed his scramble to a more measured walk across the boulders toward his boy. He was more than a little annoyed at Jack's unannounced and unbridled burst of creature-catching enthusiasm. Sam felt the need to admonish his son for such unsafe and unannounced behavior.

"Jack, could you hold off on critter catching while we deal with this dog?"

If Jack's last move almost gave his father a heart attack, the next words out of Jack's mouth would certainly finish the job.

"It's one of the snakes, Dad! I caught one! It's one of the snakes we're looking for!"

Shock and surprise registered on the faces of everyone present. Sam felt a flush come over his entire body. He stood staring at Jack, mouth hanging wide open, in stunned silence. He was dumbfounded, virtually paralyzed with surprise.

Jim was quicker to recover. Saying nothing, Jim dashed toward his canoe and grabbed his daypack from the bottom of the boat. Then he moved as swiftly as he dared across rocks to the boy with the snake. Molly was on one knee next to the dog, keeping a firm grip on Elvis, but otherwise frozen. Emily stood straight up and watched in silence as Jack carefully manipulated the foot long serpent as he struggled to retain his grip.

"Don't move, Jack. Don't move a muscle," Jim whispered as firmly but quietly as he could. "Stay right there!"

"I'll be god damned!" was all Sam could say. As Jim flashed by him, Sam finally recovered from his shock and surprise enough to chorus in with Jim's command.

"Yes! Right!" Sam stammered. "Stay there. We'll come to you. Hang onto that thing!"

"Are you alright, Jack?" Sam called. "Aren't you freezing?"

"No, the water's really warm right here!"

"It's warm?"

"Yeah. Really warm."

Jim was on his knees, fumbling with his pack. He produced a sack made of heavy white canvas. "Hold on, Jack! Just hold on to that thing. I'm almost there," Jim said as he scrambled back to his feet, canvas sack still in his hands. Sam stared intently at Jack and didn't budge. Jack obeyed the commands and remained still in the lake.

Yet another surprise was about to emerge from Jack's mouth. "There's another one! It's swimming out of the rocks! I think I can get it!"

"No!" cried the grad student. "Let it go! Just hang onto that one! Whatever you do, don't let go of the one you have!"

"I got it. I won't let go," Jack said.

"Excellent, I'm almost there," Jim said. Calmly, carefully, he crossed fractured boulders, making his way toward the boy, who still clutched the snake in his firm grasp.

Jim held the bag out toward Jack as he approached. "Right here, guy. Put 'er right here."

Jack dropped the snake in the bag. Jim drew the string tight and held the bag tight around the top. He held up his hand, palm out toward Jack. Still a little overwhelmed by the sudden turn of events, Jack wasn't sure what he was supposed to do next. Jim smiled broadly and then Jack understood, smiled, raised his hand, and 'high five-ed' Jim's palm.

Jim didn't dare open the bag until he was on solid ground. Everyone gathered around to examine the catch. In the bottom of the bag, coiled into a wad, was an iridescent green snake identical to the one they photographed in Dr. Wertz's lab in Corvallis.

"We got it!" Jim proclaimed triumphantly, raising a fist into the air. Then he paused, looked down at Jack, and in a gesture of deference and appreciation, corrected himself. "*He* got it. Jack, you're my hero. This is history…this is history, Jack, and you made it! What other kid your age, anywhere on earth, can lay claim to this kind of accomplishment. You discovered a new species. A ten-year-old kid discovered a new species."

"Eleven," Jack corrected. "I turned eleven two days ago."

Everyone laughed. They shook hands, hugged, and laughed some more. Through it all, Sam was beaming with quiet pride. He didn't want to say or do anything to detract from Jack's moment in the sun, but many thoughts relating to the significance of this find raced through his head. This was a big deal for Jack and it would remain a lifetime accomplishment. Then there was Squaw Meadow. Jack had sealed the fate of Squaw Meadow.

This was nothing short of a momentous day in the history of the whole Mt. Hood National Forest, and Jack was the guy who made it happen. Sam couldn't help but feel emotional. He got a lump in his throat just thinking about it. His eyes misted with tears of joy. But then reality and practicality returned to the forefront of his consciousness. He grabbed his digital camera from his daypack and assembled everyone for a group photo. Jim reminded them that they ought to get busy and look around the area as thoroughly as possible to see if more could be learned about the immediate area and why it constituted some kind of unique habitat. Everyone fanned out to observe and document the situation. Emily was checking the temperature and dissolved oxygen of the water.

"Twenty-five degrees!" she announced. "That's Celsius! That's hot water. Eighty-seven degrees Fahrenheit! Folks we got some kind of warm spring coming out of this talus slope. It's starting to make a bit of sense. We have a unique habitat here. No telling what else is going on back inside of these huge jumbles of rocks. There could be a cave or even a cave system back in here. There could be an underwater entrance. We could have this shoreline explored by a diver and find something even more incredible. This is really interesting. I can't understand why no one has ever found this before."

"This whole talus slope changed last winter," Sam said. "There was a big slide after all that heavy rain. All this rock is new. It came from that cliff up there." He pointed to a vertical cliff high above the lake. "See how fresh all the breaks are on these rocks and up there on that cliff. This is all new. Maybe it opened up a hot spring system that was subterranean. I don't know. But whatever is going on here, I bet they'll study this place for years to come. We got the real deal here, boys and girls. This whole thing is amazing."

"We wouldn't be here right now if it wasn't for that dog," Jim reminded them. "It's impossible, really, when you think about how we came to end up right here, right now. Through an extraordinary set of circumstances, Elvis actually *led* us here!"

He paused, looking at the pooch, "Makes me wonder exactly what happened to the dog last night. First, the dog disappeared, then it ended up way out here. Did it just wander out here on its own? I sure can't explain it," Jim exclaimed, still clutching the bag with the snake in it. I can tell you that dog was nabbed last night. By what, I have no idea. How it ended up here, I'll never know. It's like we were led here."

"And would we be standing here congratulating ourselves without Jack?" Sam wondered. First, the dog disappeared. Then it reappeared just as mysteriously.

"The more I think about it the weirder everything seems," Sam said. "Something is going on here. I can just feel it. We were led here. How, or why, I can't say, but this whole deal is just too bizarre to be shrugged off as coincidence. Somebody is steering these events. I can't help feeling that we're pawns in someone else's game."

Chapter 26

IT FELT LIKE Christmas. The last day of the school year had arrived for the kids at Redland Middle School. Despite the rain outside, students were jubilant and energetic. Only thirty minutes remained in the school year and the students were scurrying about the crowded hallway, collecting signatures and writing farewell messages to each other on the pages of their yearbooks. Teachers were spread throughout the hallways, each surrounded by a cluster of students. Each teacher was busily signing yearbook after yearbook, as though they were rock stars outside the backstage door of the concert hall.

One teacher was absent from this farewell hubbub in the hallway. Sam Ward was sitting at his desk in an otherwise empty classroom. In years past, he had dutifully signed the inside covers of an endless stream of yearbooks which were thrust before him by giddy students.

This year, Sam was not excited, he was just tired. He was more concerned with grading the last of the assignments so he could calculate grades for the 163 students he taught. In truth, the farewell messages and signatures that Sam was expected to hurriedly scrawl were tedious and unfulfilling.

"Students don't care about my signature. They want their friends' signatures, not mine," Sam told himself. "Students only ask the teachers to sign the yearbook because the teachers are standing there with pen in hand."

Sam decided he would rather make a dent in the formidable pile of work he had before him. The students wouldn't even miss him.

While Sam may have been generally correct, there were exceptions. One student was actively seeking out Mr. Ward and becoming frustrated by her failure to do so in the crowded hallway. Yearbook folded beneath her arm, Ellie Foster made her way toward Mr. Ward's science classroom.

The doorknob clicked; Sam looked up. A tall, bright-eyed girl carrying a knapsack and wearing a Nike tracksuit over a volleyball team jersey tentatively stepped into the classroom. Ellie smiled and waved her yearbook by way of announcing her intention.

Sam forced a half-hearted smile. Inside, he tried not to show it but he was not at all pleased to see this particular student's cheerful countenance grace his doorway. The popular, pretty, and athletic girl that had found Mr. Ward sequestered in his classroom was none other than Sam's former neighbor, the daughter of Bart Foster.

"Greetings, Miss Foster. To what do I owe the pleasure?" Sam asked.

"I want you to sign my yearbook!" Ellie cheerfully replied.

Sam let a moment deliberately pass before he replied. "Very well, then. Bring it here." Though he knew better than to begrudge students for past difficulties at the end of the year, Sam was still feeling stung over the complaint and the scolding he took from the principal over the bigfoot lesson. Then there was the meeting with the principal over the same issue. "Miss Foster, here, had nothing to do with that," Sam thought.

But, this was also his pal Bart's daughter; the one who generated the complaint, the student who managed to get her parents irate over the allegedly inappropriate science lesson. What's more, Ellie's dad must have heard by now that the snake Jack found had been verified by Russell Wertz at Oregon State and the whole Squaw Meadow development plan was now utterly jeopardized. Sam assumed that, right now, his name was synonymous with The Devil around the Foster household. And of all the awkward ironies, here was Bart's daughter asking him to sign her yearbook.

Sam wondered whether Ellie even knew what was taking place in respect to her father's plans to develop their family holding at Squaw Meadow. He certainly had no intention of bringing it up. It was a very awkward moment for him and he was eager to get the whole thing over with. But the uncomfortable encounter took a rather unexpected turn when Ellie said and did something that caught Sam completely by surprise.

As she handed her yearbook to her science teacher, Ellie said, "I wanted to give you a present." With that she reached into her backpack and produced a book which she presented to a stunned Sam Ward: *The Locals: A Contemporary Investigation of the Bigfoot/Sasquatch Phenomenon.*

Sam glanced down at the book then up at the tall student. "You've got to be kidding me," he said. "Kid, are you trying to get me in trouble?"

"No. I bought it for you. "

"If your parents hear about this, they're going to absolutely *freak*! I caught holy hell from them and Principal Lavelle for bringing up the subject in class. You must know that. Where did you get this?"

"Oh, they know I have it. I found it on the Internet. My mom bought it for me. I've already read it. I thought you might like to read it," Ellie said.

Sam asked suspiciously, "Is this some kind of joke?" He could feel himself getting annoyed. Once again, all the feelings of mistreatment and resentment Sam felt when he was admonished by the principal welled up inside him. But Ellie's next remark effectively defused the situation.

"Mr. Ward, I'm really sorry if I got you in trouble. I know my parents complained about the lesson you did on bigfoot."

"They said it gave you nightmares..."

"I did have nightmares, but it wasn't your fault. I was already having the nightmares before that. My parents blamed the nightmares on the bigfoot lesson. It wasn't the truth. That's what I wanted to explain," Ellie said.

Sam set the book down on the corner of his desk and sat back in his chair. "First of all, for the hundredth time, it wasn't a bigfoot lesson. It was a lesson on the scientific method," Sam stated emphatically. "But that said, Miss Foster, I trust you're going to explain."

Ellie smiled nervously, and said, "Mr. Ward, please don't be mad. Your lesson really helped me, but I didn't know why until I read this book. It's really hard to explain. It all started when we lived down the road from you on Squaw Mountain Road. When I was a little kid my bedroom window faced the woods. I used to have these dreams and I would wake up and see this face in my bedroom window... a hairy, ugly face... and I would scream and cry and refuse to sleep in my room."

The teen-ager paused. Her voice cracked with emotion. She continued, "I would only sleep in my parents' bedroom. My dad couldn't figure out what it was. My window was seven feet off the ground so he was sure there wasn't someone looking in the window, but I insisted there was. This went on for a couple years. My dad knew that his grandfather died in what became my bedroom. Since my grandfather had a stern face and a big, bushy beard, my parents thought the house, or at least my room, was haunted."

Sam's eyebrows rose. He looked at her intent eyes.

"My dad never said anything to anybody about all this, because he didn't want the new owners to know why we wanted to sell the house. As soon as we moved into the new house, everything was okay, but I still sometimes wondered what I saw in the window when I was a little kid. My parents always told me I was imaging it, but they also thought I might be seeing a ghost..." her voice trailed off.

"When Jenna's dad came in and showed the pictures and read the reports of what people saw, I had another nightmare for the first time in years. My parents were upset because they thought it was going to happen all over again, like it did when I was little. That's why they complained. But, it suddenly made sense to me for the first time. What I saw was just like that one old bigfoot movie from the 1960's you see on TV. I told Jenna and she showed me this book her dad had. In one of the chapters it talks about cases where the sasquatch looked in peoples windows. I showed it to my mom and I said, "See mom, I *told* you there was a hairy man looking in my window."

With false courage, Ellie said primly, "It's just like what they're saying in this book. That's what happened to me! My mom just sat there with her hand on her mouth and tears in her eyes. She hugged me and apologized for not believing me. She promised that she would never again doubt what her kids told her. Then she cried. You really helped me Mr. Ward. You helped us solve the mystery of what happened when I was little. And now my parents believe me..." Now, Ellie's courage was gone, her voice again cracked with emotion. She wiped a tear from her eye with her sleeve.

By then, Sam was beyond understanding; he was speechless. He felt tears well up in his own eyes as he looked at the emotion that surfaced as the kid finished her story. It was another awkward moment but for an entirely different reason. Sam looked down at the book on his desk. Ellie watched as he lifted the cover. Inside the cover, on the title page was written, "To Sam, Your science class taught us to listen carefully to the words of our children. Thank you, Judy Foster."

"My mom wrote that."

Sam smiled a melancholy smile. He sat for a moment, looking down at the inscription in the book and struggling with his own emotion. He wanted to give Ellie a hug, but then thought it improper to hug such a mature-looking student. Instead, he remained in his chair and looked up at the girl standing beside his desk.

"Your parents aren't the only ones who have learned to be better listeners. I've been going through the same thing with my son. It must be something that happens at some time or another to every family that lives on that old Squaw Mountain Road. My son was telling me what he felt was going on in the woods. I didn't believe him until just the other day. I finally understood what he had been saying all along."

"I just couldn't accept the idea as long as it carried the 'bigfoot' label. It just makes the whole strange possibility sound completely silly.

"Then I started to recognize the subtle signs that something really was there. My kid was saying it and I doubted it. Then I realized he was right. They're really there, but they're so elusive. I can see how your parents came to think of them as ghosts.

"I started calling them the 'Nowhere Men' because I happened to hear the Beatles song, "Nowhere Man," on the radio. I listened to the lyrics and I realized they're not the Nowhere Man, we are. We're all Nowhere Men at times. We don't listen, and we don't see, so we miss the subtle signs all around us that we're actually sharing our world with some kind of other beings.

"They're not just undiscovered animals, either," Sam continued. "They may actually be people. I just don't know. But there's something out there, all right. It seems like they leave us clues. The clues are so subtle and we're so busy that we never stop to notice. We're also so prejudiced, and our minds are so made up, that there's little chance of noticing the subtle signs, even out here in the country where it seems to be going on."

"It seems that the children in places like the Squaw Mountain Road see them first, and most adults don't ever come to realize that these beings are around unless, of course, they listen to what their children are saying. Ask yourself how often that happens."

Ellie smiled. Just then, from her hip pocket came the ring tone of her cell phone. "Sorry. I know we're not supposed to have our phones in school but my mom's picking me up to go to the orthodontist. I get my braces off today."

As she flipped open her phone, Sam smiled, took her yearbook, scrawled a "Good luck in high school" message and signed it. He handed Ellie her yearbook. She took it and mouthed a silent 'thank you' while she listened to her call. Then she turned and scurried toward the door, cell phone still on her ear, listening intently to whatever directions she was being given. As she headed out the door, she turned to offer a parting wave. He returned the wave and Ellie disappeared. The door clicked shut, Sam smiled and resumed his task of entering assignment scores into the computer.

Within minutes of Ellie's departure, the doorknob rattled again and into the room walked Iris' Uncle Henry. Sam grinned.

"Before you got away for the summer I wanted to stop in and congratulate the famous Sam Ward, eco-warrior. I saw the article in the paper the other day about your kid and the snake he turned over to Oregon State. Quite a story, there Mr. Ward: The snake that stopped the development. The story focused on your boy but I could see your footprints all over that one. May I offer my congratulations?"

"Henry, you were a huge help...more help than you'll ever know. But, as I told the reporter who wrote that story, I didn't do anything except drive the taxi. It was my son who pulled off the miracle.

"He found the snakes, not once but three different times, never even dreaming that those snakes were the whole key to permanent preservation of Squaw Meadow. He was just doing what he did best, and that's catching snakes. The amazing thing is the way he insisted on correctly identifying them long after the rest of us stopped caring. The irony of it all was that I wanted to stop the development somehow while my son already had the solution in his hands."

"Meanwhile, I was busy ignoring him while I barked up the wrong tree. After getting with Nick Rollo and hearing about the sasquatch, in my colossal naivety, my best idea was to stop the development by showing the world that such creatures existed."

"The only problem was, I had no real idea how to do that, and I was even less aware of *their* unwillingness to cooperate. Then, you gave me the idea of leaving them gifts and that got me going in a direction, which led to a whole series of coincidences. While stumbling around in the woods trying to buddy up to the sasquatch by leaving gifts, I found what I still think might be a sasquatch grave. The same day we found the grave, my son found the snake that we ended up taking home. But I completely overlooked the snake and got this bright idea to dig up the grave, in hopes of unearthing the proverbial sasquatch bones. What a mistake that turned out to be."

"Had I known before hand, I would have told you that was a bad idea," Henry said with a smile.

"I know. And I never would have believed you because I didn't understand exactly *why* it was a bad idea until you walked into my classroom.

"Some things," Sam continued, "you just have to find out for yourself. I still can't really believe what went on. I didn't get far into the grave before some really bad things started to happen. You better believe I put that grave back together as fast as I could once I found out exactly why you don't mess with one of their graves, even if you do find it."

"After that fiasco, I just gave up. I was fresh out of ideas and I figured there was nothing I could do to stop the resort, and I quit trying. Then, all of a sudden a thought popped into my head, "Help your kid." I don't know where it came from, but at least I listened. I dropped what I was doing and started helping him just when he was trying to identify the snake. After that, things pretty much started happening by themselves. I had this idea to call Oregon State, and just to find an expert who could get the snake identified. One thing led to another. It's like, once I stopped trying, my kid's ability did what I couldn't do. He did it just by being curious and keeping his eyes wide open.

"Still, we had to find the unique habitat the snakes required. That happened by way of another long series of coincidences that brought both Jack and I up to the meadow and, ultimately, right to the place where the snake's habitat existed. We were almost dragged back up to that meadow by forces beyond our control. That's what has me wondering, and that's why I asked you to stop by. It seems like the whole set of circumstances that led to Jack finding the snakes was just too many coincidences to shrug off. After the fifth or sixth consecutive coincidence, I think they stopped being coincidences."

"A series of improbable coincidences," Henry said, "is called a synchronicity. It may be nothing more than a series of bizarre coincidences but I tend to doubt it. Science has no answer for such things, as you know, but it begins to look like we are sometimes being guided by forces from beyond our realm."

Both men paused and reflected for a moment.

"In retrospect, it seems like the synchronicities really began to happen once I attempted to understand the whole sasquatch mystery. It definitely seems like it was some sort of trigger at that point for what began to happen. That's why I called you. You're kind of a metaphysical guy, and you understand the whole sasquatch phenomenon better than anyone else I know, so I was really hoping you could give me some insight into this. It's really been bugging me."

Henry didn't answer right away. He stared down at the floor, and thought for a moment, then he smiled. His eyes raised to meet Sam's eyes, and he said, "Like you said a few minutes ago, you have to figure it out for yourself, because you wouldn't believe me if I told you. It sounds like you've begun to figure a few things out for yourself, though. The fact that you're asking says to me you have some pretty strong suspicions."

"I sure do. But like you said, it's too much to accept, despite my suspicions. I was hoping you would confirm a few things for me."

"Ah, so the scientist in you wants validation, but as you well know, my verbal testimony, even if it agrees with your suspicions, does not constitute scientific verification, now does it?" Henry reminded Sam.

Sam smiled. "I suppose not, but right now I'm grasping at straws. I'll take anything I can get. The whole matter is already well beyond the boundaries of science."

"Remember that Indians view the sasquatch as part material being, part spirit. I think the thing that probably perplexes you the most is how the sasquatch, or whatever else it is, works behind the scenes and seems to even know what it is you want or need, so that it can help you from there. The fact that it does seem to know what your needs are, means it can listen in on your world. How does that happen?"

"You know I never thought about it, but that's an excellent point. How do they know?"

"Either they can enter our world or they can simply read our thoughts. The tribes have legends and insights as to what might be going on, but it would be good if science told us what part of these traditional sources of information has the ring of truth. But, to answer your question, I'll hazard a guess that, if the sasquatch were to know that some particular location that was important to them was somehow threatened by human activity, then I do think they would try to manipulate events in order to protect their interests. They can do a few things, but they may also need the help of certain humans if it becomes necessary to intervene in human affairs. They will not necessarily enter our world and shake us by the lapels to get our attention. They'll just tweak things, nudge things, and hopefully catch someone's attention. They cannot accomplish permanent change in the world of humanity all by themselves. They need a little help from their friends on the other side, our side, of the veil."

Sam was intrigued by his words. Henry continued to explain. "I submit that the sasquatch were well aware of the threat to Squaw Meadow and the surrounding area, as they know of many such threats, but they chose to intervene by enlisting the participation of certain very capable individuals, such as you and your son. They shared your desire to safeguard the meadow and they needed your help as much as you needed theirs. To use a baseball analogy, once they knew they could count on you to swing at the right pitch, they did what they could to throw you a pitch they knew you could hit. But whatever pitch they arranged, they still need someone to swing the bat on their behalf. You and your son were their home run hitters. You didn't know it was coming, but they sent you a 'fat pitch,' and as they hoped, you swung the bat and hit a home run. You won the game. I suspect they are grateful."

"I hope you're right, but either way, it sure feels strange to be making a place in my life for spirits. Being a career science teacher and all, I've always been a pretty literal, concrete kind of guy. Now, I'm told to accommodate this mystical element. It sort of scares me. It implies that I have less control over my own life."

"Maybe the control you thought you had was a bit of an illusion."

"That occurred to me, but I think it's necessary to assume one has control over one's own life, at least most of the time. Otherwise, one might decide to wait for the spirit beings to hand you your life's plan, rather than coming up with it yourself."

"Yes, you can't wait for the spirits to buy your groceries. You have to come up with the direction for your life. But, if you have a direction, it makes it easier, I think, for the spirits to find you and even work through you.

"Okay, then what?"

"Keep your eyes open. Remember: 'It goes as *they* allow.' If they want you to get a hit, they'll send you a nice, fat pitch: a 'beach ball' right across the plate. But then *you* still have to swing that bat, my friend, if you're gonna drive in that winning run." Henry smiled and added, "Boy, I *love* baseball analogies."

"Speaking of baseball analogies," Sam said, "that sounds just like the one I'm always saying to the kids in the dugout: 'Good things happen when you swing the bat'."

Chapter 27

THE SHRILL WHINE of a chainsaw echoed off the steep slopes of the Squaw Creek canyon. Blue smoke and saw chips spewed from the machine as it chewed through the trunk of a large maple tree. As the chainsaw labored, the entire canopy of the maple tree shuddered, as if disturbed by a breeze. Then the top of the tree began to move sideways as loud cracking noises emanated from the base of the trunk.

The familiar cry of, "Tim-berrr!" went up, though there was no one around to hear it except the man who cried it out. The treetop began a slow arc away from the house. Gathering speed, the tree plunged faster and faster earthward. A heavy thud shook the ground, followed by the crash of shattering branches and limbs. The chainsaw engine died and Sam Ward tilted back the facemask of his helmet to inspect the situation.

The fallen big-leaf maple tree now extended the length of the lawn with its canopy of branches and leaves blocking the driveway. He gave a sigh of relief. The tree in his bad dream was now safely on the ground without inflicting any damage to the log house that had taken so much work to build. Sam flipped down the facemask on his helmet, restarted the chainsaw, and began the sweaty process of lopping branches to clear the driveway. As the chainsaw barked, he carefully bucked tree limbs into firewood, just the right length for the house's cast iron stove.

But, as logger's luck would have it, as he began to clear the tangle of branches, a vehicle rolled up his driveway. Intent on the work of cutting branches and limbs, and with the chainsaw engine racing loudly, Sam didn't see or hear the approach of the big red pickup until it was just a few feet from the fallen tree.

Motion caught the corner of Sam's eye as he worked. He looked up and was startled to see the truck which suddenly appeared through the tree limbs covering the drive. He was even more surprised to see who was driving the truck. Sam finished sawing a large limb as the driver-side door of the pickup opened and Bart Foster stepped down from the raised cab of his pick-up truck. Sam clicked off the saw. The growl of the chainsaw was replaced with a deafening silence.

After a long, awkward pause, Sam finally offered a feeble, cautious greeting. "How you doin'?"

"Not bad ..." Bart returned with a shrug. Looking over the fallen tree, he said, "This big old maple was in just the right spot to fall on your house in a high wind, wasn't it?"

"Yeah, it worried me for a long time. It needed to go. Plus, I needed more firewood for this winter. I'm almost afraid to ask but, what brings you around here?"

Being a quick thinking fellow, Bart saw an opportunity to remark on the irony of the situation in front of him, "I'm trying to stop people like you from cutting down all that's left of the trees around here!"

Sam wasn't going to be out done. "I'm blocking my driveway to keep the Chamber of Commerce from lynching me!"

"Might not be a bad idea!"

"I hope I'm doing the right thing shutting off this saw. I'm thinking I might need it to defend myself."

"Don't worry, if I was here to kill you, you'd already be dead," Bart assured him, smiling a sinister smile.

Sam decided to address the obvious issue directly. "Hey, I'm really sorry about what happened. I didn't mean to ..." he began, but his voice trailed off. Sam was at a loss for words.

Bart cut him off. "Sam, I didn't come here to make you squirm. I'll make this easy for you. I'm not mad. I certainly was two weeks ago, but I'm not now. It's all good. In fact, it's amazingly good. You don't even know what's gone down in the last two weeks since the whole snake discovery was announced. As it turns out, you actually did me a big favor."

"Oh, really? That *is* news."

"Yeah, I expected to see you around the baseball diamond and give you the whole story, but now that baseball season is winding down, that might not happen. Since I was in the neighborhood, I thought I'd stop by and fill you in. It's kind of funny, really, how it all ended up. You got a few minutes to hear the whole story?"

"Sure do." He put down the chainsaw, took off his helmet, and sat down on the end of the maple log that lay across the driveway.

"First of all, the guy at Oregon State who you gave the snake to..."

"Dr. Wertz."

"Yeah, Wertz. He, of course, notified the Forest Service district ranger for the Clackamas Ranger District the day after he got the snake. Then, as you probably know, the shit hit the fan. Within hours, the district ranger had a whole team of biologists up there at the meadow."

"I knew that. About two weeks ago, my wife saw two Forest Service rigs roll by when she was getting the paper. We knew right then that it was time to circle the wagons. She recognized one of the Wertz' grad students in the rig, so she knew that Forest Service and Oregon State were sharing notes."

"Right. So here's one of the amusing parts. First, the District Ranger comes to me, in person, and tells me that the whole land swap was off. Cancelled. Ka-put. Naturally, I hit the roof. I wanted to know what the hell was going on. They said it was about critical habitat for some ultra-sensitive ecological species they'd found." Bart paused, then added, "But, they didn't say anything about some kid finding a new kind of snake up there. They didn't say anything about you or Jack. I saw that part in the paper. That was the first time I knew you two characters had anything to do with it. Well, the Forest Service turns around and says to me that it wasn't because of the kid. They said they knew that rare kind of snake was there all along!"

"I heard that, too. I don't believe it, but I heard it. Russ Wertz told me that when we talked on the phone right after it happened. Wertz thought they wanted to get the credit for finding the snake and officially naming it. It just didn't make sense to me, though. If they knew the snakes were there, why would they keep it a secret? Why wouldn't they brag about their scientific accomplishment?"

"Their story, not that I'm buying it, was that they were afraid people would go up there and mess with the snakes, you know, try to collect them and stuff, if word got out that they were there. They said they kept it all a secret to help protect them."

"Either way," Bart continued, "it makes them look dishonest. If they didn't know the snakes were there, then they're lying when they say they did. If they really did know the snakes were there all along, then they concealed important scientific information, which gives people legitimate reason to wonder what other species they are keeping secret 'just to protect it.' It's not very good land stewardship either way."

"Yeah, well, I can tell you this from personal experience," Sam reflected. "The Federal government's first priority is not protecting endangered species, it's protecting business interests. You know, boosting the old 'gross national product.'

Bart smiled faintly, then said, "Well, truth be told, they probably are. But, as a businessman myself, I'm good with that. Heck, I appreciate it. And I thought we set up a land swap that was a good deal for both sides. That's why I really felt betrayed when they unilaterally cancelled the deal. But they were adamant. After talking to that Oregon State guy of yours, they said there was just no way they could take on that fight. They'd been through the whole 'endangered species' thing too many times, and more importantly, they'd lost every time. They told me there was just no way they could win."

"Well gosh, Bart, even though I didn't welcome the idea of the development, I really do feel badly about my part in killing your land deal. Considering the amount of money you stood to make, you certainly are very magnanimous about this whole thing. I expected you would want to see me dead."

"I did at first," Bart smiled, "but what a difference a week makes. The Forest Service has been up there looking around and they found two new warm springs that have opened up in that lake. They found more of the snakes and their plant people have found a new kind of algae or something. Most of what they found was actually on my part of the meadow, so they quickly came back with an offer to buy me out. They're calling the whole area 'critical habitat' and now they're talking about making the whole place a biological research reserve."

"Wow, that's amazing. When did this all happen?"

"Just in the last few days. They're not going to announce anything for a while, but their first priority is buying me out and gaining control of the whole area."

"And you're okay with that?"

"I'm more than okay with it. I'm ecstatic."

"Why? You lost the resort."

"The resort was a big financial gamble. Getting 'cashed out' is a sure thing. To make the resort happen, I needed to line up investors and that required feasibility studies. Those feasibility studies were done and they identified several tough problems: the lake was too shallow and getting shallower all the time. It would have had to be deepened and that would have been a big extra expense and another huge permit battle."

Bart paused, inwardly reflecting on years of permit hassles. "Sewage disposal was the biggest unresolved infrastructure problem but there were a few others, too. Bottom line was, for all the time and money it would have taken, there was no guarantee the whole thing would have been profitable. I tried to get the Forest Service to buy me out years ago, but they refused. They wouldn't even consider it. All of a sudden, as a result of this whole snake thing, they changed their tune. They asked me to abandon my development plans and just sell them the entire holding. Not only that, but the 'opportunities foregone' as the lawyers say, made the value of the holding much greater."

"I don't understand," Sam said.

"My plan for developing the land was far enough along that it made the place more valuable, and that raised the selling price. Plus, they felt bad in a bureaucratic sort of way about reneging on the original deal after I spent a pile of money on feasibility studies. The papers should be signed within the month, knock on wood. I *might* have made more on the resort but it wasn't a sure thing. This is a sure thing. As they said in 'The Godfather', they 'made me an offer I couldn't refuse'."

"The Oh-Mah-fia is at it again," Sam said under his breath, referring to the sasquatches' unseen influence.

"The what?" Bart said with a puzzled look.

"Am I allowed to ask what this offer was that you could not refuse?"

"Enough that I can afford to buy you lunch next time I see you at Redland Store," Bart said, smiling.

"Wow, Really? Like a hotdog and some jo-jos?" Sam said sarcastically.

"Hell, two hotdogs, and a big order of jo-jos," Bart replied.

Both men laughed.

"Well, Bart, I can't even tell you how relieved I am! I thought we'd be bitter enemies pretty much forever! It's so strange the way this whole thing worked out. I was against Squaw Meadow getting developed, mostly for selfish reasons having to do with traffic and stuff like that, but I gave up any hope of influencing the matter. Then after we found the snakes, I was pleased about what it would do to the meadow, but I dreaded the thought of crossing paths with you around town or at the baseball field. It is really strange the way things worked out."

"Stranger than you'll even know! For starters, I figured from the beginning you'd try to lead the opposition, since you were living right there on the only access road. You had the most to lose. I was just waiting for you to try something. When my kid came home with the story about the bigfoot lesson, I began to figure you were warming up to some kind of claim that it was all bigfoot habitat up there."

"I'll admit I was desperate enough to ponder such a move. I got with local people who had information to about that and I tried to learn all I could." Sam said.

"Yeah. I heard you were talking with Nick Rollo. It's a small town, you know. That's why I was waiting for you to play the 'bigfoot' card."

"Well, you know, after all that time I spent looking into it, I still don't really even 'believe in bigfoot,'" Sam said, raising two fingers of each hand to make quotation marks. "I'm really not even sure they exist. I've never seen one and you know they say: 'seeing is believing." I will say for certain that something really strange seems to be going on around here. For example, something scared the crap out of me the other night in that woods right back there," Sam said, gesturing toward the forest behind the baseball backstop in his pasture. It was right in front of me in the forest but I couldn't see a thing. Of course it was pitch dark and I had no flashlight."

"What in God's name are you doing walking around in the forest at night with no flashlight?"

"It's just something I do from time to time when I can't sleep. I go for walks around the property. I have some pretty wide trails back there. It's easy to find my way around and it gives me a chance to think. Anyway, this thing came right up to me, and it could have had me for dinner if it wanted to. Next thing I knew, there was another one behind me. I mean, man, I was surrounded."

"When was this?"

"This was just a couple of weeks ago. Anyway, I was pretty spooked and all I could think about was that I needed to get the hell out of there, which I did. I walked out of there pretty quickly, but I didn't run, and nothing even chased me. Later, it dawned on me, whatever it was, it let me go. They could have picked me off, no problem. I mean, I was cornered. They had me. Instead, they just let me go. Whatever or whomever it is, I think they wanted to let me to know I was not alone. There's no other explanation that makes any sense."

"My daughter mentioned that she told you about the things that happened when we lived down here. It sounds like the same kind of thing. Something or someone is around and just kind of keeping an eye on things. They don't seem to do any obvious harm. They scare the hell out of people from time to time, but they don't seem to do anything else."

Sam shook his head. "I used to think that, but now I think differently. They do things, all right, but it's so subtle that it's easy to miss it. For one thing, they move things around just to test your powers of observation. The more I look around, the more I see little signs and clues that they leave around the rural landscape. It's kind of spooky, but again, there doesn't seem to be any malicious behaviors. We're not losing livestock. Sometimes, it even seems like, as you said, they're keeping an eye on things. But the strangest thing of all is the way they seem to be able to subtly influence our lives. Bart, you have no idea what's been going on. I can't even believe I'm telling you this because you're going to think I'm crazy..."

"Hey, pal, I thought I was going crazy back when I was living down here and all our stuff was going on. Then, when I saw that book Ellie bought, I couldn't believe how clueless I was. At this stage of the game, I'm totally open to any possibility. I spent too many years denying what was happening around me and not listening to things that my own kid was trying to tell me. This whole thing really opened my mind, and I've resolved to keep it open."

As Bart was speaking, Sam could feel a change was taking place in his relationship with Bart. They were cordial as neighbors, but they had their differences, owing to matters of lifestyle, politics, and so forth. Eventually, those differences became all-important, and they grew very far apart. Now, they stumbled upon a subject that they would share and discuss for a long time to come. Sam forged ahead with his main point.

"Okay, if you don't think I'm crazy after this, then you're probably crazy, too. Anyway, once I woke up, so to speak, to what was happening with this presence that seemed to reside in the landscape from time to time, things started happening that were out of my control but which seemed to be directed at me. Weird coincidences would happen.

Bad things would happen that would suddenly turn into good things. The whole thing about Squaw Meadow just seemed to be steered from some other direction. Just when things seemed to be going badly on just about all fronts, I had this incredible streak of *good* luck in my life. Knock on wood.

"I guess the question that lingers in my mind is whether there is any kind of guiding force behind these so-called coincidences. I have to admit I think there is. I mean, so many strange things have happened, so many events, call them coincidences if you like, have happened lately, right up to the fact that we're standing over this dead tree in my driveway renewing our friendship and agreeing for the first time on a future for Squaw Meadow."

"The weirdest part is the way it seems to be steered by these conscious beings. They're not just some kind of undiscovered animal, that's for sure. I think they seem more like people, except they never step out of the shadows. You might say we have some shady neighbors that we never knew we had."

"I do think I stood face to face with them in the dark that one night, and I got the distinct impression they knew what's going on around this neighborhood of ours. And if we invite them in for coffee, that is, if we acknowledge their presence, then they intervene in our world in subtle ways."

"It seems like they provide us with unexpected opportunities, but they only become opportunities when we recognize them as opportunities and act upon them. To use a baseball analogy, they send us the occasional fat pitch, but we have to be watching for it. Then we have to swing the bat."

"Well, now that it's over, I can tell you that there was one pitch I was waiting for, but luckily for you, you never threw it," Bart confessed.

"Really. What pitch?"

"The whole bigfoot thing, of course. Do you know where the name 'Squaw Mountain' came from?"

"I understand it's a disparaging reference to female anatomy."

"That's baloney. That's what everyone says who thinks they know more than three words of Indian dialect, but they're wrong. Places named 'squaw' do not refer to vaginas. I mean, think about it! Why would anyone name a place Vagina Mountain? It doesn't make any sense.

"'Squaw' is sort of 'settler-slang' for the harder-to-pronounce Kwakiutl Indian word, 'Tsonoqua.' According to my great grandfather, Indians actually called the place Tsonoqua Mountain, not Squaw Mountain. Settlers were not very literate, and language back then was spoken, but rarely written. Indian words were also mispronounced most of the time. The mispronunciations often stuck, and places like 'Tsonoqua Mountain,' became 'Squaw Mountain'. It was just easier to say. And Tsonoqua, or the alternate pronunciation, Tsunukwa, translates into something like "female giant covered with hair and having big feet."

Bart watched Sam staring as he spoke. "In local Indian lore, Squaw Mountain was where the sasquatch lived. If you talked with Nick Rollo, you know, as well as I do from my relatives, that there has been a ton of sasquatch sightings all around the Squaw Mountain area. So, when it came to challenging the resort, naturally I figured that once you learned about the bigfoot history up there, you'd try to raise the whole 'rare-and-endangered-sasquatch' ploy to stop my plan. I was just waiting for that one, but you never brought it up."

"Wow, Bart, I'm really impressed at your knowledge of Native American language. I never heard that about the origin of the word 'squaw'. Even an Indian I talked to said it was a disparaging term."

"Yeah, well, my great grandmother was an Indian, so that makes me part Indian, and you learn a few things like that when you grow up in a pioneer family, living in the shadow of Tsonoqua Mountain," Bart said.

"Anyway," Sam replied, "sorry to disappoint you on the whole sasquatch thing. It didn't take me very long to decide that raising an argument like that would do more harm than good. I figured it would be turned right back on me, serving only to make me look like some kind of *fool*, which would then discredit my whole opposition to the resort project."

"You nailed that one, friend. Now that it's all over, I can tell you that when one plans a big development deal, there really are these meetings where the planners sit around and discuss likely sources of opposition to the project and how to nullify them before they gain any traction.

"After my kid told me about bigfoot lesson," Bart continued, " I was *expecting* you to raise the bigfoot issue. So we were totally ready to do just what you said: ridicule it and make you look foolish. You know, discredit the opposition."

"So, was the complaint to the principal part of the smear campaign?"

"Sort of. I mean, presenting the subject in school did reawaken things in Ellie's mind that she was in the process of forgetting, but I quickly realized that your raising that subject was just the opportunity we needed. Sorry to get you in trouble with the principal and all that."

"There was a bit of trouble. I did end up getting a letter of reprimand for deviating from the established curriculum, but even that might have been worth it in the end. See, in the process of scolding me, the principal fell off her friggin' lab stool in my classroom. I mean, she went *down* hard. I was amazed she got up. It was the most amazing thing. Anyhow, it made her back issues worse and a few weeks later she ended up having a corrective surgery. Well, the surgery didn't work. In fact, it might have made things worse. She got these chronic pain issues and it kind of forced her decision to retire early.

"Isn't that weird? She was in my classroom, gleefully brow-beating me, and as soon as she's done, 'Boom', and down she goes. And now, 'Machiavelli' Lavelle, as we used to call her, is forced into early retirement. And it wouldn't have happened if you had not complained about bigfoot. Now, Machiavelli is gone and we get a new principal next year. Heck of a deal, eh?"

"Funny how things work out some times. And I'm just as happy we never had to play the 'bigfoot card' in the media. The more I think about it, the more I doubt it would have worked. The plan was to portray you as a wacko environmental extremist who wanted to preserve the area for bigfoot habitat. We were going to do a lot of eye-rolling and saying stuff like, "What's next from these preservationist kooks, Elvis sightings in Squaw Meadow?"

"If you only knew..."

" Knew what?"

"Knew how we ended up finding the snake."

"I *figured* you had some help."

"Oh yeah, we had help, alright."

"I knew it. I just knew it wasn't just your kid who found that snake all by himself. It just sounded too improbable. So, who helped you?" Bart had climbed back into the cab of his truck. He leaned out the pick-up truck window, eager to hear Sam's response.

Sam opened his mouth and paused. He lifted a knee and placed his boot on the step beneath the door. He leaned closer to Bart in the cab, and spoke in a low voice, almost a whisper. "I'll tell ya, but you won't believe me."

"Try me," Bart said, rolling his eyes.

"It was Bigfoot." Sam paused, smiled, then added, "… with a little help from Elvis."